Tastes Like Summer

SEASONS OF LOVE:
BOOK 4

CAROLINE FRANK

TASTES LIKE SUMMER

SEASONS OF LOVE
BOOK 4

CAROLINE FRANK

Edited by Tracey Barski and Kerri Buckley

Cover by Ink&Laurel

To the readers. Thank you for sticking with me through the entire Seasons of Love series. I loved sharing these stories with everyone.

I see it as it looked one afternoon
In August,—by a fresh soft breeze o'erblown.
The swiftness of the tide, the light thereon,
A far-off sail, white as a crescent moon.
The shining waters with pale currents strewn,
The quiet fishing-smacks, the Eastern cove,
The semi-circle of its dark, green grove.
The luminous grasses, and the merry sun
In the grave sky; the sparkle far and wide,
Laughter of unseen children, cheerful chirp
Of crickets, and low lisp of rippling tide,
Light summer clouds fantastical as sleep
Changing unnoted while I gazed thereon.
All these fair sounds and sights I made my own.

EMMA LAZARUS, "LONG ISLAND SOUND"

Chapter One

DIANA

It's always been shocking to me how quickly life can change. One minute you're living a happy life as a teenager in your beautiful, tropical home country of Venezuela; the next, your parents move you the middle of the snow-covered mountains in Colorado, USA. One minute, you're living a quiet life, married with two kids; the next, your husband's girlfriend shows up at your doorstep, revealing a multi-year affair. And one second, you have a partner in life, one that provides at least a little support when raising your children; and the next he's giving up on everything you've built together, leaving you to deal with the clusterfuck he left behind.

It's all such a fun roller coaster, isn't it?

"Hey." My sister nudges me in the side. "You've been picking at that crab cake for the past ten minutes. Do you not like it?"

"That's not it, Rosie," I tell her, taking in her intricate updo, which looks even better thanks to her pastel pink hair.

"What is it, then? I mean, it's a dumb question considering everything that's happened—of course you're not okay. But... Are you, you know... okay? You've lost a lot of weight lately."

It's a little difficult to have an appetite when your life is imploding and you need to keep it together for your two little girls.

"I'm fine." Or at least as well as I can be considering I'm a mess right now. "Just thinking, you know?" I shrug nonchalantly. I don't volunteer where my thoughts have gone because I know it would only be a matter of time before—

"If being at this wedding is too hard—"

There it is.

I lift up a hand to stop her and roll my eyes, because *of course* she would think that. *Of course* everyone thinks that newly-divorced Diana is a fragile little butterfly who's going to break at any second. But I am most definitely not. I have never been that type of girl. In fact, I was the rock for my sisters when we first moved here. The one everyone could depend on. And now I'm regarded as this sort of weakling and it's just... gross. And far from what I'm used to.

"Rosie, I'm *fine*," I insist. "Rodrigo and I were over *ages* before we even told anyone. *Eons* before we signed the divorce papers. A wedding isn't going to bring me down." And it's not even a lie. If anything, tonight has been good for me. It's Memorial Day weekend in the Hamptons, the summer is just beginning, we're at the beach at nighttime so the stars are visible, and even with my limited appetite, the food has been nothing short of to die for. Honestly? My personal life being a disaster aside, tonight has been fun. I even plan on dancing later.

Maybe.

I don't know.

Probably not, actually.

"This divorce hasn't turned me into a jaded person who doesn't believe in love or can't be happy when others find their partner. Especially Barbara, who has been nothing but nice to me. I mean, the woman isn't even *my* friend—she's yours—and she's offered me more kindness than many people closer to me ever have." Barbara Holt, former child-actress turned movie star —and also one of my sister's very close friends. "Barbara didn't need to offer her guest house in the Hamptons to me and the girls. I know she offered it under the guise of me house-sitting while she's on her summer-long honeymoon, but it's more than anyone would've offered."

"Did she also help you find a day camp for the girls?"

I nod with a smile. "Yes, thank god. It'll give me some time alone to study and complete my paralegal certification for my new job."

"Phew! Good!"

"Exactly. So I would never feel bitter about her finding happiness with someone else or resent her getting married. She's been incredibly generous to me even when she didn't have to be."

"That's who she is," Rosie says, looking over her shoulder at her friend as she glides across the dance floor with her new husband, her golden hair flowing behind her.

And this is what I mean about not being angry at love: I *know* there are couples out there who are meant to be. Barbara and her new husband, Theo. My sister and her boyfriend, Asher. Barbara's best friend Liza and her husband, Matt. They all look at their partners like they're heaven on earth. A blessing. A privilege to even be around. But Rodrigo and I, for example? We never looked like that. I mean, for god's sake, at our wedding, he got so drunk, we found him passed out in the coat closet from "celebrating so hard." (In retrospect, he was probably mourning what he called his "freedom" during our divorce proceedings.)

"Maybe I felt a little jaded in the beginning," I admit, thinking back to those first few months after we got separated.

"But I was hurt. And hiding all the things that had gone wrong in my seemingly-perfect little life. In reality, the divorce happened because we weren't right for each other—not because love isn't real or whatever. It's been two years since Rodrigo and I separated, so I think I've had enough distance and time to realize that."

"I know, but you only just signed the paperwork last month after the divorce dragged for so long. And with the whole custody thing..." She shakes her head and chews on her bottom lip.

"The whole custody '*thing*.'" I laugh, humorlessly. "What a ride."

She grimaces, and I can tell she regrets bringing it up. To say that the divorce proceedings between Rodrigo and I were eventful is a massive understatement.

"It's fine. It... It happens. It's sad, but it happens." I shrug once more, because what else am I supposed to say or do? It is what it is.

"He's a jerk. Rodrigo is a jerk." To put it mildly.

"Yes, Rosie. But I can't dwell on that. I *need* to get my life together."

With a sympathetic smile, Rosie reaches out to squeeze my hand in both of hers. "It's going to be okay."

"I know things will calm down eventually. I just need to make sure Emiliana and Cami don't feel the stress."

"How's Emiliana doing, by the way? With her diagnosis?"

My gaze drifts over to my daughters, watching as they play in the sand, barefooted, with some other kids from the wedding party. I smile, feeling relief when I hear them laugh and giggle with their new friends. They need this summer of relaxation and rebuilding as much as I do. The divorce has been difficult for Camila, my oldest. But it's been brutal for Emiliana. It wasn't enough for her parents to separate, for her whole family life to destabilize. Nope. Her body decided it was also time for it to fail on her. At least, her pancreas did.

"I don't think she gets how type 1 diabetes works yet. I mean, we only just found out ten months ago and I barely get what best practices are. But she'll get there. And I will, too. It's just been difficult. Her life is the one that's changed the most, and I just wish I could protect her from it, somehow. Protect them both."

Rosie nods, taking a sip from her champagne flute. "You're doing your best, though. And that's all anyone can ask of you. You know that, right?"

I sigh, my eyes on my kids' happy faces. Warmth spreads through my chest as I watch them play, looking more themselves and relaxed than they have in months. It brings me hope. It dismisses my previous concerns on whether or not I made the right call by taking them away from their home for the next twelve weeks.

"I hope you're right," I reply, slightly appeased. Still, I pick at my crab cake, appetite nowhere to be found.

Eventually, Rosie leaves me at the table to join Asher on the dance floor. And while I meant what I said and am happy for her and all the lucky couples holding each other as they sway to the music, there's only so much I can take. So I snuggle into my wrap and slip off my sandals. Feeling the cold, soft sand between my toes, I move closer to where all the kids run around, chasing each other. I'm not clear on what the rules of the game they're playing are, but I couldn't care less. They're happy and enjoying themselves, which is all I can hope for nowadays. My girls may not realize it yet, but I'm pretty sure they're excited about this summer, too. They're in desperate need of this distraction. Try as I might to protect them, to protect their relationship with their father, it's become increasingly obvious to me that they know he's not the man they thought he was.

Through small comments here, certain looks there, I'm starting to believe my daughters are more aware of the situation than they lead on. And that must be impossible and confusing for them.

They're strong, though. I can tell by the way they carry themselves, even at this age. They'll adapt and grow from this experience. I just need to protect them enough that they don't get hurt.

I adjust my wrap when it slips off one shoulder, wind tugging at my dark hair as I watch them with a smile on my face. It isn't until I see a man approach the children, balancing several plates with large slices of cake on them, that my stomach drops. I run over to my girls, dropping my sandals and wrap as I do, and pull them to my side.

In a panic, I pull the plates from both my daughters' grasps and toss them on the sand as if they were made of poison. A slight overreaction, I know. But you try being a parent to a newly-diagnosed type 1 diabetic daughter.

"Mom!" my oldest whines. "We were gonna eat that."

"Your sister can't have cake, Camila. I've told you guys this a thousand times. She needs to watch what she eats, on top of the medication she takes."

"Is everything okay?" the man with the plates asks.

At average height, the man stands before me in a chef's coat. His light brown hair mussed, he stares wide-eyed at me as he finishes passing the remaining plates of the cake to the rest of the kids around us.

"I was just—"

"You were just handing out food to unmonitored children without asking their parents if it was okay. Without asking whether they had any food allergies or any other health concerns," I snap.

His golden-brown eyes widen, his back straightens, and

even under his chef's coat, I can see the way his muscles tense. "I—I didn't mean to—"

"You didn't mean to, but you did. And how dare you just approach a group of children with *sweets*?" I hiss. "Can't you see the way that looks? Are you some kind of weirdo or something?"

"Whoa!" He lifts his hands in the air as if I were pointing a gun in his direction (which, to be honest, I probably would if I could—momma bear instincts, and all of that). "I am not some sick predator, alright? My daughter—Rachel, come here," he calls out to one of the girls who was playing with Camila and Emiliana and takes hold of her hand. "My daughter was over here playing, just like yours, and I wanted to offer her and her new friends the cake I spent hours making."

"The cake *you* made?" I lift an eyebrow.

He points to himself. "Uh, chef? Can't you see my jacket? I obviously catered the wedding. Why else would I be wearing this coat?"

I grow even *more* irritated with him because, dammit, his food was delicious.

"I don't know your life," I tell him haughtily.

Weirdo Chef snorts and shakes his head. "I just wanted the kids to have a piece before the adults ate it all. I didn't mean anything malicious by it. I thought I was doing something good. I was being *nice*."

"Well, if you think a normal parent would ever be okay with a stranger offering their kid food without their permission, then you're off your rocker. Or just a really bad parent yourself."

At my words, his expression suddenly shifts from apologetic to anger. "Are you calling me a shitty parent? Seriously?"

I shrug once. "If the chef's jacket fits. How else would you ever, in your right mind, think what you did is okay? Or that cursing like that in front of them is acceptable?"

I know it's a low blow for any parent to hear even a whisper of a suggestion that their parenting skills suck, so I'm pretty sure that stung. But by the expression on his face, it seems like I've pushed the right button a little too hard.

"*Mami, please,*" Camila begs. "I promise neither one of us will eat the cake. But can we go? You're embarrassing us."

I look down at my daughter as she pulls at my hand, trying to get me to move. "*Embarrassing* you?" God, when did she grow up? "Camila, I'm having a conversation with—with—"

"Michael. My name is Michael. And I'm not some weirdo or some creep. *Or* a bad parent." His eyes flash as he holds his daughter close, fingers clutching at her as if someone were five seconds from taking her away from him. "And you are a prejudicial lunatic and the most uptight person I have ever met."

"A—*What?*" I sputter.

"You heard me."

Something inside me snaps, something about his nonchalance triggering bad memories of Rodrigo and his lax and uncaring parenting. "*God, Diana. Let the girls have a snack before dinner. It's not a big deal.*" Or "*Of course they can watch* The Exorcist. *I was their age when I first did.*" Stupid stuff that would come with even stupider and completely avoidable consequences that *I'd* have to clean up on my own.

So I open my mouth to let him have it, to let this man know what he *really* is—a neglectful parent—but then I feel a tug on my skirt. Emiliana. I come back down to reality. "*Mami*, can we go? Please? I don't want you to fight."

And I realize she's right. They've had enough of watching me fight with useless men.

This summer is about them. About doing everything I possibly can to secure their happiness.

"*Sí, amor.*" I run my fingers through her dark curls, hair a mess after an afternoon of running and playing at the beach.

Before I leave, I turn to glance at Michael just to shoot him a menacing glare, daring him to say another word.

"Let's go say bye to everyone and then we can go."

As we make our way back to the main party, I stop to pick up my sandals and wrap, forgotten in the sand, when I hear him whisper an emphatic, "Good riddance."

Chapter Two

DIANA

"This looks like vomit," my ever-so-eloquent oldest daughter mutters.

Camila looks down at the plate I set in front of her on the counter as if it had called her a name and kicked her dog while doing it. So dramatic.

I suppress a sigh because I know Emiliana's diagnosis has been hard on Camila, too. For the most part, she's been fantastic. But it hasn't been easy for my oldest to deal with her parents' divorce while trying not to resent her little sister for taking more attention away from her when she most needs it.

So I reply with, "It's *scrambled eggs*, Cami. It's not like it's something weird. Plus, you've had this before multiple times. And it's good for you."

She grimaces, poking at it with her spoon while her little sister slides onto the stool next to her.

"Can't we do pancakes?" Emiliana whines, brows furrowed. "You used to always make us pancakes on the first day of school. It's the first day of camp; isn't that kinda the same? Can't we just have that?"

This time, I can't help my deep exhale. I squeeze my eyes shut. I'm sure there's more than one T1D friendly version of pancakes, but I haven't had the time to research any options, which is why I went with a recent tried-and-true. Guilt crashes over me like a tsunami because I should definitely be making more of an effort.

"Emi, please."

Camila scoffs. "Careful, Emi. You shouldn't bring up pancakes. She might blow up and throw the plates in the backyard."

"I already apologized for what happened at the wedding and— Also, you are my *child.* I will react however I feel is appropriate if I think it is in your best interest, if it's to keep you *safe.*"

She sighs, exasperated, and rolls her eyes.

"Aren't you a little young for this type of rebellion? You're *nine.* Shouldn't this type of attitude start when you're twelve or thirteen?" I shoot her a look, my hand on my hip.

"Whatever, Mom."

Oh, god. The dreaded "whatever" phase every kid goes through. Though I never did; I never had the luxury. My younger sisters, however... *they* certainly enjoyed that time in life.

I suppress a wince as I remember the fights between my parents and my sisters, knowing that I should probably nip *my* daughter's attitude in the bud before it ever gets to that. Between the divorce, having all of us adjust to a different diet, and seeing me give her little sister extra attention, Camila has had to learn how to adapt in more ways than one. It's added an extra fun level to an already mounting mass of growing pains.

Patience. The goal is patience and balance. Be understanding, while also setting boundaries.

"Do *not* 'whatever' me, Camila. And if you don't like your breakfast, you can go ahead and leave it. I'm not making anything special just because you're still angry at me for the wedding." *Two days later.* No one can hold a grudge like she can, apparently. "Please go finish getting ready for camp."

With a huff, she pushes from the stool and runs out of the kitchen. When the door to the girls' bedroom—the guest house's guest bedroom—slams shut, I'm not surprised. I've learned to expect it. Could make a soundtrack out of it by now.

I take a deep breath and run my fingers through my hair, tying it into a loose bun at the top of my head.

"Sorry, *Mami*. I'll eat my breakfast." Emi looks up at me with wide, dark, apologetic eyes.

She takes a generous bite of eggs and shoves it in her mouth, trying her hardest not to make a face. Honestly, I don't blame her. Unless we're talking about arepas, I've never been much of a breakfast person.

"Thank you, baby." At least one daughter is drama free this morning.

I WISH I COULD SAY OUR ROCKY START TO THE MORNING gets better, but it seems like hoping for the best is nothing more than wishful thinking, these days. Between Camila purposefully delaying leaving the house in protest, having to go back because Emi left her lunch at home, and the wrong turn I take somewhere, we officially make it to camp twenty minutes after drop-off time is over. As I drive up, the parking lot is empty and there are no counselors greeting parents and campers.

"Shit," I mumble under my breath.

"Bad word alert! You owe the swear jar a dollar." Emi calls from the back seat between peals of laughter.

I grimace, disappointed in myself. The jar was started originally for Rodrigo's sake, who refused to understand that cursing in front of his daughters wasn't the best example to set. The only way I was able to curb his urge was to hit him where it hurt —his wallet. And now I'm the one setting the bad example.

I sigh. "You're right. Sorry, guys."

"Where is everyone? Are you sure we're in the right place?" Camila asks, skeptical.

"Of course." Irritated, I park closest to the front gate. I look in my rearview mirror as I back up and exhale in relief when I see another car rushing into the lot. Another late parent. For some reason, it makes me feel better. Like I'm not the only one on this struggle bus.

"Are you sure, Mom?"

"Sorry, did the Sugar Maple Day Camp sign not make it clear?" I snap, and immediately regret it. "Yes, we're in the right place."

It takes a minute, but I eventually get them both out with their backpacks, double-checking once again they have everything. "You're both good? Lunchbox? Swimsuit and towels? And Emi, do you have your phone on you?"

"Yes, *Mami*."

"When do I get a phone? I'm older. I should've gotten one first." Camila huffs and crosses her arms in front of her chest.

I sigh, not wanting to have this conversation again. *Patience.* "You're still too young. The only reason Emi has one is to monitor her blood sugar. Because of her CGM. Remember? I explained it to you both? Emi's Continuous Glucose Monitor is linked to her phone so she and/or her teachers and camp counselors can reference it just in case."

The monitor is also linked to my phone, but I don't want to remind her of it. The whole thing verges a bit too much on *Big Brother is watching you,* and I don't want to make Emi feel uncomfortable. But if it weren't for the monitor and her insulin pump, I probably wouldn't be able to let her out of my sight. Thank god for modern medicine.

"You can play with my phone later, Cami," Emi whispers to her older sister. I pretend like I didn't hear her (partly because it's not the time to get into it; partly because I find it kind of sweet).

"Okay, now that that's settled, let's go. I'm going to have to walk in with you to find the head counselor."

"What?" Camila gasps. Both girls look up at me, horrified expressions on their faces. "Why? You can't come in with us like we're babies."

Um, aren't you my babies?

"Cami, I need to talk to the camp counselors and directors about Emi. They already know you have diabetes, and they said they're able to take care of you if something happens, but I'd still like to go talk to their nurse."

Emi looks down at her feet, blushing. My heart pangs in my chest.

"You know—"

"It's Emi and Cami!" a girl's voice bursts from behind us.

My daughters' faces light up, turning in her direction. When they see it's their friend from the wedding, they take off like rockets toward her.

"Well, well, well." I turn to find Weirdo Chef—Michael—walking towards us, his daughter on one hand and her pink sparkly backpack in the other. Looking smug and—it sucks to admit this—wildly attractive, he stops right in front of us. "How the tables." A wide grin spreads across his face. "You're late. Who's the bad parent now?"

"Uh, if you're calling me a bad parent for being late, then so are you. Seeing as, you know, *you're late, too*?"

He shrugs, laughing once. In the morning sun, his hair is closer to a dark blond, silver-threaded on the sides. As he smiles, lines form near his eyes, closer to green than they were the other night, crinkling in an annoyingly adorable way. And right beneath his scruff, I catch two dimples flashing.

"Touché," he says. "Still, it's nice to see you *not* be Mrs. Perfect now."

"It's *Ms.* Perfect, actually." Ugh, I don't know why I said that. That's stupid. Who cares about the clarification? "And anyway, we should probably stop chitchatting, don't you think? We're late enough as it is." I take both my girls' hands and pull them toward the entrance, ignoring the easy way Michael whistles casually behind us. Camila tugs on my hand, wanting to go to her new friend, but I drag her along. "You'll see her in camp," I mutter.

THE ONLY YEAR I EVER ATTENDED SUMMER CAMP—A TWO-week overnight experience on the coast of Venezuela—my parents simply dropped us off and drove away. I don't know if it's an American thing or a Hamptons thing, but as soon as we cross those front gates, the girls are taken to their designated cabins—small ones that look like they were purchased at the Home Depot, where they can leave their things in cubbies and change into their swim clothes—while parents are guided to a three-hour long orientation. *Three* hours. And counting. Worst of all, since we were the last two parents to arrive, Michael and I are led to the back of the room and forced to sit together.

I discretely check my watch. The long list of errands I planned on running today and *actual* work I have to do will now have to be cut down to essentials. Mentally, I remap my tasks for optimal results, moving the non-urgent ones to tomorrow's to-do list. I adjust my study plan for the paralegal certification, resolving to go through only one unit today and cram three in tomorrow. As for work, that'll have to be my priority. There are a couple of documents I need to get through for a company one of our clients is trying to acquire—the most important case on my boss's desk lately, so I have to be prepared. As for errands, I resign myself to hitting the local, over-priced gourmet grocery store instead of the better value one two towns over to save some time. Just as I'm redoing my grocery list in my head, I feel Michael lean into me.

"*Psst*! You aren't paying attention," he whispers. But he's grinning, a sly smile on his face.

"Yes, I am." *Kind of.* "But also, no offense, I really couldn't care less about how the wood used to make the newer cabins was repurposed from one of the oldest homes in Long Island that was destroyed during some hurricane in the nineties."

"Whoa. A little harsh, don't you think?" But there's a glint of humor in his expression.

I exhale, closing my eyes. "I just... had a lot of things planned for today. And now..." I check my watch again. There's only a few more hours left in the camp day. Hours that I had set aside to finish setting us up here for the next two and a half months. "How long do they expect us to stay here? The whole session?"

"Why don't you just leave?" He shrugs, sitting back in his chair.

How he manages to look so comfortable in these metal fold-out things is beyond comprehension. From the corner of my eye, I stare at him: his slightly overgrown hair, face scruffy like he didn't have time to shave this morning. He could pass for a relaxed Calvin Klein model, in a just-tight-enough white t-shirt and jeans. It's not super hot out yet, but it's still summer. How is he not sweltering in those?

"I can't. I have to talk to my daughter's counselor about... something."

He nods. "That doesn't sound sketchy at all."

This guy. *Jeez*. "It's personal," I snap.

He raises his hands in the air like he had the other night. I don't miss the bare ring finger on his left hand. "Got it."

"Why do you do that? Raise your hands like that. I'm not going to *shoot* you," I hiss.

Michael grins, green eyes wide, seemingly thrilled. "Could've fooled me. Twice I've seen you get protective over your daughters. Twice I've felt like my life was in danger." He laughs softly before turning back to the front of the room.

"I'm not *that* bad," I say, a little too loudly. A woman with fiery red hair from the row in front of us turns to glare, pressing a finger over her lips.

"Sorry," Michael whispers. "She's just *so* excited about the reclaimed wood."

I snort but try to hide it with a cough. "You're the worst."

"And you're just being a good mom. If a little overprotective at times." He shrugs easily again, his eyes straight ahead.

My breath catches, though it's thankfully inaudible. I turn to look at him—to *really* look at him—and smile.

"Thank you," I tell him.

"For what?" He raises a brow.

"For saying that. That I'm a good mom. I'm... doing this myself. And sometimes it's a little hard to believe I'm doing the right things."

"I get that. Especially since I'm in the same boat. It's why I got so upset with you that night. I'm new to this."

"Single parenting?" I take a guess.

He hesitates a bit, and nods.

What's his story? Is he divorced? Has custody over his kid over the summer which is why there seems to be no mother in sight? A widower? I'm annoyed by the fact he only volunteered a minuscule amount of information, but more than that, I'm annoyed at myself for caring.

"What's your name, by the way? I told you mine, but you never told me yours."

"Diana."

He squints at me, as if processing the information. "Goddess of the hunt."

I narrow my eyes at him. "What does *that* mean?"

Michael shrugs once. "Just that she's the goddess of the hunt."

"Will you two please *stop*?" The same woman from before hisses at us. This time, she's joined by two other parents giving us the stink eye. "Some of us actually care about our children and are trying to hear about the non-chlorinated, salt water pool the kids will be swimming in. *Please*."

I lean forward in my uncomfortable chair. "Did you seriously just imply that we don't care about our children?"

I feel Michael's hand go to my elbow in an attempt to comfort me somehow, but I shake him off.

"I didn't *imply* it. I *said* it. Because if you did, you'd be paying attention to—"

"What? What exactly would I need to pay attention to, huh? How is knowing what kinds of flowers are planted across the camp, the type of water they use to keep the grounds looking like Versailles, or the camp fight song—*sorry*, anthem, because apparently 'fight' song is too violent—affect my quality of parenting?"

The woman rears back, ready to explode. "Did you—"

"*Excuse me*." We're interrupted by a young woman in her mid-twenties wearing an official camp t-shirt. She points to the navy name tag on her shirt and leans down. "I'm Abby, one of the head counselors here. Is something wrong?" she asks in a low voice.

"Uh-oh. Someone's in trouble," Michael whispers, but I can tell he's just a few seconds away from bursting into laughter.

I steadily ignore him.

Cheeks heating, I take a deep breath before replying, "Just wondering when this orientation will be over. I need to get back to work before picking up my girls. And, well, I still need to talk to someone in charge regarding my daughter's medical condition."

"Oh, I'm sorry. I thought you knew. The orientation is optional."

"Optional?" Michael and I both say at the same time, a little too loud, sitting up straighter in our seats.

Abby looks nervously around us and shushes us some more. "Please try to keep your voices down. But yes, this part is optional. Most parents choose to be a part of it, though, because—"

"Are you serious?" Michael asks. "So I could've left ages ago? I'm not obligated to be here?"

"That's what optional means, yes," I say, irritated.

Counselor Abby presses her lips together and stares down at him. "We offer this only for parents who would like to know more about the camp and its rich history."

"Parents who are actually interested in their children's lives," the rude red-headed woman pipes in.

Michael shifts, immediately gearing up for an argument.

"Don't listen to her," I whisper.

Without really knowing what I'm doing, I place a hand on Michael's denim-covered thigh—his strong, defined thigh. The palm of my hand feels red-hot and ice-cold at the same time. A frisson of electricity shoots through my hand, up my arm, and into my chest. We stare at each other in horror before I drop my hand. Though my intention was to stop him from saying something he might regret, the result was not what I was expecting.

I clear my throat before continuing. "Listen, I just need to talk to my daughter's counselor about her medical condition. Can you help me with that? I've already been in touch with the nurse—but I'd like to meet her in person briefly as well. The camp is lovely, but I have other priorities I need to take care of over learning Sugar Maple's history." It's the most diplomatic way I can think of to say *I don't care about the camp's "rich heritage;" I'm just here for my girls to have a good time* without feeling like a horrible person.

Abby purses her lips and straightens, clearly not too satisfied with my answer. "Of course. Let me take you to the on-site nurse and then we can speak to your daughter's counselor."

Finally.

"Thank you." I get to my feet, stiff as a board from sitting in those damn chairs for too long.

Michael, on the other hand, gets up with the grace of a jungle cat. "I'm outta here, then. I'll be back at pick-up."

After an aggressive-aggressive *shh!* from Red, we head in opposite directions. I look over my shoulder once, watching as Michael jogs over to the parking lot towards his truck, his boots kicking up dirt along the way. Absentmindedly, I wonder what the odds are that the annoying chef from Barbara's wedding ended up placing his daughter in the same summer camp as I did.

It isn't until I'm backing out of the camp that I realize *he* was probably the one who told Barbara about it.

Duh.

Chapter Three

MICHAEL

"We made a bunch of these bracelets in arts and crafts today. So I made us matching ones."

We're stopped at a red light as Rachel lifts her hand from the backseat and shakes it, her grin wide. Twisting in my seat to take the bracelet she made for me, I smile a goofy, proud smile.

My fingers run over the bracelet's bright beads before stretching it over my hand, letting it snap against my wrist. It's a snug fit, but I don't tell her that.

"It's beautiful, kid. Thank you." The light turns green, and my eyes turn back to the road. "I'm glad you enjoyed your first day of camp."

Since jumping into my truck at pick-up, she hasn't stopped talking about it. About how much fun she had, about all the friends she made. About the ones she reconnected with, apparently (i.e. that woman Diana's daughters).

Despite that last tidbit, I think *Thank god*. Because as a relatively new parent, I struggle with this internal battle of wondering whether I'm doing right by her 24/7. For so long, I was nothing more than a glorified sperm donor. But things are different now. I *want* to be here for her. I *want* to make sure she's getting all the love and support she needs in life. And I want to be the one doing it.

I grin down at my new bracelet. "I love it. I'm never taking it off." And I mean it. I'll wear it 'til the elastic snaps.

I glance at her beaming face, so much like her mother it hurts. Her large crystal blue eyes, round and wide in excitement as she tells me about her day, long blonde hair a mess, remind me of what Jessie looked like when she was exactly her age. But when my scan of her face leads me to notice her ski-jump nose looking more red than pink, I frown.

"Did you reapply sunscreen throughout the day?"

"I... I don't remember. Maybe?"

I frown, narrowing my eyes at the road ahead of me. "Might need to talk to the camp counselors. Remind them they should be taking better care of you. That they should be doing their job. Especially with all the time you guys spend in the pool."

I grunt in frustration because deep down, I know it's my fault.

Here I go again, fucking up this whole parenting thing.

"I'm sorry. I promise I'll remember tomorrow." Her voice is low and small, and it makes me feel sick to my stomach.

"It isn't your fault. It's mine."

"But you're mad."

"At myself," I admit with a sigh.

"Why?"

I shake my head, trying to find the words to make a nine-year-old understand something I'm only now beginning to learn. "Because I didn't stop and talk to the people in charge. Because we were late, and I didn't think..." I sigh again. Because I'm a fucking dumbass who prioritized work over taking five fucking seconds to make sure his daughter was taken care of. Working out which dishes would best go on the menu to my restaurant shouldn't have ever come first. "I just didn't think. But it's fine. I'll fix it tomorrow."

She groans. "Michael."

I wince again. It's not like I expected her to call me *Dad* overnight. How could I when she didn't even know that's who I really was until nine months ago, when her mother died. But, despite taking on the parental role after Jessie's death, I've somehow been demoted from *Uncle Michael*—her favorite, her pal, her mother's best friend—to just plain and simple *Michael.*

My heart twists in my chest and I wince, trying not to think about last year or how devastated Rachel was. How, at thirty-four, I suddenly found myself the parent and sole guardian of a nine-year-old. The confusing time we both went through as we tried to navigate our new dynamic, as she had to process the truth: I was her father and she was coming to live with me. That Jessie had left her in my care, and care for her I would.

"I don't want you whining, Rach. I need to make sure you're safe. If they can't manage to remember to do something as simple as put sunblock on my kid, then we'll have to pull you out and find you somewhere new for the summer."

"What? No! I've only been there for a day and already made new friends!"

Part of me deflates in relief, so fucking happy she's happy, that she's having a good time. But another part of me remembers that having a good time doesn't always mean you're being safe. I would know, after all those years of long nights at work, compensating for the stress with copious amounts of alcohol, drugs, and random sex. Sure, comparing my debauchery to a day camp for kids is a stretch, but the principle remains the same, doesn't it? At least when it comes to my daughter.

"I'm happy you've made some friends, but I still want to make sure you're okay," I tell her in as comforting a voice as I can manage.

Rachel huffs and looks out the window, argument settled.

Neither one of us breaks the silence as we make the drive to my farm. She ices me out, while I fight the urge to break down and capitulate, to apologize on my knees. For what, exactly? I'm not sure. I only know that seeing her upset is like a knife in the chest, and I'd do anything to make her happy.

It's only when I turn onto the farm's gravel road that I speak up: "Do you want Lexi to make you lunch while I work?"

Gaze still focused out the window, Rach lifts her small shoulders in feigned indifference.

She barely waits for the truck to come to a full stop before jumping out and running into the main building, backpack bouncing as she does, small feet kicking up enough dirt to leave a cloud of dust in her wake.

"*Jesus*," I mutter to myself, following at a more reasonable pace. I've got a future sprint olympian on my hands, here.

When I make it to the kitchen, Rachel and Lexi are already deeply engrossed in camp talk: "...And, oh my gosh, Lexi, I made you a bracelet!" Rachel squeals, searching manically through her backpack.

I look down at mine and frown, ignoring the sting of my disappointment. I guess I'm not as special as I thought I was.

But there are no hard feelings when it comes to Lexi. On top of being my cousin and business partner, she and her wife are some of my closest friends. They've both been an invaluable support during this hectic time.

"Hey, Lex." I greet my favorite sous-chef with a kiss on the cheek.

"Hey, cus." She looks up, her dirty-blonde hair tucked into her overalls. "How was pick-up?"

I glance at Rachel, who steadily avoids my gaze. "Eventful. Apparently I can be a bit overprotective."

"I'm going to play outside," Rachel says, voice clipped.

Without another word, my kid leaves us alone in the kitchen.

Lexi puffs out a laugh. "Oh, man. What'd you *do*?"

"What did *I* do? You know, I'm starting to think there's no winning in parenting. As a kid, I had the least involved parents in the world and hated them. And I feel like now that I'm the parent and I'm trying to be the complete opposite of my own, I'm still hated."

"What happened?"

"I made the mistake of giving a shit and telling her about it, apparently."

Lexi laughs. "She doesn't hate you, then."

I exhale deeply, squeezing my eyes shut while pinching the bridge of my nose. "It sure feels that way sometimes."

"I know you don't know this because you never had a stable home life—"

"Understatement of the century," I mutter.

"—but all kids will eventually find their parents annoying, embarrassing, or frustrating on a regular basis. When you're a kid at that age, you don't get that caring comes with growing pains. You don't realize that your parents are trying to protect you by setting boundaries."

"Not all parents," I clarify.

She purses her lips and frowns. "No. Not all. Certainly not yours."

"So what do I do?" I ask, not wanting to think about my childhood. "Because sometimes it feels like I'm doing the right thing. But then other times I lie awake in bed in a panic, praying she doesn't hate or resent me the way I do my own parents."

"You *know* what you have to do. What you've *been* doing so far."

I shake my head with a grunt. "Today, two different people at Rach's camp told me I suck as a dad."

Lexi sighs. "Well, I don't know the context, but I'm sure they were wrong in saying that. I've seen bad parenting and you aren't it."

"I didn't want this in the beginning, though," I say, the guilt of it all almost knocking me breathless.

"That was before. Almost ten years ago."

"Still. Maybe those women were right."

"What the hell do they know, anyhow?"

"Uh, they were both mothers? Granted, one of them was a super snooty-looking mom, but the other seemed more down to earth. Normal." *Hot, too*, I think, remembering her angular face, the smooth skin of her exposed thighs in denim cutoff shorts. The large freckle on the right corner of her lip, every single curve of her body. And that sexy accent... Just subtle enough to go by almost unnoticed, but pronounced enough that it made me want to know more about her. But that's beside the point.

"It was rough," I grumble.

"Whatever. I'm a mother of *two* demons and I'm telling you you're not a bad dad."

I take a seat on one of the stools by the counter, looking out onto the field. "The normal one was Barbara's friend. The one I met at the wedding? The one who's staying at her place."

"How do you know she's the one?"

"Educated guess." I shrug. "But I just think it's too much of a coincidence to have seen her at the wedding and then at the camp. I told you Barb had asked for recommendations for her guest's kids. So, yeah, I think it's her friend."

"Small world."

"Hmm." I nod. "It's going to be an uncomfortable summer."

"Well, it's not like you'll be forced into social situations with this new woman. Barbara is away for most of the summer, and you can just avoid this woman at camp drop-offs and pick-ups. Pretend like you don't see her. Chances are, she'll do the same."

"Yeah," I mumble, thinking back to the look in Diana's dark brown eyes as she transitioned into protective mode. Fierce. Strong. The perfect cherry red lip pout as she stared at me in slight derision. Deadly, but beautiful. The determined expression on her face; making sure her girls were being taken care of.

So much fucking passion.

"Listen." Lexi comes to stand beside me, placing both hands on my shoulders, her dark blonde bob shaking as she shakes me. "*Snap out of it.* The fact that you're stressing about what kind of parent you are already makes you a better parent than most. It means you care enough to try as hard as you can to not mess up your kids. You need to stop thinking you're this shitty dad. You are *far* from it. You gave up your life to take care of this kid. You could've kept on being Uncle Michael, passed on the responsibility to her grandparents or something. But you chose to follow Jessie's request and take Rach in. You gave up your restaurant and your life and moved back here just so she could stay in her hometown. Amid all the trauma and all the grief, you're opening up a new business venture in the hopes of giving her a more stable life. You're *providing* for her. In more ways than one. That's not being selfish or a bad parent." She pats me on the back and lets me go. "That's being an honorable person."

"Yes, sure, *now*. *Now* that's what I'm doing. But I can't help feeling things would be easier if we had just told her from the beginning who I was, if she knew I was her dad, and I had treated her like a daughter from the get-go."

Lexi takes a deep breath. "I'm gonna say something that you're not going to like. But... you would've made a *horrible* father ten years ago."

I balk at her.

"It's true. You were selfish and career-centered and an immature ass who thought he was hot shit. But even though you were all those things, you were still self-aware enough to know you would've been the worst. Because you didn't *want* to be a father, and you would've resented that kid. Luckily, Jessie was a saint, and offered to have you be as involved as you wanted to be

—which was not at all. But trust me—it would've been a nightmare. *You* would've been a nightmare. And then you'd *definitely* have made for a terrible father. Now you're more mature, and already have a name for yourself, and—"

"But I missed so much. I missed *everything*, it feels like." I hunch over the bar, letting my forehead rest on the cool marble.

Lexi pauses for a moment, considering her words carefully before speaking again. "You were there in the best way you could have been."

No matter what Lexi says, this sense of guilt will never disappear.

"Cut yourself some slack, Michael. Look at everything you've accomplished. And what we're about to accomplish *together*."

I snort, shooting her a desperate look. "I'm starting to lose faith there, too. We're ten weeks away from opening, out of money, and I haven't been able to come up with a single fucking creative dish in months."

"Yeah, it's no secret we gotta get it together, but we can do it. We just need to find another investor and get you inspired. I'll work on finding us more catering clients to get us out of the water for the time being. And you need to get back to testing new dishes."

"I'm creatively constipated, Lexi. Like, all backed up and nothing's coming out," I nearly moan, miserable.

She bursts out laughing and slaps me on the shoulder. "Is that why you're looking a little rounder these days?"

I glare at her. "No. I think that's just my dad bod kicking in." I look down at my stomach, and while we both know she's exaggerating, I can't help but be a little vain about it.

"Michael. You need to relax. Every single dish you've created has been a hit with our testers. You're overthinking this."

She's not wrong. Still, though. I shake my head, digging my

fingers in my hair. "You don't get it." And the fact that she doesn't, sends shivers down my spine. I need my Number 2 to *Get. It.* "Perfection, Lexi. We need perfection."

She frowns and crosses her arms in front of her chest. "Perfection is the enemy of the good, Michael. So how about you take some creative Miralax or something and develop some kick ass recipes, huh?"

I grunt.

Lexi rolls her eyes and heaves a big sigh. "It'll work. The restaurant. Rachel. It will all work out. I promise."

"It *has* to." I look out the window again, my eyes landing on the one person who's become the center of my universe in such a short amount of time. "For her, it has to."

Chapter Four

DIANA

Balancing my phone between my cheek and my shoulder, I fold the towels by the lounge chairs, making sure we're not making too much of a mess. Even though Barbara is away, I don't want her to ever think I'm taking advantage of her hospitality.

"So things went well today?" Rosie asks.

"Well enough. The camp is so bougie—I think I saw a seven year-old with a designer backpack—and I got looped into some ridiculous orientation that lasted about three million hours. But the counselors and people running it were very nice."

"They liked the camp then? Camila and Emi, I mean."

Glancing at my daughters while neatly piling the towels on the table beside the lounge chairs, I watch as they squeal and splash in the pool water. They look happier than I've seen them in the past six months—since the whole divorce process started—which fills me with a deep sense of hope. It tells me that maybe this will work. Maybe coming here really will help us regroup, and we can head back to Denver in a better headspace before school starts.

"Yeah. They won't stop raving about it."

"That's good, right? I mean, obviously," she says.

"Absolutely," I tell her, nodding even though she can't see

me. "It means I don't feel *as* guilty as I should for dumping my kids in a camp while I study and work when I should probably be giving them love and attention given our whole *situation*."

"Dee..." Rosie sighs over the phone. "You're being way too hard on yourself. You need to be a bit more selfish here. And honestly? This is also good for them. You're working and getting your certification to be a paralegal and that's for them. Even though I don't get why they're making you get this thing. Didn't you say it wasn't a requirement in Colorado?"

"No, but the law firm requires me to be National Association of Legal Assistants certified," I clarify. "And they're already giving me a huge shot by offering me this job. I mean, do you know how difficult it is to find a job as a former stay-at-home mom? Especially in this economy. It doesn't matter that I double-majored in Economics and Business Management from a top 50 university at the top of my class for most of my college career. Nope. The fact that I dropped out and had to finish my last semester at a junior college ten years later only gives me the bare minimum of qualifications, apparently." I take a beat, sigh, and try to calm my heart rate. "The job market treated me like I have no job experience whatsoever. Which is ridiculous, because it's not as if I haven't been doing anything for the last decade. I've had to manage a budget, organize tasks, and raise two children—"

"Three, if you count Rodrigo," Rosie interrupts.

I laugh once but go on. "But, yeah, these are all translatable skills for a job. If that doesn't say *prime candidate for a manager role* I don't know what does. And yet, it was impossible to find something."

"Well, not impossible." And I know she's just trying to be supportive, but I really can't stand it now. "At least you found someone in Denver to take a chance on you," Rosie says before taking a sip of her champagne.

"The only reason I found a job at Porter, Jameson, & Webb is because Edgar Porter was my divorce attorney, and I impressed him during proceedings. *And* because he's dad's old friend from grad school." I roll my eyes. Normally, I'm not a fan of nepotism or calling in these kinds of favors—I like to think like I can take care of myself—but I had to do what I had to do for my kids. "I have a lot of catching up to do. Hence, the certification *and* the training program, all while I act as a virtual assistant to him."

"You are such a good mom, Dee," she says.

I heave a sigh, looking up at the clouds as the stinging in my eyes begins. I don't want to cry. Not again. Not today. It feels like it's all I do.

"Thanks." My voice cracks. "I don't know that I'm a good mom, but I'm trying. At least the girls are enjoying themselves, and that's what matters. They couldn't stop talking about how much fun they had. I was worried it might take them a minute to make new friends, but turns out they already knew another camper there."

Rosie gasps, delighted. "Seriously? How?"

"We ran into one of the kids they were playing with at Barbara's wedding just as we were walking into the camp. Turns out she's going there, too."

"Really? That's great! Maybe you can befriend the girl's parents? Make some friends for the summer?"

I frown. "Um, no. I think it's just her dad. And I don't need a *friend* for the summer. And certainly not a parent from my daughters' day camp."

Rosie snorts over the phone. "I didn't mean it like that. I meant as in an *actual* friend. Who you can talk to and hang out with. Pretty sure those still exist after you become a parent."

"I don't need friends, okay? I need to focus." I sigh, thinking of how I'm already behind on my training schedule and it's only been one day. "And the guy was the worst. I mean, he was completely clueless. And kind of an ass."

She snorts. "About what?"

I hesitate. "I don't know. He just... he rubbed me the wrong way. He teased me about my parenting style and... He showed up in a tight tee and jeans and boots, with his beard scruff and muscles and..." I trail off, shaking my head, remembering how at ease he looked, how obnoxiously okay he seemed with being late and the way his biceps just—

"Scruff can be hot." I can hear my sister's stupid smile in her voice. "Is he? Hot, I mean?"

I take a breath, feeling my cheeks heat. *Weird. Must be the late afternoon sun.* "Objectively speaking, he's... *attractive.*"

My sister laughs, and I consider hanging up. "How objectively attractive are we talking about? Are we talking conventional good looks like Hemsworth? Or dirty hot like Jason Momoa?"

I pause, momentarily distracted by the memory of this man who so easily got under my skin. The way his muscles seemed to move in slow motion when they tightened in the frustration he so clearly aimed at me; the way his mischievous grin lit up his hazel eyes as they ran over my body. The commanding presence he had, how even without laying a finger on me, I felt every inch of him pressed against the side of my body where he sat next to me.

My skin heats, my pulse races. Mortified, I shake my head, trying to clear it. So he was hot. Whatever. Lots of people are hot. Lots of really annoying, awful people are hot.

"Dee? You still there?"

"Yeah, sorry. I guess he was... less Marvel superhero, more Sons of Anarchy without tattoos. But maybe a little of both?"

Rosie gasps. "*Hot.*"

"Irrelevant since I'm not interested in any of *that* right now."

Or ever again. "He was just... annoying." Her muffled laughter makes my skin burn. I roll my eyes, frustrated. "*You're* really annoying, too, you know that?"

"*What?* I didn't say anything!" But she chokes on a laugh, clearly struggling to keep her composure.

"I hate you. I'm gonna go. I have to make the girls dinner and then get back to studying."

I almost hang up, but bring my phone back to my ear when I hear her yell "Wait! Hold on!"

"What?" I bite back.

"I'll stop teasing you, I promise. But you really should consider at least being friendly with the guy—especially if what you said is true about the girls being friends. Just do it for their benefit. So they have someone else to hang out with on the weekends beside their mother."

I heave a sigh, closing my eyes. "So I have to be *nice*?"

"It's honestly much easier than you think. People do it every day, you know."

"I guess."

Despite what I tell Rosie, however, I have zero intentions of becoming even just *friendly* with Michael. The girls can enjoy their time with Rachel and the rest of their new friends while at camp during weekdays, and then spend their weekends doing fun activities with me. But I need to focus on making sure they feel loved and let them know that they can count on at least one parent. I need to focus on my daughters' well-being and health. I need to focus on studying for the paralegal tests, studying my future boss's clients. *Not* on making new connections only for them to end after the summer.

So I steer clear of Michael for the rest of the week, looking the other way whenever we see each other in the camp parking lot, avoiding any sort of interaction.

For the most part, I'm successful—that is, until my daughters run up to me just a few days later at pick-up, Rachel in tow, big puppy eyes at the ready.

"*Mami*!" Cami greets me, and already I know it's going to take everything in me not to cave. I know that look.

"So Rachel's dad has this super cool farm with a bunch of animals and plants and flowers and food and stuff, and she invited us over to play and check it out, and we were wondering whether we could go because it sounds super fun and—"

"Whoa, hey. Hold on. Slow your roll; I can barely understand you. You want to go to Rachel's?"

"Rachel's dad's *farm*."

I practically see the physical effort it takes Cami not to roll her eyes at me when she makes the clarification, as if her summer goal is to also practice patience with her mother. The gall of this kid.

Emi tugs at my hand. "Rachel invited us. She was talking about how fun it can be, and it would be so cool because we've never been to a farm and—"

"Okay, take a breath, will you?" *Jeez*, these kids. "I know you're excited, but you're not being timed here."

"Well," Rachel speaks up. "It's just, Mic—I mean, my *dad*—will be here any minute, and we just wanted to know whether it was okay with you before he got here. So Cami and Emi could come with me and then maybe you could pick them up later?"

I cross my arms in front of my chest and narrow my eyes at all three girls. "Does your dad already know about this?"

Rachel looks down at her shoes, one of her hands moving to her hair to play with a loose strand. "Well, no. But I don't see why he would mind. He's really cool."

Yeah, I bet.

I do my best to soften my features when I speak—it's not her fault her dad and I didn't mesh well. "I don't think so, Rachel. It's really nice of you to invite the girls over, but—"

"Rach!"

Rachel's face turns so quickly her messy braid hits her cheek. In her wild excitement, she barely notices, and I can't help but be a bit charmed by her. Her face lights up like a Christmas tree when she sees her dad, running over to him to meet him halfway.

"Can Camila and Emi come over? To the farm. At least for a bit?" She practically bounces in place, doe eyes on full force. "I want to show them how cool it is."

For the first time since that torturous orientation, Michael and I make eye contact. "I don't know," he replies. "I guess it's up to their mom."

"*Mami, please.*" Emi begs, bringing her hands together.

I stare into my daughters' eyes, cursing my urge to satisfy their every need while having to balance being responsible. "Emi, you can't. I just checked the app and—" I cut myself off when I see my daughter shooting furtive glances at her new friend.

Has she not told her friend about her diabetes? Is she scared? Kids are insanely cruel, but Rachel doesn't strike me as the kind of kid who would ever judge or make fun of anyone for something like that. Or anything, for that matter. For all the crap I've given Michael or whatever negative impression he's left on me, his daughter seems like an amazing kid.

I look down at all three girls' pleading looks, feeling myself break. I promised myself I'd do everything in my power to give my girls a normal life so...

"How about this? How about if today, Rachel comes over—if her dad lets her of course—" I shoot Michael a look—"and you guys can go to visit their farm at a later time. When we can plan it out better." *When I can make sure I can go too and keep an eye on you guys.*

Because, though I'm sure that deep down—I'm thinking

Mariana Trench deep—Michael can be a responsible parent, I'm not about to entrust him with my children after everything. At least not until he can prove to me he won't pull the same stupid stuff Rodrigo pulled all the time.

The girls beam up at me, nodding.

"Michael? So can I go to Cami and Emi's house? They said they had a pool, too. And I still have my bathing suit from today in my bag."

Michael? He lets his kid call him by his first name? I try not to reveal my confusion, but I feel my face scrunch.

He glances quickly at me before turning back to his daughter, his brow furrowed. "I don't know..."

"I can make them an early dinner, if you'd like, and they can play for a while and then you can pick Rachel up."

"Please, Michael?" Rachel pulls on his t-shirt (plain white, as per usual), using the full force of her big eyes.

"If it helps, I can give you my number just in case. And you can pick her up in a couple of hours. I'll give you the address and—"

"I know where you live," he grunts, running his fingers through his hair.

"Um, what?" I pull my girls closer to my side on instinct.

Not missing a thing, he rolls his eyes at me. "You're Barbara's friend, right? The one staying at her house? Barbara and I grew up together. Well, I grew up with Vinny, Liza's brother? And Barbara's best friend is Liza. So I've known her basically my whole life. And now we're friends. Meaning, I've been to her new place. She mentioned she had someone with two girls staying in her guest house for the summer. That's you, isn't it?"

"Oh. I just thought... That you were the caterer."

"I was. I am. Though that's just a side business for now

while I get my..." He lets his voice trail off and shakes his head. "Whatever. The point is, I know who you are."

I clear my throat, suddenly anxious. What did Barbara say about me? Does he know about the divorce? About all the shitty stuff that's happened lately? *God.*

"Yes. That's—I mean, I'm not sure whether I'd necessarily categorize myself as her *friend.* More so that—" I stop myself from rambling. "Yes, I'm her. She. Whatever."

He scratches the back of his head, looks back at Rachel. "I guess we could go over to Emi and Camila's house for a bit," he tells his daughter.

"*We*?" I squeak.

"Well, contrary to what you believe, I'm not going to let my daughter spend the rest of the afternoon with some *stranger*." He spits the word out, pulling Rachel into him.

"I thought we just established that I'm *not* a stranger. That I'm Barbara's friend."

"That doesn't mean much to me. *I* don't personally know you, so you're a stranger to *me.* And you just clarified that you're not really her friend."

We glare at each other. For some dumb reason, because I honestly have no clue what's going on or how this is even an argument. So he wants to make sure his kid is okay. So what? That's normal. Why the hell does it have me so bothered? I would have probably asked for the same thing in this case.

"Fine," I say through gritted teeth. "You can *both* come over. The girls can play while you and I..." *While you and I* what, *exactly?*

I huff. Frustrated, I grab both my girls by the hand, dragging them back to the car. "Let's go. Follow me home," I say over my shoulder.

"Again, I already know where you live!" he calls out as he watches us walk away.

Chapter Five

MICHAEL

I HAVE NEVER MET ANYONE WITH A STICK AS FAR UP THEIR ass as Diana. And I have worked with some of the world's nastiest fucking chefs, many of whom had less than stellar personalities. And I'm sorry, but even though I've taken psychotic chefs screaming at me easily when I was in my early twenties and paying my dues, I have too much shit going on in my life to worry about some type-A personality yelling at me about every single thing I do or do not do.

"Um, Michael, are you okay?" Rachel asks from the backseat as we follow Diana's car to her place (even though she's taking the long way to her house and driving like a maniac).

"Yes. Why?" I try really hard to keep my voice neutral, but even I can tell I sound a bit pissed.

But really, though. She just assumed that I would let her take my kid willy-nilly? Was she really that surprised that I would demand to at least spend the first play date together? Does she really think I don't care about my daughter? Sure, this whole parenting thing is new to me. Maybe a year ago, anyone could've made that argument. But *she* doesn't know that. She doesn't know my life. She doesn't know that among all that tragedy, the one shining light was this new relationship with Rachel that I always thought I'd never want. She doesn't know that I've never worked so hard for something—to be good enough for my daughter after failing her so miserably.

"It's just, well. It kinda looks like you're strangling the wheel and..." Rachel says hesitantly.

I look down at my hands, the way I'm white-knuckling the steering wheel. Exhaling, I release my tight grip, trying to relax my whole body.

"I'm okay," I lie. "Just thinking about work. I was gonna go back to the farm and work on some recipes with Lexi after camp." And while *that* isn't exactly a lie, the current state of pure chaos that is my restaurant opening is far from my mind. For some reason, I can only focus on dissecting every single interaction Diana and I have had—from the loud argument at Barbara's wedding to the smallest of glances exchanged in the camp parking lot over the past week, pretending the other doesn't exist.

I watch from the corner of my eye as Rachel's face falls. "If you need to work, then..." she trails off, eyes on her fidgeting hands.

"No, hey. No, I want you to have fun with your new friends. I can work on the recipes tomorrow."

"Okay," Rachel murmurs.

When we park in Barbara's luxurious stone driveway, Diana and her girls are already by their car.

"Pool house's through here. It's where me and the girls are staying," she says, opening the gate to the yard.

She leads us through a sea of lilac hydrangeas and perfect green bushes before the girls squeal and quickly run off toward the pool area. They toe off their shoes, and excitedly murmur about the fun inflatables Barbara bought for them as they run off into the pool house to change into their swimsuits. It seems like only a few seconds later, they come back out and cannonball into the pool.

My heart warms as I watch peals of laughter burst from Rachel when she comes back to the surface.

At least she's having fun, I tell myself, practically dragging my feet, following Diana closely behind into the house and the kitchen.

"Can I get you anything?" she asks, opening the fridge door. "I've got flavored sparkling water. Grapefruit."

"Uh, sure. Sounds good."

She gives me a tightlipped smile as she hands me a cold can. "Last two."

"Lucky." I attempt a smile, but it's kinda bullshit.

"Yeah, it's my only vice. I know it's super silly to spend money on flavored sparkling water but... They're my favorite." She says it in a hushed tone, almost like it's shameful.

Sparkling water as a vice? The horror!

"*Mami*, can we—" Camila comes into the kitchen, but stops cold when she sees the sparkling water almost at her mother's lips. Her daughter gasps. "Oh my gosh, can I have one? I thought we were out."

Diana doesn't skip a beat. "Of course. Have this one. I haven't even touched it." Her smile is genuine, as if she didn't just miss out on the one thing she spoils herself with. A small sacrifice, and her daughters will never know.

She watches her daughters play through the glass doors for a moment before turning back to me. When she speaks, her eyes narrow. "You can just take a seat at the counter while I make us some food."

Jesus Christ, this is awkward. And painful. And did I mention awkward?

I have nothing in common with this woman, and now we're meant to spend the afternoon alone while the girls play out there? What the hell do we talk about? What do I even say?

Not to sound like an obnoxious ass, but I've never been in

this situation with someone. This immediate rejection, this strong repellant. Talking to her feels more and more like pulling teeth with each word we attempt to exchange.

Sure, there's no denying that Diana is gorgeous—even beneath the tell-tale signs of a mother who looks overwhelmed. Her dark hair is wrapped into a loose bun atop her head, stray curly tendrils framing her face. Her white and blue striped tee has a small coffee stain down the front that makes me think she hasn't even seen it yet—she's been too busy to pause and take a breath, probably. The deep circles under her eyes tell me that she's sleep deprived and likely too exhausted to notice it. But even still, even seeing her frazzled, annoyed, and a bit rundown, she's beautiful. She wears the same denim cutoffs from the other day, showing a delicious amount of tan leg and curvy ass. There's a bruise on her left thigh, and I want to ask her what happened, wonder whether if I run my hands over it, her skin will be just as soft as I imagine it.

But then I catch her throwing me a look, and I'm reminded of how cold she is and the sudden and unexpected ache building somewhere deep in my stomach quickly disappears.

I need to get a grip here.

Her hips sway as she opens the fridge, pulling out a chicken breast, carrots, and cucumber. I wait patiently to see if she pulls something else from the fridge but... that's it.

That's it? That's all she's going to make?

"I can help, if you'd like. You know I'm a chef." I plop onto one of the bar stools.

"Thanks for the offer, but Emiliana has Type 1 diabetes. Her diet is very specific."

Diana pulls out a paring knife—a *paring* knife!—from a drawer and uses it to chop the cucumber into cubes. The way she holds the cucumber, especially with how dull the knife looks, gives me anxiety. One slip of the hand and it's bye-bye to her fingers. I would never let a knife in my kitchen get to that point.

I hesitate for a moment, consider letting it go. But... "Right, but I'm sure that—"

She sighs deeply, drops the knife on the board, and lets her head hang between her shoulders. Diana doesn't look at me when she begs, "Please don't. I know you're trying to help in your own way, but it's really fine. She can't have anything too crazy to eat. So grilled chicken, steamed veggies, and salad it is. I'll throw in a very small amount of some form of carbs in there because she takes a long lasting form of insulin before bed, but that's it. She can't eat much of anything else."

I press my lips together because I know she isn't exactly right. It's true, Emiliana will forever face a lifetime of having to monitor what she eats, how she eats, and her physical activity all because her pancreas decided to stop producing insulin one day. But it doesn't have to be all dry chicken breast and tasteless vegetables. I know food. I am 100% certain that Emiliana could be eating something with more... flavor.

"I'm sorry," she says quietly, sighing again. "It's just... It's been difficult adjusting. Learning all the do's and don't's. And I need to do this my way. At least as we start getting our footing on this thing. It's not an easy thing to manage. I mean, we had only just gotten used to me administering her insulin directly, and now I'm having to learn to trust a pump. It's hard."

"I don't mean to overstep. All I'm saying is—" I run my fingers through my hair. "I went to culinary school. And while I only took a basic compulsory nutrition course, it did teach me a little about the kinds of foods she should and shouldn't be eating, and how to balance them. More than that, my roommate our first year had T1D, and he was able to eat mostly anything he wanted. I feel like I could help you find some balance. I mean, I fucking *live* to eat. Not the other way around. And I still manage to look this fit." I try for humor, but the lightness doesn't land. Nothing ever will with her, apparently.

"Yes, but your roommate had it under control. Emi and I are still learning. And as for you, you probably work out every day. Drink protein shakes three times a day." She says, a teasing smile on her face that does something to me.

I mock-shudder. "No to the protein shakes. Gross. But I do work out a fair bit, it's true. A couple of times a week at the gym. With how much I eat, I'd be the Pillsbury Dough Boy if I didn't." Diana snorts. I feel a sense of accomplishment from having made her laugh, even if it was just barely. "But I've gained weight since becoming a dad." I pat my stomach proudly.

She shrugs slightly, eyes on the cucumber, hands a bit unsteady. *It is literally painful to have to watch this.* "It's normal to gain some weight over the years. Even men's metabolisms slow down over the span of a decade."

"Oh," I say, sitting up in my seat. "No, I mean—I guess you don't know. Why would you?"

"What do you mean?" She stops chopping, looks curiously up at me.

"Well, I'm a new parent. Rachel and I... It's new."

"Oh." Diana's lips part, eyes locked with mine. *Damn, she's got beautiful lips.* "Is that why she calls you Michael, then?"

I swallow once. "I—Yeah. That's why. She's been with me for a year, but we're... We're still adapting. It's just Rachel and me. And every time I feel like we're making progress, something happens and just..." I release a breath, not realizing how tense I'd been feeling. "Anyway. It... It hasn't been easy. It's been *amazing*," I correct quickly when her expression shifts just a bit, "but it hasn't been easy."

Diana's stance relaxes and her features grow softer. Something resembling hope starts to build inside me. Could it be that me and the shrew have finally found some common fucking ground?

"I'm not new to parenthood, but definitely new to *single* parenthood, and... Yeah, it's been crazy. I get it. I guess you could say that's why I've been a bit tense about things."

I snort, feeling a wide smile spread across my face. "A bit?"

She rolls her eyes at me with a soft laugh. "Fine. A lot." Her eyes are apologetic when she meets my gaze. "And I guess I can now see why what I said the other night bothered you so much. You're learning how to be a parent. Everything must feel impossible."

Before she can go back to chopping the damn cucumber, I pull the cutting board away from her and take her pathetic paring knife from her hand.

"Hey! I was—"

I cut her off. "You're going to end up chopping your fingers off. This knife is too dull. And yes, sometimes I barely recognize myself. Sometimes I feel so lost I pray someone invents Google Maps for life or something. But Rachel's amazing. I don't regret becoming her dad."

She leans against the counter, small smile on her face as she keeps her gaze locked on my quick-moving hand. In no time, I'm done cubing the damn cucumber, despite the sad excuse for a blade.

"What else you need me to chop?"

With a laugh, she pushes three carrots toward me, and I get back to work, feeling something unwind between the two of us.

"I get what you mean, though. About feeling a little lost," she adds quietly.

I look up from my work to catch her staring out the kitchen window, swallowing hard once.

"You're divorced, though, right? So at least you had help in the beginning with the girls? You're not completely a fish out of water besides just learning to manage it mostly on your own." It's an odd and backhanded way of finding out more about Camila and Emiliana's dad, I'll admit.

"Yes, I'm divorced. But to be honest, Rodrigo never really did much. So the cooking, the driving them to school and homework and stuff—I always did that pretty much on my own. But I guess just knowing there was someone there—useless as he was —still helped with some peace of mind. It's just, now that I have to support the three of us, I have to do all this additional schooling and training and work and... My point is, it would've been nice to have someone around to help while I do all this. But he never really helped in a big way, so..." She shrugs.

"Nothing? He didn't help with anything?" There's no hiding the disbelief or anger in my voice.

She shrugs once, crosses her arms defensively in front of her chest. "Of course he did the easy things. The fun things. But never the... the more difficult ones. Disciplining, taking responsibility, doctor's appointments... Would even forget they went to them. Hasn't asked once about how Emi's been doing since her diagnosis."

"Jesus. Some people." I shake my head angrily and keep chopping, with a little more force this time. But who am I to judge? Sure, I had parents *just* like Rodrigo, if not worse. But I'm no better, am I? Until recently, I was only ever the fun uncle.

"Yeah. It is what it is, right? You can't change who people are."

Her words are like a knife in my chest because I *want* to change. I don't *want* to be the same guy I used to be. But I know that even though I feel that determination deep in my gut, my first instinct is always to think about myself. To think about how something will affect me. To choose what I want and not what I should do.

"I sure hope you're wrong."

"What do you mean?"

"Well, you're saying people can't change. But we just talked about new single parenthood and having to adapt to a whole new life. And there's just no way I can allow myself to go back to who I was before Rachel and I became a family." I don't want to be that guy again.

Diana shoots me a soft smile. "It isn't the same. We all had lives before our kids. But you chose Rachel. You wanted this. You wouldn't have adopted a kid if you didn't want this life."

Fuck.

There's no hiding the shame I feel, I'm sure. Because I *did* flat out reject it at one point in my life. And I certainly didn't ask for it the second time the opportunity to become a parent presented itself.

"I didn't adopt Rachel. I mean, I did. But she's my biological daughter. She just... wasn't my daughter before."

Diana's nose scrunches. "I'm confused."

I wince. "Rachel *is* my biological daughter. But I only recently became her father when her mother passed and left her to me. I wasn't a part of Rachel's life in that way before."

Diana brings her hands to her mouth, quietly murmuring, "Oh, you didn't know she existed," behind them.

"No." I shift in my seat, wishing I were anywhere but here, having to explain what a shit person I was. Am? Honestly, who knows anymore? "No, I mean, I knew she existed. She and I just never had a parent-child relationship. I had always been more the fun uncle type."

I feel it happen almost immediately. There's no missing the way my words shift the energy between us. We didn't like each other much before, sure. But I felt like she was finally loosening up as we talked. I felt like there was something akin to an understanding or camaraderie between parents building—a burgeoning *something*. But as soon as she processes my words, Diana shuts down.

"Oh," is all I get from her.

"Oh?"

Her lips thin, barely-there smile straightens, and she avoids any and all eye contact with me. "I get it. You weren't there for her. You decided not to be in the picture."

"I... I didn't say that," I stutter, suddenly frazzled beyond comprehension. Though she's not wrong. I *did* decide not to take on such a huge responsibility.

"But it's what happened, isn't it? You chose the selfish route. Left her alone with her mother."

"Yes—I mean, *no*. Yes, I decided not to be her father, but—"

"You abandoned Rachel. You chose to abandon her mother, too. And now, what? You're suddenly a changed man, and here to be a parent?" There's a vicious bite and venom to her words, the kind that kills you before you have a chance to make it to a hospital.

"Hey," I bite back, getting up from my stool. "That's not what this is at all. You don't even know me, or the situa—"

"Oh, I know you." She scoffs, angrily taking the damn cutting board away from me. "You're the kind of man who doesn't want to be tied down to any sort of responsibility. Who *thinks* he's changed, but in reality he's always going to be that same irresponsible guy who just—"

"Whoa, hold up. You *cannot* just start saying shit like—"

"Oh, yes I can. This is *my* house and—"

"It is not *your* house. It's Barbara's. And you wouldn't even—"

"*Mami?*"

"Michael?"

Diana and I turn to see all three girls staring back at us, pale-faced. They shiver beneath the thick pool towels, Rachel on the verge of tears.

"What's going on?" Diana's oldest—Camila, I think—asks.

"I—We were just..." But my voice trails off, so I look desperately to Diana for assistance. But she's frozen to the spot, guilt-ridden eyes locked on Camila's.

"I—I'm sorry. We were just making food and..."

"We were just debating what to eat," I cut in. "Your mother wanted to cook dinner and I tried to help, but she said she wanted to make something special, so..."

"I wish you *would* cook," Camila says with an eye roll. "Mom says she can, but she's not very good anymore. She's not good at being anything. She's definitely not good at keeping promises to her daughter like not embarrassing her."

"Cami!" Diana scolds, but Camila ignores her mother and stomps away in frustration.

I expect another outburst from Diana, especially after seeing her explosive reaction to our conversation. Instead, she crumples against the marble counter, eyes watering.

"...can't seem to do *anything* right..." I think I hear her murmur.

Emiliana walks over to her mother and takes one of her hands. "*Mami*. It's okay. She didn't mean it."

Diana forces a smile at her youngest, runs her fingers through her wet hair. "I know, *amor*. I'm fine. Just... tired."

And she is. I can tell. Because I am, too.

Besides the basic assumptions I've made through observations alone and everything we've talked about, we're both struggling. Being a parent is no fucking joke. It's thinking about another human being—a small, opinionated, delicate, means-everything-to-you human being—constantly. It's about putting them before your personal life and work every single time. And while I'm devastated it took losing Jessie for me to get here, it's also the best thing that's ever happened to me. But it is fucking exhausting. And I realize I'm coming into this with no experience, so it would be normal to say that it's hard. But to do it with two kids? One of which was just diagnosed with a serious medical condition, and you have no present second parent to help with the heavy stuff? I don't know how she does it.

And it's because I can appreciate to an extent what she's going through that I say, "Why don't you girls dry yourselves off while Diana finishes with the food and I help her set everything up?"

Quietly, they go back outside, heads hanging a little low.

"Thanks," Diana murmurs. "I'm sorry I—"

"No, *I'm* sorry—"

She laughs and shakes her head, waving her hands in front of her. "Please stop."

I press my lips together, trying not to smile, and nod once. "Okay."

Diana heaves a huge sigh before meeting my gaze, the exhaustion in her eyes even more pronounced. "Listen, it's clear that our girls are going to be friends for the rest of the summer. And I, for one, think that's fantastic for them. I'm sure you're happy Rachel has friends, too. So can we put aside the fact that we don't like each other, and just have a truce?"

"I need to explain. I can't let you—"

Diana sighs heavily, dropping her face in her hands. "*Please*, Michael. You don't need to explain. You don't owe me anything. Just... truce?"

I want to say no. I want to go back to when we were arguing and tell her that I'm not that guy who runs away from responsibility. Not anymore, at least. That my whole thing with Rachel... Yes, it started off like that in a way. But it's different. I was different.

Wasn't I?

Guilt rears its head once more, my stomach dropping as I understand why it is that she bothers me so much. And it's because every negative thing she's said, every awful thing she's probably thought of me, is what I feel deep down about myself sometimes. That I could've been there. I could've been Rachel's dad from the get-go.

But then I think of the man I was then, and how much I would have let her down...

And I'm torn.

I had the shitty parents. So I never wanted to be one. But was I still a shitty parent by assuming the role of the fun uncle, and never the father? Or would it have been worse to try to be part of this kid's life, knowing full well I wouldn't have been able to give my all to her *or* my career and grown to resent them both, like Lexi said?

Still, I'm done with this sick tension. It's not good for the girls to see it, and it's not good for us in general to place so much blame and stress on each other.

Which is why I shoot her a tight smile and stick out my hand for her to shake. "Truce."

Chapter Six

MICHAEL

I WIPE THE BACK OF MY HAND OVER MY FOREHEAD, already feeling the summer sun beat down on me despite it only being eleven A.M.. An hour of set-up time and three more of actual feeding frenzy, and I'll be out cold tonight as soon as I get home. Leaving me with no time for additional work or recipe research, unfortunately. Not unless I want to be even more wiped for work tomorrow.

Sighing, I try to follow the camp counselor's instructions as she walks me through Do's and Don't's of feeding people. I want to tell her—Daisy—that I've worked Michelin starred restaurants and am the last person who needs instruction on this. But then I realize, yeah, she's not talking about goat cheese foams or deconstructed fig and cherry tarts or any of the type of molecular cuisine we used to experiment with in my old restaurant. She isn't even talking about the fine catering I've been doing on the side to support ourselves while we get the restaurant off the ground. She is talking about *feeding* children and their parents. As if they were cattle. *That* is something I certainly do not have experience with.

"Just remember to put the gluten free stuff on the right side of the table and the dairy free on the left. We can leave the normal stuff in the middle to separate them. That sound good?" Apparently fancy cattle with a million food sensitivities.

When I got the brief for this request, I was shocked to find out just how many allergies were found to be so common with kids, and the liabilities the camp could incur if they were to provide any foods with certain allergens. It was difficult to come up with an inclusive, yet varied kid-friendly menu, but I did it because I'm awesome at my job.

Daisy grins up at me, her cheeks blushing when I meet her eyes. Unconsciously—or maybe fully consciously—Daisy tilts forward, pushing her chest out.

"Er, yeah," I say, turning away, fidgeting with the disposable tongs.

"We should probably have signs, right?" she asks.

"We do. They're somewhere in the baskets with the rest of the utensils and napkins."

Daisy tugs at her bottom lip with her teeth as she moves even closer still.

Immediately, I stiffen and take a step back.

"Don't worry; it shouldn't be too difficult to handle! You're a big time chef, right? You must be so used to this type of craziness."

I grimace, leaning away. "A kitchen of adults who act like children? Yes. A large group of *actual* children? No."

She bursts out laughing, several octaves too high for it to sound natural, and reaches out to place a hand on my shoulder. Did she just... Yes, she definitely squeezed my bicep. *Jesus.*

"Uh." I hesitate, trying to find the right words to let her down easy, gently grabbing her wrist and pulling her hand away. "I'm good here, if you want to move on."

In more ways than one, please.

Daisy bursts into laughter once more, batting her lashes so hard for half a second I fear she's trying to tell me something in morse code. *Shit. Does she think I'm flirting with her?* I was just trying to be funny!

"I'm sure you have more people to help out," I tell Daisy, internally begging her to leave me alone. "More volunteers to guide."

I use the term "volunteer" here very loosely, given that the email the camp sent out "asking" the parents to assist with the Field Day was passive-aggressive at best and served out enough of a guilt trip to make the purest of saints feel shame at worst. Even if I hadn't been hired to do the catering, though, I probably would've ended up doing it. The camp did not hesitate to mention I will fail as a parent if I don't sign up to be part of this amazing day. That I will be "missing out on being part of one of Rachel's most important core memories." And I'm done not being part of them anymore.

"Now, just remember to use the biodegradable bamboo plates Mrs. McCallister brought and *not* the plastic ones Mrs. Santini did." Daisy rolls her eyes at me as if to say *Typical Mrs. Santini, amirite?*

I simply nod because I don't have a fucking idea who Santini or McCallister are, and there is no way I'm opening up another painful round of conversation with this overeager woman by asking. "Right."

"I'll send over the catering volunteer when they get here. Let me see who it is..." She checks her clipboard, scanning the paper in front of her, but a part of me somehow already knows. "Diana Castillo," she confirms with a smile. "She's really nice. She has two amazing kids, Camila and Emiliana Guerrero. *Divorced,*" she whispers with a disapproving expression on her face.

Defensiveness creeps up on me, my irritation with this counselor finally reaching its limit. The only reason I don't call her inappropriate and judgmental is because I'm too busy pretending to be unaffected by the news that Diana will be my partner for the next four hours. Which I am, obviously. Unaffected by it, of course. It's why, when Diana shows up just a few minutes later, a small cooler in one hand, my heart doesn't beat *too* far out of my chest; my stomach doesn't drop *all* the way to my feet.

Okay, so maybe I'm not completely unaffected by the news of having to spend the rest of the afternoon working together. But it's only because our interactions, though civil since calling a truce, have not gone past a *Hello* or *Goodbye* at camp drop-offs and pick-ups. And I've hated it. I've hated the way we left things. I've hated the fact that she already made up her mind about who I am and doesn't like it. Above all, I've hated the way I hate the situation itself—the fact that I give a shit at all.

My chest tightens as I watch Diana walk towards me, a slow, hesitant smile on her face. Her hair is up in a loose bun again, exposing her beautiful, slender neck. I wonder what it would feel like beneath my lips, whether it's really as soft as it looks. I try not to be too obvious as my eyes travel down her body, taking in her soft curves, her tan thighs—the way they look as they slowly make their way to me. Or maybe she's not walking slowly. Maybe life has just started moving in slow motion. Because that's what this feels like.

"Hey there."

Her soft voice—like she's doing her best to pretend everything is okay when we both know it's been incredibly awkward —breaks through whatever the hell was happening in my brain right now. And *thank god* because what the actual fuck.

"So you're my task buddy, huh?" she asks, giving me a wry smile.

"Don't sound too excited," I harrumph, handing her a branded Sugar Maple Day Camp apron to slip on. I turn my back on her, pretending to busy myself with set-up when really

I'm freaking the fuck out. My breathing is ragged, so I do my best to control it, to push whatever intense reaction I just had to her to the back of my mind.

She takes the apron, staring down at it as if enthralled by the stitching or something. Either that, or she really can't stand to look at me. The latter seems to be the more likely of the two, given our last real encounter. This false truce of ours has been a nightmare. Especially now that I just realized I'm attracted to her.

Fuck.

I hate myself. I truly, truly hate myself.

Though I can't deny, given the current pressure building between my legs, maybe it's for the best that she avoids looking me straight in the eye. The emotional separation helps lessen the physical need. Barely, but it helps.

"I'm just joking," she murmurs.

"Are you?" And now I hate myself even *more* because why the fuck do I need to ask her these questions? Why put myself through more of this shit? Just let her hate me. I deserve it. She's not wrong when she said I was selfish.

She heaves a sigh and finally looks up at me. "Yes. I was. Kind of?" She scrunches her face, tilts her head.

Cute, I think.

I laugh once at her expression, feeling myself unwind a bit, and nod. "Fair. I get it. Things have been weird. I know you haven't wanted to talk to me, so if this is really uncomfortable for you, maybe we can ask Daisy to switch you out for something else. I would offer to switch only I'm being paid to cater this thing and—"

"No, I'm okay. Really. And I've been avoiding you because I've felt so ashamed of how I acted. I don't know if I would've had the courage to reach out to you to apologize, honestly. So I'm glad we're 'volunteering' together." She air-quotes the word, and I smile. She felt the threatening undertones of that email, too, then.

Great minds and all that.

"Forces me to be a big girl and tell you that..." She takes a deep breath and blows it out. "Tell you that I'm sorry. That I was an ass. That some things you said reminded me a little bit about my ex and so..."

Now my stomach *really* drops. I remind her of her *ex-husband*? Jesus. So she does hate me. I feel my face drain of blood, and I can no longer look at her.

"Right," I say, busying myself by stacking some plates at either end of the picnic tables.

"Shoot. No, that's not what I meant! You're not as bad as my ex—"

"*As bad*? Fuck." I scoff.

"I mean, no. I mean, yes. *Ugh*. Just let me explain."

She exhales, hands on her hips. Wisps of dark brown hair loose around her face, wild and beautiful. They pair perfectly with her coffee eyes, large and doe-eyed.

"Well? Explain," I demand after a painful thirty seconds.

"I just meant that the story you told me about your past—"

"Which was just surface level, by the way. You're missing a lot of important details," I mutter, crossing my arms in front of my chest.

"—reminded me a bit about how cavalier Rodrigo used to be about our children. And just life responsibilities in general. When it came down to what *he* wanted, what was best for *him*... Well, he sure went after it. Whether it was taking a job that forced us to move and resulted in me marrying him way too young and dropping out of college a semester before graduation, or whether it was the twenty-five year-old blonde he met on a flight to Phoenix and left me for. Either way, he never *really* stopped to consider his wife or children. Or anyone else for that matter, especially since he soon after cheated on said girlfriend, too. And you were talking about only recently taking ownership of the things you'd done—not that Rachel is something you did, like crashing a car or something—but..." She shakes her head, frustrated. "I'm not explaining myself properly. Again." She catches her breath, brows pinched, luscious lips pressed tightly closed. After a few seconds of silence, she tries once more: "I'm sorry. That's what I really want to say—what I really want you to take away from this verbal diarrhea I can't seem to control. I don't know you—not really—and I was too wrapped up in my own stuff to give you the benefit of the doubt."

"Thank you." A knot unwinds in my stomach and I smile back at her. I don't know her well, either, but something about Diana tells me that this apology didn't come easy to her.

"You're welcome, I guess." She sighs, as if relieved to get this over with.

Her apology is more than welcome, even though I keep reminding myself I shouldn't give a shit. This woman literally has no bearing on my life. The best way to deal with this situation would be to go on as we have: let our girls be friends, maintain a *very* surface-level relationship, occasionally see each other at camp pick-ups and drop-offs, and make polite conversation over playdates.

But then what I can only assume is an alien takes over my fucking brain and next thing I know the words "I know we already called a truce the other day, but... How about we actually start over?" escape my lips as I stick out my hand and grin expectantly. "My name's Michael. I'm thirty-four years old and a former workaholic. I grew up around here before moving to New York City to be a chef. After my best friend passed away unexpectedly, I inherited Rachel, my biological daughter, and moved back to the area. Currently, I own a farm with my cousin Lexi. We're opening a fine dining farm-to-table restaurant here in Long Island, but it's been a bitch to do as I learn to navigate and balance single-parenthood with work."

She stares down at my hand, biting down on her lip to keep from smiling. After some internal battle, she laughs once and takes it. "Diana. I'm thirty-one and from Denver, though I was born and spent most of my childhood in Venezuela."

I raise my brows at that brand new information, a piece of the puzzle that is Diana, falling into place: her soft accent. I ache to ask her more about herself, to tell me the story behind that, but choose to let her continue to share whatever she's comfortable with.

"I am *also* new to being a single parent—kind of. The concept of *Married Single Mom* was invented thanks to me. My kids, Emiliana and Camila, are my whole life, and it's been really difficult managing my recent divorce and my youngest's recent T1D diagnosis on my own. Especially while finishing my degree, applying to new jobs, and now studying to complete a certificate as a paralegal for the state of Colorado. My life is a mess and I'm trying to keep it together, so I apologize if I can get persnickety sometimes."

I laugh, her small, soft hand still in mine. "Persnickety?"

"Persnickety."

"Okay, then."

"Friends?" She looks up at me with a hopeful expression that tugs at something in my chest—weird—her caramel cheeks flushed in anticipation.

Friends. Something about the word doesn't sit right with me, and I'm not sure why. Regardless, *friends* would make my life easier. Being *friends* with Diana would make Rachel's life easier, too.

So: "Yes, let's be friends."

"Oh, good!" Daisy pops up once again out of nowhere. "You've introduced yourselves. Saved me the hassle!" She laughs as she looks nervously between us, then at our still-held hands, and back again. "Wow, that sure is a long handshake." Daisy laughs once more, though her disappointment and discomfort is impossible to hide this time.

Jesus, this is awkward.

Diana pulls her hand from mine with a little too much force, though her expression remains unchanged—the perfect picture of zen. As if she meant to hold my hand for longer than usual, and she stands by it. As if this young counselor isn't acting out of line.

"Right, well. I just came over to see if you two needed some help, but it looks like you're doing just fine. So I'm just gonna..."

"Yup. No issues here," Diana says, voice saccharine. "Thanks *so* much for checking up on us."

Daisy clears her throat once, visibly uncomfortable. "Okie dokie. Let me know if you have any questions, alright?"

Once she's out of earshot, we burst out into laughter.

"God, that's so fucking embarrassing. I am so sorry for her," I tell her, shaking my head.

"Is she always like this with you?" Diana asks, slipping her apron over her head and tying it behind her back. The movement pushes her chest out, forcing me to look away even though I really, really didn't want to. It's not a conscious effort, like it was with Daisy. And it's certainly not one that isn't well-received. Diana has a perfect set of—

Whoa! Slow down there, cowboy.

"I don't know," I say with a sigh, a little frazzled by my own train of thought. "But it's bordering on harassment. She kept touching my arm while she was helping set up right before you got here. She also always seems to catch me at pick-up to give me an update on Rachel. Which, at first I appreciated but, like, I don't fucking want *her* to tell me what they did at arts and crafts every day? Unless it's something important about her safety or happiness, I want my *daughter* to tell me about it. So Rachel and I can bond over it. I think it's pretty evident this seemingly-innocent crush she has on me has turned into a full on inconvenience."

"Oh my god," she says with a laugh. "That's crazy. You're like twelve years her senior! What is she thinking?"

"You calling me an old man?"

"No," she smiles. "Just saying that's a big age difference. Duh. She must be, what, twenty-one? Twenty-two?"

I dig through the basket of utensils, find the food signs, and place them in their respective spots. "Here." I take a few items and hand them over to her so she can help set up. She takes them from me with a smile. "But yeah, absolutely. She's way too young. I would never date anyone who doesn't pass the 'half plus seven rule,' you know? Too weird."

"The *what*?"

"The 'half plus seven' rule? It's what determines whether someone is age appropriate for you. The minimum age you can date someone has to be half your age plus seven. So the youngest I could date without any weirdness—or too much of it —would be—"

"Twenty-four."

I nod and she takes a beat to think about it.

"I still think that might be too young for you."

"Now you're telling me who I can date?" I poke her in the side with a pair of tongs with a laugh.

She swats my hand away and shoots me a menacing look. Still, though, she suppresses a smile.

"No. I'm just saying there is a huge difference in where someone is in their lives in their mid-thirties and their early twenties."

"Not necessarily. I could find myself a twenty-four year-old looking to have kids and settle down immediately."

She presses her lips together and thinks on it for a moment. "You're right. You could. And honestly, intellectually and emotionally you could also pass for a twenty-four year-old, so you'd be a perfect match."

I sputter a laugh. "Wow, really? High compliment, coming from Diana Castillo," I say sarcastically. "What about you, though?"

"What about me?"

"Would you date a half-plus-seven?"

"A twenty-two, twenty-three year-old?" She winces. "I don't have time for babies. Already got two kids—don't need another one." I burst out laughing, watching her smile at her own joke. "I'm not looking for anything now, but when I'm ready, I'll be looking for a real man."

"*I'm* a real man." And as soon as the words escape my lips I want to die. Want to hit myself in the head with the tongs, and bury myself in the bowl of vegan coleslaw I spent all morning making.

"Um," Diana looks up at me, face flushed to her hairline.

My jaw drops as I scramble, tongue-tied, for something to say, how to save this awkward encounter.

"I just meant—"

"No, it's okay," she says with an awkward laugh. "It's fine; I know what you meant." Which is great, because *I* have no idea what I meant. Would love for her to explain it to me.

"Right."

The silence that falls between us is painful as we just stare at each other. I hold her gaze—or maybe she holds mine—and that's when I notice how beautiful her brown eyes really are. The depth of color in them, the variety of different hues. Coffee black and dark chocolate, with mahogany and flecks of gold—even a splash of hunter green. Never in my life have I seen such beautiful, complex eyes. Never in my goddamn life have I *noticed* someone's eyes like this.

What is going on with me? So she's hot. Big deal. So many other women are hot, too. But I've never had this... reaction before.

As if out of my control, I take a step toward her. Diana inhales sharply, tilting her head back to look up at me better, the wind tugging at the loose tendrils of her hair as if trying to untie them from that bun. A wave of honey and peaches—and is that mint?—overwhelms my senses. Unconsciously, I step closer. And just as I'm about to speak, to say... something, anything—

"Are you getting ready to serve lunch soon?" one of the campers interrupts.

Chapter Seven

DIANA

"So this is vegan?" I hear one of the kids in the buffet line ask Michael.

"Yes," he practically grunts out.

"And does it have any added sugars? Any preservatives?" The kid pokes at the small amount of coleslaw on his plate, as if checking for poison.

Michael gawks at the boy, who does not look a day older than seven. "Uh. It's all freshly made. Farm to table." He shoots me a glance and shakes his head in disbelief before turning back to the boy. "That means that—"

The boy raises a hand to cut Michael off. "I know what farm to table means." The kid rolls his eyes in frustration while I do my best to suppress laughter. "I just want to make sure you're not putting any garbage in our food."

Michael crosses his arms in front of his chest and glares at the kid as the line behind the boy begins to grow by the second, hungry children and parents quickly growing impatient.

"Listen, kid. I know my stuff. I know how to treat food and what's healthy. I know—"

The boy rolls his eyes once more and sighs. "Fine. Just tell me what's gluten free. I'm not allowed to have anything else."

Michael grunts and serves the boy another scoop of the most

colorful coleslaw I've ever seen—a delicious kaleidoscope of purples and oranges that makes my mouth water—and a piece of barbecued chicken cooked to perfection—far from the breast that I made this morning for Emiliana's lunch.

The boy glances down at his plate and leaves with an exasperated sigh before walking over to the nearest picnic table, poking at his food with hesitation.

"I cannot believe that just happened," Michael mutters. "The absolute *gall*."

I burst into laughter, unable to keep it in any longer. "Seriously? Did you just use the word *gall*?"

"I'm not used to anyone questioning my culinary skills."

"I'm sure you get 'Yes, Chef' all day—"

"And night," he cuts me off with a smirk.

My breath catches, and I clear my throat before rolling my eyes as if somehow that didn't affect me. "But you just need to understand that kids can be as picky—if not more so—as adults."

"It was freaking *coleslaw*," he grumbles.

"These kid's palates are far more demanding than your former customers," I say between giggles. *Giggles??* But I can't help but find the situation funny. And Michael's frustration is a little adorable. "You can't really hold it against him too much."

"The food I made is perfection, and far better than anything I ever ate at his age. I'm telling you, I grew up on Rice Krispies treats and microwavable meals and did just fucking fine."

"That's a bad word, mister," a little girl says, looking up at him with wide eyes.

He sighs and looks down at her. "You're right. I'm sorry. Here. Have an extra cookie as an apology." Michael places a piece of chicken and a scoop of coleslaw onto her plate, but drops two cookies right beside them.

The little girl grins from ear to ear. "Whoa, cool! Thanks!"

"See?" He points at her retreating form as she makes her

way to sit with her friends at another table. "That's the kind of excitement I'm looking for! That's the kind of reaction I'm used to getting for my food."

"The cookies are for later! And aren't they store bought?"

He glares at me, and I stifle a laugh. I bite my lower lip to keep from smiling too much, my cheeks already sore from an afternoon spent joking around with him. How did we get from not being able to stand each other to having the best time I've had in a while? I mean, we've been standing under the sweltering sun for a couple of hours, serving food to campers, parents, and counselors, all while battling an unreasonable amount of picky eaters, yet I've been having a good time.

"You just need to realize that kids are *not* fine diners."

Michael sighs. "One of my current struggles in life. My daughter prefers dinosaur-shaped chicken nuggets to my Cajun chicken with a beurre blanc sauce."

I laugh. "Dino nuggets are a classic staple in any home with children." *And some adults*, I think. "And I bet you save a ton of time cooking them. Can't beat an air fryer."

He grunts in acknowledgment.

"How're things going by the way? With Rachel, I mean?"

He smiles at the vegan and gluten-free mac 'n cheese he slaps on another girl's plate before telling her to enjoy her food. "Good. Better. We had a great day last Saturday. I took her to this summer fair a few towns over. They had a petting zoo and a bunch of other activities. She whined that it was for little kids, but I could tell she was having fun." His eyes take on a far-off glance, as he remembers the outing with fondness.

I can't help the smile that spreads across my face.

"That's amazing. I'm sure she was happier about spending quality time with you than the actual fair, though."

Michael shoots me a bashful smile. "I hope so. We used to be buds, you know? Before her mom... Whenever I'd come into town, I was fun Uncle Michael. And now the dynamic is so different... For a moment there, I thought she cared less for me. Was too angry at me for lying. But considering everything, I think she's taken it like a champ. We've both come so far, but things could have been much, much worse." His head shakes in awe. "She is truly incredible."

I smile widely at him. I barely know Michael and Rachel, but hearing about how they've healed their relationship makes me so happy for them—even though it sends a slight pang of jealousy through me. I wish my girls had a father like that. One who made a conscious effort to improve their relationship. Rodrigo might be an absolute ass who made me question every single life choice I've ever made, but I still want him to be there for our girls. I don't want them to ever feel unloved by him or like this divorce was in any way their fault. And yet, Rodrigo has only grown more cavalier with his daughters. While Michael...

"I'm sorry, by the way," I tell him, reaching for another kid's plate.

When he turns to face me, it's with a raised brow and pointing tongs in my direction. "Didn't we already do this? Don't get me wrong, hearing you apologize is amazing. I feel like it's slowly starting to become my new kink." His cheeks flush, and so do mine. *What was that?* We both choose to ignore it, clearly, because he keeps going: "But... You don't have to do this for a third time."

I nod, scooping some more food onto another kid's place. "The first time was barely an apology. It only led to a truce. The second one was more genuine because I felt bad for how things were between us when our girls seem to love each other so much. And I think you deserve this third one because it's *specific.* I need to apologize for putting you on the same level as my ex."

He winces and gets back to his task, muttering a *You're welcome* to those who thank him for the food. "Yeah."

"I guess it did anger me a bit to hear that you chose to... not *abandon* Rachel, exactly, but maybe chose to not..." I pick my words wisely. "Well, *choose* her, I guess. Does that make sense?"

He flinches, keeping his eyes on the food trays in front of him.

"I think part of me wasn't willing to understand where you were coming from. And while I still believe it was... not a great thing to do." I grimace, wording things to the best of my ability. "I can admit I shouldn't make any judgments considering I don't know what the circumstances were. And I can't deny that you aren't doing your best to change things *now*. To make up for lost time and own up to your responsibilities. And that's better than never doing so." *Like some people I know*, I almost add.

Michael takes a deep breath before facing me head on, leaving an eager child lifting his plate up for food in Dickensian fashion. "Diana. You should know that—"

"*Mami,* do you have my lunch?" Emiliana pops up beside me, followed by her sister and Rachel.

I immediately crouch in front of her. "Sweetheart, have you been drinking water? I've told you that you have to stay hydrated in the sun." God, I can't believe I haven't checked her glucose levels in the past hour. My stomach rolls, guilt flooding my system as I pull out my phone and open the app.

I am a horrible mother.

Emi gently pushes my hand off her cheek. "I'm fine," she grumbles.

"Emi, please," I beg.

With a sigh, she lets me lead her to the closest picnic table where I offer her a cold bottle of water, leaving Michael to manage the rest of the hungry crowd on his own. When I've double-checked Emi's levels are okay and she's hydrated, we walk back to the buffet table, where I pull out the cooler of prepared food I made for her early this morning. I don't miss her wince when she peers into the containers.

"Thanks, *Mami*," she says with a forced smile.

I don't blame her. How many times can she eat the same thing every day? But I haven't had the time to learn new recipes that are quick and easy and work for her, so I've been sticking to my tried and trues.

Diabetes is hard.

Michael clears his throat beside us, whispering. "I, uh, actually made something special for her, if you wanted to give it a shot?"

I gawk at him for a moment. "You... what?"

"Well," he starts, his cheeks flushing a deeper red. "I figured you'd have her bring her own food and stuff, and maybe she'd feel a bit left out, so I made some friendly options." He grumbles something under his breath as he pulls out his own small-sized cooler from under the table, the line of people waiting for their regular food growing.

"How..." I clear my throat. "How do you know all the nutritional value and everything?"

"I wrote it down. Here." He shrugs once, pointing at a bright yellow Post-It taped to the lid of the container. "I don't know if that's okay, because I know it's all like a delicate balance and stuff. And you need to adjust her bolus, right? But I googled a bunch of recipes and used what I already knew and... Yeah. It's dumb, now that I think about it. But I just didn't want her to feel left out."

"It's anything but dumb. It's... very considerate of you."

I look down at the cooler in my hands, inspecting the containers.

"I'm not trying to poison your kid," he whispers. "I promise it's all legit and accurate."

"It's not that. It's—" I try to control the stinging behind my eyes. "I... don't know what to say. Thanks for wanting to help and for being so considerate." *Considerate being the standout word.* I can't remember the last time someone did something like that for me. For *us*.

I think I hear him whisper *Fuck* under his breath as he looks away. Watch how he quickly busies himself by getting back to feeding impatient, hungry campers. "Don't—Don't even mention it, okay? It's dumb. I... I just wanted to help."

Emiliana looks between us, a slow smile forming on her lips. She walks over to him and tugs at his apron until he looks down at her. "Thank you," she says. "Mom and I really appreciate it." She takes the container from me and waits for her sister and friend to get their food, while I stare blankly at a tense Michael, a frown on his face.

I double-check the nutritional value of everything, check her blood sugar, and adjust Emi's insulin bolus before letting her dig into the food. But when I get back to the buffet table to finish serving the last of the campers, parents, and counselors, Michael and I don't go back to the easy conversation we had going before. We're silent as we finish up our task, avoid each other's gaze as we clean up the table, and are almost indifferent as we pack everything up at the end of the afternoon.

The awkward tension is nearly painful by the time I finish tying up a trash bag. But before I can figure out what to say or even begin to understand why something nice suddenly shifted our entire dynamic *again,* he takes the bag from my hands with a deep sigh.

"Okay. I'm sorry. I know I crossed a line and stepped over a boundary I probably shouldn't have. But I promise I was just trying to be helpful, and it wasn't intended to be a dig at your parenting skills. I don't know why I did it, but I swear I just wanted to help. Maybe because I know I can? And I could tell you needed it? And I hated the thought of you feeding them the same depressing shit over and over again when I know they can still eat delicious food and have a ton more variety even though Emiliana has T1D. So I'm sorry if—Why are you smiling?"

I laugh once. "Honestly, I wasn't aware that I was smiling."

He frowns. "I don't understand."

"I don't either. But I wasn't mad. Not at all. It just caught me off guard, is all. I think that was very kind of you. And given our short past, it was unexpected. I've... I've really misjudged you, Michael Haynes. Thank you for proving me wrong."

Michael sputters. "Are you serious? Did you just thank me? For proving you wrong?" A heartbreaking smile spreads across his face.

I shake my head and take the garbage bag from his hand, but he takes it back.

"I'm taking the trash out, are you kidding me? But seriously, did you just admit you were wrong again?"

I roll my eyes and shove him once. "Don't get cocky," I say, pointing a finger in his direction. "It's not often that I'm mistaken."

He laughs. "I believe that. I just feel honored."

"Thank you for being so thoughtful. Now, will you let me help you take out the trash, or what?"

"I will, on two conditions," he says, pulling the bag just out of reach.

I narrow my eyes at him. "What conditions?"

He smiles mischievously. "First, you tell me how you found out my last name."

Now it's me who flushes viciously—I can feel my cheeks practically aflame. "I—I googled your catering company. I remembered the name from Barbara's wedding."

His grin widens. "Cool."

I roll my eyes and put a hand on my hip. "Don't go thinking

you're special. I needed to check who my daughters' friend's parent was." Which is true, but that's not the entire reason I googled him a couple of nights ago. My having a glass of wine too many and thinking about how attractive he was, however, did add to it. I need this part of the conversation to be over. "What's the second condition?"

"That you let me come over and teach you some recipes—quick and easy ones. Let me help you. Help *Emi*."

For a split second, I almost consider it. But my instincts overpower that part of me that is screaming for help because I was always taught it's rude to do so.

"No, I'm okay, thank you. You're right, though—I should be doing more research." I sigh internally because the idea of adding one more thing to my mental load makes me want to scream. I reel it in, feeling the weight of guilt from that thought press down on my chest. What kind of mother am I? Of course I should be doing all this research. I have to do better, though. *Be* better.

"Okay, well. If you have any questions... Just know I'm here."

"Thanks," I say, slapping on my best smile.

We stare at each other in silence for a minute, unmoving. I take in his features, noting the way the sun hits his hazel eyes, making them look almost emerald green. Vibrant, full of life. But also tired. Overwhelmed. And it makes my heart ache just a little. Because, despite having annoyed me at first, I can see how big of a life change this has been for him, too. That, I can empathize with.

"Hey, so. Do you guys have any plans for Fourth of July?" he asks.

This takes me by surprise. "Um. No, actually. I mean, I was thinking of taking the girls to the next town over's parade—some people have recommended it—but nothing other than that."

He scratches the back of his head and looks down at his feet as the words rush out of his mouth: "Well, I'm hosting a barbecue with a bunch of people at a beach in Southampton—just about twenty minutes from here. Good food, corn hole—other activities. You know. I've already invited Barbara, though she hasn't really RSVP'd yet. Do people still RSVP? Anyway. We're gonna do the whole seafood and hot dogs thing and see the fireworks over the ocean and have a bunch of people over. And I was wondering whether you'd like to come. The girls and you, I mean."

Is he... is he *nervous*?

"Barbara won't be back until the last couple of weeks of summer. But, yeah, I'm sure the girls would love to come hang. That sounds like a lot of fun."

"They'll be other grown-ups there, too. Not just me. So you won't be bored out of your mind."

I laugh. Did he use the word *grown-ups*? Adorable. "Listen, we might not have gotten along in the beginning, but it's never been boring between us."

Us.

"No, it hasn't," he says quietly. He stares at me for a moment before breaking the unexpected silence between us. "Can I get your number? So I can text you the address, I mean. And you can call me if you get lost or anything."

My chest tightens while I pause for a second, eyes roaming his face, taking in his expression—so kind; such a difference from our first few interactions. Do I want to give him my number? "Yes."

Chapter Eight

MICHAEL

"Tell me exactly why you're doing this? I thought we were having a low-key Fourth of July at the beach." Lexi raises a brow, setting down two beach chairs on the white sand next to the four I already set up. She eyes me skeptically when she should be monitoring her kids as they play catch with a football. I mean, she's acting like this whole thing is a huge deal when it's not.

At least that's what I'm telling everyone.

"This *is* low-key," I lie, hoping my aviators hide the anxiety in my eyes.

She looks meaningfully at the portable Weber grill I bought for the occasion, the new umbrellas and towels I got from Costco yesterday, the beach games I borrowed for the afternoon from my neighbor, and the three coolers full of food and beverages I spent all last night preparing.

"Bagged sandwiches and sodas and water in a cooler is low-key. A whole barbecue, fire pit, and prepared foods is *not* low-key," Lexi's wife, Lauren, adds.

"Not to mention the amount of people you invited. It's crazy. Call it what it is—this is basically a full-on party at this point."

"It isn't a party. And I only invited people who are close to us."

"Right. And this new woman in your life." Lauren snorts.

I wipe a bead of sweat from my forehead before laying out the blankets and beach towels. "Can you help with these, please? And she's not a *new woman in my life*. I didn't invite *her*. Yes, she's become a sort of friend—kinda." Maybe? "But it's only because her daughters are Rachel's best friends at the moment. I invited *them*. And considering everything Rachel's been through this past year, I am super grateful for their existence." The fact that Diana is their mom is just a bonus. A very hot one. "Last year was super difficult for Rach—it was a new school and she didn't have many friends. This summer has been great for her."

Lexi gives me a hesitant smile. "That's great that they've gotten so close. Though aren't you concerned about what it will do to her at the end of the summer when they go back home? Because they aren't from around here, right? So, it's not like these will be permanent friends."

"Yeah, what happens when they leave?" Lauren asks.

I frown, readjusting the umbrellas for the millionth time now for maximum coverage. "I know. They're from *Denver*." I almost spit out the word like it's a dirty one. "But I'm trying to focus on the now. If this is what makes Rachel happy, then I'm not going to stand in her way. Her well-being is my number one priority. We'll deal with her friends leaving when it comes." Lexi grins at me, so I groan. "What now?"

"Nothing." She shakes her head with a smile on her face. "It's just so nice to see you this way. Being a parent definitely suits you."

My heart swells with pride, but I can't help the bout of imposter syndrome I feel every day. "She's an amazing kid. It's all her. And hopefully, last year was just a fluke, and the kids at her new school will realize this, too."

God, I hope so. I can't stand the thought of my daughter hurting even more than she is. Though we haven't spoken much about it. I've been patiently waiting for her to come to me—to talk to me about what's been going on.

"I'm sure they will." Lexi pats me on the back. "And I'm sure she's excited you set up this party. And hopefully *you're* also excited for it?" She smirks.

I roll my eyes. "I never should've told you guys about Diana. Admitting I found Rachel's friends' mom attractive was the worst mistake of my life."

Lexi snorts. "Really? The *worst* mistake of your life? I've known you forever; are you sure you don't want to include the ridiculous frosted tip hairstyle you had in high school?"

I cringe. Thank god I've gotten rid of all the photos from back then, all evidence of that horrible hair color gone from existence.

"Or that time you thought it would be a great idea to go rock climbing with absolutely no training whatsoever, and ended up with a broken arm and leg? Not to mention the stitches on your forehead!"

My fingers unconsciously reach for the scar just above my right eyebrow, barely visible to anyone but me. "Those were questionable choices, not mistakes."

"Oh, buddy. Believe me when I say that hair was a serious mistake—far from *questionable*. The only questionable thing is whether or not we're even related."

"It was the aughts. Everyone was doing it. And I was going through my rebellious phase."

Lexi scoffs. "And the rock climbing?"

"That was..." *A cry for help?* I almost say. Something I didn't realize until well into adulthood. Maybe part of me wanted to see if my parents gave a shit about whether I hurt or not. What they really gave a shit about was the medical bill that stunt I pulled came with. "That was a stupid thing to do."

"Understatement of the century," she mutters, crossing her arms in front of her chest.

I hear Lauren gasp behind me. "Michael. Are... are those flowers sticking out of that beach tote? Did you bring flowers to a beach barbecue?"

I flush bright red, staring at the white daisy arrangement I picked up on my way here. "I... I wanted the set-up to look nice," I say, trying to act cool but all too aware of the defensiveness in my tone.

"Oh, Michael. No," Lexi says softly, shaking her head.

"Will you just help me finish setting up these umbrellas?" I ask with a huff.

"Pretty sure you've moved them in every statistically possible position, but okay."

It's not long after that the others begin to trickle in, joining me and the women. Vinny, the Castelli sibling closest to my age, helps me heat up the grill while Danielle, his wife, wrangles their children.

"You're tense," Matt, Vinny's old college buddy and his little sister's husband, whispers. When he slaps me on the back, I flinch a little. "And jumpy. What's with you?"

I look nervously around us, making sure Lexi and Lauren are out of earshot, and therefore able to keep their noses out of my business. I'm not safe from them giving me shit. "I'm fine. Just trying to make sure everything is set for today and tonight. I want everyone to have a good time."

He narrows his eyes at me. "You sure?"

"Of course I'm—" But my words turn to ash on my tongue when my eyes fall on Diana. She's a vision—a fucking *dream*—walking toward us from the path between the dunes in denim shorts, a white tank, and with what looks like a red bikini underneath.

Lord, give me strength.

I try to swallow the rock in my throat once. Twice. Three fucking times. But fail miserably as my eyes stay fixed on Diana's moving figure, her lithe, curvy body walking through the sand, beach tote in one hand, sandals dangling from her fingers on the other. My concentration only breaks when her girls come barreling toward us, screaming for my daughter.

The girls crash into each other in a group hug, and for the first time, I wonder whether my cousin and her wife were right. Whether this friendship I thought was a blessing might end up being a curse—for all of us. Because I'm realizing that Rachel has come alive since making new friends, and maybe this *thing* I have for Diana is definitely more of a crush.

How high school of me.

A drum beating against my ribs, I can't help my smile when I greet her with a simple, "Hey."

"Hey back." She grins, eyes fixed on mine.

After what could've been an hour or a second, Matt breaks through our silence—*thank god*—by sticking his hand out to her. "Hey I'm Matt, by the way. Matt Wilson."

Diana greets him with her most beautiful smile, making me have to calm down the sudden feelings of jealousy coursing through me. I realize it's irrational for *so* many reasons—we're not dating and most of our interactions up until now have been tense. Not to mention the fact that Matt is married, for Christ's sake—but it's instinctual. My lizard brain yearns to yell *Mine!* and take her by the hand, maybe sneak a make-out session by the dunes.

It's a new feeling, this possessiveness—it catches me off guard. In general, I've never been a jealous guy. The idea of barking the words "Get your hands off my girl" has never even crossed my mind. And yet, the second their hands meet, I feel a shift inside me.

Idiot, Michael. You're an idiot.

"Hey, yeah. We've actually met. At Barbara's wedding?" She smiles at Matt, who blushes in embarrassment.

"Oh, man. You're right. I'm so sorry." He facepalms.

Diana shakes her head softly, the wind blowing at the loose, soft tendrils framing her face. "No—don't worry about it. It was a busy night, and we only spoke for five seconds." She's being way too kind to him. I can't imagine anyone meeting Diana and forgetting about her—even if it was only after a five second conversation. "I also met your wife, who's great, by the way."

Matt smiles wildly, a goofy grin. I realize in that moment my jealousy is even dumber than I thought, because Matt is still head over heels for his girl and everyone knows it. "Yeah, Liza really is," he tells her with a sigh.

"So how has your summer been?" he asks.

She blows a puff of air. "Well, it's been good. Barbara has been amazing in letting us borrow her guest house—which, like, is the size of a normal-sized house, if you ask me." The three of us chuckle in agreement. "I'm really bummed she couldn't make it today, though."

"That's the life of a movie star," he says with a grin.

"Ha. I guess so. I just feel bad because she's been so good to us, and I have no idea how to even thank her. My daughters have been having an amazing time at camp and stuff this summer, and I definitely owe that to her. I mean, just ask Michael! They've definitely kept themselves busy with Rachel, too."

"So we covered your daughters. But how has *your* summer been?"

I suppress a smile, because Matt was able to catch onto

Diana's habit to downplay the importance of her own happiness just like I have.

"Um," she says, scratching the side of her nose. "It's mostly been busy for me, too. I'm either working or with the girls, so I haven't had much time to explore the towns or anything. This is actually my first time at the beach in the entire six weeks I've been here. Or at least since Barbara's wedding."

"Wait, really? Well, thankfully you have this guy over here to invite you out to these types of events, am I right?" Matt slaps me on the back. I glare back at him. "He's just *so* nice and generous."

Diana presses her lips together, suppressing a knowing smile when her gaze meets mine, right before turning back to Matt. "Oh, yes. Michael has been an absolute *treat*." She laughs.

"Hey," I grumble. "I thought we were in a truce. Or at least moving towards a friendship?" *Sigh.* I hate this. I hate that I want her to like me.

"I'm just joking." She lightly elbows me in the side with a laugh. "Michael has been really nice. Lately, at least. And inviting us to this was super sweet of him. Otherwise, my daughters and I probably would've just stayed at home after hitting the parade."

"Not a chance. I never would have let that happen." I say it with such conviction, I even surprise myself.

Matt laughs and raises his brows at me. "Alright, then. Well, I need to go find my wife and ask whether I can get her anything to eat. Food is her love language. It was really nice seeing you. I'll tell Liza to come say hi."

"I'd love that." She smiles—that perfect, open smile I wish she'd give me just once.

Matt leaves us by the edge of the group of umbrellas, walking away with a knowing smirk.

Fucker.

Diana looks around our set-up. "This looks incredible. Like something out of Martha Stewart or Ina Garten. Did you do all this?"

I turn and look around, filled with pride. A normal man might feel insecure after being compared to those two legendary women, but I'm not closed-minded to let it affect me. "Yeah, but Lexi and her wife helped."

"Lexi?"

"My cousin. Business partner, too. She's married to Lauren, over there." I point to where they both stand, huddled next to one of the coolers. When I catch them staring, they quickly turn and face different directions.

Smooth.

"Ah." Diana shifts her canvas tote from one shoulder to the other, and that's when I see the welts it's left on her skin.

"Jesus, that's just from carrying this from the parking lot to here? It's that heavy?"

"It's got all the girls' stuff. And mine."

"Give me that; let's set it down." In an uncharacteristic move, Diana lets me help her by gently pulling the bag off her shoulders.

"Careful. There's an apple pie in there, too."

"You shouldn't have—really. I told you in my text last night we were more than good on food."

"I know. And I know it's extremely lame to bring a store-bought apple pie compared to all this, but it goes against every grain in my body to just show up with three hungry people and nothing else."

I laugh, and pull out the pie box from inside the tote and place it over one of the coolers. "Two kids is the equivalent of, like, one adult, so it's not a big deal at all," I joke. She snorts. "And I'm sorry to disappoint you if you guys are already hungry, but the food isn't ready yet," I say with a grimace, cursing myself for not setting up earlier. "We were hoping to have the actual food for sunset, and that's a few hours away. But we have snacks and drinks and stuff. Can I get you anything while we get the grill going?"

"What is everyone having?" She looks around the group. The wind whips at her loose curls, finally free of a bun. And I love it. Am *obsessed* with the way her long, dark hair falls over her shoulders, the way it makes her look a bit more unwound—*carefree*. As she always should be.

I take this time to look at her—*really* look at her. Soak in the glow of her skin and the small mole right above her lip. The delicate curve of her neck. The way her chocolate brown eyes squint in the sun while she holds a hand up to protect herself from the rays.

"Michael?" she asks, breaking through my wayward thoughts.

"Mmm?"

"I was just asking what snacks you have?"

"Ah. Yes. Well. Hummus and carrots and chips and some other stuff."

She makes a face. "Do you have something a little more refreshing?"

I laugh. "Would you like to see a menu?"

She blushes and shakes her head. "Sorry, I didn't mean to sound ungrateful. It's clear you've done... so much work for this." She looks around at our set-up.

I laugh, and reach out to touch her wrist, but immediately pull my hand away. "Hey, I was just joking."

She sighs. "Sorry. I'm just having a particularly exhausting day. I was trying to catch up with work and some coursework. And it's really so hot..." She shakes her head. "I honestly can't wait to get in the ocean."

I suppress a groan because I just *know* I'm going to fucking die the second I see her wet in that red bikini like some sort of scene out of *Baywatch*. But better.

"So you obviously need a pick-me-up," I say, trying to steer my brain away from my imagination and back to the present. I lead her over to one of our larger coolers, pop it open, and dig through the ice almost all the way to the bottom, wincing at the cold ache in my joints, the blade-like slice of ice over my skin. After a few moments of painful digging, I pull out just what I was looking for. The look of pure happiness on Diana's face brings me more satisfaction than I'm comfortable with, the way my chest tightens leaving me a bit disoriented.

"A bomb pop?" She gasps, reaching quickly for the red, white, and blue popsicle.

Her enthusiasm makes me laugh again. She's so fucking adorable when she's happy, and it's addictive to help make it happen. "Yes and no. It's one of the healthy ones because I'm trying to be a responsible parent. Sugar free. But yeah."

"Oh my god, *yes*. When we first moved to the US, these quickly became one of my favorite things."

"How old were you when you moved to the US?"

"Mmm, around thirteen?"

"Really?" I inhale sharply, a surge of happiness coursing through me from peeling back another layer of who Diana is. She's been such a mystery since the beginning of the summer, only showing me pieces of her—and reluctantly so. The thrill of this discovery is surprising.

"Mmhmm. We moved here because of my dad's job. And because it really wasn't very safe for us back home."

"So that's where your accent comes from." I grin.

Diana glares. "I don't have an accent. I've worked really hard not to have one."

I exhale a laugh. "You do have one. But *barely*. And what's wrong with having an accent? It shows you know more than one language, which is super cool. Honestly, it's—"

Diana licks the cherry and lemonade popsicle from bottom to tip, my entire system short-circuiting. Is she doing this in slow motion? Is this a fever dream? Am I dead and in heaven? Or possibly hell and being tortured? Because in the split second it takes for me to process the fact that she's going to keep *licking* the popsicle, I realize it's going to be next to impossible to continue to formulate any type of rational thought, let alone carry a conversation.

"Michael? Are you okay?" she asks, finally pulling her lips away from the popsicle.

Seriously, what the fuck was I thinking giving her one of those? It's an *obscene* food. She's too hot for it.

I make a mental note *not* to offer her a hot dog or any other phallic shaped foods in the future. At least not while we're in public. "Uh. Yeah. Just... lost my train of thought."

She narrows her eyes at me. "I can see that." She reaches out to place the back of her hand against my cheek, but I physically recoil. "Have you been drinking any water? You've been out in the sun for a while, right? Why don't we sit under the umbrellas in the shade and get you something cold to drink?"

Chapter Nine

DIANA

WITH SHAKY LEGS, MICHAEL FOLLOWS MY INSTRUCTIONS. He settles in a chair under the shade—one that's still far enough removed from the group so that we have our own space to talk. I toss my popsicle in the trash and run to the coolers and find a cold water bottle. When I bring it to Michael, I press it to his face in an effort to lower his body temperature.

He closes his eyes and hums, leaning into it, taking it from my hands to press it to his other cheek. After a moment, he cracks it open and finally takes a long swig. "Jesus, that feels good."

"Better?" I ask after giving him a moment to cool down.

He nods once, lifting his backwards facing hat and running his hand through his hair before placing it back. "Yeah. Thanks. Must've been the sun, like you said."

"It happens. When I was a kid, my family and I used to go to this archipelago called Los Roques back home. It's all white sands and clear, turquoise water. The most beautiful place on earth. True perfection. But it's easy to get dehydrated without really noticing because the sun is so aggressive, and the wind makes it so that you never really feel the heat. So we had to always remember to keep drinking water."

I try to control my mind from going down memory lane, but I can hear the nostalgia and ache in my voice. Normally, I'm good about controlling it—a habit I had to pick up when we first moved here in order to survive—in order for my sisters to survive, too—but something about having the beach close by these past six weeks has triggered a yearning for home. Except, after all these years, I don't really even know where that is.

"Do you miss it?" he asks.

I look away, staring out to the ocean in front of us. "Sometimes," I reply after a minute.

"Sorry, I don't mean to pry. It's just... I want to know more. About you, I mean."

I look back at him, at his flushed cheeks, the way he scrunches his nose in embarrassment.

"Shit, I'm sorry. I mean that it would be nice. To get to know you better. Because we see each other all the time, you know."

My lips twitch, almost upturning into a smile. But this topic weighs heavy on me, filling me with guilt and nostalgia. "It's been more than fifteen years since I moved to the US, but it's never truly felt like home. And I know that if I were to go back to Venezuela now, I wouldn't feel at home, either. Not fully." I sigh deeply, gently grabbing the bottle of water from his hands and taking my own sip. "It's gotten better over time. Still, it's hard knowing what I've left behind. Knowing that so much of who I am has changed. My sisters... they were younger than me when we left, so I'm pretty sure it must have been easier for them. I could've struggled the most, but I'm the oldest. So I guess I always thought I had to lead by example. Really teach them that we had to assimilate and do so quickly. So I did."

"In which ways?"

I pause. "My name, for example." I wince, not sure how I feel about it even over a decade later.

"Your name? What do you mean?"

"I sort of changed it."

"You mean your real name isn't Diana?" He raises a brow, sitting up in his seat.

"It is. And isn't. It's *Diana*," I say, pronouncing it like Dee-*ah*-na. "*Not* Diana." I exaggerate my American accent, which makes us both chuckle.

"*Diana*," he says, trying to pronounce it Spanish, letting the word tumble out of his mouth.

My name sounds delicious coming from his lips—foreign and all too familiar at the same time—and I want to taste them. Inhaling sharply, I try to suppress whatever has my cheeks flushing a deep crimson.

Even so, a smile on my face widens when I look at him. I pull my knees up, wrapping my arms around them.

"Almost perfect pronunciation," I tell him.

A big, adorable grin spreads across his face.

My god, when did he get cute? And are those dimples in his cheeks right beneath his scruff?

"I want to get it right. Be respectful of you," he tells me.

"Thank you. But it's unnecessary. I've gotten used to the English version, and, in a way, I'm glad only my family and relatives are the ones who call me that now. Serves as a way to compartmentalize everything."

He deflates a bit. "Shame. It's a beautiful name."

I lean my cheek on my knee, staring up at him as my chest tightens at the soft expression on his face.

"You're not as horrible as I thought you were," I murmur, voice so low I wonder whether he even heard me over the sound of the children laughing as they play and the waves crashing on the shore.

"Neither are you."

"Are we officially friends now, then?" I ask, my voice a bit too hopeful for my liking.

An odd look passes over his eyes, but it's gone in a heartbeat. Quickly replaced by mirth. "Yeah, I guess so."

He sticks his hand out toward me, and I place mine in his to shake it. I don't know whether it was the refreshing coolness of his hands from holding the water bottle or the way he looked at me when I slipped my hand in his, but chills run up and down my spine at his touch. My lips part as I gaze up at him, speechless. I'd be embarrassed if I weren't the only one without words.

I'm not sure who lets go first, but we eventually slip our hands away. The warm breeze blows between us as we grin at each other before Michael kills his water bottle.

"Are you feeling any better now?" I ask, after a couple of minutes of companionable silence.

"Yeah. Yeah, I think I am."

For a moment, we quietly watch the girls play paddle tennis on the beach, laughing without a care in the world. Something inside me unwinds and relaxes, and for a second, I feel like the girls are going to be okay.

As if reading my mind, he says, "Your daughters are amazing. Pretty sure they made Rach's summer. Truly."

I smile, reaching out to readjust his cap to face forward. "This is the *correct* way to wear a hat." He mock glares at me. "And I could say the same about your daughter. It's obviously been rough for both our families, but it looks like things are getting better, right?"

Michael frowns.

"What? Did I say something wrong?"

Michael shakes his head but sighs. "I'm happy the girls found each other," he starts. "But I'm concerned what it'll do to Rachel once the summer is over. After Jessie, her mom, passed away, I moved back home for Rach. But even still, the place I got... It's in a different school district. So she kind of lost a lot of her friends and has been struggling to make new ones. Any, actually. That's why I'm extra grateful for your daughters. I just hope that her making new friends this summer will give her the courage and confidence to make new ones in the next school year, and not have her missing the friends she made at camp."

I nod, absentmindedly making shapes in the sand with my index finger, loving the soft way it trickles from my fingertips when I cup some in my hands. "I understand what you mean."

"Any advice? You've got more experience, and seem to be kicking ass at this single parent thing."

I burst out a laugh, dry and sad. "You're asking me for advice? I thought this entire time you've been telling me I suck as a parent."

"C'mon. You and I both know you're not a bad parent, and there wasn't a second I believed otherwise. You're a rockstar."

"A washed up rockstar, maybe." I sigh. "Most days, I feel like a failure."

"What? Are you joking?"

I bite my lower lip and look away as my eyes begin to sting, not able to bear seeing the expression on his face as I admit that every time he doubted my parenting, I was doing it, too. "Well. I keep trying to keep it together for the girls, but I feel like I'm drowning half the time. Between this new job and juggling taking care of them, managing Emi's medical condition and learning more about it, I'm exhausted. I don't want them to see, but sometimes I feel like I can barely keep it together."

To my horror, a tear slips down my cheek. I manage to quickly wipe it away with the back of my hand, but I'm sure he saw it. "Shit. I'm so embarrassed, sorry. I just had a rough work week, that's all."

From the corner of my eye, I watch as he instinctually stretches out an arm—I assume to pull me into him and offer some comfort. But Michael pulls it back, and shifts in his seat instead.

Part of me feels practically *deprived*. To my embarrassment, I realize I would've loved to have been comforted. But I remind myself I'm acting insane, because we aren't even friends, for Pete's sake. Not really. Just summer pals.

"I can help," he says, his voice dripping with something akin to affection.

I sniff and laugh once. "What? How? Why?"

He shrugs. "Because I can. And it could be something as simple as babysitting the girls to give you time to work or catch up with your studies. Whatever."

I wipe at my cheeks. "You'd do that?"

He sits up straight. "For you, I would."

"For me?" I ask quietly.

"Yeah," he replies, voice deep.

I turn to face him head on, lifting my hand to shield my eyes from the sun.

"Don't you have any sunglasses?" he asks with a frown.

I sigh, appreciating the sudden change in subject. "Left them at home like an idiot."

"Here." He takes off his aviators and gently places them on my face.

I promptly take them off and offer them back.

"What are you doing?" I ask. "Take them."

"I'm trying to help you." His voice is soft, if a little hurt, by my unexpected rejection.

"What about you? Don't you need them?" I twirl the glasses around in my hands.

"As you've pointed out, I have my hat. See? I only brought my sunglasses in case I needed them, and I'm fine." He points at his faded blue Yankees cap.

I smile, bashfully putting them on. "Thank you. You're sweet."

His smile is broad and open, the look on someone's face

when they get something they worked so hard to achieve. It throws me off for a moment. Suddenly, I'm thankful for the dark aviators covering half of my face, hiding my expressions.

"So, tell me. Is everything okay at work?" he asks, looking genuinely concerned.

And screw him for that, because I'm starting to really like him as a person, and I don't need someone else in my life to care about. The fewer people in your life, the simpler things are and I really don't need complicated now. It's just basic relationship math.

"It's actually amazing, which is the weird part. I'm *good* at this. And I like what I do."

Sure, I currently work in a corporate law firm, but it's not all evil corporations and billionaires living in secret lairs, petting white cats in their laps. It's interesting contract law, problem solving, finding creative solutions around someone's language. It's fascinating work. And I've been kicking butt, doing better than most first- and second-year associates. Catching their mistakes, finding alternative solutions which, thankfully, Edgar is willing to hear me out on. So much so, he's included me in several meetings and email exchanges on the case.

"Diana Castillo. Kicking ass and taking names," Michael says with a heartbreaking grin that looks angelic and sinful at the same time.

I laugh at that. "I wish. Though I do actually have this meeting thing in New York City my boss asked me to go to, but..."

"But what?"

"The trip will probably be an all day thing since it's a newer client, bigger than we've ever taken on, and will require a lot of schmoozing. And I have no one to watch the girls after camp."

Michael scoffs. "I can do it."

"What? No, I could never ask you to—"

"You didn't ask. I offered."

I lift a brow. "No, I couldn't. It's... a lot. And I don't know you *that* well yet. Not well enough to leave you my kids, I don't think."

A little hurt flashes through his eyes, but he's quick to control it. Though I certainly don't miss it.

Michael nods thoughtfully. "Okay. Heard. And fair. We haven't known each other that long. But how about you think it over before rejecting my offer? You don't have to say yes now."

"I will. Think about it, I mean. And I really appreciate the offer, either way. This is kind of a big opportunity for me. To be honest, if I hadn't married young, I probably would've gone to law school. And I guess maybe that's what's making work so difficult? Knowing that I would've kicked ass as a lawyer."

He grins at me. "I can see you kicking ass at it. Except I'm sorry you're living with the whole regretting-marrying-young part."

"Yeah, but as big of an ass as Rodrigo is, I can't fully regret him or the way my life turned out. It brought me my girls, after all."

"It's okay to regret not doing something without feeling guilty, Diana. Just because it wouldn't have led to a specific thing doesn't mean you can't regret how *some* of the parts of your life turned out. Like, I've been trying to come to peace with how I chose to forgo a parental relationship with Rachel years ago. I think of all the things I missed out on. But I also know who I was back then, and I would've been the worst parent. Resentful, absent, angry. I had that growing up—from *both* of my parents—and it certainly did not make for a happy childhood. I wanted more for her—not just for me."

Michael takes a deep breath and closes his eyes as if steeling himself to say something important. "I've been thinking a lot about what it means to forgive yourself. About how it feels incredibly selfish of me to do so. But I also think that if I don't do it, I'm going to fail Rachel. Because she needs an involved parent who is able to stop living in the past and be able to be present while thinking of the future. I can only control what happens now, not what I did or didn't do before. If I had stayed, if I had done the, quote, 'responsible' thing, I probably wouldn't have given her the dad she deserved. Because even if I was never her *dad*, I was never not there for Jessie or Rachel. Anything they needed, I gave them. I think that while I caused some damage, I can change my situation now. I have to." I watch as he white-knuckles the beach chair's armrests, his gaze far away and almost haunted. "And that means you can do that, too —but with yourself."

"Yeah." I nod, but I'm not too convinced. "Maybe you're right in your case. But it's not like I'm in this position where I can pursue a completely different life now. Sure, law school sounds like a dream. But that's exactly what it is. I can barely handle the current state of my life *now*—how am I supposed to handle law school on top of everything else?"

"What about your ex? I mean, he's there, right? I assume he co-parents at least to *some* degree."

"Rodrigo?" I snort. "Please. I can't even get him to reply to his daughters' messages. The girls have been sending him letters twice a week all summer, and he hasn't called or replied once to them. All I do is lie to them, and tell them the post office keeps losing them, and Daddy's phone doesn't work. I have no idea how Rodrigo could do this, treat his children that way. It's not something I would've ever thought him capable of, even at his worst."

His face softens as his gorgeous hazel eyes—looking more like a peaceful meadow under the sun—travel across my face. "I'm sorry to hear that. He has no idea what he's missing out on."

"Yeah." I laugh once, shaking my head.

"It kills me to think I reminded you of him." His voice is soft, but I can feel the pain in it. Guilt floods my system, because I know now he isn't like Rodrigo.

"I misjudged you, Michael. Please don't think I still have that impression of you. Your thing wasn't the same," I say, wrapping a hand around his bicep, trying really hard not to notice how muscular it is, how warm and soft yet still strong it feels beneath my fingertips. "You stepped up when you were needed. And you weren't when Jessie got pregnant.

"Rodrigo... This man just... *disappeared.* He went from being there to taking off. I literally had to negotiate a *lower* alimony and child support payments—which he has yet to pay, by the way—to get him to spend *more* time with his daughters—something unheard of—and he hasn't even lived up to that. If it were up to him, he'd spend the least amount of time with his girls and pay no child support. It's like he got this taste of what life would be free attachments and would give anything for it. I swear, sometimes it feels like if it weren't because he's scared of what his family or friends would say, he'd give up total responsibility over the girls."

"Like giving up parental rights?"

"I know that sounds crazy, but... Anyway, trust me when I tell you that you are nothing like him. There's a difference between a man who steps up and takes ownership after making a questionable choice or mistake, and one who retreats and abandons his family." In an uncharacteristic move, I reach out and rub his back. "I didn't know you before, but you're a good man, Michael. At least you are now."

Michael blows out a deep breath and nods. "I hope to god you're right. Or at least I hope I'm good enough that I can give Rachel the good, stable, happy life she deserves—the one I didn't get as a kid. That's what matters most to me right now."

The urge to hug him is so strong I have to cross my arms in front of my chest, because I know what it's like to feel like you aren't good enough. That you're giving everything you can to try to be the best parent and still feel like it isn't enough. In a messed up way, it's comforting to know someone's going through the same thing. Sure, our situations aren't exactly the same, but the feeling of inadequacy is there for both of us. Knowing I'm not alone in this is life changing.

"We ready to get back to the party?" I ask suddenly. When he nods with that heartbreaking smile of his, I do my best to ignore how it steals my breath. "Cool. How about we let Matt and Vinny handle the grill while we take a victory lap of sorts for all of our hard work and go into the ocean?"

Michael's eyes widen, but he quickly recovers. He clears his throat before adjusting the cap on his head. "Um, now? In our bathing suits and stuff?"

I laugh, utterly confused by his reaction. "Uh, yes, our bathing suits." Am I hideous? Unattractive to such a degree that seeing me in my bathing suit should be embarrassing? I've never paid much attention to the way I look, possibly because I considered it a luxury in a way. But all of a sudden, I feel self-conscious about my body. Before I can help it, I look down, taking myself in. Sure, I have pregnancy stretch marks, but... are they really that bad?

I swallow the knot in my throat, suddenly regretting my decision to wear a two-piece.

God, this is so stupid.

With more effort than I'd care to admit, I control my hurt expression and ask, "Is that a problem or something?"

"No!" he says quickly, loudly. I can't help flinching. Michael clears his throat again. "Sorry. No, of course not. No problem with that. Let's... Let's go for a swim I guess."

He gets to his feet and outstretches a shaking hand to me.

Confused by his reaction, I take it and pull myself up with his help.

"Okay, then."

Without another thought, I pull my tank top over my head and slide my shorts over my hips, folding them both neatly before stuffing them inside my beach tote. The sun on my bare skin feels amazing, the excitement of spending the whole day at the beach fills me with light and hope. Despite standing on the precipice of not wanting to take off my clothes in front of Michael not thirty seconds ago, I can't help the smile that spreads across my face as soon as I turn to watch a wave crash onto the shore.

That is, until I turn back to Michael and am faced with a wall of tan, ripped, perfection of a man. I try as hard as I can to keep a poker face, but I'm pretty sure there's no hiding the surprised and wild expression in my eyes. I mean, I knew the guy was attractive, but this... this isn't fair. Broad shoulders and a light smattering of hair, the surprising array of tattoos that remained hidden beneath his shirts until this very moment. They're unexpected, and reach all the way up to his shoulder, stopping below a corded, muscled, and delicious-looking neck... Jelly-kneed, I attempt to say something—anything—but the sudden and unexpected attraction has derailed every other thought in my head besides, *Oh my lord, this man...* My stomach tightens, my cheeks heat, and I'm mortified to admit that I feel a foreign tightening low in my belly.

Michael Haynes is hot. More than hot. As scalding as the summer sun beating down on us hot.

I swallow once, trying to hide the way I look him over, head to toe. But I guess I'm not subtle enough, because when I look back at his face, a knowing smirk has spread across it.

Shit.

"You ready?" he asks, his eyes roaming over my body as well, bright eyes darker as they trail every inch of me.

No.

I clear my throat and force a smile, the tightening in my belly increasing, the look of hunger in his eyes... incredibly satisfying. "Yeah. I'm ready."

Chapter Ten

DIANA

The sun begins to set over the most perfect Fourth of July I've had in a long time, and while I'm filled with mild sadness over the end of this amazing day, I'm not disappointed it happened. I spent the entire afternoon watching my girls look happier and lighter than they've been in a long time, playing in the sand with Rachel, making new friends with other children on the beach. Enjoying their summer so much more than I ever thought would've been possible when we first got here weeks ago.

But they weren't the only ones who had fun: I can't remember the last time I enjoyed myself so much. A huge part of it has to do with Michael and how attentive he was, of course; how much he made sure I felt comfortable with everyone and that I was having a good time. The truth is, I'm not really a shy person, but I wasn't at the Fourth of July gathering for myself—I was there for my girls. I would've been fine sitting on my own, watching them play, happy to enjoy the salty wind blowing my hair and the sun warming my skin. Michael, however, had no intentions of letting me blend into the background. He made sure I felt comfortable with everyone, made me feel like the girls were safe while I enjoyed the beach for myself. Together, we went into the freezing ocean (which made me miss the warm, clear Caribbean waters more than I expected, but I still enjoyed it), played beach volleyball with the adults (which I was terrible at, but mostly because I kept getting distracted by how much he belonged in a *Top Gun* montage more than at some beach in Long Island), and walked along the shore as we learned more about each other (I told him a little more about life back in Denver, and he told me about his time as a head chef).

After everything going on at work and with Rodrigo, it felt good to unwind. And if I'm being honest, it didn't hurt to have someone as gorgeous as Michael to have around.

Thinking back to the times I think I caught him staring at me, I smirk to myself in satisfaction, because I know I wasn't the only one feeling a physical attraction.

But as I sit on a log by the fire pit Vinny and Matt built while I attempt to warm my feet without burning my toes off, I try to push it out of my head. Even if we were both attracted to each other, it's not like anything could ever happen. Or that I'd even *want* it to happen.

Right?

Sighing involuntarily, I watch Danielle and Liza. Each one has a child in their arms, wrapped in a towel as they rest on their mothers' chest. I can't help the big smile that spreads across my face when Liza's three-year old sucks her finger.

"They're exhausted, aren't they?" Liza asks, smiling at me.

"And thank god," Danielle says with a sigh. "The amount of energy this kid has is gonna be the death of me. I could handle it with my twins, but now that I'm older..."

I laugh, remembering when both of my girls were toddlers, how exhausted I would get even in my twenties. "Tiring as they are, you have to admit they can be so much fun."

"Oh, one hundred percent. Sometimes they act like mini-teenagers, which is super frustrating because it's either hilarious or incredibly annoying. Or both." But even as she says it,

Danielle looks down tenderly at her girl, Alessandra. "The other day, I was going to sit down to play with her, and she raised her hand and went, 'Mama, I need my space.'" She scoffs. "Can you believe that? I wanted to laugh and cry at the same time."

"Three-nagers," I say with a grin.

"You know, I'm so happy you came," Liza says. "We didn't get to spend much time together at Barbara's wedding, so I'm glad we have today to get to know each other a little more."

"Yeah, especially since we're all ninety-nine percent sure Michael has a crush on you," Danielle sing-songs under her breath.

"What?" I ask, a bit shocked. After today, after seeing the way he'd look at me when he thought I wasn't paying attention, I wouldn't deny that he'd feel attracted. But a crush?

"Danielle! Don't." Liza shoots her sister-in-law a glare.

"No way." I laugh, but it comes out high-pitched and uncomfortable. "Michael doesn't have a *crush* on me." But I frown and pause as I look down at my bare feet. There's been a sort of harmony between us. Especially lately. I mean, we had fun today. Though it's all been in the name of our daughters, of course. Right? It's not a *crush.* "I think you guys are confused. We're just friends. Actually, not even that. Our daughters are the ones who are friends. We're just the parents to really close friends."

Danielle snickers and looks away. "I'm just saying. I don't see him looking at other women the way he looks at you. And this BBQ?" She whistles "This is not something he usually does."

Liza lightly elbows Danielle in the side, trying not to wake either of their daughters. "You have a serious addiction to meddling in other people's love lives, you know that?" she hisses at her.

"I didn't hear you complaining when it came down to yours," Danielle says, lifting a brow.

Liza sighs once before saying, "Point taken. But she's not your sister-in-law. And you don't know whether she even likes him or not."

Danielle turns to me with a kind, but determined expression in her eyes. "Well... Do you?"

"Do I... what?"

"Danielle—seriously!" Liza whisper-yells. "You do not need to ans—"

But Danielle cuts her off. "Like him. Michael. Do you like Michael?"

My jaw drops, my eyes flashing between the two of them. To be honest, my instinct is to reply an immediate and resounding *NO*. But something stops me. Instead, I go with a cowardly "I mean, he's a nice guy?"

Danielle rolls her eyes. "C'mon, girl. You know that's not what I mean. There's something between you two. And everyone can see it, no matter what either of you say." She smiles, eyes shining under the light of the fire. My cheeks heat at that piece of information, the thought of other people discussing a possible connection between Michael and me making me self-conscious.

I sigh. "I don't know. I haven't thought of him that way before." Which isn't exactly true, but it also isn't really a lie. I've obviously noticed how attractive he is—today especially. I mean, how could I not when he spent all day shirtless, skin practically glistening from the ocean water? I'm not blind. And those dimples, visible even beneath the stubble... "Never even considered having that type of relationship with him."

"Really?" Danielle asks, surprised. "Well, how about now that someone has flat-out asked you? What do you think of him?

Do you think he's attractive? Do you think you could ever like him?"

"Danielle," Liza warns.

I shake my head, heart racing in my chest. "I—I don't know." Truthfully, life has been so crazy ever since I separated from Rodrigo, that I haven't even had the time to stop and think about the possibility of entering into another relationship ever again. Not really. And now that the topic has been brought to the forefront of my mind, I'm a little dizzy and overwhelmed. Letting another guy into my life sounds as dangerous as jumping off the tallest bungee jump in the world—you hope that it'll catch you, but there's always the chance that the rope will snap.

There's no denying the rush felt during the fall is something else, though...

"You're making her feel uncomfortable," Liza tells her, standing up for me. Except not a second later, she looks at me with hesitation and asks: "Well... But *do* you think you could ever like him?"

When I realize there's no way I'm getting out of this, I decide to answer. At the very least just to get them off my back. "I mean, he is... objectively attractive," I tell them, repeating the same assessment of him I gave my sister. I look over my shoulder, watch him smile as he jokes around with Vinny's son by the grill. "And he's a good dad. And a nice guy, like I said. Nicer than I expected." I hear how my voice has grown soft, feel the way my chest has tightened. But I snap back to reality when I hear Danielle laugh softly. Shrugging once, I turn back to them. "He's okay."

Liza presses her lips together, trying not to smile. "Just okay, huh?"

"I thought you were on my side, here," I mutter.

Danielle and Liza chuckle, though not unkindly. More so

like they're seeing something bloom before their eyes. And I don't know whether I like it or not.

"Well, regardless of how you feel—"

"Or *don't* feel," Liza cuts Danielle off.

"—I think he likes you. I mean, he did all this for you." She nods meaningfully at the luxurious set-up.

"Oh, I'm sure you must be mistaken. He's a chef and caterer. He probably does this kind of stuff with his eyes shut, like it's second nature."

"Mmm. I don't think so. This afternoon is far from the beach barbecues he's thrown in the past. I've never seen him so stressed out about getting things right, about making what was supposed to be a simple Fourth of July thing look like it belonged in a magazine or movie. I mean, Michael is an amazing guy, but this... this is something new." Danielle smiles at me.

I bite my lower lip and look down at my hands, considering her words. My stomach tightens as I think back to the relationship we had at the beginning of summer and where we are now. What I thought was a camaraderie of sorts has shifted and evolved, and begin to wonder whether they're right.

"I'm sure you're misreading the situation," I tell them, heart racing as I try to process my own feelings in the matter. "He's nice and we're definitely getting along, but—"

"Hey guys," Michael's voice comes from behind, causing me to jump at least a foot in my seat. "Whoops, didn't mean to scare you." He takes a seat beside me, a blanket in his arms. Smiling widely, the apples of his sun-kissed cheeks dimpling in that adorable way of his.

My stomach drops, and I turn back nervously at Danielle and Liza, who look like they're seconds away from bursting into laughter. Thankfully, Michael is too distracted to notice.

"Here, I got you a blanket. It's starting to get cold out."

My lips part as he unfolds a navy, cotton cable knit blanket and drapes it gingerly on my shoulders. I have never sat more still in my entire life.

"Um, thank you," I mumble, suddenly unable to look him in the face. My skin is on fire—it must be—but I still wrap the blanket tighter around my shoulders, instinctually inhaling the scent of it in a deep, long breath—citrus, maybe grapefruit?

Shoot. Danielle and Liza can't be right, can they? I *cannot* have a thing for this man. For a million and one reasons, I *cannot* even be one bit interested in any other type of relationship with Michael aside from him being the father of my daughters' friend.

"Oh, no, thank you, Michael. *Liza and I* didn't want any blankets. We're good," Danielle says sarcastically.

He laughs and shakes his head. "Nah, you guys are basically family. You can get your own blankets. Diana is the guest here."

Liza scoffs and looks at Danielle. "You know, I think I get the message here. We're not really wanted," she says, teasing. Still, Liza gets to her feet and readjusts her drowsy daughter in her arms. "C'mon, Danielle. Let's get out of here. He doesn't deserve our presence."

Michael laughs as they walk away, but I remain still and silent, because I know it was all a ploy to leave us alone.

Chapter Eleven

DIANA

AFTER DANIELLE'S REVELATION, PART OF ME WANTS TO BEG them to stay, while the other is ecstatic to have them gone, to give me the opportunity to figure out what it is I'm feeling now that this idea of a romantic *something* has been planted in my head.

"Did you have fun today?" Michael asks with genuine interest.

I swallow once and consider what Danielle said, about how he organized this afternoon for me. Even though I'm not sure I believe her, I want to make sure he knows I appreciate everything he did. Because regardless of *why* he did it, it was great, I felt welcome, and so did my kids.

"I had an amazing time, Michael. Really. I... I honestly can't believe you pulled off such a barbecue. I mean," I look meaningfully at the groups of people around us. "I feel like we're the envy of everyone at the beach. This looks like a professionally catered event."

"Well... It's been kinda my job lately." He chuckles and runs his fingers through his hair, hat discarded now that the sun has almost gone down completely. It's almost dark now, but in the light of the bonfire, I catch the way his eyes light up, the way the green hue has changed once again to a lighter one—the same green they were earlier today when we talked about the wildly different experiences we had in our twenties as we walked along the shore. The need to figure him out, to match a hue to every mood is almost visceral. I get lost in his eyes, pulled in by the dancing colors reflecting the fire beside us, keeping us warm.

Before I can stop myself, I say "Your eyes are like some sort of mood ring."

A single laugh bursts out from him. "Excuse me?"

"Oh, god." I laugh, facepalming. "I just mean... I've noticed that your eyes—they're more green than hazel—"

"Yes, I know that." He grins, thoroughly entertained.

"—and they change hues, and sometimes I swear it's related to your mood."

"To my mood?" Michael seems thrilled to hear this theory, but I personally want to die. Did I seriously just say that? Did I really word vomit to this guy what I think about his *eyes*?

God, maybe Danielle and Liza are right. Maybe this physical attraction is evolving into something else. It needs to end.

"Yeah. Like, when you're excited about something they look really bright, the flecks of gold standing out. And when you're frustrated with me—" I say with a chuckle—"they turn a kind of mossy green."

He grins. "That's it? I only have two moods, then? Excitement and frustration?"

"Well, no. Your eyes also look a deep emerald normally, which is kind of... beautiful. But then, today, it was the first time I saw them turn a deep color—almost forest green. Right before we went in the water." *When your eyes roamed over my body, when you smirked at me in that way I felt down to my toes.*

"Oh, yeah? What do you think that one meant?" His voice drops a few octaves, some kind of mischief building in his expression while still darkening at the same time. His gaze drops to my lips as he moves closer to me.

Suddenly, our breathing speeds, and my heart races as something warm and delicious spreads through my body. Without meaning to, I lean in closer, the combined scent of citrus and sea salt falling over me, intoxicating. He's so *handsome*. And he smells *so* good.

"Diana," he murmurs, scooting closer to me on the log.

"Yeah?" I breathe, eyes on his mouth, daydreaming about what it would feel like to have it on mine or grazing my skin.

"I—"

An explosion of colorful lights flood the night sky above us, the loud sound causing us to jump apart as the Fourth of July fireworks go off. My cheeks blush as I look away, but I still feel his gaze on my face, my body as tense as a bow string. Slowly, I turn to face him, unsure of what I might find. But all I see is a man with a furrowed brow, confusion etched into his expression, as his face dances in red, blues, and golds from the lights above us.

"You're so beautiful," he whispers, his eyes never leaving mine. There's an ache in his voice, and I think it matches the one building inside me.

I inhale sharply, speechless.

What is happening?

My gaze roams over his face, looking for any hint that he's playing me, making fun of me for this buzzing feeling that's spreading all over my body. But there's no trace of humor—no signature smirk, no teasing smile. It's him. It's Michael, raw and vulnerable, and in that second, it officially becomes my favorite version of him.

"Michael," I say, not really knowing how to keep going. I rack my brain for how to follow it up, because it *feels* like we're having a moment. But I've been out of the game so long that I have no idea how to respond.

Luckily, the vision of Camila running toward me in my periphery brings my parental instincts to the forefront, distracting me from whatever the hell just happened. Or didn't.

When an out of breath Cami reaches me and looks nervously at Michael, I wonder briefly whether she saw our interaction, whether a part of her knows that something was going down between her friend's dad and her mom—whatever it was. Thankfully, though, I shouldn't have worried.

"*Mami*, can I talk to you super quick?" she asks, biting her lip. "Over there." She throws a thumb over her shoulder, where I see Emi and Rachel huddled by the dunes.

"Uh. Sure." I get to my feet and throw Michael an apologetic look before walking away, only looking back once as I feel the cold sand beneath my feet to find him holding his head in his hands, looking glumly into the fire pit.

"So, please don't tell Michael or anything," my daughter says, pulling me by the hand, "but Rachel's been really sad because Fourth of July was kinda her and her mom's thing? I don't know. She was super cool all day, but then I guess the fireworks made her even sadder because she started crying out of nowhere and I wanted to call Michael but she said she didn't want to and then I asked if I should call you and she said no, but I thought you'd know what to do because she won't stop crying." Cami rushes through her words, looking up at me as she walks, brows pulled together.

I smile wildly because my daughter came to me when she needed my help, and that feels big. It means she trusts me. All happiness dissipates, however, when I see Emi holding Rachel in her arms while she sobs.

I drop Cami's hand and jog over to the girls, who separate

once they hear me ask what's wrong. But Rachel can barely get words out, so Emi decides to speak for her.

"Rachel really misses her mom, and she's sad she's not here. It's the first Fourth of July they aren't together."

My heart breaks for Rachel, not knowing quite what to say.

I take Rachel by the hands and have her face me. Using the sleeve of my sweatshirt, I wipe the tears off her face, only to have them quickly replaced by fresh ones. "Do you want me to call your dad? Ask him to come talk to you?" I try to sound as comforting as possible.

"No!" She sniffs. "No, it's just gonna make him feel bad. He's been so great, and he made sure everyone had fun today. But the fireworks were my mom and mine's thing. And I'm just sad." She shrugs once, trying to act strong. "I just—I just need to get over it."

"Get over it?" I gasp. "Honey, you have *every right* to be sad today. And your dad is not going to think you're being a burden or whatever crazy thing is running through your mind right now. He loves you so much, and wants what's best for you. He would want to know if you're sad—I know I would want to know if one of my girls were going through a rough time."

"I don't know how to talk to him, though," she cries.

My heart twists for them.

"Okay." I nod. "I understand that. Talking about feelings isn't always easy and sometimes we don't even know how to start. So would it be helpful if I bring him over and guide you guys through it?" I ask.

Rachel hesitates a moment before nodding.

"Perfect." I turn to Emi and ask her to go get Michael, making sure she lets him know it's urgent, but doesn't alert the other adults. He comes running in seconds, brows pulled together.

"Rach? What's wrong?" He drops to his knees, kicking sand

everywhere, and pulls her quickly into his arms. "What's going on?"

She starts crying again, wrapping her little arms around his neck as she sobs into his chest. Michael looks helplessly at me. He pushes Rachel away just enough to meet her squarely in the eye. "Talk to me. Please."

Rachel bites her lip and looks back at me.

"Um. She misses her mom," I whisper. "Fourth of July fireworks were super special to them, apparently, and she got very sad."

"Why didn't you tell me?" he asks her. "I would've loved to have sat down and watched them together. You could've told me all about what you and your mom used to do. We might've been able to recreate some of it."

Rachel sniffs again and runs the back of her hand over her nose. "You never asked."

Michael looks away, ashamed. "Fuck," he mutters. "You're right, Rach. I am so sorry. I should've known better. I-I'm still trying to figure this parenting thing out, but I want you to know that I love you *so much*. It seems impossible, but I love you more every day. I know this whole thing is still new, but I can't imagine a world without you now. Please, please, *please* know that you can come to me no matter what. Next year, I promise we can continue you and your mom's tradition. Or start a new one."

"I don't want a new tradition. What if you leave? I'd have to start another one all over again with someone else."

"Leave?" Michael looks horrified, his eyes glazing over with unshed tears. "Kid, I know we had a rough and confusing start, but I promise you there is no freaking way I am ever leaving you again. I am here to stay."

Rachel starts crying again and throws herself at her father. "Do you promise?"

"I swear." He squeezes her tightly. "Nothing in this world is ever going to keep me from you ever again."

"Okay. I love you, Dad."

I wipe a tear across my cheek before pulling my two girls into my sides, watching Michael and Rachel have this breakthrough moment. After a few seconds, he opens his eyes and looks at me, mouthing a *Thank you.*

Chapter Twelve

DIANA

"Alright, girls. Let's make it quick—I need to get back home and back to work," I say when I pick the girls up at camp.

"Yes, *Mami*," my girls reply in unison as they climb into the car.

"What are we having for dinner?" Cami asks.

"Probably chicken breast and veggies," I tell her, loading up the car.

Both girls grimace, but it's Cami who speaks up. "Ew. Gross. Again? Can't we try something new this time? We always eat the same things. Can't we have *pabellón* or something?"

I sigh, hanging my head in my hands. *Pabellón* is the Venezuelan national dish and used to be a staple at our house: white rice, black beans sprinkled with a bit of sugar, *carne mechada*, and fried sweet plantains. Not exactly diabetes friendly.

"Sorry, Cami. Not this time."

I miss the days when I could just prepare the staples I learned from my mom—*arepas* and *empanadas*. Carb heavy meals that soothe the soul... They're not always the healthiest options when eaten fried or every day, but they're delicious no-brainers for days when you don't want to think too much. And while having T1D doesn't mean Emiliana will never be able to have any of that kind of food—especially now that technology has progressed with CGMs and insulin pumps—minimizing consumption of those meals is preferable. Especially as we pay attention to the different ways Emi's body reacts to certain foods as she grows. Which is why it's been grilled chicken and roasted veggies almost every day.

I mean, it's fine. There are some people who love that. But I grew up in a family where decadent yet simple food was a part of our DNA, and every day felt like a culinary experience. And now... I'm a horrible mother, I know, but for the time being, this is the only thing I can handle.

"That's what we're having, and I won't hear anything else about it," I say with finality.

Cami huffs and crosses her arms in front of her chest as I shut the door behind her.

I'm just putting the girls' backpacks in the trunk when I see Michael jogging over to me from his truck with a smile on his face.

"Hey," he says, his breathing perfectly even, as if running from one side of the parking lot to the other was nothing. "I'm so glad I caught you guys before you left."

"Oh, hi," I say with a forced smile, my stomach tightening. The things I'm starting to feel for him are still incomprehensible to me. I wouldn't say I've been *actively* avoiding Michael over the past few days since the party, but I've also not stopped to say hello during pick-ups and drop-offs like I normally would've since our truce. "Where's Rachel?"

He nods back to the camp. "Restroom."

"Oh. Okay." I wait for him to say more, but he doesn't. Is he just going to stand here next to me while he waits for her? Are we supposed to make small talk? God, please no. "So... What's up?"

"I just wanted to thank you for what you did the other night." He laughs awkwardly, scratching the back of his head. The way his cheeks flush does something to me I'm not quite ready to admit aloud now or possibly ever. He's so... *adorable.* When did that even happen?

"I didn't do anything," I assure him. "That was all you. All I did was encourage her to talk to you."

"Regardless, you played a part in getting her to feel comfortable enough to talk to me. And I'm eternally grateful."

"It's not a big deal, like I said." I wave a hand in the air. "Seriously."

He presses his lips together and nods. "Either way, I'd like to do something to express my gratitude."

"Michael, you don't have to do anything for me, I promise. I'm good."

"I—I can carpool for the rest of the week. Or even the summer."

I laugh uncomfortably. "Tempting. I could definitely use the free time but, you do not need to carpool for me."

"Are you sure? Because I'd be saving you from afternoon traffic. You can use that time to focus on work?"

"It's a good time for me to run smaller errands. Even though I could probably be using that time to study or work, I like doing it because I get to bond with the girls in the end."

He sighs. "C'mon. Work with me here. How about if I cook for you? Or give you a free cooking lesson or something? Your knife skills need some help. Teach you a few recipes?" Michael smiles; my knees weaken.

Two girls' voices in the background cut into the conversation before I can get a word in: "Yes! Yes, please!"

I stare at the girls, slack-jawed. They'd just overheard everything through the open trunk door. Cami sits up on her knees and twists in her seat to look at us. "Yes, Michael, that'd be so cool. *Mami*, you should totally let him come and cook for us. Let him teach you how to cook something different. Please."

"I—I don't—"

Laughter bursts through Michael. "Perfect. Thanks girls." And with a dimpled grin, he tells me, "I'll see you tonight with groceries and a meal plan."

"Michael, you don't—"

"Diana." His hands come up on my shoulders, then drag down my arms, until he takes mine in his. I gawk down at our clasped hands, skin heating everywhere. "Let me do this for you."

I nod wordlessly, giving in.

Michael smiles and shuts the trunk door. "See you at five-thirty. We can start cooking then."

"Oh my god," Rosie laughs on the other end of the line. "Oh my *god*."

"You know, this isn't helping," I whisper over the phone, hoping the girls can't overhear my conversation from the living room.

"I'm sorry, but how would I *not* find this hilarious? Between the girls roasting you and you ending up in this situation in general... I mean, I *told* you, didn't I?"

"You told me to befriend him. You didn't say this would happen."

"And what is 'this,' exactly? Because all I'm hearing is he's coming over for an innocent cooking lesson as a thank you. Right?" But the suppressed giggle in Rosie's voice is obvious, and I want to murder her for it. "Unless there's something more you want to tell me..."

"I know you know the cooking lesson is not why I'm freaked," I whisper through gritted teeth. "I-I... his friends said he had a crush on me. Or that they *thought* he had a crush on me. Now, unless Liza and Danielle were saying that just to mess with me—"

"They'd never do that," Rosie assures me.

"Fine, whatever. Then he's either just a super duper nice guy, or maybe they're right, and he *does* have a crush on me."

"You gotta stop saying crush; it's giving me the ick. We aren't in grade school."

"Danielle and Liza started it!"

"Well, let's end it, because gross."

I sigh, pinch the bridge of my nose as I squeeze my eyes shut in frustration.

"Would it be so bad if he did, though? Like you, I mean?" she asks.

"Yes!" I sigh in exasperation.

"Why? If you like the guy—"

"I don't *know* if I like the guy."

Sure, I find him attractive. With his Scott Eastwood good looks, who wouldn't? And, despite our initial interactions, Michael turned out to be a considerate, sweet man—something I haven't seen in a long time. His actions and our conversations during the Fourth of July have led me to believe that Michael is more than an okay guy I misjudged when we first met. He's actually an incredible man I consider myself lucky to know. And the fact that he's offered to come to my house and cook for my family as a thank you... Well, it speaks volumes. The men in my life haven't historically ever acted that way. Rodrigo was an entitled ass who expected everything to be done for him without even a whisper of a thank you. And while I love my father and respect him, he still lives under an old school, machismo mentality: women raise the family and are in charge of the home; men work and bring home the *tocineta*.

So, yeah. You could say that Michael has been a breath of fresh air.

"You like him—you know you do—or you wouldn't be acting this way. Even if it's just on some level, you like him as more than the dad to your daughters' friend. So why would it be so bad to just... kinda see where it goes?"

"Because," I start. "Because I'm not even sure *how much* I like him. Because I live about five thousand miles away from here. Because, even though my marriage has been over for years, I only just now got divorced and have to figure my life out. Because I wouldn't even know what to do."

Rosie snorts. "Sis, you are out of your mind. You're not one to get worked up, and I don't think I've ever seen someone get under your skin quite like this."

"Stop," I beg.

"I'm serious."

"I know you're serious, which is the worst part." Rosie scoffs, but I keep us on track: "Can we get back to the reason I called you, though? I need some advice on how to handle this. How to control whatever the heck is going on here."

"Okay, we also need to put a moratorium on 'heck'—it's okay to curse sometimes; your girls aren't even around. Second of all, you're overthinking things. Just go with the flow. He clearly has a thing for you, and a little flirting might be the best thing for you and your self-confidence right now. Just lighten up. You're getting adult company for once *and* what sounds like a delicious free meal from a gorgeous man. I don't know what the hell you have to complain about, girl."

"I think you're missing the point." I sigh.

"Maybe. But I think you are, too."

I squeeze my eyes shut and rub my forehead.

"Listen, Dee. It really isn't that hard. Wear something cute, be nice and polite. If you say you're not looking for anything, then I'm not sure why you're stressing at all. However, if you wanted a summer fling—which no one would blame you for, by the way, because I totally think you deserve to have some fun for the first time in your goddamn life—I think you should wear something hot, be a little flirty and mysterious, and still be nice."

"Hot? I don't own anything *hot*. And I am always nice."

"You know what I mean."

"No, I don't know what you mean, apparently. Because if—" A knock on the sliding kitchen door cuts me off. My stomach drops and suddenly taking in a breath seems to be much harder than normal. "Shoot. Rosie, I gotta go. He's here, and I haven't even changed!" I look down at my stained t-shirt, my worn denim cutoffs, beat up Converse, and sigh. This is as good as it's going to get.

"But—"

I hang up and run into the kitchen, where I find a smiling Michael—two giant grocery bags in his arms, a black canvas bag strapped across his chest—and Rachel, both bathed in the late afternoon summer sunlight.

With more force than even I expected, I slide the doors open, eyes on Michael's smiling face, dimples hiding just below his scruff. He holds my gaze as Rachel slips by me with a, "Hi, Mrs. Castillo," before shooting off to my daughters' room.

Rude as it may sound, my brain barely processes the interaction. I'm hooked on the way Michael's eyes look so green under the setting sun. My breath catches, cheeks blaze, something warm starts to build low in my stomach, and suddenly I realize that, *oh no*, maybe Rosie was right.

I do have a little crush on him.

Maybe bigger than little. Medium?

"You came," I can't help but breathe.

A dimpled grin turns me a bit jelly-kneed and the warmth spreads to that place between my thighs. Okay, maybe my crush is bigger than medium, but not quite large. Is there such a thing as extra medium?

"I told you we would. And I'm a man of my word."

I laugh once, waving him into the house. "You're a rare breed, then."

His grin widens. "I'm glad you see me that way. It would kill me to be just another guy to you."

Oh no. I'm in trouble.

"Here. Start chopping these green onions," he says, passing me a bushel. Our fingers touch as he does, hands freezing momentarily in the middle of the air. But after a moment, he loosens his grip and I take the onions to the sink to rinse.

I clear my throat, picking a spot on the kitchen island to start chopping. "So what are we making?"

"I'm going to be teaching you how to make T1D-friendly Venezuelan food. All it takes are a few adjustments, but once you have it, you'll be able to have her living a semi-normal life again. At least with food at home."

"What? I mean, I know there are some foods she can still eat, obviously, but—"

"They're not going to be the same. But eating for her condition is all about balancing sugar and fiber, right? Kind of? So that's what we're going to do. And just how you memorized the same three go-to recipes, we'll have you memorize these adjustments so you can add three more to your repertoire. Like, she can still have *arepas*—we just need to add something like flax seed to the mix in order to increase its fiber content. So, yeah. All about replacements and adjustments."

I stare wide-eyed at him. Because it sounds obvious. And it is. And I want to cry from the shame I feel for not realizing it earlier.

"Hey, wait. What's wrong?" He reaches a hand out to grab one of mine but pulls back just in time.

"It just... it doesn't *sound* like a hard thing to do. But for some reason, the mental load makes it almost impossible. Like... I know the principles. I know what she can and can't eat. And yet... I need to be sure what she's eating so it *has* to be stuff that I've measured, that I've calculated prior, even though now we can enter all that into an app, and the pump and CGM work together and—" I heave a sigh. "I'm just saying. She's not even your daughter and you were able to do the research. I'm not used to failing, and here I am, my entire life falling apart. I'm usually so organized and on top of things." The shame in my voice is pretty evident, especially since I don't try and mask it. I deserve it.

"Hey." In a completely surprising turn of events, he pulls me into his arms. In an even more surprising turn of events, I like it. "You are dealing with *so much* right now. More than one person can handle. With everything on your plate, I wouldn't blame you if you were giving your kid the same shit for breakfast, lunch, and dinner. I mean, a fucking divorce? An ex who you have to protect for your daughters' sake? Finding a new job and an apartment? Having a kid be newly diagnosed with a dangerous chronic condition while making sure your other kid doesn't feel left out? Diana, I am in awe of you."

I press my forehead against his shoulder. Citrus fills my lungs, but it isn't from any of the lemons or limes lying on my counter.

It's a lot, yes. But: "I don't even know what I'm doing half the time."

He sighs and wraps his arms around me, pulling me into the sweetest hug I think I've ever received from a man. "Your best, Diana. You're doing your fucking best."

It only takes a few minutes for me to settle, but I manage to do so beautifully. Mostly, thanks to Michael. Quickly, we're able to move on to the actual "lesson," though there's not much he's truly teaching me, regardless of what he says.

I roll my eyes at Michael as he *tsks* at my chopping. Again. "You know, I'm actually a fantastic cook. My mother taught me when I was a kid, so I've been doing it since forever."

"I don't care if Gordon Ramsay himself taught you—you're doing it wrong." He takes the knife from my hands and pulls a honing steel from one of the bags. With careful precision, he begins to sharpen the eight inch chef's knife, swiping the blade over one side of the steel rod from the bottom to the top and switching sides. He repeats this motion about five times, and it's only once he's done that I realize I didn't breathe once throughout the entire process.

I shake my head to try and clear it before attempting to get us back on track. "Are you saying that my mother was wrong? That *she* doesn't know how to cook?"

He huffs out a laugh as he rinses the knife and wipes it clean. "No. I would never insult any mother's cooking, even if I don't know her. I'm just saying your *technique* is wrong."

"God, you love disagreeing with me, don't you?

Michael smirks when he hands the knife back to me. "No, I think you're confusing me with yourself."

He moves behind me, reaches around to adjust my hold on the knife. "Here. It should be easier now that it's sharp. With your right hand, pinch the blade with your thumb and forefinger, then grip the handle with the rest of your fingers. And then with your left hand, hold the veg or whatever the hell it is you're chopping in a claw shape. Like this." He gently takes my left hand in his and shapes it to his liking. "That way, your fingertips are safe since your knuckles act as a protective barrier." He runs his fingers over them, a current of electricity shooting up my arm.

Michael crowds me from behind, my body between the hard marble of his chest and that of the countertop. He is predator and protector at the same time. The way he curves over my spine leads me to believe he'd stand between me and an avalanche without hesitation, but would love to eat me simultaneously. I'm surrounded and... it feels amazing. I feel his hot breath on my neck and close my eyes, imagining the feel of him in this position—only in bed with considerably fewer clothes. I can't help the whimper that breaks free from my lips.

Yeah, this definitely isn't a little crush.

"Michael," I murmur his name, though I barely hear it over my heart's loud drumming.

Suddenly, I feel the tip of his nose drag up my neck. Soft as a feather, but with the intensity of a laser beam. Heat blooms low in my belly and I nearly whimper when he takes a deep breath, holding it in for several seconds. "You smell," he whispers low in my ear, "like the most fucking delicious summer peach."

My breath hitches, his hand sliding up my left arm. Without thinking, I lean back, giving in, and realize that his chest isn't the only marble-hard thing about him.

Chapter Thirteen

MICHAEL

Did she just—?

My arm bands around her waist as I groan and squeeze my eyes shut. I've wanted her for weeks—I can admit it to myself now after being in denial for so long—but now isn't the time and it isn't the place. So while I am on cloud fucking nine, I know I have to force myself to come off it.

I gather the strength of a million Greek gods and begin to loosen my hold on her, part my lips to say *something* that will stop this before it starts, to say something that will make it clear that while I *do* want to keep going, we can't have it now. But then she looks over her shoulder, stares up at me through thick lashes with those beautiful, dark eyes of hers, and I can't help it. I lose any hope of self control. Heart beating against my ribs, I lean in, half an inch away from kissing the most gorgeous lips I have ever—

A phone rings in the background. It's fuzzy in my head, but I can hear it, and it brings us both to a stop.

We freeze as we gaze at each other, waiting for something or someone to tell us what to do next. Is it right, kissing her now, like this? I don't think so. But do I want it? Fuck, yes. It feels like I haven't wanted anything as much as I want this in my entire existence.

"That's my phone," she whispers after a few seconds, her sweet breath on my lips almost making me forget every logical thought in my brain.

"You—you should probably get that, then. Before the person hangs up. Might be important." I loosen my hold on her, and she clears her throat. When she slips out of my arms, I'm left with the most hollow feeling in the world. The loss, though short, is almost seismic.

"It's my boss; I have to take this. I'm sorry," she says, looking genuinely apologetic.

"It's alright. I'll just..." I'll just *what* exactly? Go die of embarrassment, maybe?

I exhale deeply and step outside into the pool area to take a breather on one of the lounge chairs. And to wait til my dick calms down, because, yeah, that was one of the hottest moments of my life, and there wasn't even kissing. Just *feeling* her like that...

I shut my eyes and lie back, listening to the crickets chirp as the sun goes down, Diana's voice faint and muffled in the background, while I try not to think about all the ways in which I would've liked that moment to have progressed.

It's a while before I hear the sliding glass door of the pool house open, but when I do, I sit up in a panic, not knowing what to expect. I never intended for this to happen, and definitely not like that.

"Hey," she says, walking up to me with a wry smile.

The sun is a kaleidoscope of oranges, yellows, pinks, and purples—breathtaking in its own way—but it's nothing in comparison to the way she looks tonight.

It's a few seconds before I can breathe again.

"Hey."

She takes a seat in the lounge chair beside mine and faces toward me, so I sit up and face her.

"Sorry about that. Colorado is two hours behind, so I'm technically still on call for work, you know? Usually, I'm not done until maybe eight or nine P.M."

"Oh. That sucks. I'm sorry." And I am. Anyone who's met Diana for even a second will know that she is not one to shirk work responsibilities or give anything less than one hundred percent of herself in anything she does. I'd bet my entire professional chef knives collection that she's been running herself ragged—and still thinking she isn't doing enough.

"It's okay; I don't mind," she says with a shrug. "It's for that in-person meeting in the city I told you about. The one for a big new case we've been working on, and I can't go. That's what the call was about." Diana stares off into the sunset, chewing the inside of her cheek.

"Yeah, I remember you telling me about the meeting." *I remember every single thing you've ever told me.* "I also remember telling you that I would help you watch your girls while you were away, if you needed it."

"I..."

"This sounds like a big deal. Let me help you. I know you said you didn't know me that well, and I get that. But I've got references—you can call Barbara again. And I think we've gotten to know each other better since the barbecue. At least a little."

I mean, my hard cock was literally against your back just now. And, had we not been interrupted, and you had let me, I swear I would've thrown you on top of your kitchen island and eaten you out just how I've imagined it a thousand times since the Fourth of July. Maybe even before then, if I'm being honest with myself.

Diana sits up, back ramrod straight, brows scrunched in that cute way she always does.

"Are... are you serious?" she asks after a heavy moment of silence passes between us. "You'd take them for the day?"

I clear my throat. "Yeah. *Yes.*"

Let me help you. Let me give you the support you deserve but have clearly never received.

"I can't ask you to do that," she whispers.

I huff, frustrated. "You're not asking—I'm *offering*. It sounds like you need help, and I'd be happy to do it."

"But... you're doing that now. Helping me, I mean." She points over her shoulder toward the pool house. "You showed up and are cooking us dinner. Teaching me a couple of good recipes and whatever."

"I mean, sure. But I could also help with the girls if I can. It's not a big deal. It's not like they're moving in or anything. It would just be like a playdate or something. Are they too old to call it a playdate?" She smiles and I'm not sure whether I like what it does to me. "When is your meeting supposed to be, anyway?"

"Um, day after tomorrow."

"Let me check my schedule." With her gaze on me, I pull my phone out of my back pocket and check my calendar, knowing deep down that I would reschedule anything to help her out. She often gives all of herself to others, and rarely takes anything. She deserves someone to do the same for her once in a while. And if I can do that even once... Well, at least I know I will have made her load a bit lighter. "So would you need me to pick them up from camp, too?"

"Yes?" I can hear the hesitation in her voice. Can hear how tempted she sounds, how much she wants to accept help but isn't used to doing so.

"My day doesn't look too busy. I have a couple of test kitchen hours scheduled with Lexi, but I could probably move that to earlier in the day when the girls are at camp. And then, once I pick them up, I can take them to the aquarium or something."

"The aquarium?"

"The Long Island Aquarium in Riverhead? I used to go when I was a kid, and I've been meaning to take Rachel." I shrug. "This could just be the perfect opportunity to do it."

"Um... I don't know." She shakes her head, biting her lower lip. "Emi... I've never left her alone with anyone before. Not since her diagnosis. And though we're not exactly strangers anymore—" she clears her throat once—"we've sort of only just met."

That stings because, even though it's true, it doesn't feel that way with her most of the time. Not anymore, at least.

I nod. "I understand you're nervous. But just know that if you reconsider, I am down to help. I might not have firsthand experience with type 1 diabetes, but I can follow instructions better than anyone."

She chuckles, relaxing a bit, causing relief to wash over me. "Thank you. I really appreciate that. More than you know."

Another one of our silences passes between us. "Are you—" She stops herself mid-sentence and shakes her head.

"What?"

"Nothing. It's fine."

"Tell me. What were you going to say?"

A sigh. "Are you just offering to help because of what happened back there? Which I guess we're both avoiding talking about but should probably address sooner rather than later?"

I look over my shoulder at the pool house, and then back at her. "I offered to help, remember? I want to help you because I like you, yes. But also, because I feel like you go the extra mile for everyone all the time, and you deserve someone to come through for you once in your fucking life. And... I want to give you that. I want to be the one who comes through for you."

Diana's eyes glisten, her brows scrunching together again. "I… don't know what to say. To any of it."

"Say you'll let me be there for you—at least this one time—so you can get exactly what you deserve for once."

I notice she doesn't address that I've all but confessed how much I like her, but none of that matters when she breathes, "Okay. Thank you," and gives me the most beautiful smile I've ever seen.

If you'd have asked me five years ago where I'd be today, I would not have answered The Long Island Aquarium. In fact, five years ago, in an interview for the *Times,* I *was* asked where I'd be today, and my answer was far from what my reality is now. Back then, I believed I'd be head chef and owner of my own restaurant in a city like New York or London or Paris. But here I am, herding three children—Rachel and Diana's two girls—through a packed aquarium while a mountain of work piles up for the farm-to-table I'm trying to open, and there's not a single thing I would change about it.

I'm more than happy to help babysit Cami and Emi while Diana is in Manhattan. The fact that her boss flew in all the way from Colorado for this meeting signified that it was a big deal, which in turn meant that her being invited was even bigger. And I want Diana to be happy—for so many reasons. The first being that she's always there for her daughters, sacrificing her happiness for their own. But it's not just for them that she goes the extra mile. I think back to the Fourth of July barbecue, the way she helped me and Rachel achieve this very pivotal breaking point in our relationship. Without her help, without her influence, there's a chance Rachel would've never opened up to me fully. There's a chance we would've had a relationship limited in communication, both of us starved for it for the rest of our lives. But Diana knew better, and she helped my daughter and I talk. She made us listen to each other and express how we felt.

I know that sounds extremely simple in theory, but understanding what you're feeling and subsequently expressing those feelings is not always a simple task.

Rachel called me "Dad."

I smile down at my daughter, gazing at her as she watches the stingrays in the open, shallow pool right by the aquarium entrance. Gasping, her eyes shine with excitement.

"Guys! Look!" She squeals, jumping up and down as she gets Cami and Emi's attention. "You can *pet* the stingrays!"

The other two girls gasp as well and immediately make a run for the "petting area." I run behind them because that can't be right, can it?

"You can pet stingrays?" I ask, looking around at the other children sitting on the edge of the pool, some of them, indeed, letting their little hands run over the backs of swimming stingrays. My first thought is how awful it must be for the animals to have to endure humans all day every day. But as I take a closer look, I see that most, if not all, stingrays seem to enjoy the attention, playing with the children, coming up and peeking out of the shallow water before going back in.

"Dad!" Rachel waves me over. "Come pet one! It's so gross and slimy and cool!"

"Well, I would've never thought those first two words would go in the same sentence as 'cool.' Still, I'll take your word for it, kid."

I smile at the girls' awestruck expressions, and think to myself *Today is gonna be a good day.*

It takes longer than expected to get three girls to abandon petting a slimy fish (are stingrays fish?), but I manage to pull them away from the shallow feeding pool to check out the rest of the aquarium.

Watching Rachel pay absolutely zero attention to me because she's so busy having fun with her friends feels like one of the best things a person can experience. Seeing your child happy and just being a fucking kid is an indescribable feeling. My happiness is momentarily disrupted, however, by bitterness. Because *my* parents apparently never gave a shit about me enough to make sure whether I was happy or well taken care of. They never made me feel the type of joy or peace I see in Rachel's eyes right now. I was never anything more than a burden.

The resentment I feel toward my parents has increased steadily every day since Rachel has come into my life under this new dynamic. I've grown more and more indifferent about the fact that no one has any idea where my parents are now—I don't even know whether they're together or not—but the anger I repressed as a young adult and in my early twenties has come back full force. Despite the rage, I try to reframe the feeling into a positive one. It's something that will ensure I will, for the rest of my life, do everything in my power to make sure my child is happy and well.

It's around snack time when we finally get tickets to see the seal show. The girls convince me to sit in the first couple of rows, so we naturally get soaked during their hilarious show. Normally, I feel weird about aquariums and zoos, but all the animals here seem to be happy with their new digs. Before I know it, I'm laughing, lost in the moment, feeling something warm course through me as my daughter looks up at me and thanks me for bringing her and her friends here.

"Of course, bud. Plus, I'm on babysitting duty, too, remember?" I tell her.

"Yeah," she whispers with a shrug. "But you could've just left us playing at the farm while you worked. Instead you decided to take us somewhere fun and spend time with me. And that's kinda cool."

Kinda cool? From a nine year-old? Even *I* know that's high praise!

"Well... I just wanted you to have a good time. Plus, it's a really pretty afternoon. Woulda been a shame to waste it on work."

Would've been a shame to waste it on work?? Who am I?

"Still. Thank you."

"You're wel—"

"Michael?" Emi's soft voice cuts me off. "I don't feel so good." I twist in my seat on the bleachers to get a better look at her and realize just how pale she looks.

My stomach drops as her phone beeps loudly in her bag. *Her insulin levels. Check her insulin levels. Or is it her blood sugar? Fuck.*

Moving as fast as I can, I reach her and unzip her backpack, rifling through it to get to her phone. Just like Diana taught me this morning, I open the app, and check Emi's blood sugar and insulin levels.

Shit...

Chapter Fourteen

DIANA

Few things in my life have felt as painful as watching this first year associate from our firm mumble his way through our presentation and findings, desperately rifling through paperwork for the correct contracts—and I've been through a very messy and painstaking divorce. But the frustration running through my veins at watching someone who went through three years of school for something that comes so easily to me is incredible.

"Max?" Edgar asks, clearly sharing my frustration. "I thought you were prepared for this," he whispers.

Max, a baby-faced twenty-something year-old, looks like he's two seconds away from a panic attack. "I-I was. I *am*. I just need to find this one file that—"

I can't take this anymore.

"Um. If I may. I believe what you're looking for is the initial construction agreement with the builders? I have a copy in my folder if you'd like to see it while Max looks for the original." I slide the contract across the conference room table to my boss, the company's own internal legal team, and Jonathan Bloom, our big fish. The one who insisted on seeing us in person.

Edgar sighs in relief and smiles. "Thank you, Miss Castillo. And now, Mr. Bloom, you can see that we've adjusted this clause, as per your request—but we also added this consideration."

I smile to myself as I look out the conference room window over Edgar and Mr. Bloom's shoulders, a wave of appreciation for Michael crashing over me. There would have been no way I would be here without his help.

The view from the seventieth floor is magnificent and unlike anything I've ever seen. Definitely a different kind of view than the ones you get from the Colorado mountains but still just as awe-inspiring. My mind drifts for a moment to the sheer amount of engineering and architectural talent, to the decades of innovation that it took to create one of the most legendary skylines. But my whole world comes to a halt with the chilling sound of a notification from my daughter's CGM app.

I gasp and pull my phone from my purse, chills covering every inch of my skin as I read the banner across my phone: "*Urgent - Low Glucose*"

"Excuse me," I mutter, pushing away from the table, knocking the chair over.

My heart beats so loud in my chest, I can barely hear Edgar's words or process his concerned expression. All I know is I need to call Michael now, and I need to know how my daughter is doing.

I search for his contact in the hallway just outside the conference room, cursing myself for making such a colossal mistake. I should never have left them. I should never have left Emi alone with Michael. I should've—

"*Mami?*" Camila's voice comes through Michael's phone.

"Cami? Why are you answering Michael's phone? What's going on?" *Tell me, because I can barely breathe.*

I hear Michael's voice in the background, speaking to my daughter.

"Michael says to tell you that everything is going to be fine. That he's got it handled."

"*What?*" I screech, causing some people passing by me in the hall to shoot some well-deserved looks in my direction. "What do you mean he said he's got it handled? Let me speak with him right now."

He's supposed to be taking care of my girls. He's the one who offered to do this for me. If he can't even make sure she's okay...

"Um," Cami says to Michael. "She's yelling. You should probably take the call. She wants to talk to you."

I hear Michael's frustrated sigh. Hope he enjoys it, because it will be his last one.

"Put the phone on speaker while I help your sister, please."

"Help her how? What is he doing to her?" I nearly scream into the phone. I'm two seconds away from jumping out of my skin, from taking the first train, bus, taxi, or helicopter out of here to get to my daughter as soon as possible.

Cami apparently does as she's asked because I hear Michael say, "Emi's going to be fine. I'm just helping her sit up right now. We're checking her pump and monitor." His voice sounds a bit far from the receiver.

"What the fuck is going on, Michael?"

He gasps. "Whoa. I've never heard you curse before."

"Don't try to be cute. What is going on? I've asked this question about three times too many. In fact, any time is too many. I shouldn't have to ask it at all. You said you would take care of them. You said that—"

"I *was* taking care of them. I *am*."

"That's my daughter's life you're playing with."

"Playing with?" He scoffs. "We didn't calculate how much sitting outside to watch the seal show would affect her and her blood sugar levels. How the sun would dehydrate her. We were about to hit the cafeteria after the show when it happened. But everything is fine now. Emi is resting, I gave her some of the candy you had in her backpack and gave it to her like you said to get her blood sugar up quickly, and a cold bottle of water to rehydrate. Once she feels better, we're going back home to have real food, and a rot day."

"What the hell is a rot day?"

"It's when you stay home and rot on your couch. Watch TV. Don't do anything."

"*Mami*, I'm fine," Emi says, her voice faint.

My heart jumps, tears building in my eyes. "Emi? Are you sure you're okay?"

"Yes. It was just an accident. But Michael is being super nice, and he's doing all the right things. Don't be mad at him, *Mami*. Or me. It was just an accident," she repeats.

I stifle a sob. "I'm not mad at you. I just wish..." *I just wish things weren't like this. I just wish I didn't feel this alone.* "I just wish I were there with you."

"Well, Michael says we'll see you later this afternoon, so don't worry about it."

"Later? No," I say, shaking my head. "I'm headed home now. Michael, can you drive them to my place, and I'll meet you there, please? I just need to excuse myself from this meeting and grab my things and—"

"*What?* No," Michael says loudly. "Absolutely not. You are not coming home now. Not while you're still in the middle of this thing. Not until you're done with what you went there to do." His voice sounds clearer, like he's taken me off speakerphone, but there must be a problem with the connection because there's no way he just told me not to come home after what happened.

"*Excuse me?*"

"Diana, you are not leaving in the middle of this meeting.

You told me how important it is, and I am not going to let you mess this up."

"Michael, my daughter is *unwell.* I have to go to her."

"Your daughter is not unwell. At least, not anymore. I did everything you taught me to do and the situation has been handled. Her glucose levels are under control—or on their way—and I will be taking all three girls back to your place so she can rest—where is the spare key hidden by the way?—and you're going to stay there and wow your boss because you know your shit and are good at what you do. Do you understand?"

"I-I-I can't," I stutter, shocked he would even suggest it. "What kind of mother would that make me if I just stay here? A selfish one. An irresponsible one. I can't just abandon them and—"

"You're not abandoning your children, Diana. Believe me—I know abandonment. I know this is going to be really difficult for you to hear," he says, lowering his voice, "but you deserve this. You deserve a career, and you deserve this time, and taking it doesn't make you a bad mother."

"But I am! I should be there with Emi, and I should be—"

"First of all, Emi is fine. You were an amazing mother and explained everything I had to do if an emergency situation arose, and I followed your instructions, and things are good. She's got some color in her, she's sitting up and talking with the girls. And like I said, we're gonna head home, slap on a movie, and everything will be fine. Second, I'm going to tell you something I've heard about a million times since becoming a single parent."

"And what's that?" I sniffle, my heart breaking.

"The fact that you're even a little bit stressed about what kind of parent you're being already makes you a far better one than most. And believe me when I say that no one who knows you for even a second would ever dream of thinking you're subpar. At anything, really, but especially at this whole parenting thing."

I struggle to stifle the soft cries rising through my chest.

"Don't waste this opportunity. *Please.* You deserve this, and your kids deserve this. They deserve to see their mother's success, too. I know this isn't easy for you, but trust me. Let me be here for you. I *want* to be here for you so you can succeed."

His words rock me, a sob I pray he didn't hear over the phone bursting from my lips.

He waits patiently for my response as I weigh all options in silence.

Finally, I speak: "Okay. Okay, I'll do it. I'll stay. But text me every step of the way back. I want a progress report every five minutes."

I practically hear his dimpled smile over the phone. "Yes, of course."

"And I want regular updates as soon as you get home, too."

"Obviously."

"I mean it!"

"Okay." He says calmly. "Don't worry. I got this."

I blow out a breath. "Yeah. I think you do."

He chuckles softly.

"Michael?"

"Yeah?"

I sniffle once again. "Thank you."

"You're welcome. Now tell me where the spare key is."

I'VE NEVER BEEN ONE TO LET GO EASILY, WHICH IS WHY when I hang up with Michael, it takes everything inside me to walk back into that client meeting with my boss and not bolt right out the front door instead.

I squeeze my eyes shut, and press the phone to my forehead, trying to gather myself.

Today is important. This meeting is so important. For my boss and myself. It's a chance to prove that I am more than an executive assistant. It's a chance to prove to Edgar that he can trust me with things other than scheduling, especially since he's hiring me as a paralegal. And Michael was right. While I can say that staying here is selfish, the only reason I'm here, the only reason I took this job to begin with, was for my daughters.

So it's a good thing.

I'm just not used to people helping me with childcare. Maybe my parents, when they could manage to come down to Denver and help me, but my ex has certainly never pitched in much. Or at all. So it's difficult to accept that this man—this man who I didn't even like when we first met—would willingly offer to help. That Michael would not only be capable of handling a delicate situation, but was happy to unload it from me in order for me to have the tools necessary to succeed today.

Wiping the tears off my cheeks, I check the CGM one last time. After taking a deep breath, I push the conference room door open, praying my makeup isn't that big of a mess.

Quietly, I slide back into my seat at the long, oval table with a murmured apology. "I'm so sorry for the interruption. It was a family emergency." I shoot Edgar a pleading look. "It won't happen again," I assure everyone in the room.

"Is everything all right? Do you need to excuse yourself?" Edgar asks.

"No, no. It's been handled." At least, I'm trusting that it has.

The meeting wraps up smoothly an hour later, leaving both parties pleased—thank god. Edgar is happy with how our presentation went, and I'm ecstatic that my personal emergency didn't affect our business—or so it seems. With a smile on my face, I gather up our documents and ready myself to leave.

When Edgar and Max excuse themselves to go to the restroom, and the rest of the Bloom Inc. legal team leaves, I'm left alone by the elevators with the man who has unknowingly kept me up late working on his case. Not that I'm complaining; I've actually found it quite fascinating. But it's odd to have spent so much time wading through his sensitive information without ever having really met him until today's meeting.

"Are you joining us for drinks?" Jonathan asks.

"Oh. I didn't know I was invited." I clutch the documents to my chest, and look up at him.

"Of course you are!" He laughs, his blue eyes shining. "I was the one who made you guys come all the way here. It would be horrible of me to not even take you guys out for a drink."

"That's very kind of you, Mr. Bloom, but you're the client. We're supposed to be taking you out for drinks."

That makes him laugh. "Please, call me Jonathan. And you think I'm going to make you pay on top of having the entire team travel all the way here?" He shakes his head. "I'm not that type of guy."

No, he doesn't seem like that type of guy. In the hour I've known him, Jonathan Bloom hasn't given me Evil Billionaire vibes. He actually seems... nice.

"Well, that's super nice of you, but I'm pretty sure we would've just billed you for it later," I say with a smirk. "Still, I think I'm going to have to pass this time around. Remember that family emergency? It's not an emergency anymore, but I should probably make sure everything is okay."

"I understand," Jonathan tells me. "Family should always take priority over work."

I guess I must be visibly surprised that a billionaire would say that, since he asks "What? You don't think I could ever value family over work?"

"Um, well, you're Jonathan Bloom. You're a media mogul and you're self-made. I'm sure you had to make a lot of sacrifices in order to get to where you are. I've read your bio—you didn't get to where you are easily."

Running a hand through his thick, dark hair, he chuckles. Piercing blue eyes bounce around my face, searching for… something. His smile is perfect and straight, inviting and kind. The guy is basically Superman in a business suit—Clark Kent without the glasses—but it's not doing much for me. Have I gone insane?

"Yes, it's been years of hard work. But recently I've realized that the sacrifices I made may not have been worth it. It's been a lot of lonely nights and empty holidays. It's a cliché, but what's success if you have no one to share it with?"

I smile up at him. "I suppose you're right."

"You look like the type of person who carries a lot of weight and self-blame around. So, I just want to make sure you know that you didn't cause a big interruption in the meeting today. You did the right thing, and you had your priorities straight. And if Edgar says anything to you, I'll be extremely disappointed."

I grin at him and shake my head. "You're really nice, but he would never. He's probably the most supportive boss anyone's ever had. He was my divorce attorney, too, so he knows me pretty well. That's why I think he won't mind me skipping out on our drinks to go back to Long Island."

He perks up. "You're from Long Island? I thought you were from Colorado."

"Oh, I'm from Colorado, that's true. But I'm spending the summer in Sag Harbor at a friend's house for now."

"Sag Harbor, huh? I actually have a house around there."

He scratches the back of his head, his cheeks suddenly a pale pink. "If you're around and free... I don't know. Maybe we can take a rain check on today's drinks, and I can take you to dinner sometime?"

My jaw drops. He can't be serious, can he? "Like a... date?"

"Yes." He smiles, suddenly marginally more confident than he was just a few seconds before.

"Um. I... I don't know if that will get me in trouble. Isn't that a conflict of interest or something?" I gnaw on my lower lip, not knowing what to say.

On the one hand, what? On the other, maybe this will be good for me? It could be an opportunity to find out whether whatever crush I have on Michael is only because he's attracted to me like Jonathan, and I haven't been with anyone who has shown any interest in me in years, or whether what I feel for him is real.

"If it's a conflict of interest, then..." Jonathan shrugs, "Then I guess we won't do it. But I think you're nice and smart and beautiful. And I'd really like to see you again. I can come to you —you don't even have to worry about coming into the city. I have some stuff I need to take care of out there, anyway, so you'd really be saving me from a boring trip. And there's this special place I could take you to—a place I'd love to take you to." He smiles and it's tender, his eyes soft. Like he really does mean everything he says.

Odd.

"You don't even know me," I say, shaking my head, almost in awe.

"No. Not yet. But I have a feeling."

But I don't, I almost say. Though to be honest, who am I to say? The last time I went on a first date was a million years ago. I mean, low-rise jeans were still in, and we were all for it, for Pete's sake. And maybe this will be a good way to get Michael out of my head. Not that I'd admit to him being there to begin with. Because he's not.

Ugh.

Stupid Michael and his stupid dimpled smile and perfect body and the adorably considerate speech he gave me and the way he makes me feel and that hot almost-kiss.

Uggggghhhh.

"Um. Okay. I guess that would be fine." My voice is small, hesitant.

Jonathan laughs softly, his eyes warm. "I'll try not take offense to that level of enthusiasm."

I laugh and shake my head, feeling a blush creep up my neck. "No, no. I mean yes. An enthusiastic yes."

But is it enthusiastic? Is it really, Diana?

His eyes shine with humor as he presses his lips together. "How about this: how about you think about it? I don't want you to feel pressured or coerced into it. You can give me your number or I can give you mine. Or both?"

"Okay," I say softly. "I appreciate that."

"Okay, then." He nods and asks for my number, which he saves right before immediately sending me a text with his name.

"We ready to go?" Edgar comes up behind me, Max in tow, and I jump, lucky they weren't there to overhear the conversation. I'm not sure exactly what my boss's reaction would be, but chances are, he'd rather I not date the biggest client he's been able to score in decades.

"Yes," Jonathan says.

Chapter Fifteen

DIANA

I HEAD HOME ON THE LONG ISLAND RAILROAD, SO LOST IN everything that's happened today I almost miss my stop. Between the meeting, Emi not feeling well, how amazingly Michael handled her crisis, and now Jonathan asking me on a date, I'm exhausted. All I want is a glass of wine and a shower, but I need to make sure my girls are fine before I can even consider relaxing tonight.

"Hey, there she is!" Michael greets me as I walk through the pool sliding doors into the house.

There's a wide smile on his face, green eyes bright, as if the day had gone as smoothly as butter. Momentarily, the deep happiness reflected in his expression at my arrival distracts me. It throws me off, something inside me tighten and loosening at the same time; it makes my skin heat but covers me in goosebumps. I still don't understand this new thing blooming between us, and I know it's something I'm going to need to really analyze soon. But right now, there's something much more pressing I need to attend to.

"Hey. How's Emi?" I ask as I shrug off my blazer with one arm and hold my purse with the other.

Michael takes both from my hands after placing my bag on

the kitchen counter and hanging my jacket carefully on the back of the island stools.

"She's fine," he whispers. "She's in the other room with the girls watching TV. I didn't want to make too big of a deal about it when we got home because she was really sad and felt self-conscious with Rachel. I heard her crying in the bathroom, so I waited until she came out and reassured her that Rach wasn't going anywhere because of this and that these things happen. So I know you want to go in there, mom guns blazing, but, if I may, I think it would be best to keep the anxious questions in private for her sake. Like, pull her aside or wait 'til we're gone. I don't know."

I stay rooted to the spot, stinging building behind my eyes. "Are you sure?" My voice cracks. "Because I feel like running into that TV room right now, bursting into tears, and hugging my daughters forever."

He takes my right hand in both of his. "Hey. I know. And you can absolutely do that. I just think you should let her have this."

My tears spill over down my cheeks in quiet sobs. I'm bone-tired. Weary. My brain, heart, and body are a minute away from collapsing from this nerve-wracking day. As if reading my mind, Michael pulls me into his arms, holding me tightly to him. The tears come more easily now when I wrap my arms around his waist. He whispers comforting words in my ear, and I've never felt this grateful for anything in my life.

"Shh. It's okay. Everything is okay. Your girls are okay and so are you. I'm here to help with whatever you need."

I try to apologize between sobs, my mouth muffled by his shoulder. "I'm s-s-so sorry. You've been so great, and I y-y-yelled at you. But I'm just *s-so* tired, and wish the girls and I could just get a break for once."

"Hey. Don't worry about me. Seriously. I would've been just as terrified as you. Now, let's go outside before they hear you."

He takes me by the hand, but I pull away. "But the girls. I want to see them, and make sure they're okay, and—"

"I told you, the girls are fine. But if they see you like this now, they're going to get upset. You can't keep repressing this shit, though. Let's sit outside, and we can talk about this."

We take a seat on one of the lounge chairs by the pool, his arm around me.

"Tell me what's going on. And not the Diana I-don't-need-anyone's-help version. The *real* version."

My tear-covered face is buried in his neck as I begin to word-vomit. "Work is exhausting and handling all this s-s-stuff on my own is exhausting. And Rodrigo won't even answer the damn phone or Cami and Emi's letters." My heart aches when I think of how easily my ex-husband has cast his daughters aside, how heartless he's become. "It's been *months* since they've heard from h-h-him, and they keep asking where their dad is and *I don't know what to say*. And we're gonna have to go back to reality soon. But I still haven't found an apartment in Denver and work is great but I feel s-s-so frustrated because I *know* I'm so much more capable than these kids that get to boss me around, and it makes me feel like a horrible person, but I *do* feel that way. And then there's Emi's diagnosis and how much I wish I knew how to manage it better. How much I want to give her the most normal life. How am I gonna give her that? How am I going to give either of my girls that when their mother is a mess? Especially when their mother is the single most selfish person in the world, obviously, since I'm here *complaining* about—"

"*Diana*." The assertiveness in Michael's voice brings my manic rambling to a stop.

"What?" I whisper, looking up into his dark green eyes.

He reaches up to cup my face with both hands, wiping the tears from my cheeks. "You are the strongest woman I have ever met in my life. I am truly in awe of everything that you do every day for everyone, and I will never allow you or anyone else to ever call you selfish. You are the most *selfless* person—to a fault, I believe. Those girls in there? Yeah, they fucking adore you. They love their mother. And maybe they give you shit, but guess what? That's kids. You are not only doing your best, but you are also doing a great job with them. It's reflected in who those kids are. And if I hear you call yourself selfish or a bad parent again, I'm going to get so mad at you. I never want to hear you put yourself down again. Not you. Not ever." His eyes are fierce. I have never seen anyone look so determined, so *serious*.

I stare with wonder at Michael's handsome face as he looks back at me with reverence and loyalty. Like he's a knight from the Middle Ages ready to go to battle against an entire army for his queen. His breathing grows ragged, and I notice mine does, too. In the heat of it all, I can barely catch my breath while my heart takes off and the need for him I've been repressing rears its head.

Want.

I stare up at him, his face just inches away from mine, dumb-struck. "I—I don't know what to say."

And that's when I see that same hunger I've been carrying with me, hidden away, is clearly reflected in his face.

"Don't say a thing," he murmurs.

And without another word, Michael's hands slide to the nape of my neck, they tangle in my hair. He brings his face closer still, lips only millimeters away from my own. His gaze bounces from my mouth to my eyes in question, and I want to scream *Yes!* from the top of my lungs. I can taste the scent of him on my tongue, fill my lungs with it on every inhale wishing it stays with me forever. I nod once on a sigh and just with that, he murmurs my name before bringing his lips to mine.

It's... the best kiss I've ever had. The best kiss that has ever existed in the history of the universe. It starts off slow, but the heat of it immediately starts to build everywhere—especially low, between my thighs. I sink into him, his body warm and hard and soft at the same time. He groans into my mouth when I pull at him, running my hands over his shoulders, scratching him with my nails and secretly hoping I leave tracks on his skin —marking him physically in the same way he's marked me emotionally. My breathing is already embarrassingly ragged when he moves to my neck, his hand sliding beneath my shirt, settling over my ribs in a commanding hold. I moan at the touch, the ache between my legs, the feeling of emptiness growing with every second. His lips feel incredible everywhere, but I need them back on mine, need to taste him.

With every passing second, we pull each other closer, but the position is uncomfortable and it's like we can't get enough of what we need. Always the mindreader, Michael wraps his arms around my waist and, in a move that can only be described as acrobatic, manages to flip me on my back, adjust the lounge chair to lay fully flat, and crawls over me in a matter of seconds.

"Yes," I hear myself moan, one hand in his hair, another on his (perfect) denim-clad ass.

"God, *Diana*," he groans into my neck. "I've been waiting to kiss you since..." A sigh. "Since what feels like forever."

One hand is under my bra, thumb rubbing over my nipple, driving me crazy. The other travels over my waist and hip, moves down all the way to my knee, where Michael proceeds to hook my leg up over his hip.

I inhale sharply when he readjusts himself to fit perfectly in between my legs and pushes forward once, my clit throbbing. "Oh my god." The ridge of his cock hits my sensitive nerves just right, making me throw my head back in pleasure.

"I want to feel how wet you are. I dream of tasting you and driving you wild."

I whimper, and I think I beg him for exactly that. If I weren't so lost in the delicious way he thrusts his hips into me, I'd be a bit more embarrassed. But I just can't bring myself to care.

He's hard. And *big*. *Big* big. Like, he *must* have an *actual* eggplant in his pants or something *big*.

I want that. I want *him*.

Close. I'm so close.

But I want it all. I want to go back into the house, have him throw me on my bed, and—

"Oh my god!" But this time, I'm not moaning it in pleasure. *The house. The girls.* "Get off," I yell, pushing against his chest. "Get off, get off!"

Michael doesn't hesitate, immediately sitting up and giving me enough space to think a bit. "What's wrong? What did I do?" His chest rises and falls almost as quickly as mine does, his cheeks are bright red, pupils blown with the same hunger I feel, and his hair is a mess from how aggressively I must've run my fingers through it. Adorable and absolutely edible.

I try not to look at his jeans because I *must've* been imagining what I felt between my legs, but then my gaze slips down and—

Nope. Didn't imagine anything at all. There it is. And...

Want. Want so bad.

"We need to stop."

"Why?" He clears his throat and shakes his head. "Sorry. I mean, if that's what you want, then—"

"No, it's not what I want! Or... Actually, I don't know what I want. That was amazing, and you're amazing, and we're gonna need to talk about this eventually. But the girls. They're in there and they could come out any second and we were just dangerously close to... *something*."

He exhales deeply and rubs both hands down his face, nodding. "No, you're right. Holy shit, you're right. Like, what if they'd walked out and..."

"Exactly." My cheeks are sensitive from beard burn, but I don't hate it. I shiver, part of me ashamed from the pleasure I feel in knowing I've been marked, even if it's accidentally.

"Right." He scratches the back of his head before looking back up at me with a dimpled, bashful grin. "Bummer. I was... I was really enjoying myself."

"Yeah." A slow smile grows across my face. "Me too."

"Yeah?" He raises his brows.

"Duh. Did me moaning your name not give it away?"

Michael laughs. "Not really. Maybe you dry humping my leg did, though."

"Oh, god." I pull a towel from the table beside the chair and cover my face with it.

"C'mon." Michael gently pries the towel from my hands. "Don't be embarrassed—dry humping is severely underrated. That was amazing. But you're right. We should probably get inside."

"Right." I get to my feet and readjust my shirt, tie my hair up in a ponytail and take a deep breath.

I slide the door open, but Michael stops me with a hand around my wrist.

"Wait," he pleads. "We're going to talk about this later, though, right? We're not just gonna... I don't know, forget about it?"

I swallow, because part of me suddenly wants to forget about it. I mean, where can this even go? But the other side wants to have that talk. It wants to ask him why I'm feeling this way because maybe he knows.

"Like I said before, I promise we'll talk about it later."

He blows out a puff of air and nods, relieved. "Okay. Okay, good."

Inside, the girls chatter away on the couch, watching YouTube makeup tutorials. They're not even teenagers yet, and I already have to worry about this.

"Hey, girls. I'm home." I smile, and reach for the remote, pausing their video.

"*Mami*!" My heart warms in my chest when my girls get to their feet and hug me just as I crouch in front of them, their affection a bit unexpected but very well-received. I hug them extra tight.

"How was your day? Emi, I heard you had a bit of a hard time."

Emi glances furtively at Rachel, and I realize that Michael was right. "Um, yeah. But I'm fine now."

"It's okay. We can talk about it later, if you'd like," I whisper to her.

Emi nods gratefully.

"Guys, I thought we agreed on *Masterchef Junior*. Why are you watching makeup tutorials on YouTube?" Michael asks, his eyes wide and horrified on the television screen. "You're nine years old. Emi, you're eight!"

"*Masterchef Junior*? Really?" I chuckle.

"I'm trying to convince my daughter that I'm cool, okay?" He sighs as he rubs his forehead.

"So you thought *forcing* her to watch old episodes of *Masterchef Junior* would help?"

He presses his lips together, but his eyes are alight with humor. "Yes. I thought it would."

Rachel walks up to him and takes his hand. "*Cooking* isn't cool. But that doesn't mean *you* aren't, Dad."

Michael basically melts on the spot, his face spreading into a goofy grin that makes me want to die it's so adorable.

"R-Really?" he asks, his voice high-pitched. It's clear from her body language that Rachel is thinking twice about her choice of words because Michael looks like he's five seconds away from bursting into tears. "That's, like, the nicest thing you've ever said to me."

Rachel rolls her eyes, definitely regretting causing this big moment, before Michael pulls her into a big hug.

"I've told you you were cool before, what are you talking about?" She tries to pull away from him, but it only makes him hug her harder.

"Yeah, but that's when I was your uncle. Not now. You haven't said I was cool." He squeezes his eyes shut, his smile pure ecstasy. "I love you, Rach."

"Oh my god, gross. Get off me. I'm never giving you a compliment again." Rachel finally manages to scramble away, but Michael is laughing.

"That's fine. This one will probably last me like ten years. I can wait until the next one."

She crosses her arms and glares at him before muttering, "Not likely."

They stay for another hour while the girls finish their videos and have dinner. When they start to fade, he carries a drowsy Rachel to his truck and sets her in the backseat, buckling her into place before walking back to me.

"Tonight was..." He sighs, hesitation in his eyes.

"It was great." I try to smile, but the truth is my stomach is in knots. I really don't want to talk about this. I'm not ready. I'm not even sure I know how I feel. "Thanks again for all your help today."

"You're welcome. Let's talk tomorrow?" His voice is pleading, his eyes wide. The expression on his face tugs at my heart, but I'm half filled with excitement and terror at the same time.

"Yes. Sure. Tomorrow. I'll call you."

But I never do. And it makes the next time I see him all the more complicated.

Chapter Sixteen

DIANA

"Okay, Diana. So, I'm going to need you to send our client the addendum for them to review," Edgar says over our daily morning Zoom touch base. "Max prepared it, but you have such a good eye and attention to detail, I'd prefer to have you take a final look over it before we send it."

My eyes widen. "You want... *me* to review it?"

He smiles over the screen. "Yes. You have a problem with that?"

"I just... I mean, shouldn't you be the one reviewing it? Making sure that it was done right?"

"Well, Max is an associate, so in general I shouldn't be checking his work at all, should I? But alas, he's proven to be... somewhat useless at times."

I wince at his blunt words, but he isn't wrong. Sometimes Max actually creates even more work than necessary.

"You understand the basics, you're a quick learner, and have natural instincts for this type of thing, so I want you to review it. Plus, I think it will be a great learning activity for you."

I bite my lower lip and open the attachment in my boss's latest email, quickly scanning the first paragraph.

"If anything, you can check it for typos and grammar," he adds.

A broad smile stretches across my face, my heart shining from Edgar's encouragement. He believes in me, trusts in me, and every day that passes, I grow to love the law more and more. But with it also comes the disappointment that I've missed my shot.

"Okay. Yeah. I'll look it over this morning and have it back to you with notes by the end of the day."

"Perfect. I think that's all we need to review for today's to-do. Is there... anything you'd like to talk about besides work?"

I sit up in my chair, feel the color disappear from my cheeks. Does he *know*? "Um... no?"

Edgar sighs, and crosses his arms over his desk. "I want to talk to you about Mr. Bloom."

"Oh? I thought we were." I play dumb.

"Not about his *business*, and I think you know it. In retrospect, I should've started this morning's conversation with this, but I got distracted."

"And... what is it that we should be talking about?"

Edgar takes a deep breath. "After Max left early for the hotel, Mr. Bloom approached me at drinks. About you. He mentioned he asked you out on a date? And I just want to make sure he didn't make you feel uncomfortable. If so, I can speak to him as I don't think that was appropriate behavior. I told him, I didn't condone that. He assured me he tried to be as respectful as possible, but I wasn't pleased. This client... Please know that you can tell me if you felt uncomfortable. We can figure something out, pull you from the case or limit your contact with him. We can even—"

Mortified, I hold a hand up to stop him. "Mr. Porter—Edgar. *Please* don't worry. Yes, he did ask me out, but... but he never made me feel uncomfortable or... or harassed or anything. He was super respectful, even when I said no because you'd probably find it a conflict of interest or something. You've been so generous with me in giving me this opportunity and I don't want to do anything to risk my position with you—"

"Did you want to say yes, Diana?"

"I—" I stutter. "I already kind of did. I'm sorry, because I should've asked. But we never really solidified our plans, so I can just—"

Edgar raises a brow and cuts me off with a nod. "I was there during your divorce, in case you forgot. So I know everything you've gone through—at least in that sense—and I know what kind of man your ex-husband is. I've known Jonathan since before he hired us, and I must say, I can assure you he is nowhere near whatever your ex-husband was."

I snort. "Well, of course. Rodrigo isn't a billionaire and—"

"That's not what I meant, though that's certainly something to consider as well. No, I meant that Jonathan is definitely one of the good ones. I suspect that the reason he's still single has nothing to do with who he is as a person, and more to do with the fact that he has little time to give to a relationship—which is why him asking you out surprised me. But even still, the fact that he asked for *permission*... Even if it was after the fact." Edgar shakes his head with a smile on his face. "It just proves he's always trying to do the right thing. I just wanted to make sure you were okay on the off chance he was inappropriate—you never know these days. The nicest people can end up being the worst devils. But if you were interested in going out with him... Well, I'm not going to stand in your way. I'm not going to encourage it because of how it might affect our business, but I'd turn a blind eye."

I smile, my cheeks blushing. "That's very nice of you, Edgar."

Thumbs hovering over my phone screen, I chew on my lip as I try to formulate the right thing to message to Jonathan. The right way to say I've thought about it and am willing to let him take me out. It should be simple, right? Just a *hey* or *hello* maybe, add in a *I've thought about it and would like to go out.* But somehow it feels disingenuous.

Maybe because deep down you know he's not the one you really want to go out on a date with?

Rubbing my forehead, I sigh, hesitating. After an hours-long conversation with Rosie (I couldn't help panic-calling her), I decided to go for it.

She had whistled over the phone. "Oh, man. I just googled him. He is... something else."

"Of course he's devastatingly attractive," I told her. "But that's not everything, is it? That's not all I should be looking for in a partner."

"Well, duh. But is that what you're doing here? Looking for a partner? I'm so confused."

I groan. "I'm confused, too."

"Do you like him?"

I shrug, throwing myself on the couch, switching my phone from one hand to the other. "He's fine."

There's a silence over the phone. "Is this about Michael?"

"Um..."

"Did something happen between you guys?" she says, her voice brightening.

"Um. Maybe. Yes. We... kissed. But just a little bit!"

"Oh. My. *God.* Are you serious? And you're just telling me now?"

Sighing, I close my eyes and roll onto my side, pulling a blanket over my legs. The girls are still at camp, and I couldn't be more thankful. It gives me the chance to openly talk about this. "I don't know how I feel about it. It's... it's not something I'm used to."

"But you told me about Jonathan."

"Yeah. So?"

"So you can tell me about this guy but not about the one you made out with?"

I clear my throat. "I never said I made out with him."

"But you did?"

I sigh. "Yes, of course."

Rosie laughs once. "Of course?"

"Can we get back to the topic at hand? Or, you know what? Better yet, let's forget about the whole thing. I'll just figure this out on my own. Tell me about California. How are things?"

"Oh, abso-fucking-lutely not, sis. Tell me what happened."

Truthfully, I considered telling my sister off, but I found myself in no position to handle this alone. It was evident I was in new territory. So I did. I told her all about Emi's crisis, how amazingly Michael handled it. I told her about how the tension had been building since he came over to cook, but even before that. I told her how we ended up making out on a lounge chair by the pool, under the stars, and the amount of unanswered texts he had sent me over the past twenty-four hours, asking to meet, to discuss what had happened.

"Okay, so it's clear you have some feelings for the guy. And he has feelings for you."

I sniffled, on the verge of tears. "Maybe."

"Do you not want to maybe, I don't know, *try*?"

A tear runs down my cheek, but I quickly wipe it away. "I don't want to ruin things. I don't want to end up hating each other. He's been... such an amazing friend. And a big support. Losing that..." I shake my head. "I can't afford it, right now."

"You know... Asher and I are together, but—and bear with me, because I know it sounds trite—we're still *best* friends. And I swear to god it makes for a better relationship, I think. Because no matter what, we're friends first, which I think adds an entire layer to our relationship that regular relationships don't have. It's like... we're partners first and lovers second. So no matter what's going on between us, we're never going to stop being there for each other or stop considering our feelings. So sure, you might be risking a friendship. But also, you might be gaining the best relationship of your life."

"I just don't see it working. What's the point? He lives here; I live back home in Colorado."

"Then what's the point of dating the rich guy if you're in the same situation?"

I take a beat. Think it through. "He'd act as the first pancake, maybe? Just... rip off the Band-Aid for dating in general. I can be honest with him, tell him I'm just looking for fun, and just... hang."

"When have you *ever* been the type to have a casual relationship?"

"Maybe *that's* the point. I never have been that type of person because I married so young. Because I was so eager to have my own family. Maybe *now* is my time." I pause. "You know what? *Yes*. That's exactly what I'm going to do. I'm going to text him and tell him he can ask me out again if he wants. And then, at dinner, I'll tell him the truth."

"This is... a horrible fucking mistake, Diana."

"I don't think so." But even as the words leave my mouth, my stomach rolls, filled with doubt.

"You know what I think? I think you're freaking the fuck out over your feelings for Michael and want to go out on a date with this billionaire dude to distract yourself from it."

"I think you can fuck right off."

Rosie gasps, and so do I. I'm not one to curse, and we both know it. But I'm upset and she's not wrong.

Sigh.

"Dee—"

"Thanks for your advice," I say, embarrassed by my outburst. "I'm gonna text him now."

"Dee, I really think that you should reconsider. This sounds like a bad idea."

I groan, kicking my legs on the couch. A little bit childish, but this whole situation is throwing me off. "You're the one who suggested I get a special friend at the beginning of summer!"

"Yeah, but that was before you caught feelings for—"

"I—I didn't *catch feelings*. I—" I sigh in frustration. "I'm hanging up now. Talk later."

Which is how I find myself now, determination wavering. Should I listen to Rosie? Is this a mistake?

But then just as I delete the few words I'd managed to type out, I get a banner notification of another text from Michael:

MICHAEL

Diana. We can't keep avoiding this. Can you please call me? Send me a text? Smoke signals? This isn't right.

You can't avoid me forever.

Fine. I'll see you at drop-off.

THE TIGHTNESS THAT WAS BUILDING IN ME REACHES ITS limit, which is why I decide to push through my doubts and text

Jonathan. I cannot continue whatever this is with Michael, and maybe going out with another man will help. Somehow.

DIANA

Hey, Jonathan. You mentioned something about a date?

Chapter Seventeen

DIANA

I WEAR THE NICEST THING I BROUGHT WITH ME: THE RED top and midi-skirt combo I wore to Barbara's wedding. It's not overtly sexy, but the silky tank shows a bit of skin and the soft satin clings gently to my curves. It's light and airy and perfect for a summer's night. At least I hope.

It's my first first date in over ten years and to say I'm freaking out is an understatement—though not for the same reasons I would've freaked out all those years ago. This time, it isn't just about the nerves of going out with a new guy, but about a million other things, too.

For one, I'm not too happy about leaving Cami and Emi with a new babysitter—even if said babysitter is Catterina, Liza's mom. But I couldn't ask Michael to watch my girls tonight. I mean, after everything that happened between us, how was I supposed to ask him to take them for the night while I go on a date *with another guy*? But when Barbara called for our weekly check-in, and I mentioned getting asked out, she suggested her (even without me having mentioned what happened between me and Michael).

"She practically raised me, so she's had experience with kids with chronic conditions. There was more than one instance she had to take care of me post-seizure when my parents just...

wouldn't. Sure, she's in her sixties now, but she's still very physically agile, and is an experienced mother and grandmother. She'll be able to take care of the girls and monitor Emi all through the night, I promise. You just need to give her clear instructions."

"And you think she'd do it? I don't even know her. I've only met her that one time."

"Yeah, but you and Liza have sort of become friends, right?"

"I mean, I'd say we're friendly, but it's not like we've gotten to the 'spilling life secrets' part of our relationship."

Liza and I have hung out since the Fourth of July weekend; we went out for lunch with our kids last weekend and had gotten to know each other better. It had been amazing having someone to talk to who wasn't Michael, to be honest. Barbara and I had grown quite close over the weeks during our weekly conversations and occasional texting, and I was in constant communication with Rosie, but there was no question that I've been in desperate need of some in-person girl talk. I just wasn't quite sure whether our relationship was there yet.

"Regardless, Catterina is, like, the best person in the world. She'll do it—especially if I ask." I could practically hear Barbara's excitement for me on the other end of the phone, and it was damn contagious. Suddenly, the paralyzing nerves I felt whenever I thought about the date weren't as paralyzing. Just a bit debilitating.

So when Jonathan picks me up in his green Range Rover, I'm not too nervous to leave the girls with her, a woman who's had experience in following medical instructions and taking care of children with chronic conditions.

She puts her hands on my shoulders, and offers a comforting, "I'll take care of your girls. Enjoy your night—you deserve it."

And with that, I step out into the driveway in the only pair of high-heeled sandals I own.

"Hey," Jonathan whispers, taking my hand and bringing it to his lips.

The gesture shocks me, my cheeks turning a blazing red. Did he seriously just do that? I want to cringe, but I stop myself just in time.

"You look so beautiful."

My stomach tightens, but not in the same way it does whenever Michael smiles at me, or even whenever I remember the kisses we shared just outside by the pool, right beneath the stars.

As soon as the thought of Michael pops into my head, I shake it. This whole night is supposed to be about *not* thinking about him. It's supposed to be about having fun *with someone else.*

"Um, thank you. You look good, too," I say, my voice barely audible over the sound of my beating heart.

He *does* look good. He looks incredible, actually. Even though it's close to a million degrees out, Jonathan looks perfectly comfortable and absolutely delicious in a full suit. Even through his clothes, I can tell he's athletic—there's no doubt in my mind that a shirtless Jonathan would be a sight for sore eyes. But it does nothing for me. Not when the physical pull Michael has over me has grown exponentially since first meeting him.

God, will it always be like this?

Jonathan chuckles softly once and runs his fingers through his unaffected-by-the-sauna-like-humidity hair. "Thanks. I drove directly from work."

"But... it's a Saturday."

He shrugs, and with a hand on my lower back, leads me to the passenger door. Holding it open for me, he says, "I normally work a bit on Saturday and Sunday mornings, and since I'll be spending the night in town, and not working tomorrow, I wanted to catch up on a few things."

"Gotcha." I settle into my seat, and he shuts the door.

Before starting the car, he turns in his seat to look at me. "I just want to make sure that you know that I'm trying to kick the workaholic habit. If I had a relationship," he shakes his head, "I wouldn't risk it over work. I'm done with that life. I don't mean to come off too strong, but I'm ready to get into a serious relationship."

I stare, wide-eyed at him, utterly and completely speechless.

So I guess the whole casual thing with him is out the window, huh?

"Oh." Because what else am I going to say? Now certainly isn't the time to tell him I want the complete *opposite* of that. He drove all the way out here for this dinner, and now I'm just going to send him packing? *God*, I am a horrible person. I should tell him to stop, should tell him we aren't on the same page.

But then he pulls out of the driveway with a small smile playing at his lips, and I decide to go along for the ride for the rest of the night. I did go through all the trouble of setting up someone to babysit the girls, after all. And who knows? Maybe he'll end up being the love of my life.

But I grimace as something knocks the air out of me, because now that the word "relationship" comes to the forefront of my mind, that I let myself play around with the idea of one, it isn't his face that pops in my head. It's someone else's.

THE SUN IS LOW IN THE SKY, CASTING A PERFECT WARM ombre light over the road, the beauty of it mesmerizing me to distraction. But as the homes around us turn into long stretches of land and farms after a few minutes of driving, I'm pulled from my trance.

"In retrospect, I probably should've asked you this already, but where are you taking me? Because—and I hope you take no offense to this—it kind of looks like you're taking me to some farm in the middle of nowhere to murder and bury me, never to be found again."

He snorts once, but doesn't take his eyes off the road. "I'm not going to kill you—don't worry."

"I mean, that's probably what a killer would say, but okay. It's just, this doesn't necessarily look like a neighborhood where you'd find a lot of restaurants. I just want to remind you I have two daughters who will lose the only capable parent in their lives if you *do* kill me, so..."

This makes Jonathan laugh. "I'm taking you to dinner, but it isn't to a restaurant."

"Oh?"

"I have this friend who's a chef and is looking for investors for the new restaurant he's trying to open out here."

No.

No, no, no, no, no.

NO.

"You have a chef friend?" My voice comes out high-pitched, no graver than a mouse's.

"Yeah. We used to be buddies when he lived back in the city, but he had to move out here some time ago, and now... Well, I won't get into too many details. But anyway, he's rebuilding his life, and asked me to invest in his restaurant. Michael—that's his name—is bleeding money, and doesn't have enough to get a brick and mortar no matter how many side jobs he's been pulling."

Michael's bleeding money? I didn't know he was having a hard time opening his restaurant. He never mentioned it. Or maybe I was just too wrapped up in my own thing to even realize it.

I really am the worst.

"I automatically agreed to invest, obviously—he's super talented, only he's had a bout of bad luck—but he insisted on having a trial dinner anyways. Since I knew he was gonna make a huge deal and pull out the stops, I thought it might be a good idea to take you with me."

I attempt to swallow the knot that's formed in my throat, but it won't budge. This is too much of a coincidence. This is... This is... *torture.* I cannot go on a date with Jonathan at Michael's farm—*especially* not when it's also a business meeting. And *especially* not when I've been avoiding him after the hot make-out session we had. There's just no way.

I consider faking an illness or something—though with the sudden onset nausea I feel, I'm pretty sure there won't be much to fake soon—but when Jonathan flicks his blinker on and turns onto a dirt road, I realize I'm too late. I'm having dinner at Michael's farm with my date. And I have a feeling it is not going to go well.

The sound of Jonathan pulling the parking brake simultaneously sends shivers down my spine and makes me jump in my seat. Because standing on the porch of a beautiful red barn, which itself stands in front of acres of farmland, is Michael. In the fading sun, it's difficult to see his eyes, but there's no missing the way his expression changes when he realizes that the date his friend—and possible investor—brought to this dinner is the woman he kissed just a few days ago.

"Michael. Hey." Jonathan steps out of the car to greet his friend, hugging and slapping each other's backs in that weird way men do.

Over Jonathan's shoulder, Michael shoots me a look that could burn down entire empires.

"Shit," I murmur.

"Diana, come here," Jonathan waves me over with a warm smile. "Come meet my friend."

My body decides now is really not the time to move, actually. It would rather remain seated in the comfort of this luxury SUV, thank you very much. But I guess Jonathan has other ideas because, like the gentleman that he is, he offers his hand for me to take. I look at it, and then at Michael—Michael, who looks like he would bite off Jonathan's hand off in a heartbeat.

This is not good. Not good at all. For anyone.

"I... I'm okay, thank you so much."

With a quizzical brow, Jonathan nods and pulls his hand away, giving me space.

For a split second, I consider pretending like Michael and I don't know each other, sure he'd play along. He needs Jonathan's money at the end of the day, right? So why wouldn't he? But then I think back to all those romance movies where the main characters play the same game, pretending they have nothing to do with each other, and all hell breaks loose. Every time, I'm left frustrated for the entire movie wondering why they couldn't be grown-ups and just tell the truth. So I do: "Michael and I actually know each other already."

"You do?" Jonathan asks, thrilled by this information.

"Yes. Um, our girls go to day camp together."

Michael's eyes flash, his hands fisting at his sides, lips pressed together into a thin line. I thank god Jonathan's back is to him, because there's no denying that, if I really were to be murdered tonight, it would be by Michael. I begin to wonder whether maybe it might've been better to just deny his existence at this point.

"Fantastic! Have you tried his food then? If not, you're in for a real treat."

"Yes, he's great," I tell him. "You're great, Michael." I clear my throat.

Michael laughs once, humorlessly, and nods like a madman. "Right. Fucking fantastic. Well," he says, clapping his hands. "Let me show you guys what I have in store for your *romantic dinner* tonight." He spits the words out like they're the most disgusting things he's ever had to say, leading the way into the barn's makeshift dining room.

When he dips into the kitchen after seating us at a set table for two, I do everything I can to avoid Jonathan's gaze. And because he didn't become a self-made billionaire by being an idiot, he clears his throat once and asks, "So I'm assuming you guys dated at some point?"

"Um," I say, looking down at my hands. "Not exactly, no. But also, not no?" I chuckle awkwardly, praying we're all evolved enough to get through the night. "We've never dated but... There might've been a *thing*."

Jonathan nods thoughtfully.

"If this is too much, if it's too uncomfortable for you or Michael... Maybe you should drop me off at home. I don't want to risk this opportunity for him. He... He definitely deserves the chance to be able to launch his new restaurant. I've already messed up by showing up with another man; I don't want to ruin his night by inadvertently causing more conflict and ruining his chances at making his dreams come true. I already know how much this means to him and all the hard work he's put into it."

Jonathan stares at me, silent. "You care about him," he says finally.

"I—" I can't help the way my voice catches, the stinging in my eyes, or the knot in my throat that hasn't gone away all night.

"You do." His voice is softer now, eyes kind. And that's all he's ever been with me—kind, patient, understanding. "I think, perhaps, you might be on the wrong date, Diana." He smiles, taking the bottle of champagne from the bucket beside the table and fills both our glasses.

"Maybe," I admit.

Jonathan laughs, surprising me. "You look terrible."

I sniff once. "I *feel* terrible."

"Don't."

"You're such a good guy, and I'm—"

"Here," he says, taking both glasses and passing one to me. "Let's toast to our new *friendship*—nothing more. And then I think you should probably get up and go talk to him. I've known Michael for a while, and I have *never* seen that reaction out of him. Never seen him look at another woman like that."

This makes me laugh, a little awkward, wet and sniffling. We cheers once, just like he says. The champagne is crisp and cold and just what I need to scrounge up enough courage to talk to Michael when Jonathan says, "Go to him."

Chapter Eighteen

MICHAEL

I PUSH THROUGH THE KITCHEN METAL DOORS IN ONE SWIFT movement, scaring my staff and Lexi. Gritting my teeth, I lean over the counter, hanging my head between my shoulders as I stare down at my work boots.

She is on a date.

With another fucking guy.

And it's going to happen right before my eyes.

All night I'm going to have to look at her, so fucking beautiful, laughing and enjoying the company of one of the best guys I know.

Fan-fucking-tastic.

I can't believe I've been worrying like an insane person, thinking of nothing but her and her kiss and her scent and just how fucking incredible that night was and now—

How do they even know each other? How could she just have ignored me? How can she just go out on a date after what happened? How can she—

"*Michael,*" Lexi breaks through my internal rage, shaking my shoulders, the tone of her voice suggesting this isn't the first time she's called my name. "What's wrong? What happened?" I see the fear in her eyes; the concern that something might have happened with the potential investor sitting outside—our last shot at finding someone to help us out. "Is it Jonathan, your friend? Did he say no? I mean, that's impossible! We haven't even served him an appetizer! Was it the champ—"

"*Stop*," I practically growl. "It's not Jonathan. He's fine. It's..." I sigh and shake my head, squeezing my eyes shut. "He's here with her." I open my eyes and look at Lexi, hearing the hurt in my voice. Diana is the first woman I've ever felt like this for, and it's clear from her actions that she must not feel the same.

Lexi looks over her shoulder at the line cook and server we hired to help us for tonight before wrapping an arm around my shoulder. She leads me into a corner of the kitchen for some privacy.

"What do you mean he's here with her? What are you talking about?"

"Jonathan. He's fucking here with Diana."

Lexi inhales sharply. "*No*."

"Yes."

"Like, on a date?"

I raise a brow. "What do you think?"

"You could be wrong," she says, shaking her head. "Maybe they're just friends."

I snort and rub my eyes. "They're not *just* friends. When he asked if he could bring someone to the tasting, he mentioned a *date*. Plus, she's..." I sigh. "She dressed up—I think that's the same outfit she wore at Barbara's wedding. She's always so fucking beautiful, but tonight... It's more than that." The ruby red of her silky outfit contrasts with her tan skin, her dark hair falling like a waterfall down her back in beautiful loose curls. Diana doesn't wear a lot of makeup, usually, and tonight is no different—save for the enticing red lipstick calling my name. It's clear she's dressed to impress tonight, and she's succeeded. Diana looks devastatingly beautiful in a torturous, agonizing way.

My chest tightens, my hands fisting at my sides. I'm not sure whether I want to run outside, pull her from that chair, and claim her from Jonathan, risking everything that's on the line, or whether I want to run away and never see her again. Neither of those options are possible, however, because the ache of the situation has made it impossible for me to breathe. Diana hasn't texted or called since we made out at her house, making something quite clear: "She doesn't want me."

"Michael," Lexi whispers. "That can't be true. I saw you guys at the beach; saw how she looked at you—how you looked at *each other*."

"It doesn't matter; she's made her choice. And now I have to watch her fucking laugh and flirt the entire night with the guy I'm counting on to give us the money for the restaurant."

"Well, what if I host them? What if I'm the one to guide him through the menu and answer questions, and you just stay back here? I can tell him you're the one manning the kitchen, being a total control freak, and—"

"Stop, that's not going to work. Jonathan and I are close—it would be too weird if I avoided this dinner. And not showing up would be counterproductive. I'd rather just one thing be fucked up tonight instead of two. This dinner is too important."

Lexi sighs and wraps her arms around me. I tense at first, but let myself lean into the hug after a few seconds, not able to recall the last time someone held me. "It's her loss."

Sighing, I squeeze her hard once. "Thanks, cus."

She pulls away and smiles. "Now let's give them the best dinner of their lives."

I nod once. "Give me a minute, will you? I need a moment alone," I murmur, before heading out of the kitchen, and leaning against the hallway wall.

I sigh and run my fingers through my hair, trying to control my deep disappointment. I thought Diana and I would *be* something. For the first time in my life I wanted this, and now it's all gone. She doesn't like me the same way I like her, doesn't feel the same way, and I'm just going to have to deal. Though I don't know how I'm supposed to last the rest of the summer with her around. Because there's no avoiding her, is there? Not when Rachel has found happiness in her daughters after the worst year of her life. No matter how much it'll hurt to constantly see Diana, there is no way I'm going to let it affect my daughter's emotional well-being. I'm just going to have to work through this. I'm just going to have to—

"Michael," Diana's soft voice breaks through my thoughts. My spine straightens, every muscle in my body tightening, but I still can't open my eyes. Can't bear to see her in that fucking outfit that she wore for another man.

"No," I tell her. "I don't—*can't*—talk to you right now."

"I—" She sighs. "I know you hate me. I know I probably hurt you, and—"

"You didn't hurt me," I lie, opening my eyes and facing her head on. And it's a mistake. It's a fucking mistake because she's *gorgeous* and heartbreaking and, standing in front of me right now, I realize there's nothing I want more in life right now than her. Screw the restaurant, screw Jonathan—I'd rather have Diana.

"Um. Okay. So, maybe you're just upset with me. Still, I want to talk to you. About this. Right now."

"Sorry, but don't you have a fucking date to get back to?" I seethe, pointing in the direction of where we set up the dinner table for them both. "Won't *Jonathan* start to wonder where you've gone?"

"No, actually. He's the one who sent me to you."

"I'm... confused."

Diana looks away, sighing impatiently. "Obviously, he could tell something was up between us. I mean, the man is a proven genius. I think I read an article about him one time where it mentioned his IQ was something like 143?"

My jaw ticks, not liking her complimenting another man one single bit.

God, I hate this jealousy—it's so foreign to me.

"Anyway. He could tell how upset we both were. So much so that, as soon as we sat down, he asked point-blank whether we dated. I said no, but... but I told him something had happened between us. And that I—" She sniffs, quickly rubbing away a tear as it streams down her cheek. She shakes her head once. "That I really like you. That I... that I really care about you."

I suck in a breath, my heart jumping in my chest. "Did you just..."

She laughs once and rubs the back of her hand over her nose. "*Yes,* okay. I care about you. I mean, obviously. We haven't known each other long, but I'm sure you know me well enough to know I'm not one to casually make out with someone, am I?"

"No, you're not. Which is why seeing him with you tonight after having you ignore my calls... It ripped my heart out." I grimace, because I'm not usually one to get this poetic, least of all one to speak about my vulnerabilities. Yet here we are, discussing how her dismissal of the events that transpired only a few days ago almost ripped me to shreds. "I went from the highest of highs, from flying on fucking cloud nine after what we did by the pool... To feeling the lowest I've felt in a long time. I... I put myself out there, Diana—just like I am now—and I didn't just get ignored. No. I also have to see you show up with another man looking so fucking beautiful I can't even think straight." In the moment, something takes over me—something foreign that grabs ahold of my sanity, of everything I've ever known about myself. And it's her and *us*—it's the possibility of *more* with her. It takes over, pushes me to the extremes. It leads me to declare something I know to be true with everything that I am: "You aren't his. You aren't anyone else's. You're *mine*."

Without thinking, I reach out to wrap an arm around her waist, pulling her roughly against my chest. One hand slides into her hair as I turn to push her against the wall right before pressing my lips to hers.

She melts into me, her hands sliding up my ribs before tangling into my hair. With a moan, her perfect lips part, her sweet tongue sliding against mine. Having her in my arms like this is intoxicating, so much so that I lose all sense of self-control. Because, after just a moment, my right hand slides down her neck to her breasts, where I rub my thumb over her pebbled nipple right there where anyone can walk in on us.

"*God*, you're all I can think of anymore," I growl in her ear. "You're all I want."

She moans my name as my lips travel to her neck, kissing a trail down to her exposed collar bone.

"Say it again. I need to hear you say my name again." I graze my teeth across her delicate skin, eliciting a moan from her.

"*Michael*," she breathes. "Michael, Michael. Michael Haynes. *Michael*."

"*Fuck*, Diana."

"Yes." Her voice is breathy, almost pleading, as she lifts a leg and wraps it around my waist. I wrap a hand beneath her knee and keep her leg right where it is, opening her hips a bit wider so I can fit between them. In a fog, lost in her voice and scent and perfect body, I press my own hips forward, rubbing my hard cock against her. Even through our clothes, I know I've hit the right spot when she moans in my ear, begging for me to do it again.

"Yeah. Anything you want," I assure her, voice gravelly. "Anything you need, baby."

The hand that was wrapped around her leg travels up her

thigh and over her ass. I somehow manage to dip my fingers beneath her underwear, teasing her by playing with the hem. There's no one around to stop me from inching to the front, right where I want to be. I want to feel the heat of her, find out just how wet she is. I want to touch her and make her feel good *—so fucking good—*

A crash from the kitchen causes us to break apart, our secret hallway tryst leaving us both wanting more, panting like we've just finished a marathon.

"Holy shit," I say with a laugh, bracing my hands on my knees as I attempt to catch my breath. "That was the most life-altering kiss of my fucking life."

Almost gasping for air, Diana leans against the wall, fingertips over her lips as they spread into a gorgeous smile. "I think that was slightly more than a kiss, don't you?"

Chapter Nineteen

DIANA

A SMILE FLASHES ACROSS MICHAEL'S FACE, HIS GREEN EYES dark and mischievous, while I smooth my now-wrinkled red satin skirt. There's no denying that I've just been kissed within an inch of my life—or how embarrassingly close I was to actually coming from it. Old Diana would be mortified. But current Diana is *starved* and *aching* and feels so empty she wants to tell the whole world they're going to have to wait because there's something she needs to do before she gets back to it, and that thing is Michael Haynes.

"That was—"

"Everything," he says, taking my face in his hands, and placing a soft kiss on my lips. "It was everything." I look up at him, unable to help the goofy grin on my face. "But it's clear this isn't the time or the place to have this conversation."

"No, it really isn't," I tell him, fisting his chef's coat in both my hands. "But Jonathan *did* tell me to come talk to you."

He snorts. "I don't think this is what he meant by it, though."

I chuckle and press my forehead to his chest, inhaling his scent—grapefruit and lemon, with a bit of smoke from whatever it is he's been grilling in his test kitchen back there. "What do we do now?"

He wraps his arms around me, pressing a kiss to the top of my head. "I think you go back out there with Jonathan and let me serve you both the best dinner of your lives—but you do it as *friends*." I laugh once. "He's really cool, and what you see is what you get with him, so if he told you to come find me, well, then he meant it. Just go out there and hang. I'll join you soon and walk you both through the dishes. Hopefully, he won't be too upset about me stealing his date. Pray he's still considering investing in this." He sighs, but there isn't a hint of regret in his voice; he wants this, too. "After dinner's done... Well, that's up to you."

"What do *you* want?"

He's quiet for a moment, pulling back to stare back at me, green eyes fierce with determination. "I want this, whatever it is. I want you to stay behind tonight so we can talk it out. And after we're done figuring out what we're going to do or *not* do..." He shrugs once. "I'll drive you home."

A slow smile plays on my lips. "Okay. Deal. But you better cook for your life, Michael Haynes. You don't just have Jonathan Bloom to convince you're the real deal. You've got to prove it to me, too."

"Oh, sweetheart," he growls in my ear. "Believe me, by the end of the night there will be no doubt in your mind that there is no one better for you than me."

And while I know he meant that to be sexy, no combination of words has ever terrified me more.

"There are no words for what tonight was. An out of body experience, maybe. Cosmic love. Utter, ethereal happiness?" Jonathan is on cloud nine after Michael served us well over fifteen courses of the most incredible food I've ever tried in my life.

The three of us laugh, standing in the middle of the farm's driveway, the breeze cooling the night air.

"I agree. I didn't know you were so good," I tell Michael with a smirk.

"Oh, you didn't know, did you? What was that meal that I cooked at your house, then? Fast food?"

I scoff. "It was not this. I've been spoiled now," I tell him, playfully elbowing him in the side. "Make no mistake, I *will* be expecting this level of cooking from here on out."

A shiver runs through me, the previously warm night having turned cool. My reaction to the change doesn't go unnoticed by Michael.

"It's gotten chilly. Let me get you something," he says, running into the barn before giving me a chance to turn him down. I mean, what's the point? I'm going back inside as soon as Jonathan leaves so Michael and I can talk about things.

"Ah, so he's cooked for you before?" Jonathan asks as he plays with his car keys.

And with that question, reality sets in once more. Because despite having spent the entire night enjoying truly exceptional food and fantastic company (because Jonathan *is* fantastic company), we still haven't *really* addressed the fact that Michael and I are... *something*. Not really. Not the three of us together, at least.

"Oh. Right. Yes, he has. With our daughters. *For* my daughters, actually. Not me."

Jonathan chuckles. "You don't have to be nervous; it's okay. It was one date, if that. Half a date—maybe a quarter of one since we only made it to the dinner table before realizing that it wasn't going to work between the two of us. I'm not mad. I'm actually kind of happy that Michael found someone. Back in the day, I used to believe he and I would be the only ones who would always remain single because we were both such workaholics. But things have changed—for both of us. And that makes me really happy."

I smile and reach out to squeeze Jonathan's hand once. "You really are an amazing man."

This makes him laugh. "Thanks. You're pretty fucking great, too. And it's obvious in the way Michael looks at you that he thinks so too. That he's a little more than just interested."

My stomach rolls as I look over my shoulder at the barn. "We'll see. I have a ton of baggage."

"Hey," he says in a soft voice. I turn to stare back into his aqua eyes. "It's not baggage—it's life. And if he cares to be in yours, he'll accept whatever it is as his own."

"Here, I brought you a blanket." We turn to Michael's voice, watching him run to us, stopping only to wrap me as tight as a burrito in a soft, gray plaid blanket.

Jonathan smiles between the two of us. "I'm gonna head out, you guys. So you're giving her a ride home?"

Michael smiles. "Yeah."

And without another word—just a small wave as he pulls out from the driveway—Jonathan leaves us both beneath the twinkling stars.

"I'm right here, you know. What if I wanted to go with him?" I huff.

Michael wraps his arms around my waist, presses his forehead against mine. "You already agreed to stay behind after dinner. And there's no way I'm letting you out of my sight yet. Not after you avoided me for so long."

"Maybe it was with good reason," I tease, but the regret that follows is immediate. The hurt on his face reminds me of how stupid and inconsiderate my actions—or lack thereof—have been. "I'm sorry," I shake my head. "That wasn't funny."

"No, it wasn't." Michael frowns and sighs. "Let's go back inside and talk. I'll give you a tour of the kitchen and make you some tea—you're clearly freezing somehow—while I make sure the staff put everything back in its right place before leaving for the night."

"Everyone's gone already?"

He nods, pulling me behind him by the hand. "I don't know if you noticed, but we were done with dinner a while ago. I guess the conversation was so good, time flew by." He shoots me a smirk over his shoulder. "Can you stay a bit longer?"

I pull out my phone to check Emi's glucose levels and relax once I see they're stable.

"Maybe half an hour? Forty-five minutes more?" I don't want to push it.

Michael leads me into the industrial kitchen, and while it's not something that would appear in Architectural Digest, I can't help but gawk at all the gadgets and different types of cooking appliances that fill the room. For anyone who's a fan of cooking, it's a dream.

"Whoa," I breathe, setting the blanket on the spotless metal counter before running a finger over it. It's not pretty, but something about the utility of it all impresses me. It could take what you give it—anything at all—and not budge or bend or creak or break for anything or anyone—the antithesis of how I feel sometimes.

Michael fills an electric kettle with water and starts it. From a utility rack, he pulls a mug down and hands it to me.

"One sec," he says before heading into what looks like the pantry. After just a moment, he's back with a box of tea and a jar of honey. "This good? It's dandelion tea."

I shrug. "Sure. I've never had dandelion tea before."

He reaches out and grabs hold of my hips, pulling me up onto the counter with a surprising amount of ease. The contrast of cold metal and his heated touch sends shivers up my spine. Michael presses a soft kiss against my lips while gently pushing my silk skirt up my thighs, making room for himself between my legs.

"Really? You'll like it. It's good for you, too. Lots of antioxidants." He presses a kiss to the side of my neck. "And anti-inflammatory properties."

Michael presses a kiss to the other side, this time with an open mouth.

My eyes slide shut, and I move my head to give him more room.

"Are you—" I inhale sharply when his teeth graze my skin. "Are you selling this tea or something?"

This makes him chuckle, so he pulls away to give me an indulgent smile. Without breaking eye contact, he unbuttons his chef's jacket before tossing it behind him carelessly on the floor.

I press my lips together—though the urge to do so disappears once my eyes travel south and they land on the fitted white t-shirt stretching over his broad shoulders. And *god*, how does he manage to look so good in the most basic article of clothing?

"No, I'm not selling it. Just thought it was appropriate."

"Appropriate?"

The kettle automatically turns off as the water reaches its boiling point. Michael nods and takes the cup from me, gently opening a tea bag, and dropping it inside before pouring the water. "Dandelions symbolize resilience and healing—hope and strength. I thought it was appropriate since you embody those qualities every single day."

I can't help the grin on my face or the way it fades just as quickly as it appears. "I wish that were true."

"Believe me, Diana. It's true. You are..." He inhales deeply, shaking his head as if in disbelief. "Incredible."

Speechless, I watch as he pulls the wand from the pot, the golden syrup drizzling and shining under the overhead lighting.

"Would you like some? It's local honey," he offers, his voice deep.

I nod, the only way I seem to be able to answer right now.

Wordlessly, I watch him drizzle honey into my cup before putting the wand back into the glass container.

"Shit, my fingers are all sticky."

And though he begins to pull away to presumably go wash his hands, something foreign comes over me leading me to wrap my legs around his waist to stop him.

"Let me," I whisper, taking his hand. I bring his index finger into my mouth, tasting the sweet honey on his skin as I suck it off. Michael watches, slack-jawed and rapt, a slow moan building in his chest.

"*Fuck.*" And in that moment, I know it's both an expletive, and a promise.

Chapter Twenty

DIANA

I HOOK MY ANKLES TOGETHER, PULLING HIM INTO ME, feeling him hard and hot between my legs as I run my teeth over his finger.

"Jesus, Diana." When I release it, he cups my face and runs his thumb over my lower lip so gently, it almost distracts me. But then he presses his lips to mine, his tongue diving deep into my mouth.

The sounds coming from him are driving me to within an inch of madness, making it impossible to think straight.

"I can taste the honey on your tongue." His breathing is ragged as he holds my face between his hands. "I can taste it, and I want more."

"*Yes.*" I want it all and I want to give him whatever he wants.

Michael pushes the straps of my top off my shoulders, kissing from one side to the next. Without moving his mouth from my skin, he whispers, "Your scent drives me fucking *insane.*" He moans against my tits, flicking my nipple before kissing a path to the other side. "It's what inspired that summer salad—the one you had tonight? The pomegranate and grilled peaches with the sweet honey dressing. It's how I imagined you'd taste. And now..."

"Yeah?" I breathe, but I honestly can't focus on anything other than the devastating feeling of emptiness I feel between my legs.

"Yeah." His voice is rough and wild and I'm in love with it.

Blindly, Michael reaches for the honey wand once more with one hand, while the other pushes my shirt and strapless bra over my breasts, down to my waist. He stands up and drizzles the honey over my chest, focusing on my nipples. "Now I get to try you for myself."

Michael carefully sets the wand back into the glass container before diving back into me, his tongue lapping up the honey from my tits, lingering playfully on my nipples, teeth tugging.

I can't help the moan that breaks free from my lips, the way my hands move into his hair to find some grip or purchase in reality. I'm seconds away from exploding in a way I never have before, and it's mind-bending and confusing and the best thing I've experienced in years, if not ever. I feel almost guilty, reveling in this pleasure because it's for me—just for me—and no one else. It goes against who I am, against the way I live my life every day.

On top of that, I can't remember the last time I did this with someone else. My sex life with Rodrigo ended years before divorce proceedings were even filed, years before I found out about his girlfriend.

God, what if I suck? What if the sexual chemistry is great now, but when it comes to the actual action, I won't know what to do anymore? And do I really want to do this with him for the first time on a kitchen counter? Not that it isn't hot, but maybe he'd like for us to have a better set up?

I squeeze my eyes shut, wishing I could get my mind to stop racing, praying I can find a way to let myself enjoy this moment.

But I can't.

As if he were able to read my mind, despite being very clearly occupied, Michael straightens. "Where did you go? Come back to me." He cups my face in his hands and gives me another drugging kiss, his lips sweet and syrupy.

"I'm..." At a loss for words.

"You're shaking. Do you want to stop?" His breathing is ragged, his green eyes dark and ravenous, and I know the last thing Michael Haynes wants right now is to stop touching me. But I also know that he would in a second if I asked him to.

My first instinct is to brush it off, but he's giving me the chance to be honest about what I want and need. So I take a beat and really think about it before responding: "Just... overwhelmed. In a good way." I pull him down for a peck. "Thanks, though. For checking in."

"Always. I always want to make sure you're okay," he tells me, his eyes more sincere than I've ever seen them before.

My heart pirouettes, so I kiss him, sinking into him and this moment, marveling at the speed with which this thing between us seems to be evolving now that we're letting go.

Suddenly, his shirt is off and he's kicking off his shoes. His pants and my skirt follow.

"I haven't done this in a while," I whisper into his chest.

"We can stop whenever you want, Diana. I can keep going, or we can get dressed, and I can drive you home. Either way, I feel..." He exhales, his gaze on mine. "I'm happier than I've been in a long time. Knowing you care about me, too..." he says with an awed smile on his face, shaking his head. "Well, I don't think I could be happier. So if you want to press pause, I'm okay with that. You don't need to worry about me being a dick and getting upset."

I place a soft kiss to his lips and pull back to smile at him. "I think I might not be ready for sex just yet. But... other things..."

His grin is wicked, eyes gleaming in delight, and if I were standing, his dimples would have my knees buckling.

"Other things? Yeah, we can do other things." Michael wiggles his brows, making me roll my eyes. But then he kisses up my neck and puts his lips to my ear as he whispers, "I can make you feel so fucking good with *other things*."

I can't help the whimper that escapes my mouth.

"Would you like that, baby?"

I gasp as he bites my neck, feeling so empty all of a sudden I could cry. "Yes, Chef."

"Oh, *fuck*." He groans and sucks on my neck while his hand skims up my thighs until they reach my underwear. With the back of his fingers, he grazes the delicate lace between my thighs, groaning when he feels the moisture.

"*Fuck,* you're so wet." His voice does things to me, heating my already ignited skin. With a slow, frustrating pace, Michael slowly moves my underwear aside, moving his fingers up and down my wetness. "This for me?"

"*God*," I call out, leaning back on the steel counter, supporting myself with my hands.

"No, not god. You know who I am, don't you?"

It takes me a second to grasp what he means—the lust fog caused by the way his fingers play between my legs not helping the situation—but then: "Yes, Chef."

And with those words, I know I've fully unleashed Michael. He drops to his knees and pushes my legs apart, making room for himself. His torturous, slow kissing up my thighs drives me to the edge of insanity, but he thankfully does not hesitate once he reaches his intended target. With one slow swipe, I melt over the counter, hair spreading everywhere. My hands fly to take hold of the edge when his tongue reaches my clit, and my back arches when he slides two fingers into me. Breathing ragged, my mind blurs as it tries to process this pure, unbelievable pleasure.

As it tries to parse the loving words he breathes against where I'm wet and pulsing—*So fucking beautiful* and *been wanting to do this since the day I met you* and *most perfect woman in the world*—and the rough way his fingers wrap around my thighs as he holds me down.

I'm close. So close. So goddamn close.

And I think I've said the words aloud because Michael's movements grow faster, more intense. His fingers are magic, tapping in just the right spot and pulling me under as his mouth on my clit finally sends me into sensation overload. And I'm *there*, clenching around his fingers, calling his name over and over again like a prayer. Because, my god, this is the closest thing I've come to a religious experience in my life.

I never want to be without it again.

After a few minutes of trying to catch my breath, I somehow manage to sit up. Michael helps me clean up the remnants of honey all over my chest with a smirk on his face and a damp, clean dish towel. The way he puffs up his chest in pride is so adorable I pull him in for a soft kiss. When our lips meet, he inhales deeply and holds the breath in, as if wanting to keep my scent with him always.

The need for him builds almost immediately once again, a hunger that might never be satiated.

"I need to take you home. And I need to get home, too," he whispers against my lips.

With a sigh, I nod, and pull away.

"This kitchen is wild," I tell him, hoping the complete change in subject will knock my one-track mind in a different direction.

I pull my shirt over my head and try not to ogle Michael as he looks around at the room for his t-shirt, bare-chested.

"It's good for now, but I'm hoping for something better for our brick and mortar. *If* we find the space." He sighs, finally putting his t-shirt on.

My pout is immediate.

All of a sudden, my conversation with Jonathan about Michael's current financial situation pops into my head.

"Jonathan mentioned you were having financial issues," I tell him.

His head whips in my direction. "He *what*?"

"Relax," I say, putting my hands on his shoulder. "This was before he knew I knew you. When we were on our way here and he was telling me about his super talented friend who was opening a restaurant and was hosting this dinner for him in order to get him to invest."

"He said that?"

"Yes. He also said it was an unnecessary dinner because he already knew how talented you were, and that there was no question he was going to invest in your place."

Michael takes a step back and runs his fingers through his hair with a sigh. "That was before I took his date from him. Even though he said it was fine..." He shakes his head, looking at me with weary eyes. "It still wasn't cool for him to show up with the most beautiful woman in the world and then have her be taken away from him."

I roll my eyes. "Okay, first, I'm not the most beautiful woman in the world. Second, no one *took* me; I left willingly. And he's not going to back out. Jonathan doesn't seem to be the type of person to hold a grudge. Plus, he seemed genuinely happy you'd found—" I stop myself, because we're both making very big assumptions.

He stole his date? Jonathan was happy Michael found someone? Are these all givens now? We haven't even talked about what's going on between us—at least not really—and there are already so many absolutes being casually thrown around in conversation. Weren't we going to use this time after dinner to discuss what this is?

"Have I?"

"Have you what?" I ask.

He takes my hands in his before bring them up to his lips, pressing a kiss to them. "*Found* someone, I mean. Have I found that someone?"

I inhale sharply, a rope around my heart tightening at the idea of him and I *together*.

This. I want this.

"I—" I clear my throat. "There are... things to consider. To talk about before we decide anything."

"Such as?" His voice is soft as he brings my right hand to his chest, before moving the left one to wrap around the back of his neck.

Michael presses a soft kiss against my lips, and I lose all ability to speak. How can he still do this to me after what just happened? Shouldn't I be desensitized or something?

"You were saying?" he murmurs.

"I have a hard time speaking when you touch me like that," I try to say, but the words come out breathy and ragged at the same time.

"I have a hard time, too." I can feel his grin against the skin of my neck as he presses his hard cock where I'm already hot and wet again.

I half laugh, half moan, the knowledge that he wants this just as badly almost even more intoxicating than the moment itself.

"Michael, I'm serious," I say, hating myself a little for pushing against his chest.

He stops immediately and gives me space, though his hands never leave my body, sliding instead from my waist and tits down to my thighs. He does, however, remain snuggly between my legs.

"I like you," I whisper, as if it weren't already obvious.

"I like you, too. Very, *very* much."

"And this *feels* good, but..." I exhale and shake my head. "The more I think about it, the more I wonder whether this is the right thing to do. No matter how much either one of us wants it."

"What? Why?" He frowns, the fog of lust clearing around us.

"Well, for starters, I live almost two thousand miles away from here. The girls and I go back to Denver in late August."

At least that's the plan. The temptation to stay for Labor Day weekend is big, especially since the girls don't start school until the week after. But... No. I have responsibilities. I need to find a new apartment and get settled before the school year starts.

"I—" He exhales, eyes wide and frantic as he searches for the right words. Finally, he pulls his brows together and stares at me in determination. "That doesn't matter to me. I don't care."

It's like a blow to the chest. *He doesn't care?*

"Uh—" I stutter, taking a moment to organize my thoughts. "I think there's been a disconnect here," I say, my heart breaking. If he feels a fraction of what I feel for him, he *would* care. This just shows we shouldn't be doing this—shouldn't be alone like this together, shouldn't be touching each other in ways that light our skin on fire. "While I respect that you *don't care*," I say, suppressing the sudden urge to vomit the fantastic dinner I enjoyed earlier tonight, "I'm not that type of person. You're the first guy I've liked since—" I clear my throat. "It's fine if you want to do the whole casual thing, but that's not me. I don't think I could manage that. That isn't what this is to me, so I should probably lea—"

"Wait, no," he cuts me off, holding me on the counter before I can jump off. "That's not what I meant. What I meant was that I don't care that you live somewhere else because I really like you and I'm sure two intelligent people like ourselves can figure out something by the end of the summer."

I grimace. "Like what?"

He shrugs, helpless. "I don't know. But I want to try. Please." He swallows once, hands shaking as he brings them to my face. "*Please,* Diana. Don't let this die before we even give it a chance to start."

I search for something in his eyes, unsure of what exactly, but enough to tell me that this won't turn into a massive mistake.

"I like you so much, I don't think I'll be able to keep my feelings from deepening," I whisper, this admission ripping at my chest. Shaking, terrified I've exposed too much of myself and my aching heart, I put my hands on his chest.

He moves closer, his mouth millimeters from mine. With his eyes on my lips, he breathes "Diana, I'm already in so deep, I can't see sunlight. I'm here, waiting to catch you whenever you're ready."

Chapter Twenty-One

MICHAEL

I LOOK AROUND THE EMPTY SPACE, BOBBING MY HEAD AT everything the commercial realtor says as if I've been able to process a single word that's come out of his mouth. I've been doing my best, but my mind is a bit preoccupied reliving last night—from the pain of seeing Diana arrive for a date to my farm, the ache of taking in how beautiful she is and thinking she wasn't mine, the absolute bliss of what we did in my kitchen (which I had to deep clean in the morning, of course), and flying high on my way home after dropping her off with a goodnight kiss and a *Talk tomorrow*.

"Great. That's great," I say with a nod, feeling a grin nearly split my face in two.

"Great?" Lexi breaks through my daydreaming, her face pinched in a frown. "Michael, are you even listening? He just told us that the water main will need to be repaired before opening, significantly delaying our preferred start date. Meaning, this isn't really the ideal space for us, no matter how good the location."

"Oh." I pause, looking between John, our realtor, and Lexi. "So, that's *not* good, right? It means we shouldn't pick this place?"

Lexi's eyes widen, hands on her hips. "Would you give us a sec, John? Michael and I need to have a little chat." Once he steps out and we're alone, Lexi glares at me. "Okay, what's up? Your head has been up in the clouds all day. Did you even pay attention to the previous two spaces we saw this morning? We've both put everything we have into this business. I've sacrificed a lot of time with the boys and Lauren, and I know you've done the same with Rachel. So can you please tell me what the hell is going on?"

I laugh once, scratching the back of my neck as I sheepishly answer like a fucking teenager: "She likes me."

Lexi blinks. "Who?"

I raise a brow at her. "Who the hell do you think? Diana. You've only been giving me shit about her for the past couple of weeks. Who else would it be?"

"I don't know your life."

I sigh. "Well, it's her. She likes me and I like her."

"When did you find out? During third period Math?" Lexi snorts. "You're so cute I could throw up."

"Shut up," I say when she mock-gags. "I'm serious. She told me so herself last night."

"Last night? Last night she was on a date with another man. I'm not sure I'm excited about you liking a woman who can so easily go from one dude to the next."

Irritation sparks in the back of my mind. "She wasn't on a date with another man. I mean, she was, but it's complicated. You left early last night, so you didn't see that she stayed after dinner with me. And we talked and—" I stop myself before I let my dopey smile rat me out. "Anyways, things are good between us. Really fucking good."

She groans. "Ah, that's gross. You had sex didn't you? Wait, no, don't tell me. I don't need that image in my head."

I snort. "Well, *she's* the image I've had in my head all fucking day, which is why it's been kinda impossible to focus. So I'm really sorry. I promise to try harder." I don't know how I'll manage, though, because I'm currently fighting an impossible battle—which is to say, fighting the urge to message her every five seconds.

Give her some room to breathe—to process.

From what I gathered, last night was the first time in years that Diana had been with someone physically, which is why I've only texted her *once* today (a good morning text with a winky face emoji). Her response (*Morning, I had fun last night*) came almost immediately—just like me once I got home.

"I'm glad you were able to get the girl, but can we try getting through today before you start writing your initials in hearts all over your notebooks? We need to lock a place in by the end of this month, and we still need financing. I'm assuming last night was a bust given that you stole our latest potential investor's date?"

"Wrong." I smile. "That's the other great news. Despite me being a total dick and—your words, not mine—*stealing* our potential investor's date, I'm pretty sure he's giving us the money. He was really nice about the whole thing last night. Plus, I just checked my email and saw I have something from him. I'd bet the recipe to my famous beef short rib that it's good news."

"Are you joking?" Lexi glares again. "Are you telling me that you have, right there in your pocket, Jonathan Bloom's final decision on whether or not he's going to invest in our restaurant, and you've been too nauseatingly happy to care enough to read it?"

"I—Yes?" Now that I think about it, it might've been a bit idiotic of me to skip over Jonathan's email this morning. But then the image of Diana—gripping the edge of the counter as she moaned my name, my head between her thighs and fingers deep inside her feeling her tight and wet—popped into my head and I grew distracted.

Understatement of the year.

Lexi slaps me on the back of the head. "Read it, you idiot."

Pulling my phone from my pocket, I laugh, not letting even Lexi's bad mood shake me. Today is a good day, no matter what. How could it not be after what happened last night?

From: Jonathan Bloom
To: Michael Haynes
Subject: Dinner last night

Bud,

What a meal! You really outdid yourself with your tasting menu. I know you said there were more dishes you were experimenting with, but I think you and Lexi are headed in the right direction (though I've never doubted your ability to cook for a second—not since we first met that night when I sat at the chef's table at the old place you worked at ten years ago. Can you believe how long it's been?).

I like your idea of bringing fine dining to the Hamptons while making it accessible. There's no reason why eating at a Michelin-starred restaurant should cost upwards of $300 per person. If you're using seasonal ingredients from your own farm, I'm sure you'll be able to keep costs down.

Your business plan is solid—I looked over your deck this morning—so that's good, too. And I trust that you have the ability to handle the business side of things but also have the self-awareness to hire someone if you're too overwhelmed.

In conclusion, I'm down to invest, man. I know you were worried for a second there with Diana, but you two are really good people who deserve the best—just make sure that's what you give her. Understood? Last night, I saw a grown-up version of you I'd never seen, and I really enjoyed it. That's the guy who made me want to double my investment (that's right, man; I was always going to invest no matter what because we're friends, but now I really want to invest because I think you're going to do great things).

I'll have my financial manager and lawyer reach out to hammer out the final details, but yeah.

LFG!!

Best,

Jonathan

"It's done," I tell Lexi. "We fucking did it, Lex."

I park my truck in Lexi's driveway, hug her goodbye, and keep the engine running while I wait for Rachel to run out of the house, where Lauren was babysitting her all day. Taking advantage of this brief moment of alone time, I decide to text Diana:

MICHAEL

Can I take you out tonight?

Her response is nearly immediate:

DIANA

I'd love to, but I've been working and studying all day, and I promised the girls we'd do some mother/daughter bonding time. I'm taking them to the movies in town.

I almost ask her whether Rachel and I can join but decide against it, not wanting to intrude on their family time. The disappointment hits me unexpectedly, though, because I never would've imagined I'd ever feel hurt or sadness for not being included in their family activity. But over the past three weeks, this solidarity or camaraderie we've developed has certainly brought us together in more ways than one—not just in a romantic sense. And it kills me because I realize now that their return to Colorado will hurt ten times more than I expected.

MICHAEL

Sure, no problem. How about tomorrow night?

DIANA

I'd love that ;)

Where are you going to take me? If you're thinking dinner, I'm not sure how you're going to top last night.

This makes me laugh.

MICHAEL

We can do something different. Just be ready tomorrow by seven. If you need a babysitter, I'm not available. I'm going to be too busy taking out this hot, brilliant woman I met at the beginning of the summer. But I can ask my cousin to three-for-one babysit?

DIANA

I'd rather not. Nothing against your cousin, but if Liza's mom is up for it again I'd rather have her do it since I already gave her the rundown, and she has experience taking care of kids and people with chronic conditions.

From the corner of my eye, I see Rachel run out of Lexi's front door with a grin on her face.

Initially, the idea of dating Diana seemed perfect. But now I wonder how the hell we're supposed to explain our date to the girls and—

"Fuck it. We'll figure it out," I say out loud with determination. I've never wanted something more and I'm not just going to give up because things are hard.

Chapter Twenty-Two

DIANA

Since arriving in Sag Harbor, the girls and I haven't *really* spent any bonding time—not the fun activity kind, anyway. Sure, we hit the beach on the Fourth of July, but any time we've spent alone has been while they come with me to run errands, or just spending time at home while we watch TV or eat dinner. So I cancelled the stay-at-home pool day I had planned for us and switched it out for a girl's day out with Emiliana and Camila in town. I thought we could window shop around Sag Harbor, maybe even buy something as a keepsake for our summer in the Hamptons.

Besides spending time together doing something outside the house, I owe it to my daughters to ask them whether they'd be comfortable with me going out with another man—especially when that man is none other than their best friend's dad. Once I find the right time, I'll address the possibility of dating —maybe even tell them that I specifically mean their friend's dad.

My heart flutters just at the thought of it. Of how this conversation I'm hoping to have makes it official: Michael and I are doing this. We're going for it. The exact parameters, rules, and expectations haven't been hammered out yet, but what's certain is that we want to explore it.

I'm both terrified and feel more exhilarated than I have in a long time.

I was hoping for a beautiful beach day, followed by a fantastic movie and dinner, something to soften the blow—but the powers that be failed me. The sky is overcast, the weather muggy, the movie was, as kids say, *mid*, and dinner was *meh* and a bit of a headache due to having to be extra careful of what Emi could order.

It's only after we're having our post-movie stroll around town, walking up Main Street, that I dare to bring the topic up at all: "So," I begin. "I have to talk to you girls about something big." With a nod, I lead them to an empty bench, where we all settle comfortably. "How would you feel about me going on dates? Or possibly, you know..." I take a deep breath, steel myself. "Having a boyfriend?"

Emi gasps just as Cami whips in her seat to look at me.

"What are you talking about?" Cami looks up at me, brows pinched in suspicion. My oldest has *always* been smarter than your average bear. "Is that where you went last night? On a *date*?"

This makes Emi gag and grimace; she shakes her head slowly as she keeps her eyes on the ground.

I swallow. "Yes. I guess, so. Yes?"

"With that guy in the suit?"

"I—" And then I freeze. Because I want to correct her—I *should* correct her—but Michael is their best friend's *dad*. And if they say no? Well, what will that mean for their friendship? Will the girls pull away from Rachel because I've decided to selfishly follow something *I* want for the first time in years? I need to check whether they'd be okay with me dating *anyone* first.

"I mean, it's no one specific," I lie with a shrug. "It's just a thought."

Emi visibly relaxes with a nod. But Cami? Cami has narrowed her eyes at me, and I can tell she's evolved into some form of guard dog. She's bitten into this piece of information and will not let go until she gets more of it.

"I don't understand."

"Well," I say, clearing my throat. *God*, when did nine year-olds get so terrifying? "You know how Dad has a girlfriend now?" *Does he?* Honestly, who knows at this point. The man has disappeared into the ether without a second thought. "Well, he's found someone else he wants to spend time with, and I was thinking it might be time for me to do the same."

Cami looks away, face and neck red. When I watch her raise a hand and wipe a tear away, I realize with horror how my words must've come out.

"*He's found someone else to spend time with,*" and she thought I meant he'd abandoned them for someone else—which, for all we know, he has. At least the abandonment thing we know for sure.

I turn quickly in my seat to face her and take her hands in mine. "That's not what I meant—" the words burst through me, loud enough to cause some passersby to turn and stare. "I don't mean I'd rather spend time with someone other than you guys—*never* that. You and Emi will *always* be my priority. Always." *Not like your dick of a father*, I don't add. "I just mean that I would like to spend time with another man—one who cares about me—instead of your father. We are not together anymore, after all."

My eyes jump from one daughter to the other, back and forth, making sure they understand my meaning.

"I don't know..." Cami finally whispers. "You're just going to do the same thing he did. Forget we even exist."

The pain in my chest is visceral, the rage coursing through my veins burning through me like acid.

Fuck Rodrigo. Fuck Rodrigo to the deepest depths of hell.

It's the first time we've spoken about their father outside of our weekly card-writing sessions when they write and send him letters that always go unanswered and it takes everything inside me not to throw up. If I'm angry and upset, I can't imagine how my girls feel.

"Hey." I grab her gently by the chin, forcing her to look at me. "I will *never* do that. I will *never* allow anyone to come between us. It's why I'm even having this conversation to begin with. Your happiness and well-being will always be more important than anything else."

Cami's lower lip trembles, her eyes filling with tears.

"Please don't leave me, *Mami*."

My heart shatters when she throws herself into my arms, sobbing into my chest. Emi hugs her sister from behind. I reach around my oldest to clutch at my youngest's shirt, bringing her closer and closing our group hug. It's in that moment that I realize that *this* is my family now; *this* is who we are as a nucleus. Rodrigo is long gone, not just for me, but for them, too.

"I will *never* leave you," I say through soft tears, my nose runny and gross. I can't even begin to imagine what people around us think as they walk by. "But I deserve to be happy, too, I think." It's not the first time someone says that about me, but it's the first time I say it about myself. And I believe it. I *do* deserve to be happy. So long as my girls always feel loved and taken care of by their mother, then this can, of course, work out for everyone.

I hope.

"So are you ready for tomorrow?" Michael's deep voice, low and gravelly, sends shivers down my spine.

I can't help the way my heart tightens in my chest when I think about going out with him, or the way my stomach fills with *actual* butterflies when my mind runs through what we did the other night and whether we'll do it again. Whether I'm even ready to do more. "Yes. I think."

This makes him laugh. "You think? Did I stump you with that question?"

I bite my lip as I flip the seasoned chicken from one of the new recipes he taught me. "No," I say with a blush. "Why are you whispering, by the way?"

"Ah. I... haven't exactly told Rachel about my date tomorrow. So I'm hiding in my room."

I snort and shake my head. "Coward."

"You told your girls?"

"You sound surprised! You didn't think I'd be able to tell them I would start dating again?"

Michael sighs. "I shouldn't be. You're the strongest person I know. But it's different for you. I just need to tell my daughter that her biological father who was never in a relationship with her mother is going to go out with the hottest woman in the world—" I scoff, but he ignores it. "You had the more difficult job. You had to tell your daughters their mother, who recently got a divorce, is going to start dating another man who isn't the father they grew up with. Who isn't the man they always saw as *your* partner."

"He wasn't much of a partner," I mutter. I peek through the kitchen door to make sure the girls are too distracted by their movie to hear me talking to Michael. "But you're right. It wasn't easy. At all." I sigh, switching the phone from one hand to the other. "It was a pretty intense conversation, I'm not gonna lie."

"Did you tell them it was me?" His voice is soft, tentative.

I know part of him wants to be as honest as possible with the girls after all the lying he and Jessie did to Rachel, but the other part understands that, due to my circumstances, we need to ease into this. *Especially* since we don't even know where this might lead given our geographical challenges.

"No. No, I think it would be counterproductive. I think they need to sit with it a little."

I can practically hear him nod. "Agreed. At least for now."

"So what are we doing tomorrow?"

As if on cue, the sky outside crackles with lighting, followed by a deep rumble of thunder, rattling the pool house's windows. The intensity of it all makes me jump and gasp, bringing a hand to my chest when sheets of rain suddenly begin to hit the windows with such force, the sound echoes throughout the entire house. The girls scream from the other room as well, calling out for me.

"It's okay, girls," I call back, feeling *not* okay at all. "It's just a little thunder." I'd love someone to tell that to my heart, however, since it's five seconds away from beating out of my chest and running away to take cover.

"Oh my god," I say in awe.

"Did you hear that, too?" he asks, his voice laced with concern.

"Yeah. I mean, it was a horrible day out today, but I didn't expect *that*. It scared the girls, too." I peek back in. "But they seem to be fine now."

"Didn't sound too loud from here, and Rach seems to be okay. Let me check my weather app," he says. On the other end of the line, I hear him tap away at his screen, searching for something. "Shit," he mutters, his voice clear now. "There's a sudden storm coming in the early morning and it's supposed to last until the following day."

"*In the early morning*?" I gasp. "Meaning it's going to get worse than what it is now?" I walk over to the window and stare out into the pool area, but can barely make out anything past the chairs.

"How did I miss this?"

How did we *miss this?* I want to ask. But I know how. The distraction that came with what we did and the nerves from telling the girls definitely threw us both off track.

"I don't know how the hell this came out of nowhere, but... Diana, you *need* to put all the pool furniture inside. It says the winds are going to get pretty strong. Up to fifty miles per hour." I try to keep calm, but I can sense the panic in his voice, and it's not helping to keep mine under control.

"*Fifty*—What?"

"Hey, listen to me. You're going to be fine. It's—It's just a summer storm. They happen. You'll be okay."

"Yeah," I try to swallow the knot in my throat, but it doesn't budge. "The thing is, I don't do well with storms." My voice sounds far away to my own ears as a montage of wild memories flash before my eyes. Currents of mud destroying everything in their path. Entire homes disappearing into the dark waters. My sister, a baby in my mother's arms, crying. A fear so intense, it coursed through my four year-old system and marked me for the rest of my life.

"What do you mean you don't do well with storms?"

I force myself to breathe, unable to answer the question.

"Do you know if Barbara has a generator?"

A sharp gasp escapes my lips. "A generator? You think the power could go out?"

His silence is deafening.

I squeeze my eyes shut, try to control my breathing. "I don't know," I whisper, frustrated once again that this is all on me. It's always all on me. And I can do it—I *know* I can—because I *am* strong, just like Michael says. And I can overcome this fear. But, my god, I'd like for the universe to cut me some slack for a change. "I guess I have to go and make sure the house is storm ready. Fill the tubs with water and stuff. That's what you're supposed to do, right?" I look out once more at the pool, watching the tables and chairs outside start to shift with the rain.

Shit.

This isn't the same, I tell myself, attempting to stay sane. *It's just a summer storm. It'll be okay.*

"Dee—" It's the first time he calls me by a nickname, and I hate that it's when I'm five seconds away from a panic attack.

"I need to go check on the girls and handle this before it gets worse. I'll talk to you later." I hang up and turn off the stove, brace myself for what's to come. "I'm okay, Michael. I promise."

Chapter Twenty-Three

MICHAEL

But she isn't okay. I *know* she isn't.

Maybe on a normal day Diana could've handled this easily with her hands tied behind her back, but something's up. Something that goes deeper than just a fear of taking on a sudden summer storm on her own.

I look out the window at the purple-blue skies and gray clouds hammering rain down over us and debate what to do. There's not a doubt in my mind that Diana can handle herself in a crisis, but something in the tone of her voice set off alarm bells in my head.

She said she didn't do well with storms.

I swipe through the weather app and, according to the radar, see I have about an hour and a half of okay driving time before things start to get *really* bad.

"Rach?" I ask, pulling her attention away from her tablet (educational games only). "You up for a road trip?"

If my daughter weren't in the car, I probably would've made it to Diana's in under ten minutes. But because I want to be safe, I make sure not to speed, to be even more aware of my surroundings as the trees sway wildly from the ever-growing force of the winds. I know there's danger in going out during this weather, but my gut is telling me Diana and her girls are in even more danger. And that they're more scared than they would be at my place.

When I finally make it to her house, the wheels on my truck splash in her driveway, the usually pristine, light gray gravel already covered in mud.

I turn in my seat to face Rachel. "Kid. Normally, I'd say we'd have to make a run for it. But the last thing I want is for you to slip, so you're going to get wet. That okay? It's that or leave you alone in the truck, and that's just not going to happen. Not in this weather."

"So you're saying I have no choice but to walk out in that and get soaking wet?" she asks, pointing out the window with a casual shrug.

This makes me laugh. I nod and scratch the back of my head. "I guess so. Let's go."

By the time we make it through the gate and to the pool area, we're both drenched, the winds starting to gain even more force. I push Rachel toward the pool's sliding door, and tell her to go find her friends and ask for dry clothes. After that, I run toward Diana who doesn't seem to have noticed my arrival as she struggles to close a pool umbrella. I can tell by the redness in her eyes that she's been crying, though the rain beating down on her hides it well.

I wrap my hands around the umbrella and steady it, bringing her attention up to me.

Her jaw drops before she swallows, her brows pulled together before a sob breaks through her. "You're here."

And I can't bear it any longer. I wrap her in my arms, pull her to my chest, not giving a shit that the world seems to be falling apart all around us. All that matters is us, here, now, and that she knows she's not alone.

"I keep trying to close this so I can move it to the storage shed where all the pool furniture is supposed to go," she wails into my chest, "but the wind is too strong, and the water is making everything slippery. I don't know what to do."

"Shh. I'm here." I kiss the top of her head and cradle her in my arms, letting her cry against my chest for a few more moments before releasing her. "We need to move quickly, okay? Before it gets worse. I can do the bulk of the work, but I'm going to need help maneuvering. You okay with that?" When she nods, I tell her, "Okay, let's do it."

It doesn't take us longer than fifteen minutes to store the remaining pool furniture. Teamwork definitely made the dream work.

We call for the girls to bring us towels as soon as we walk into the kitchen, and then I catch Diana staring appreciatively at my now-transparent white t-shirt. I grin mischievously. Her deep blush when she realizes I've caught her makes me laugh despite this crazy situation.

"Don't worry," I whisper. "It's not like I wasn't doing the same thing." I nod towards her own top, where I can clearly see her pebbled nipples through the fabric.

"I'm wet," she whispers back. "That's why."

"Oh, I'm sure you are."

She snorts and shakes her head, but not before slapping me on the shoulder. Laughing with her like this after everything that happened, as the adrenaline begins to wane, makes me want to kiss her more than I ever have. But the moment is interrupted by three girls running into the kitchen with a stack of towels each.

"I think you guys should come stay with us," I tell her once she's changed into dry clothes. Mine are in the dryer while I'm wrapped up in a robe.

"What? No. Why?"

"I texted Barbara, and she said this house doesn't have a generator, and with these winds and the old cables around the area, I don't trust that your power won't go out. My house, on the other hand, *does* have a generator. Plus, your house is closer to the shore than mine. I'm more inland, so my place is better protected."

She shakes her head, and looks over at the girls as they play in the living room, making sure they don't hear us. "No way. We're fine here, I promise."

"Dee," I sigh, reaching out to cup her face, taking a step closer to her. It's a risk, I know, but I can't help it. "*Please.* For me. For my peace of mind," I beg. It's a fucked up move, because I know her first instinct is to help people, so I know that by asking her this way it will be harder to refuse. But there it is. I'll do anything to keep her safe, anything to make sure she and the girls are protected.

She looks back at her daughters then back at me. "I don't think—"

And, *thank god*, that's when the lights go out.

"Okay, so the girls can have a sleepover in Rachel's room," I say, carrying Diana, Cami, and Emi's bags all in one hand into the house. "I've got a couple of air mattresses they can use, or if you guys want to feel like you're glamping or something you can use a couple of sleeping bags. I just need to get them out of the attic."

The girls giggle in excitement and run into Rachel's room, apparently uninterested in their sleeping arrangements for now.

"Okay, then," Diana says with a laugh.

I grin at her as I settle the bags by the door. "*You* will be sleeping in my room—"

Diana's eyes widen with panic, swinging both her hands in the air. "Michael, *no*. There's no way—"

"Calm down, Dee," I laugh. "I'll be sleeping on the couch—not in the bed. The thought didn't even cross my mind." Which isn't exactly a lie or a truth—I sure as fuck have imagined her in my bed, but there was no way I was going to ask her to do so while the girls are under the same roof.

"Don't be silly. I'm not going to force you out of your own bed! I should take the couch. After all, I'm smaller than you."

"You know there's no way in hell I'm going to let that happen, right? I would never do that. I'll go drop your bags there, and change the sheets—"

"Oh my god, at least let me do that—"

"No way. I need to get out of these damp clothes that never dried, and then change the sheets. Once I'm done, I'll cook us dinner."

"Michael..." She sighs. "Thank you."

Those last two words are felt deep in my bones because I know the weight behind them. I understand how difficult it is for her to accept help.

I reach out to cup her face, run my thumb over her lower lip. "Of course. Anytime. Anywhere."

A smile plays on her lips until realization hits her. "Oh shoot. This means our date tomorrow is cancelled, isn't it?"

I drag my fingers down her neck, over her arm, and take her hand, my eyes following their trail. *She's so soft*. "Not cancelled. Just needs to be rescheduled, maybe."

Her answering smile feels like a tight rope around my heart. *Jesus, what* is *this feeling?*

I look over her shoulder to make sure the girls are shut in

Rachel's room, the laughter coming from behind the door signaling just how unaware they are about our situation.

Taking advantage of it, I lean down and press a gentle kiss to her forehead. "Let me take care of you," I whisper, my mouth moving to her lips. "Let me be here for you and your girls tonight."

Eyes closed, she whispers, "Yes" on a sigh.

Chapter Twenty-Four

DIANA

The wind rattles Michael's house, heavy sheets of water sluice over the shingles and fall onto the bushes below the windows. The rain coming down is too hard to even be considered relaxing white noise. If anything, it's one of three reasons why I'm finding it impossible to sleep tonight. Why I'm so restless. The others being, of course, that I'm not at our place and that Michael, this amazing man who made sure my daughters and I were okay today, is just outside in the living room, snoozing away on the couch, when I very much want him in bed beside me. Or on me.

Either way.

Most of all, though, I want to talk to him. There hasn't been an opportunity to do so yet, what with the girls around. We spent all night trying to hide the chemistry from them—or at least I was. After we made it to his place, I was able to calm down a bit. In his house, surrounded by him, I felt safe. *Feel* safe. I feel at home.

It was difficult repressing the urge to flirt back whenever he'd say something that made me blush or touched me so gently and subtly it drove me within an inch of madness, but I made it work. Thankfully, I don't think any of the girls noticed.

And now, lying in his bed, surrounded by his scent of smoky citrus, my brain can't help but run a marathon around itself, searching for answers and comfort. Frustrated doesn't cover what I feel right now—physically and emotionally. I want him, yes. But I also need to talk to him. Explain why I flipped out. So with a heaving sigh, I pull the comforter off and tiptoe out of the bedroom in search of him.

"Michael?" I whisper from the living room's doorway, suddenly incredibly aware that I'm only in my PJ shorts and tank top set.

His head pops up over the back of the couch, his blanket sliding off his chest—his *bare* chest—when he sits up. "Diana? What are you doing up? It's two A.M. Is everything okay?"

"I—I'm so sorry. I'm so *stupid*. You're sleeping. Of course you'd be sleeping; I don't know how that didn't even occur to me." I groan and turn to go back to the bedroom, but not before he stops me.

"Wait!" he whisper-yells. "Come back. I wasn't asleep; I was playing sudoku on my phone."

I snort and turn back to him. "I didn't take you for a numbers guy."

He's fully sitting up now, feet on the floor, a goofy, sleepy grin on his face. Even in the darkness, I can see his dimples beneath his stubble, the way his eyes shine with happiness at me even if I am showing up in the middle of the night. *God*, he's so adorable.

I tiptoe over to the couch before taking a seat on the coffee table in front of him. It's nearly impossible not to get distracted by the muscles of his chest, nearly impossible not to remember how his skin feels beneath my fingertips, but I manage to keep it together.

"I'm not a numbers guy—pretty sure I failed math in school

—but I find the game... *stimulating*." We both chortle like children when he wiggles his brows, taking care not to raise our voices enough to wake the girls.

"You have such a dirty mind." I shake my head, a grin spreading across my face.

"I meant *mentally* stimulating. *You're* clearly the one with the dirty mind if you understood something different." His smile is mischievous, and it makes my heart do that pirouette thing it loves to do around him lately.

He reaches out to hold my hand, staring down at it. "I was really worried about you today."

I sigh, squeezing his hand in mine. "I know. But you came for me. You came and got me right before the power went out, and things got worse."

His brows pull together, and he shakes his head. "That's not what I meant. I mean, sure, yes, I was worried about your and the girls' physical wellbeing. But it wasn't that. Your voice over the phone..." He sighs. "That's what I was worried about. You seemed so scared."

There's a heavy pause between us as I look out the window at the pouring rain and think of what headspace I was in when it all went down.

"I was."

"You said you don't do well in storms?"

I inhale deeply, gathering my strength so that I can tell him this story, hoping he doesn't think I'm being ridiculous. "It may sound silly without context, but heavy rain like this is a bit terrifying to me. When I was a kid, I went to something kind of traumatic—*very* traumatic, actually—and it sort of scarred me. I still remember every detail."

"What happened?" Michael's voice is cautious, which I appreciate it. Nothing in his expression reads impatience or insistence. All he wants is for me to come to him, to open up, on my time. And it makes me want to do it even more.

"I don't know if you even remember this, or whether they even aired it on the news in the US. But when I was four years old, over the course of almost two weeks, the state where we lived in in Venezuela was affected by torrential rain. This all led to incredibly dangerous flash floods which ended up killing tens of thousands of people as well of the disappearance of whole towns. We managed to make it out alive—just barely—but..." I shake my head, squeezing my eyes shut. I don't remember much about being four years old, but there's no way I could ever forget that day. "I remember my dad pushing me onto this aid truck, and my parents and I scrambling in and—" The currents of mud destroying everything in their path, homes disappearing into the dark waters, entire families displaced and crying...

"Are you serious?"

I open my eyes and nod. "The Tragedy of Vargas went down as the deadliest mudslide ever recorded. It led to a complete infrastructure collapse, and took the state years to recover. It's why my family ended up moving to the capital. We didn't have clothes or a house or—" I feel myself choke on my words, the stinging in my eyes threatening tears. The tremble in my voice is clear, and I hate it. I hate that I can't be stronger than this. It happened almost three decades ago in an entirely different country, and yet my body still remembers.

"Hey, it's okay." He brings my hands to his lips and presses a gentle kiss to my knuckles. "You're safe now."

"It's dumb. It happened so long ago and I was so young. But I *remember*."

"Of course you remember. Traumatic is an understatement. You were a kid and your whole life got turned upside down."

I laugh once, watery. "It seems that's always been the theme in my life, then."

He raises a brow at me, displeased. "Don't say that."

"It's not all bad. You turned my life upside down—but in a good way."

His smile is so buoyant, I swear it could light up the whole house in this rainy darkness.

"Thank you for not thinking it's dumb."

Michael frowns as he laces his fingers with mine. "Why would I?"

"I don't know. In the past, not everyone has been as understanding as you. Some people think it's just me being dramatic and that it shouldn't be a big deal."

"Who the hell would—" His expression shifts from confusion to anger. "Are you telling me all those years you were with your ex, he never once understood that living through a natural disaster could've had long-term effects over your psyche and he just, what, didn't take you seriously?"

I shrug, embraced.

"I want to fucking punch him out."

My laugh is soft. "It wouldn't be worth the effort."

Michael drags the back of his fingers slowly down my cheek, down my neck, before landing it on my exposed knee. "Your fears are valid. But I get the feeling that there's more to it now. Something more? And it wasn't just that you were scared of the storm, but of being alone, too. I *think*... you're lonely."

"I'm not *lonely*," I say, a bit taken aback.

"I don't mean lonely, exactly. But maybe just tired of dealing with everything on your own? A little overwhelmed?" He grimaces, as if terrified of offending me. "Please don't be mad—I don't mean anything by it—but I just want us to be honest. I wanted to make sure you were okay and felt supported because I get the feeling you rarely get that. And... as I've told you before, I *care* about you. I don't know..." He scratches the back of his head in that way he does when he's bashful or insecure. "I want you to know that I'm here. For whatever. Not because I want sex or anything—though believe me, I'm trying really hard to control myself because holy shit these PJs of yours are filling me with all sorts of ideas—but because I care about *you.*"

My lungs have stopped working, Michael's words rendering them completely and utterly useless. I feel the stinging in my eyes build, the space in my chest that holds my heart shrink, and the way I want him grows tenfold. "Michael," I whisper, the ache in my voice surprising us both.

"I'm serious." And there's so much weight to those two words, so much meaning behind them.

With a sniff, I stand. "I know." I use my grip in his hands to tug at him, wordlessly leading him out of the living room and into his bedroom.

I STOP AT THE FOOT OF THE BED, EYES LOCKED ON Michael's bare chest. When my hands hesitantly reach up to touch him, to feel his pecs beneath my palms, a smattering of chest hair tickling me as I explore him, he inhales sharply. Even in the stormy darkness of the bedroom, I can tell his eyes have grown fierce, his hands at his side flex and release over and over again as if wanting to reach out and grab me, too.

We've done this before—kiss and more—but, for some reason, this feels like *everything*. Like a defining moment in who we are and what we could be together.

Michael brings his hands up to cup my face, moving even closer to me, our lips brushing as he says, "I never knew I could feel this way, *Diana*."

I gasp at the sound of my name—my *real* name—not the

anglicized version of it, but the Spanish one. The way his voice wraps around the two soft syllables heat my skin and melt my heart. Such a small gesture with such huge significance to me.

A bashful laugh bursts through him. "Was that any good? Or did I butcher it? I've been practicing, wanting to pronounce it the way it deserves to be spoken. I want to be part of that special group of people in your life that get to call you by your *actual* name."

I swallow to hold back the tears, taking a deep breath before answering because he understands perfectly how something so small can mean so damn much. "It was perfect. You're perfect," I breathe.

"I think *we're* perfect. Together. I want this so much. I want *you* so much." With an intensity I wasn't expecting, Michael's lips press against mine, his tongue eagerly parting them, a low moan building in the back of his throat.

Without further hesitation, I let my hands travel, both knotting into his thick, blonde hair. I tug forcefully when Michael bands an arm around my back, arcing me into him, his other hand making its way up my sleep shirt to my tits.

When he kisses my neck, I let my head fall back—both to give him more room and because I've lost all control of the muscles in my body. If it weren't for Michael's tight grip around me, I'm positive I'd be nothing more than a melted puddle on the floor—syrupy and blissful from his touch and words, but a puddle nonetheless.

"Can I take your shirt off?" he asks with so much caution I almost laugh.

Feeling me naked seems so mild after what we did on his kitchen counter. But I suppose the tremble in his voice that matches the one taking over my body is justifiable—like he said, this moment right here feels like *more*.

So I raise my arms in invitation, letting him pull at the hem of my sleep shirt, slipping it easily off over my head.

Lighting strikes nearby, illuminating my skin as I stand vulnerable in front of him, even if for a brief second. When the thunder follows, his hands are grazing me at my sides, caressing my ribs with such reverence I can't breathe.

I'm not scared, though. I'm safe.

Michael's lips part, his eyes wide on me as he shakes his head. "I still can't believe this summer happened—*is* happening. I can't believe you're here with me now, like this." He frowns, conflicted. "I know this is fucked and what lead to you being here in my bed is a scary situation, but I'm so happy you are."

I press a soft kiss to his lips, hoping to free him from whatever conflict is brewing behind those eyes, before pushing his boxers down over his hips. When I start kissing down his chest, down his abs, he reaches out to grab hold of my shoulders.

"Not now. Not tonight."

I laugh once at the serious expression on his face. "What? Why not?"

He swallows once and frowns. "I don't know. I felt wild last time we were together, but tonight feels different."

"Different how?" And despite the hunger in his eyes, the beautiful words he breathed against my skin, and the amazing support he was today, a large part of me immediately assumes the worst: he's lost interest or changed his mind.

Sensing my insecurities, he pulls me quickly to my feet, covering my face in kisses as he whispers, "No" in between each one. "I only meant this feels more special. And while I'd love to do *that* soon, it's not what I want now." His lips trail down my neck, sucking and biting as he walks me backwards to the bed. When the backs of my knees hit the mattress, we slowly move onto it. I back up all the way, but Michael takes his time to look at me as I lie there, half naked, waiting for him.

"You know, I've imagined you in my bed about a thousand times."

"Yeah?"

He nods, that signature dimpled smirk of his turning me into putty. "Yeah. In a million different ways. But nothing has ever come close to this moment right here to the real thing." Like a panther ready to have his prey, he climbs over me. Only this predator kisses his way up my stomach and sternum, stopping to kiss each breast before kissing me softly on the lips. "Whenever I thought of you here, I thought of it rough."

"And is that what you want tonight?" I whisper.

He seems to think it over, his eyes studying my face. "Maybe later, before morning comes. Right now, I mostly want to show you how much I—" His brows pull together, body tenses. "I just want it to be *us*."

"Then let's be us; let's live in this one, perfect bubble."

He smiles, but it quickly turns almost sad. "At least for tonight."

Hating the ache in his voice, I pull him down over me, pressing my lips to his in an almost desperate way I've never felt in my life. Every bone in my body is begging me to forget anything that isn't Michael and me—work, tests, diabetes, shithead exes—and allow myself to enjoy something that's just for me for the first time in years. This isn't the same as what the kitchen was. This isn't two people who had built a desperate sort of attraction and wanted to satisfy it right then and there.

No.

Whatever is happening between Michael and me in this bed is about something else entirely. An acknowledgment of sorts that this thing between us? It's real. It's messy, and only going to get worse. But it isn't going anywhere.

It terrifies me, it has me shaking in his arms, which is why when my hips lift off the mattress so he can pull my shorts and underwear off, Michael presses his lips to my ear: "I'm scared, too. But I'm yours. I've never been anyone's, and I think it's because I've always been yours. I'll always belong to you, *Diana*. If we do this now, there's no turning back."

I close my eyes to keep Michael from seeing the tears pool in my eyes, but as usual, he knows me better than I expect. He's already hard and ready, but he takes the time to kiss both my eyelids, drag his lips down my throat and to my collarbone. He whispers my name over and over again against my delicate skin —so low I almost can't hear him over the sound of the rain hammering down on us.

When he finally pulls away just enough to meet my eye, he says, "Trust me."

And for the first time in a very long time, I give myself truly to someone else.

When he pushes into me, it's slow. My lack of practice over the past few years makes me feel self-conscious, but all of that is eviscerated when Michael pushes in to the hilt, my back arching off the mattress.

He groans deep in his throat, head dropping to my shoulder as we both pause to take this moment in for what it is: *everything*, just like he said. Because there's no going back from this— not for me, at least. No matter the distance between us, in this moment, I know we will find a way to make our relationship work.

Before I can let that thought terrify me, I give in to the overwhelming waves of emotions, every sense being stimulated at the same time: his rough stubble against the soft skin of my breasts; the heavy breaths and grunts that echo throughout the room as he pushes into me over and over again; his signature citrus scent mixing with mine as we move on his sheets; the taste of him, salty and heady, as I kiss down his chest when he lets me straddle him; and finally, the look of wonder and disbelief on his face as we both come at the same time, my fingers curling into his chest for support as I ride him just before we both fall.

In the quiet moments after, when he holds me against his chest, I beg the universe to let this go on forever, to never let tomorrow happen.

Chapter Twenty-Five

MICHAEL

THE SUN IS HIGH IN THE SKY, THE WEATHER FAR FROM THE blistering heat of the past couple of weeks or the storm that came suddenly out of nowhere two days ago. The restaurant is coming together quickly, especially now that my creative constipation seems to have resolved. My mind is no longer blocked—instead, it's brimming with new ideas and concepts, ready to make a splash on our menu.

Life has never felt this good—not even when I was at the top of my career. The pep in my step as I walk around our kitchen prepping some more experimental dishes is almost comical, according to Lexi, who cannot stop giving me shit about it if I paid her.

"It *has* to be this Diana chick, isn't it? Did you guys finally do something about these feelings you were repressing? Because, cousin, you look like a walking toothpaste commercial you're smiling so much," she says, raising a brow as she chops some shallots for our next recipe experiment.

I do my best to hide the smile on my face, but there's no denying that just thinking about Diana heats my skin and tightens my chest at the same time.

Lexi makes a gagging noise. "Oh, god, you're disgusting. Look at that goofy grin! You guys fucked, didn't you?"

My smile drops, cheeks heat. "We didn't *fuck*," I almost spit.

Lexi's brows pull together in confusion. "You guys didn't have sex?"

"I mean, we did," I mutter, digging through our pantry for some cardamon. "But we didn't *fuck*."

Lexi drops her knife on the chopping block with a clatter, moving her hands on her hips as a smug grin spreads across her face.

"Hey," I call out. "Watch it! That's *my* knife you're using. It's a Shun. If you fuck up the blade, I *will* make you buy me a new one."

"Did you just correct me over my use of the word '*fuck*'? Michael... are you saying you *made love*?"

I choke and mock gag, but Lexi throws her head back in laughter.

"Shut the fuck up," I tell her.

Even though, that's what it felt like—I'm just terrified to admit it. I've been 'fucking' women since I was sixteen, but what Diana and I did a couple of nights ago? That was not fucking. It was something else. An entirely new species of physical connection I had never experienced. And I hate the way it sounds—even in my head—but there is no other way to describe what happened but by calling it what it was.

"All I'm saying is that it was more special than that. I don't want to debase it to what I would say about a girl I picked up at a bar for a one night stand. Diana deserves something more special."

Lexi laughs once. "Oh my god, look at you! You're adorable. I'm gonna get a cavity, you're so sweet!"

I grab a few carrot tops, and throw them at her.

Lexi expertly dodges them with a chuckle.

"I hate you. You're an asshole."

She shakes her head and continues chopping before scooping the contents of her cutting board and placing them in a small bowl, prepping her *mise en place* before starting to work on our new dish.

"Fine. I'll just go about my business, continue to do prep for this stew idea you have—which sounds far from elevated fine dining."

I grin and take a bite from a leftover carrot. "I have a specific vision for this one," I tell her. "It'll be a beef stew like you've never seen before—comforting, familiar, and beautiful. Something to keep your heart warm and make you feel at home. We're trying to revolutionize fine dining, remember? Not elevate it."

Lexi gawks at me. "Oh, Jesus, you're in love, aren't you?"

I roll my eyes and scoff. "Shut up." But I make a desperate exit because even the suggestion of it has my heart racing, beating a loud drum against my ribs. When I finally retreat into my office, I'm half terrified, half exhilarated. This thing is so new, but I think it's real—I sure as hell want it to be. It's the first time I've ever been interested in something serious, something long-term, and I won't let a silly thing like *distance* be the thing to fuck it up.

Diana and I haven't talked about specifics yet. Our night together mostly centered around doing *other* things—very quietly, since the girls were in the house. By the time morning came, the storm was in full swing and our priority became distracting our daughters from the strong winds and rain outside, keeping them entertained and comfortable—managing any type of cabin fever without letting on that we had just spent the night in bed together and I was absolutely gone for her.

There was one problem, however—one that I hadn't told Diana about yet—which is that, just as I was tiptoeing out of my bedroom to get back to the couch, I ran into a bleary-eyed Camila. I stopped dead in my tracks and hoped her grogginess would aid in believing me when I told her I was just coming from the bathroom. I thought about telling Diana about it, but between one thing and another, it slipped my mind. Now, as I remember the incident, I take comfort in the fact that Diana hasn't mentioned anything about it, meaning I'm sure her daughter barely registered it.

As if summoned by my thoughts, my phone vibrates in my pocket, Diana's name popping up on the screen.

"Hey," I say, leaning against my desk for support. "I was just thinking about you."

"Oh, yeah?" she whispers. I can practically hear the way she bites her lip, trying to stop a smile from spreading across his face.

"Yeah. Was thinking about maybe taking you out on a date? It's kind of about time I followed through with that, don't you think?"

I hear her laugh over the phone, the sound thrilling. Knowing I get to make her happy like this is more than I could have ever imagined.

"Sure. Where do you suggest we go? And *how*? It feels like I'm always working or studying or taking care of the girls. It's not like I can ask you to babysit. I kinda need you to be at this date, too." She chuckles. "We can ask Catterina again, but I feel weird about it."

"What if I ask Lexi and Lauren to watch them? That way they can hang on the farm, and I can take you out to lunch—it doesn't have to be anything special."

"Gee, thanks."

"C'mon. You know what I mean. You can talk Lexi through exactly what you talked me through for Emi. She's a mom of two heathens, so she's not inexperienced, either. She can handle your two daughters—they're practically a pair of angels. All I care about is spending time with you. I didn't even get to see you this morning at drop-off. I just want us to be together."

Her inhale is low, but I hear it nonetheless. "I really, really want to. But we had a scare last night, and it's not something I want to risk now by leaving Emi alone."

I stand, body tense. "You *what*? Is she okay? What happened?" Emi is such a good kid; the idea of her having another crisis is like a punch in the gut.

Diana sighs, and suddenly, I can hear the exhaustion dripping from the other end of the line. "She's fine, thank god. Her CGM app went off at like 2 A.M., and I had to wake her and make sure she was okay, and..." Another sigh—deep and sad. "She's fine. It was a false alarm caused by a compression low, which happens—"

"When the person rolls on the CGM in the middle of the night which moves the interstitial fluid and makes the CGM misread blood sugar, I know." I exhale and run my fingers through my hair as I will my heartbeat to come back down. "I read it could happen."

There's a weighted silence on the other end of the phone. Did she not think I'd do my own research? Does she still not know how much I care about her kids? About her?

"Yes, that's right. Anyway, I had them both stay home today after I had a mild freak out—that's why you didn't see me this morning and why I'm keeping my voice kinda low. I don't want them to hear me."

I hesitate for a moment, consider telling her about what happened the other night with Cami but decide against it. She doesn't need more stress in her life.

"Okay. Then how about I let you rest today. Tomorrow, though... I need to see you."

"I need to see you, too..." she whispers, a smile in her voice.

"I just don't know how without raising any weird suspicions. Plus, with all this work I have..."

"Let me figure it out, okay? You have enough to worry about right now."

Chapter Twenty-Six

DIANA

Through the living room window, I watch him park in the driveway and pull two bags of groceries from the backseat, his muscles flexing almost in slow motion under his ever-present white t-shirt. When he catches me checking him out, the smirk on his face almost knocks me over, knees weakened without hope of revival.

Before going to greet him at the sliding door, I check my hair in the hallway mirror hoping I look halfway decent for our clandestine lunch meeting. Between work and not wanting the girls to find out about us yet, scheduling a date has proven much harder than either one of us thought it would be. Which is why Michael came up with this solution: I work, he cooks, we eat. It's not a long walk on the beach beneath the stars or a romantic dinner at a fancy restaurant, but it's whatever we can do to make it work, and I love that. I love that we're both fighting to figure out whatever this is. I love that, for once, I'm not the only one trying to make things work.

When he greets me at the door, my skin is electrified, buzzing with anticipation. We're doing this—*finally*.

He greets me with a deep "Hey," the sound of his voice reminding me of what we did last night over the phone. The way it felt like his words reached all the way down to my bones;

the way they seemed to become part of my makeup for that moment in time. Without hesitation, he leans down to press a kiss on my cheek in greeting. "I had fun last night," he murmurs in my ear.

My lungs paralyzed, I lose all ability to breathe. Ironic, given how much he made me pant with just his words, my phone pressed to my ear, as he commanded me to imagine my fingers as his, as he begged me to *come for me, baby. Imagine it's me fucking you and come.*

And I did, biting down on my lip so I didn't moan his name into the darkness of my bedroom after letting myself go.

"Hey," I say back, knowing that he's remembering the same thing I am. Sure, we haven't been able to be alone, but it's only a matter of time, and the knowledge that we'll eventually get to have a repeat of that stormy night is everything.

"You ready for our date?" he whispers.

I run my fingers through my hair, an intense blush creeping up my neck. "Yes, more than ready." I wrap my arms around his neck and press a soft kiss to his lips. "I blocked off some extra time for lunch, too, so I should have more than my usual thirty minutes."

"Perfect," he says with the press of a kiss on my nose. "Go sit down and wrap up work while I make us something amazing."

With a goofy grin, I walk back to the kitchen table where my work is neatly spread out. He helps me scoot in my chair and brings me a cold glass of water. When he sets it by my computer, he drops his head to my neck from behind, placing a kiss on the delicate skin behind my ear. His hands briefly rub my shoulders, though there's no need for that—he's successfully melted me into a pile of goo with one kiss. "If you need anything, I'll be right over there," he whispers in my ear.

Heat spreads like wildfire all over my body and, for the first time ever, I resent my work. What I once revered and had prayed for so many nights is now keeping me from jumping back in bed and losing myself in him. When I turn in my seat to kiss him, I throw every last bit of myself into it, but I feel his lips curve up in a grin right as he pulls away before letting it get too wild.

"You need to work and I need to cook."

My face falls into a pout and he laughs.

"Seriously, get back to work. I'm here to serve you, remember? I'm your own personal, private chef. You should be completely ignoring my presence."

"I think it's kind of hard to ignore your presence."

He snorts as he begins to unload the groceries onto the kitchen counter. "Flattery? Wow. You must be really hungry and desperate for lunch."

I laugh, marveling at how easy this all feels, at how far away we seem to be from those days where we merely tolerated each other for our daughters' sake. "Oh, I feel a little desperate, but it's not for whatever incredible meal I'm sure you'll prepare."

He shakes his head and smiles. "Get back to work, you. I'm here to satiate real hunger. *Maybe*, if you're good, I'll satiate the other kind that's overtaken you after lunch."

It's not long until the delicious smells coming from the stove begin to distract me from my work. My stomach rumbles as I listen in on a conference call with our internal team, taking notes for my boss, while trying not to drool all over my keyboard. Through it all, Michael waits patiently, smiling across the kitchen at me every time I look over to check on how he's doing. I worry whether he'll start to resent my job for keeping me from paying attention to him now—I did tell him it was going to be a light day today, after all—but his mood never seems to shift. Michael is never far, always offering an encouraging smile.

"Just one more meeting and I'm done until after lunch, I

promise. I just need to touch base with my boss about this case and the call I was just on."

"Hey, I'm good. Don't worry about me—this can wait. I can wait."

And he does. Patiently so. He sets the place settings at the bar while I speak to Edgar, give him updates on the case.

When I'm finally done, I shut my laptop with a soft thud, pushing out of my chair, stretching my arms up in the air. Once I get to my feet, I feel a pair of muscular arms wrap around my waist, banding to pull my back against a hard chest. Michael's lips trail from my jaw down my neck and up again as a chill skitters down my spine.

"You have no idea how sexy you sound on your meetings," he growls in my ear. "It took everything in me not to ask you to turn off your camera and let me fuck you from behind while you were on them."

My eyes roll back as I suppress a moan when he drags his tongue up my neck. "That... would've been... difficult to do."

His teeth grab hold of my ear, his hips press his hard cock into my lower back. "We would've managed."

"Managed to get me fired, more likely." I try to joke, but the lack of oxygen to my brain makes it quite difficult to concentrate on anything other than the feel of him all around me, crowding me like an animal ready to eat its prey.

"Well, we can't have that. I don't think I've ever been more attracted to anyone ever in my life." As he speaks, one of his hands travels from around my waist up my sternum, wrapping lightly around my neck.

"So let's go into my bedroom and you can show me. Or better yet, let's do the whole bent over the table thing. That sounds like fun."

His laugh turns into a groan when he presses his face into my hair. He inhales deeply before admitting, "There's nothing I would love to do more right now than fuck you, but I promised you a nice lunch, and that's what you're going to get. You're going to need energy if you want to keep kicking ass at work like that."

I snort and turn in his arms. "Please. I'm just an assistant."

"Being an assistant is hard work—don't downplay it. Plus, you're almost a paralegal, too," he reminds me, the heat in his eyes slowy cooling. "And I really think you should revisit the whole lawyer thing. I mean, besides the fact that you're brilliant and even your boss seems to think you'd be good at it, can you imagine how fucking hot you'd look in those pencil skirts?" He groans again. "Actually, I take it back. No pencil skirts. I don't want anyone staring at that ass but me."

"You know pencil skirts aren't part of some uniform for female lawyers, right? This isn't *Suits*."

"Please, let me dream a little." He kisses me again.

"You heard Edgar and I's last part of our conversation, though? About considering law school?"

"Diana. I was two feet away from you. It was a little hard to ignore what you were talking about. I don't think I can forget how your boss was encouraging you to do something we all think you would be great at."

I exhale and look out the window. "I don't think that's true at all," I admit out loud for the first time.

"What do you mean? Your boss just waxed poetic about the amazing work you've been doing and the incredible instincts you have and—"

"Listen," I cut him off, eyes back on his. My hands drop to his ribs, tightening as I finally speak these words aloud. "Corporate contract law is fun to me because it's like a game. Like, you have to find these loopholes in contracts or create iron clad contracts that benefit your client in ways that you have to think about one, five, *ten* years down the road. It's fun and something I know I'd be good at. But every time I even begin to entertain the idea for even a second I think 'It took me *years* to leave my husband—and that was only because his *girlfriend* showed up at my doorstep—so who the hell am I thinking I can stand up for other people when they need me when I failed myself so miserably?' I let myself rot in that horrible marriage for years, never standing up for myself or my kids through his neglect. Who the hell am I to do it for someone else when they're in trouble? Or when they need their lawyer to stand up for them?" I close my eyes before I start crying and press my forehead to his chest, hands fisting his t-shirt as I pull myself closer to him.

"Diana," he sighs, his eyes fierce as they roam all over my face. "I know you. You probably thought you were doing what was right for your daughters. You probably thought half a dad would be better than a divorced dad, than one they'd rarely see."

"And I was right, wasn't I? I mean, my girls have not been able to speak to their father *since we left Colorado*. They've gotten *nothing*. So now I'm raising children who used to believe their dad at least cared about them. Now they *know* he doesn't. Thankfully, they seem to be too distracted by the end-of-summer talent show lately to notice. That choreography for Cruel Summer by Taylor Swift has them in a goddamn chokehold," I say trying for a joke and failing. He shoots me a look, like he knows what I'm trying to do, so I get back on subject. "I mean, I thought before we got a divorce that he just didn't love me. But now to find out it was our entire family he didn't love? He made mention one time of giving up all parental rights, but I thought he was doing it to rile me up. But now I'm beginning to wonder whether he was being serious." I scoff, tears streaming down my cheeks. Michael cups my face and wipes them away with his thumbs, letting me finish. "And then I just sit in bed at night wondering whether I made a mistake, whether we should've just agreed to have a kind of arrangement or something, so my girls wouldn't have to grow up like this. I've spent countless sleepless nights wondering whether my girls are going to be negatively affected by this well into adulthood, how it's going to change the fabric of who they are and—" The sobbing intensifies, making it nearly impossible to speak. So Michael just holds me, arms wrapped tightly around me as he waits for me to calm down.

"As someone who grew up with shitty parents," he says, breaking the silence after letting me cry on his shirt for a few minutes, "your girls are better off. *Knowing* that my parents didn't give a shit honestly would've been better than having to constantly wonder about it. It's better than doing everything in your power to please them and never succeeding, never getting a thank you or good job or shit. Or worse, do what I did, which is *negatively* try to get their attention by doing stupid shit. At least your daughters know now. At least they know and they won't have to try and live through that shit in their teenage years, wondering why Dad can't show up to their school activities or why he's always on business trips or why his eyes glaze over whenever they talk to him. It's better this way."

"I'm not sure you're right," I tell him.

He shrugs once, a sad smile on his face. "I'm not sure, either. But I think I would've preferred it that way. I would've loved the freedom of not having to care because they didn't care first."

More tears streak down my cheeks, but this time they're for him. "I'm so sorry. People are just... shitty."

My simple statement makes him laugh once. "Yes. But it is what it is. I'm sorry for Emi and Cami, though. They don't deserve to feel unloved. Hopefully they do know how fucking amazing they are and that they have an equally amazing mother who loves them with a fierceness I've never seen in anyone else."

I sniff and wipe my snotty nose with the back of my hand, clearly throwing any type of modesty or demureness out the window. "Who knows? Sometimes I feel like Cami hates me or blames me for this, even though she doesn't know the details. The amount of attitude she's been giving me lately..." I attempt a pathetic whistle. "It makes me fear her teenage years."

"I think maybe it's easier to be mad at you because you're actually *here.* But as she matures, she'll realize what really happened. Hopefully, she'll grow to realize that you were never the problem."

I sigh deeply, feeling the weight of the world on my shoulders. "You don't know that."

"Fuck yeah, I do." He presses a kiss to my forehead. "C'mere," he whispers, pulling me into him again. I nuzzle his neck and breathe him in, feeling the weight on my shoulders lighten just a bit—enough to where maybe I can relax a bit and enjoy the rest of our time together today.

"I'm sorry I ruined our date with a breakdown. I don't know what that was exactly. I never really..." *talk to anyone*, I want to say. "Anyway, I promise to be a functional human from now on. No more drama." I grin, finger-combing my hair.

"Sometimes we need to break down in order to rebuild better versions of ourselves, and that's okay." He pushes me away just enough to look me straight in the eye, brows furrowed. "And I'm not here because of any notion I may have that this is *easy,* or that it should be just for funsies, Diana. I'm here to be with *you.* And that includes the good, the bad, and the ugly. I'm here because I want to be a part of your life, and I hope that you want to be part of mine, too." He pauses when I inhale sharply at his words. "Isn't that what you want?"

I bite my lip and consider his words before speaking. Do I want him to be part of my life? *Yes.* Do I want to be part of his? *Yes.*

But...

"But what about after the summer is over?"

He swallows once, his muscles tensing with a flash of concern in his eyes. "We'll check back at the end of summer. See what we want to do."

"That's playing with fire," I whisper, my lower lip trembling once more.

"Maybe. But I'm not about to let that stop me from enjoying my time with you while you're here."

Chapter Twenty-Seven

MICHAEL

FIVE WEEKS LATER

"Doors will open in t-minus two minutes, chef," Danny, my head maitre d' announces.

I look over at Lexi, who's elbow deep in whisking one of the sauces for our entree. She smiles nervously at me and nods. "We've got this."

"We've got this." And I think, for the first time since the beginning of the summer, I mean it.

Lexi and I had been preparing for months, developing recipes and sourcing investors. At one point, though, things started to look quite bleak. It felt like we were stuck, creatively and financially.

As head chef, I'm in charge of developing our plates and the vibe of our place, but I was creatively burnt out. One day, though, it all came to me—the direction in which I wanted the restaurant to go, the type of food we *really* wanted to serve, and the type of environment we wanted to have—clean, but not cold; modern, but cozy. And though I'm not sure whether I'd admit it out loud, much of it has to do with Diana, I think. Something about being with her unleashed a creative side within that I'd never experienced before. You can feel the passion in the spices, the comfort in the base of the recipes, the devotion in its execution, and the beauty of it all in the plating.

She's my muse, in more ways than one.

Then, once Jonathan gave us the money, everything sort of happened at lightning speed. As soon as the cash hit our bank account, we put a deposit on a space that needed minimal renovations. Lexi and I finally agreed on a name, H & H, which stands for Haynes & Haynes. Through Jonathan's connections, we were able to find a designer to redo our space, and because we were going for minimalism, it didn't really take a long time to source things to style the restaurant according to the aesthetic we were going for.

Honestly, it's insane what money and influence can do.

Five stressful—yet equally blissful—weeks later, and we have a restaurant soft launch for friends and family only.

"Are there any people at the door already?" I ask Danny.

"Your daughter, I believe. She's with another woman and her children."

I suck in a breath, stomach rolling. "They're here already?" I turn to look at Lexi, who gives me an encouraging smile. With a nod, she tells me to go and meet my daughter—and Diana and her girls—at the door.

When I see the four of them outside the restaurant holding hands, I stop dead in my tracks before they even spot me. Diana holds Cami's hand on her right, while she holds Rachel's on her left, who in turn holds Emiliana's. Diana smiles down at Rachel as she talks to her, my daughter rapt by her words. The imagery of it all, of seeing the four of them together, there to support me in arguably the most important moment of my career, hits me like a cannonball to the chest.

We belong together. We could have this life together. It feels more right than anything I've ever felt before.

The girls love each other, Diana's kids are amazing, and over the summer I've grown to care about this woman more than I could've ever imagined. Diana and I haven't decided on the final fate of our relationship, but as the final days of summer near, I know I've made my decision. There's no way I'm letting this end. We'll find a way.

Just because she's moving back to Colorado, and we won't get our daily lunch dates, our intimate moments, or the almost family-like days we share with our children, doesn't mean we have to end.

I will find a way to make it work. *We* will find a way to make it work.

"You ready to come in?" I ask when I open the door of the restaurant for them.

Diana beams at me, the girls' energy buzzing around as well. "Are *you* ready? I mean, I'm sure you're prepared, but emotionally," she whispers.

The nervousness in her voice, the concern for my wellbeing, is heartwarming. Without thinking, completely forgetting that the girls still don't know the intimate details of our relationship, I lean down and kiss Diana once on the cheek.

I stop dead in my tracks, realizing my mistake, a cool chill running through my entire body.

Fuck.

I pull away suddenly and stare into Diana's eyes, whispering a quiet apology. Her skin blazing red, she smiles softly and shakes her head, telling me we'll talk about it later. I try to avoid the girls' stare, to play it cool, but my gaze drops to Camila, and something about the way she stares at me through narrowed eyes tells me we definitely won't be able to keep this from the girls for much longer.

That's fine, honestly. It's what I want.

So I clear my throat and personally lead them to their table, taking four menus with me as we go. I pull out the chair for Diana and each of the girls, and hope they all have an amazing meal before heading to greet the second group of diners waiting by the door.

LEXI, THE KITCHEN AND WAIT STAFF, AND I WRAP THINGS up at two A.M. with a glass of champagne and a toast to the future of H&H. Exhaustion runs bone-deep, but rather than go home and have a well-deserved goodnight's sleep alone, I drive to Diana's, where my kid is sleeping over.

I sneak around the back of the guest house and tap lightly on her bedroom window, waking her with a jolt. When she sits up in bed looking at me like I'm a madman, one hand over her chest, I know she's where I belong.

"Hey," she whispers after pushing her bedroom window open. "Everything okay?"

I beam up at her—I can't help it. Tonight, I opened my restaurant, with my daughter and dream girl by my side, and a sense of family I never hoped to have.

"I'm on kind of a natural high, and wanted to share it with you."

This makes her laugh with a nod. "Okay. Come in."

She steps aside, and lets me climb through her window like a teenager, only with less grace. I fall with a thud while she stifles a giggle, but I don't care—nothing can stop the buzz of happiness coursing through me.

"You were incredible tonight," she whispers against my lips before kissing me. "I don't know much about fancy food, but I know it looked and tasted amazing, and even my picky girls loved it. And thank you for making something special for Emi. I really appreciate that, and she did too."

She goes in for another kiss, but I pull away. "I gotta warn you, I'm super sweaty. And I kinda smell like smoke."

"Let's take a shower, then." Her grin is mischievous, her eyes sparkling even in the darkness of the bedroom.

I fucking love it.

"It's late. Won't the girls hear?" I ask, looking over my shoulder at her bedroom door. Still, the thought of having her now, with all this adrenaline coursing through me, makes the blood rush to my dick.

Diana shakes her head as she slips her hand in mine, leading me to the bathroom. "They were practicing all day for tomorrow's talent show, and even did the full routine a few times after we got home. Once I put them to bed, they were out like a light."

With care, she unbuttons my chef's coat and pushes it off my shoulders, letting it drop onto the tiled floor with a thud. She reaches for the light switch while I kiss down her chest, pushing her underwear and pajama shorts over her hips.

I reach over and turn on the shower while she begins to kiss up my neck, pulling on my earlobe before whispering, "I'm so proud of you, Michael."

I groan, in love with her praise. "Thank you, baby."

"Please. I want you so bad," she moans against my lips.

With my hands on her hips, I walk her backwards into the shower, pressing her up against the cold tile.

"I've waited all day for this," I whisper into her neck as we let the hot water fall over us.

She laughs, a little breathless, as she digs her fingernails into my shoulders. "How? You had your opening today. I'd think you'd be more concerned with that."

I growl and bite her clavicle. "You're all I think of anymore.

Whether it's fucking you, or just being with you, you're always in my head. I've had to learn how to multitask."

I press a leg in between hers, and move her up and down my thigh. Diana moans, her hips taking a life of their own as she fucks my leg.

"God, you're already so fucking wet, baby."

"You're not the only one who—" She gasps once, her eyes rolling to the back of her head.

My laugh is smug. Dark. Hungry. "What were you saying?"

It takes her a minute to focus, to answer. "You're not the only one who can't stop thinking about us."

Us.

There's no way I can help groaning at the word. It sounds too good.

"I want you so much," I tell her.

"God, Michael. *Please*," she begs again.

"Don't worry—I've got you."

I start kissing down her chest again, stopping at her breasts. I take one nipple between my teeth while I roll the other with my hand. Above me, she calls out my name.

"*Shh*! You'll wake the kids."

When I get to my knees in front of Diana, to worship her like she deserves, she stops me. She runs her fingers through my wet hair once, before tugging at my nape, forcing me to get to my feet.

"This is *your* night. *Your* time to celebrate. Let me do something for *you*." And like the goddess she is, she sinks to her knees, never breaking eye contact, and takes me into her mouth.

"*Fuuuuuck*," I groan, slamming my hands against the tile wall to keep from falling over.

As she works me, I try not to focus on how good her mouth feels, try not to look down to see her lips around my cock. Because I know the second I do, it's all over. And I want this to last as long as it possibly can. But when I feel her tongue play with the tip, my eyes roll to the back of my head, and I almost lose it.

"Stop," I puff out. My hands dig into her hair to pull her off me. "Jesus fucking Christ, Diana."

She beams up at me, and I'm positive the steam from the hot water is not the only thing fogging up the mirrors.

"You okay?" she asks, getting to her feet.

I pull her to me, relishing in the feel of her wet body, perfect tits pressed against my chest.

"Am I okay? Fuck, yeah, I'm okay. Better than that. I feel like I'm dreaming right now. I've just opened the restaurant I've always wanted to have, and I've got the perfect girl in my arms. Naked. Wet in more ways than one." I snicker when she blushes. "I'm fucking amazing, Diana. And you've played a big role in that. So thank you."

Her brows pull together, eyes bloodshot. "Anything. Anytime."

Without another word, I press a kiss to her lips and hitch one of her legs over my hip. I hold both her wrists over her head against the wall with one hand, while the other lines my cock to her entrance.

Part of me wanted to drag this out, make it last longer. But the other part can't wait another second to be inside Diana. So in one swift movement, I push into her to the hilt.

She moans my name. I groan into her neck, licking the drops of water off her tits.

"Fuck."

It's all I can say, all I can think, as I start to fuck her. Right here. In her shower.

In the back of my mind, I'm mildly aware that, any second now, I could slip on the tile and crack my head open. But my body wants it—this—so much, it uses every bit of adrenaline stored in its system to make sure my muscles are locked in tight. Besides my hips and tongue, my body has become an immovable force. Nothing is stopping me from this.

When her moans grow louder, when the words coming out of her mouth stop making sense, I know she's close. And thank fucking god for that because I'm not sure how much longer I could take.

"*Michael.*" Diana gasps, her arms breaking free from my grasp to wrap around my neck as she comes. She holds onto me for dear life, and fuck if I don't do the same to her.

"Let me come inside you. I *need* to come inside you."

She nods frantically, whispers yes in my ear before kissing me just below it.

With a groan, my hips start a desperate rhythm, fast and rough and hard toward the finish line. When I feel myself start to lose control, when my mind begins to blur, I pull her closer into me just before emptying myself inside of her.

After we come, we're quiet. When I pull out slowly, she whimpers and I kiss her on the tip of the nose. Diana and I take turns soaping each other, and I take special care when I wash her between her legs, conscious of how sore she might be after our little tryst. When we're done, we towel off quickly and slip into bed. Immediately, I pull her into my chest and press a kiss on her forehead, inhaling her scent, holding it in for several seconds, memorizing it.

After a while, just when I'm about to fall asleep, she pulls back to look me in the eye.

"What are we going to do? I can't leave Colorado—Rodrigo would never allow it. And I don't even know if I want to, honestly. Not yet, at least. And you just opened a place here in Long Island. You're not exactly going to up and decide to leave after one day, are you?"

And I know exactly what she means. Because things have

changed. Yes, we agreed to continue to do this thing and see where it goes. But it's evolved into something more than we ever could've expected. She and the girls will go back to Colorado soon. Me and Rachel will stay here.

Still, that isn't even our biggest problem. It's that the girls don't even know we're together. They don't know we meet up almost every day. They don't know we talk on the phone for over an hour before going to bed after they've fallen asleep. And they sure as fuck don't know that I've been falling for Diana since the beginning of the summer.

"No. But we're staying together," I say with confidence. There's no way I'm letting this end. "We're staying together even though we'll be miles apart. We'll figure it out. There's no way in hell I'm letting you go. No way in hell I'm letting *us*—the girls included—go." I don't want to come off too strong, but we're a family. Or at least the beginning of one, aren't we? "We're going to stay together and see what happens and you're going to kick ass at work and maybe even go back to school and become a lawyer." She laughs at that and calls me crazy, tells me that's not happening, but I keep going. "And when the time is right, we'll figure out how to be together geographically."

Diana pauses for a moment to think it through before breaking into a smile. "Okay," she whispers. "Okay. We'll tell them tomorrow. After the talent show. At dinner."

"Perfect." I pull her into my arms and fall asleep with a smile on my face, dreaming about the years to come.

Chapter Twenty-Eight

DIANA

I WAKE SLOWLY, BRAIN FOGGY FROM AN INTENSE WEEK OF work and studying—not to mention yesterday's late night activities—rolling into a hard pillow that smells suspiciously like citrus. I nuzzle into it, inhaling the comforting and familiar scent. But when a pair of strong arms wraps around me, I realize it isn't a *pillow* I'm nuzzling—it's Michael.

My eyes fly open, because: "The girls!" I whisper-yell. "You need to leave before they see you here!"

He smiles down at me, his dimples visible beneath his scruff under the morning sun. "Hey, good morning."

"Seriously, Michael." I push against his chest, reluctantly freeing myself from his hold. "You need to go before they wake up."

"We talked about this last night, remember? We're gonna tell them today."

"Yeah. At dinner. *After* their talent show thing. I don't want them to find out by having you walk-of-shaming out of my bedroom first thing in the morning. That's not how we should be handling this." I don't think. I've never been in this situation, obviously, but logic is telling me this isn't the way.

Michael throws himself back onto the pillows, his eyes on the ceiling. "I know you're right, I just would love to have breakfast here with everyone. Together. Like a real..." He swallows once, and I feel my stomach jump.

Whoa. Was he gonna say—

A loud banging comes from the guest house front door—the one we never use.

"Who the hell could that be?" I sit up and quickly put on a pair of shorts and a t-shirt.

Michael follows my lead, dressing in the same clothes he came in last night. "Could it be Barbara?" he asks.

I shake my head. "Barbara won't be back for another week. She has a couple of more days of filming to do. It's why she couldn't make it to the opening."

"Right."

The speed and strength of the knocking grows insistent, and when I hear the voice that starts calling out for me, I go as still as a statue. A cold chill runs through my entire body as I realize the person huffing and puffing outside of the house is none other than my ex-husband.

"What the hell are you doing here?" I ask when I pull the door open and find myself faced with the man who abandoned my children. My skin simultaneously heats from rage and indignation while a current runs through me from fear and uncertainty of what this might do to the girls.

Rodrigo stands in the doorway, a smug smirk on his face that turns my stomach over. "What do you mean? I'm here to see my daughters."

Something I've learned about Rodrigo since our divorce is that there has to be something in it for him in everything that he does—he doesn't know the meaning of the word "selfless." I'm not sure how I never saw that side of him—or if I did, how I was able to find the strength within me to suppress the realization. Maybe I just had to in order to survive? Maybe part of me thought that a quarter of a partner was better than no partner at all? But now that I've had time and separation from him and our relationship, I can see that all he was doing was dragging me down emotionally.

"You're here to see your daughters?" I ask, my voice flat. "Well, that's hilarious, considering you have been absolutely MIA from their lives over the past couple of months. Or have you not received any of their letters or calls? We definitely haven't heard from you once." I cross my arms in front of my chest and glare at him, trying to scare him with my best evil eye. In the back of my mind, however, I'm praying Michael doesn't feel the need to come out and meet my ex.

Rodrigo, at six-foot-four and a large build, looks down at his nails. "I saw their letters—how do you think I found you? I used the return address. I've just been super busy, so I haven't been able to reply."

"You've been too busy to even answer one fucking text?"

His neck snaps up to look at me, surprise in his eyes. I'm not one to curse often so he knows I'm close to boiling over. Honestly, if I were him, I'd go find cover before I erupt all over the place and burn him down.

"With the divorce and everything," he starts, "I've been settling into my new home. You know how I rented that place downtown? Well, I've been doing this whole move alone so..."

"How sad for you," I say sarcastically. "Well, I've been doing the whole parenting thing alone and let me tell you, I'm pretty sure that's a little bit more difficult than building IKEA furniture for a studio apartment."

He scoffs. "*God*, why do you have to be so bitter? I'm sorry I found someone else. It just didn't work out between us."

I practically choke, stutter through my words, not knowing where to even begin to reply to that statement. "*It just didn't work out*? That's all you have to say? It's not even about that anymo— And you think that's the only reason I'm upset? I don't give a—"

"Hey," Michael's voice comes up behind us. He wraps an arm around my waist, the look he gives Rodrigo filled with such resentment and protectiveness I wonder if it physically causes my ex any pain. "What's going on here? Everything okay?"

"Ahhh," Rodrigo says. "This is the new boyfriend, huh? I've heard about you."

I narrow my eyes at my ex, heart dropping. "What do you mean you've heard about him? From *who*?" I ask, a bit horrified.

"Well, my dear, you might think that I haven't had time to read our daughters' letters, but Camila sure had a lot to say about the man who sneaks out of my wife's bedroom in the middle of the night. Even for a seven year-old, she sure has a way with words."

I stop breathing, while Michael inhales sharply beside me. "First off, Cami is *nine*. And second, how did she even find out about us?"

"Shit," Michael mutters. "I meant to tell you about that, but then you never mentioned it so I assumed she thought nothing of it and—"

"What are you talking about?" My eyes flash to him.

Rodrigo whistles and laughs once with an, "Ooh, trouble in paradise," but I ignore him.

"Well," Michael starts, scratching the back of his neck. "That night of the storm, after we..." He glances nervously at Rodrigo before looking back at me. "Well, when I went back out into the living room, I ran into Cami. But she was groggy and kind of out of it, and I swear to god I thought she didn't suspect a thing. I was going to tell you, but..."

My jaw drops in disbelief. "How could you not tell me?"

Michael shakes his head, speechless.

"That's highly inappropriate of you, Diana. I mean, have you no consideration for our daughters? You're sleeping around with this man I haven't even met while the girls are under the same roof?"

Shame crashes over me like a tidal wave, skin flushed in embarrassment and disappointment because, my god, what *was* I thinking? As much as I hate to admit it, Rodrigo is right. My actions were inappropriate and disrespectful, even if I thought the girls were in the dark. And now to find out that Cami knew all along...

"Hey," Michael's sharp voice breaks through my shame spiral. "Don't talk to her like that."

I lean into Michael a bit, needing the support as my balance wavers. His arm tightens around me in response, but I quickly pull away once I hear the girls' bedroom door open.

Rodrigo pushes between Michael and me, forcing himself into the house as if he owned the place. He calls out for our daughters while walking through the front hall and the living room, all the way to the kitchen.

"*Papi*?" Cami's sleepy voice comes from inside.

I follow behind Rodrigo closely while I try to prepare myself for the storm that's about to hit us. Not only did he decide to drop by without any warning after disappearing for the past three months, but now I need to address the whole Michael situation in a wholly different way than I'd planned.

When I reach the kitchen, I watch as Cami runs into her father's open arms, closing her little eyes and fisting her hands behind his neck when he squats to hug her back. My heart tears in two, because I can see the sadness in her face when he lets go much sooner than she'd hoped. He looks over his shoulder at me, almost smug that his daughter would still want to spend time with him. But when Emi comes out of her room, Rachel behind her, and makes no move to greet her father, there's no sense of satisfaction that washes over me as the evidence of their hurt becomes apparent. Because, while part of me feels validated that I was right, that I wasn't exaggerating, and that Rodrigo's behavior this summer has been unacceptable, an even bigger part just wants them to never know this kind of pain. The kind where you learn to believe you'll never be good enough, no matter what you do.

And in that moment, I realize why Cami did what she did. Why she wrote her father about our relationship. Maybe a part of her thought that this would be a misguided attempt at getting her parents back together, but I don't think that's necessarily true. Cami has never once mentioned us to get back together throughout our entire separation, which is surprising. So part of me wonders whether she told her father as a way to bait him into a reply, test whether he'd been reading their letters or not.

And the little genius did it.

"Hey, kid," Rodrigo says to Emi. "You gonna say hi to me or what?"

But Emi doesn't move, expression cautious.

Rachel runs over to her dad, who takes her hand and leads her aside, giving us space to deal with this incredibly awkward family reunion.

"Why don't we go out for breakfast? I can take you guys out to a diner and get some waffles or pancakes? Load up on some syrup and whipped cream, huh? Your kid can come too, if you want," Rodrigo tells Michael, who looks like he might actually growl.

"They can't; they have to get to camp. Today is their summer talent show and the girls are doing a dance. And you might think twice about giving Emi a plate of pancakes or waffles smothered in syrup and whipped cream. I don't know if you know this, but she has type 1 diabetes," Michael says, narrowing his eyes at Rodrigo, his cheeks reddened in anger.

Rodrigo gets to his feet, all pretense of being a nice guy finally out the window. "Don't talk to me about my kids. My kids' lives are none of your fucking business."

I gasp, getting in between Michael and Rodrigo as they quickly move toward each other.

"Maybe it technically isn't, but it's clear that I care more about them than you do."

"*Michael*," I say with a groan, because he doesn't know he's just awakened the beast. "I'm gonna need you to leave."

He turns to look at me, hurt. "What? You're asking *me* to leave?"

Rodrigo laughs, while all three girls look like they're on the verge of tears, the expression on their faces begging for answers neither one of us can give yet.

"Girls," I say, before continuing. These two are seconds from going nuclear, and it's not something any of them should see. "Why don't you get changed for camp? Rachel, you can still come with me, if your dad's okay with it. You have your things, right?"

"Yes, Mrs. Castillo," Rachel replies, voice soft and meek.

"Sweetie, I've told you to call me Diana a million times, now." I smile encouragingly. "Why don't you three go back into the bedroom and get ready?" I usher the girls into the room and shut the door behind them. When I get back to the kitchen, Rodrigo and Michael seem to be in the middle of a testosterone-fueled staring contest, each one nearly shaking with rage or frustration.

"Michael," I whisper, touching his shoulder gently, trying to get him to look at me. "Please. Please go, and I'll see you later at the talent show."

"You're kicking *me* out?" he asks, eyes wide with shock.

I sigh and run my fingers through my hair. "There's just... a lot we need to deal with as a family right now. And this fighting is not helping."

His brows pull together as he looks from me to Rodrigo and back to me again. "I don't want to leave you here alone with him," he whispers, low enough only I can hear.

"I know," I say, rubbing his bicep. "But I'm going to be fine. And you need to change before today. You're still wearing last night's sweaty clothes." I try to throw him a smile, but even I can feel how weak it is. "I'll take Rachel to camp today, and we'll see each other there for the performance just like we planned, okay? Nothing is going to change."

"Promise?"

"Promise."

With great reluctance and without another word, Michael exits through the kitchen door, leaving me alone with the *actual* smallest man who ever lived.

Chapter Twenty-Nine

DIANA

"You know, you really should lighten up. I thought all you wanted me to do this entire summer was show up for the kids. Here I fucking am and you're *still* not happy. As per usual," Rodrigo whispers as we find our seats in the audience.

Michael and I were supposed to sit together, but he seems nowhere to be found.

"And child support. I also wanted you to pay child support, remember?"

Rodrigo rolls his eyes and whispers, "I haven't forgotten. Your lawyers have made sure of it. You need to relax—I already told them I'll get to it eventually."

I scoff. He's so lucky this isn't the right time for this conversation.

We haven't had the chance to discuss the events of this morning or his pitfalls as a father. Once Michael left, I had to get the girls ready for camp, make them breakfast, and make sure they had their costumes and everything in their backpack. With everything that had gone on, I barely had any time to make myself look presentable. And it's not like Rodrigo could be bothered to even ask whether he could be of any help at all—god forbid he thinks of someone else for a change.

He tried to pull me aside while Cami and Emi finished their

breakfasts, but the second he reached a hand out to wrap it around my arm, I sidestepped him, putting all my attention on the girls. My two daughters, who didn't know what to make of their dad's sudden appearance after going MIA for more than three months.

Cami asked him where he'd been, asked why it took so long for him to reply to their letters, and it absolutely gutted me.

Because Rodrigo smiled through his answers as if none of it had been a big deal and said, "Sorry, kid. I've been busy."

Too busy for his own kids?

"I wanted you to show up for our *daughters'* sake," I hiss at him, shifting uncomfortably in my chair (the same ones from that torturously long orientation Michael and I suffered through). "I wanted you to show up for *them.* Not out of some twisted sense of ownership you have over me. I didn't want you to come and act like some primitive ape trying to mark his territory the *second* you find out I might be moving on. In case you've forgotten, we're divorced, Rodrigo."

He snorts. "No shit. And you wish I cared that much for you. That's not why I'm here; I don't give a shit about who you're dating."

"Oh, yeah? Then why did it take our daughter telling you I'm starting to date for you to come out here? For you to talk to them again? And why are you giving me so much crap for having a boyfriend?"

"So he *is* your boyfriend, then. Confirmed?" He raises a brow, challenging me.

I sigh, and cross my arms in front of my chest, looking away. "I can't do this. Can we just enjoy the girls' dance, pretend to tolerate each other's presence for their sake, and then go back to our regularly scheduled program?"

He laughs once. "Which is what, exactly?"

"You go back to your debauched life back home, while I

raise our two daughters. I don't tell the court you've been neglecting your agreed-upon parental duties, and all is well," I whisper, my words coming out with more fire than I was ever able to muster throughout our entire marriage.

"And the boyfriend? How does he fit into the equation? He coming back with you to Colorado, then? Don't think opening up a restaurant a day ago and having a kid in school here is exactly compatible with a big move, is it?"

It takes everything in me not to slap that smug smile off his face, but I manage. I bite my lip, thankful for the dimming lights as my eyes begin to water.

Last night, we agreed to give long-distance a chance. But if there's any hint at all that the girls aren't okay with us dating, then... then that's it. And given that Camila felt the need to write her dad, all signs point to a continued single life on the other side of the country.

"Where is he, by the way? The boyfriend, I mean. I thought you told him to meet you here," Rodrigo whispers as the introduction to the talent show begins. "Shouldn't he be sitting with his *girlfriend*?" Rodrigo snorts once before laughing softly at his own comment. Someone in front of us turns in their seat and shushes him.

The emcee introduces the show, tells the audience about Camp Sugar Maple traditions and what an amazing summer it's been. They discuss what kinds of acts will be performed and how many age groups are included in the end of season talent show.

Beside me, Rodrigo groans, muttering, "Are you fucking kidding me?" when he realizes just how many acts there will be.

I scoff once, because he's so clearly inexperienced in this kind of stuff, never once having showed up to a single school event.

While he squirms uneasily in his seat, likely regretting his decision to come here in the first place now that he's faced with having to watch three hours of acts from kids he couldn't care less about, I look around for Michael again. I do my best to act natural as I scan the audience, struggling to see much of anything from my chair, but it's nearly impossible. Just when I'm ready to give up, I spot him from the corner of my eye, leaning against the auditorium wall, arms crossed in front of his chest.

As if sensing my gaze, he turns and looks back at me. I'm not sure exactly what I expected to see in his face, but I don't think it was hurt. The way he stares back, the way his eyes meet mine even in the darkness of the auditorium, hits me like a bat to the chest. It makes my lungs seize. Before turning away from me, he frowns and shakes his head once. After that, I don't focus on anything else until I hear my daughters' and Rachel's names being called to the stage.

To say that my girls are hardcore Swifties is an understatement (although there really is no middle ground when it comes to being one). Throughout the worst part of the divorce, her music was the only thing that kept them singing in the car during pick ups, bobbing their heads cheerfully as they did their homework at the kitchen table, and making up dances like the one they're performing tonight during those weekends when they would wait for their father to come and visit them. Her music has been a distraction from the pain of their parents' separation, and for that, I will forever be grateful.

So when I see them take the stage with their close friend in matching sparkly t-shirts, pink tutu skirts over jeans, and pink sneakers, my eyes water, thinking it's only fitting that they close this chapter by performing a dance to a song called *Cruel Summer*. They made it through. *We* made it through the summer. Even though there were moments these last couple of months when I felt like we would never survive, a lot of it was about growth.

But as my eyes flit for a second away from the stage to where Michael stands, enraptured by his daughter, expression filled with pride, my heart breaks. Because my daughters and I didn't make it through this summer alone; we had help from him and Rachel. From the very beginning, Michael and Rachel were there, and despite our rocky start, we stuck through it, worked things out, and later spent almost every day of the season together.

And now that's all over. The little unit we've formed is coming to an end; the girls and I are going back to Colorado, and Michael and Rachel are staying here. And I'm going to miss them more than I ever thought I could.

Once the dance is over, I clap as hard as I can, tears in my eyes. I'm not sure what we have to face next, but I know we'll be able to get through it—I just don't think my heart will be able to survive it if everything Michael and I decided we would build together will never come to be.

Chapter Thirty

MICHAEL

I wait for Rachel just outside the auditorium at our previously-discussed meeting spot, feeling like crawling out of my skin. With the subtlety of a bulldozer, I turn around in place looking for Diana, not sure whether I want to talk to her or avoid her altogether. Sure, last night and this morning before everything happened was amazing, but something about her reaction to Rodrigo's ill-timed arrival told me not to bet my life savings on everything going to plan.

We're supposed to go out to dinner together at the restaurant tonight right after the show. But are we even going out now that this tool was here, or was she going to cancel? Diana wouldn't do that to me, right? Or to Rachel? Or her daughters? She wouldn't abandon our plans last minute for an absentee piece of shit father who decided to show up only because he felt threatened, right?

Rachel saves me from spiraling any further when I catch her running towards me, beaming like I've never seen her before—at least not since her mother passed. "Dad! Did you see? Did you see how cool we were?"

The way she calls me *Dad* will never stop feeling incredible to me.

"It was amazing, kid!" I tell her, squatting and wrapping her tightly in my arms, needing to feel her support likely more than she needs to feel mine now. I squeeze my eyes shut, and relish in this love I never thought I would have or even want. It's horrible to think it took Jessie dying to get this, but I know she'd be happy that what came out of it was this amazing relationship Rachel and I have. "You looked incredible up there! Taylor Swift herself would've been so proud to see the dance."

"And people were singing in the audience! Did you see?"

"I know," I say with a laugh. Even I can admit the song is a banger. "It was amazing."

"Are we headed home first to change, or going straight to dinner?" she asks, practically bouncing with glee. "Because I know the restaurant is kinda-fancy-but-not-fancy but I *really* don't want to change from our costumes because, like, when else are we going to wear them, you know? And I *loooooove* my sparkly sneakers." She looks down at her pink rhinestoned shoes with as much adoration as I feel for her.

"You're *my* kid and that's *my* restaurant. You can dress however you want, and so can the girls."

She beams up at me. "Awesome! I'm gonna go tell Cami and Emi that we can leave them on, then!"

Rachel starts to loosen her grip on my hands to turn and go in search of her friends but I stop her, pulling her back to face me.

"Um, wait. Are... are they with their mom? And dad?" I try not to wince.

Rachel's previously glowing expression fades, her smile drops. "I don't know if their dad is with them... Are you guys breaking up?"

I stand, every muscle in my body tense. "Breaking up? No, I — But— The thing is—" I stop stuttering for a second and take a deep breath. "You knew? That we were together, I mean?"

Rachel rolls her eyes at me—something Diana warned me I

should get ready for before she enters her teenage years—and laughs once. "Dad, it is so obvious you guys, like, love each other." She gags. "I mean, it's kinda cute but also kinda gross?"

"I..." I shake my head, not knowing what to say. She knew? And... *love*?

"Wait, are you not dating? I'm confused."

"No. I mean, yes. I mean, I *think* so." We were. We *are*. We fucking spent almost the entire summer together. Her and I. And the girls. *Us*.

And last night...

"You *think* so?" She frowns, hands on her hips.

I sigh once. "Grown ups are complicated, Rach. But I *think* we are."

She hesitates before smiling once more. "Okay, well that's great, then. Right?"

"Yeah?" I sigh, relief flooding my system. "You think that's great?"

"Yeah! Diana's the best. She was super nice all summer. And I love Cami and Emi. And, like, it would be *so* cool to have sisters, you know? Because I don't have any and—"

"Whoa, hold up. Sisters?" My heart begins a strong gallop, my breathing grows fast and shallow.

Rachel's face falls. "Well, that's why people date, right? To get married? And if you get married, wouldn't that make Cami and Emi kinda like my sisters?"

"I— People don't necessarily date to get *married*. Some people just want companionship, others believe that marriage isn't necessary to make a life-long commitment to someone so they just stay together as partners. There are a ton of reasons not to get married, and a ton to get married. Everyone is different." This is not how I thought this conversation would go and the topic of marriage is not something I thought I would be discussing with my daughter until much later in life—at least not until the whole birds and the bees thing needs to be addressed (god save me when *that* time comes).

Rachel pauses and carefully thinks my words over. "Okay... But, then, what do you want? Do *you* want to get married?"

"Whoa, okay." I take a deep breath and stand, running my fingers through my hair. "I—" I hadn't really thought about it lately, but until recently I lived my entire life finding the idea of me *married* almost hilarious—at least marriage in the conventional way. Committing to one person for the rest of my life? Having to think of someone else's needs other than my own? No, thank you. I was always far too focused on my career and making my own life for that. But now that I've slowed down, that I've seen what it's like to have a family, that I've met someone I really care about... The idea of belonging to someone —to many someones—sounds almost utopian and euphoric. "I don't... think... I mean, I don't *know* if that's something I can answer right now."

Rachel frowns, her brows pulled together. "But... don't you think it'd be so nice to be, like, a family together?"

"*A family*?" Now my heart is on a full sprint, running for its life.

"Rachel!" Cami calls out to my daughter, (thankfully) interrupting our conversation, thereby successfully avoiding a full-blown panic attack.

Rachel pulls away from me and gleefully runs over to her friends, leaving me crouched in the grass, mind racing so fast it could rival the best Formula 1 driver.

And as the seconds tick by, the thought of it—of all of us together—transforms from a nebulous cloud of *ideas* of what a family would look like into a surprising amount of *clear visions* of what it could be for us. What it practically *has* been for us over the summer. Always together, always having each other's back. Always there to care and protect the other, to make sure our children are well and happy.

"Hey, Rach! You were amazing!" Diana's voice cuts through my blissful daydreams and realizations, and suddenly all I want is to tell her that I've finally *got it*. She and I and the girls—that's what we are, what we've become: a family. And there's no fucking way I'm going to let some fucker who doesn't care about his kids come and destabilize that. And how could he, anyway? We're solid. Nothing has changed since we spoke this morning other than his arrival. Our lives are still the same. We're staying together despite the distance and will find a way to make it all work.

With a smile so wide my cheeks almost hurt, I walk quickly over to Diana, determined not to let anything stand in our way. When she sees me walking toward her, her breath catches, eyes widening as if bracing herself. And by the way I looked at her earlier and how I completely avoided her, I can understand the expression in her eyes. But she has nothing to worry about.

When I finally reach my love, I lean down and press a kiss on her cheek, wrapping an arm around her waist to pull her flush into my side as I inhale her signature scent of peaches and summer and absolute perfection.

"Don't worry," I whisper in her ear. "I know I was upset before, but I was just jealous you kicked me out over him. But it's okay, I get it now. He's their father, and you had to deal. We have our whole lives to be together."

I move to meet her gaze, expecting to find the same love and adoration I currently feel overwhelmed by. Instead, her shoulders are hunched inwards, brows pulled together as she looks up at me with apologetic eyes.

"What?" I whisper again, hoping the girls don't catch on to our distress. "What's wrong? God, is it Rodrigo? Did he do something?" I look around, desperately trying to find him. When I catch him a few feet away flirting with a counselor ten years his junior, I make to confront him for whatever he did to upset Diana.

But she holds me back, wrapping a hand around my bicep. "Stop. He didn't do anything."

I take a beat, studying her expression. "Then I'm confused. Why do you look like a puppy died or something?"

"I… I'm—" She looks around us as if searching for help, but I keep my eyes on her, ignoring the hustle and bustle of parents congratulating children on their performances. "I'm just stressed, you know? With their dad here?" she says only loud enough for me to hear before glancing at Cami and Emi. "It's kind of left me rattled."

"Do you want me to ask him to leave?" *I really wouldn't mind kicking that guy to the curb.*

"No, it's fine. The girls should spend some time with him. Even though he seems to be preoccupied with something else at the moment," she says, looking over her shoulder where Rodrigo is currently performing the "wall lean" for an entirely *different* counselor.

"Yeah, well. Then we should invite him to dinner, right?" See? I can play nice. Look at me being all mature, putting what I want aside for the needs of Diana's girls. Because even though I hate to admit it, having Rodrigo here *is* what's best for them after months of nothing but crickets.

"You'd do that for me?"

I nod. "Of course. But if I'm being honest, it's mostly for Cami and Emi. I care about them, too, you know? I hate to admit it, but they should spend time with their dad. Even though I think he's a dick and he's only chosen to show up now, after all this time."

Diana shakes her head, a small smile on her lips. "Michael," she whispers.

For some wild reason, I've never wanted to kiss her more. Maybe it's because everyone knows we're together now (kind of) or that I got the green light from Rachel. Or maybe it's just the high of standing here with a whole future ahead of us. Sure, there's still so much to figure out, but that's the exciting part. Because there's no bone in my body that's telling me that this isn't right.

"I want to kiss you wildly," I confess in a low voice, "and it's taking everything in me not to."

This makes her laugh once, her cheeks flushing. "Not gonna lie, I'd love that. But it's a pass for obvious reasons." She nods towards the girls who are still talking about the dance, about coordinating another one as soon as possible. "I still haven't had the chance to really address what we are with them. And given that Cami was the one to tell Rodrigo about us... I need to proceed with caution. But yeah, I want that, too."

I sigh, a bit frustrated, a bit thrilled.

"What's the plan now?" Rodrigo's voice comes up behind us, his entitled tone grating.

I control my features, though, since all three girls follow close behind him.

The tension between the two of us is obvious—especially when Diana pulls away, breaking herself free from my hold. I try not to take it personally, to feel hurt, however... It's easier said than done. But I get it. It's obvious the girls know about us now, but we still haven't discussed what a relationship together will look like or how they feel about it.

"Well, we were going to go to Michael's new restaurant to have an early dinner," Diana tells him.

"You have a restaurant?" He raises a brow as if he needs to see it to believe it.

"I do, actually. Just opened it yesterday."

"You opened it yesterday, and you can just take your second day off like that?"

I grit my teeth. "This is an important day for the girls. I wasn't going to let anything come between me and my family."

Rodrigo doesn't like my answer, hearing every single layer of subtext I managed to include in that statement.

"You already knew about the restaurant. I told you this morning," Diana hisses at him.

Clearly he's just trying to get a rise out of me, but I won't let him win.

"You should come," I tell Rodrigo, trying to be the bigger man, lightening the tone of my voice when I see Diana tensing beside me.

"Yes, *Papi,* come!" Emi cuts in.

Rodrigo scoffs. "Of course I'm going to come. I'm here to see my daughters." Ironic, since he doesn't even address them when he speaks. Instead, he keeps his narrowed eyes on me. "The real question is whether we're going to accept your plan or not, not the other way around."

"*We*? Excuse me? Going to dinner after the talent show was something *Diana, the girls, and I* agreed upon *weeks* ago. Before you even got here. So, yeah. It *is* this way. You *may* join us."

"*Papi.*" Cami tugs at her father's hand, but he barely acknowledges her.

Diana puts a hand on my chest, her eyes pleading when she says "Michael, *please.* The girls," she whispers glancing nervously at where Cami and Emi stand, their faces devastated.

Immediately, I feel like shit. Because I care about them, and they don't need to see me and their father argue, they don't need to see their mother caught in the middle. I mean, for fuck's sake, we haven't even sat down as a family to discuss what me dating their mother means, and we're already fighting.

I need to reel it in, even if Rodrigo is a total asshole.

Filled with irritation, I take a deep breath, slap a smile on my face, and state "Let's go eat, then."

Chapter Thirty-One

DIANA

I STARE DOWN AT THE BEAUTIFULLY PLATED TOMATO, cucumber, and feta salad in front of me with a sense of despair. It sounds like a simple enough dish, but something about the vinaigrette Michael created and the quality of the ingredients he used made me fall in love with it when I first tried it last night. Today, though, I can't appreciate the way the rich cherry tomatoes' flavor bursts in my mouth, or the freshness of the cucumber and its satisfying crunch. I can't relish in the sweet and tangy dressing that had my tastebuds wanting more of something so simple yet beautiful. And I know I won't even get to enjoy the entree and dessert I ordered, either. There are no words to describe how amazing last night's dinner was, or how excited I was to have more of Michael's amazing food with our girls, and now it's been ruined by my ex.

My ex who cannot stop making snide comments or remarks.

My ex who keeps trying to belittle the amazing work Michael and Lexi put into this endeavor by using backhanded compliments like "cute restaurant" and "the food is *so* simple" and "did you guys run out of cash, or did you mean to decorate the place like this?".

My ex who hasn't spoken to his daughters all summer but tries to gaslight us all into thinking there was nothing wrong and he was just "busy." Luckily, none of us buys it—not even the girls, I don't think.

My eyes flash to Michael, whose muscles are wound so tight it's a wonder he can even breathe. His eyes are on his plate as he grits his teeth while we are all forced to listen to the Rodrigo show.

"...So anyway, after that weekend Elizabeth and I spent in Palm Springs, we decided we should visit the West Coast more. So I was thinking you girls—Cami and Emi—should come on a trip with us the next time we go."

"Whoa, hold on." I say, raising a hand. "Elizabeth? I thought your girlfriend's name was Katie."

Rodrigo purses his lips and takes a sip of his drink before responding. "That didn't work out. Katie grew a bit too... attached."

I scoff. "So who's this new woman, then?"

"Just someone I met through work. She's an intern through our company's MBA program."

"*An intern*? Rodrigo, really?"

He groans. "Here we go again. Another made up drama for your Lifetime movie." Rodrigo rolls his eyes and takes another sip of his wine. "She's twenty-four. An adult. It's not the end of the fucking world, Diana," he hisses.

"It's not even about her age. It's so inappropriate! And I'm not letting you take my daughters on a trip with a woman I've never met."

"Oh, like you fucking this dude right here is any different? Or did you not let him spend the entire summer with my girls?"

I gasp, appalled. Between the language he used and the blatant disrespect in front of his kids and Michael and Rachel, I don't even know where to start. But even though I want to go off on him, I can't tell him he's wrong. I *did* leave them alone with

Michael when I left for New York, and he took them to the aquarium.

Still, I open my mouth to let him have it, but catch the look on my girls' faces before I do. Devastation. Stress. The beginning of tears building in both their eyes. So I grit my teeth and bite back the words that beg to be spoken.

Michael pushes back from the table, the legs of the chair scraping across the floor in a way that makes most patrons turn to look at us with nervous curiosity. "Rodrigo? I think we should step outside for a moment."

"What? Michael, *no*." My stomach drops—it twists and turns. The Michael I know today would never start a physical fight, but I know he has a past. I know he was a troublemaker when he was a teenager (a bit of a euphemism based on the stories he told me). So I anxiously reach over and take his wrist in my hand, doing my best to pull him back down. "Please," I beg.

"Fuck, yeah. Finally. Let's do this." Rodrigo gets to his feet and rubs his hands together like a villain in an old school spy movie. "I'm going to kick your ass."

"*Papi*, no! What are you doing?" Cami tugs on her dad's shirt and tries to pull him down, but he's an unmovable force, his rage blinding him to the fact that his little girl is even speaking to him. Emi cries in earnest now, unrelenting tears building. But it isn't their father who calms them down.

Michael runs over to where they're both seated and crouches beside them. "Hey," he tells them in a soft, soothing voice, grabbing one of their hands in each of his. "No one's going to fight anyone. I just want to talk to your dad for a second." His eyes flit to mine. "I promise."

But Rodrigo scoffs, making me believe that, though Michael has no intention of starting something, he may have to finish it. "Yeah, okay," my ex says with a sarcastic laugh. "Let's *talk*."

Chapter Thirty-Two

MICHAEL

It's already 6 PM, but the sun and the temperature are still high on this late August evening. You wouldn't be able to tell by the gorgeous day we had today, but fall is fast-approaching, and with it, the end of the most incredible summer of my life. The sadness of it has become a near-constant ache in my chest, but I put it aside for now when I lead Rodrigo to the side of the restaurant to have a little talk.

"By 'talk' I legitimately meant '*talk*,'" I clarify once we're face-to-face and alone.

His face droops slightly in disappointment, which shocks me. If I'm honest, despite knowing everything I know about Rodrigo, I wouldn't have *really* pegged him for someone violent. Especially not in this case, when I feel like I'm more justified in my anger than he is. He mistreated the woman I love and neglected their children, whom I also care deeply about. Rodrigo, on the other hand, is only angry because I exist. Because by me being there for Diana and his daughters, he's no longer needed. And narcissists don't like to feel irrelevant.

"Talk? That's all you want to do?" He scoffs. "I should've known Diana's next pick would be a beta."

I grit my teeth, not letting him bait me even though there's nothing I would love more than to show him just how bad this *beta* could fuck him up.

I cross my arms in front of my chest in an effort to restrain myself. "I'm not going to fight you."

"Why the hell not?"

"First of all, because it would upset Emi and Cami, and they've been through enough trauma. Second, it would upset Diana, and I really don't want to hurt her. And third... well, honestly, I don't think it's worth the effort."

He snorts. "So Diana isn't worth the effort?"

"No, that's not what I meant. Diana is worth *everything*. But beating your ass—and make no mistake, I could very easily beat your ass—is not worth sore knuckles, *or* upsetting the girls."

Rodrigo rolls his eyes. "Yeah, okay, sure."

But I'm not going to argue about this. It's dumb and a waste of my time and completely irrelevant.

"I want to talk about what you're *really* doing here."

"What I'm doing here?" He raises a brow. "I'm here to see my daughters at camp. To visit my wife."

"*Ex*-wife. And based on your performance this summer, it doesn't seem like you give two shits about your daughters. Or Diana, for that matter."

"Oh, and you do give a shit about my daughters?"

"Abso-fucking-lutely I do." And I mean it. Over the last two and a half months, I've gotten to see how amazing Diana's daughters are. How smart Emi is, how passionate Cami can be. Both of them so strong, both overcoming their own set of challenges at such a young age. And while I know Cami must've felt conflicted about whatever role she thought I was playing in their lives, I know she didn't mean to harm me or her mom by telling her dad about us. I know she didn't intend for drama to follow. She's just a kid, struggling to manage a mess created by adults. And I won't fault her for that.

"Please," he scoffs. "This isn't serious. Diana's only with you because she's upset I've moved on—"

"Several times over, apparently."

"—and she can't deal. So she just picked the first guy who showed some interest in her. And you—you were probably just looking for a summer fling and a baby sitter for your kid. Because that's what she did, right? Helped you with your daughter all summer?" He snickers. "This whole thing is temporary and a joke."

"It's not a fucking joke. And we're going to make it last. I'm going to be part of Diana and Cami and Emi's lives, which means you need to get used to me. It's why I'm trying to have a civilized conversation here, but you're making it increasingly difficult."

"What? You're gonna try long-distance with Diana? *Please.*" He scoffs.

"This is real," I say through gritted teeth.

"Oh, sure," he says sardonically. "I'm positive it will all work out, despite the thousands of miles between you two. *And* the time difference. And the fact that both of you have children and are therefore not a flexible schedule. *Please.* This is ridiculous and all you're going to end up doing is hurting my daughters. You two won't last more than a month."

"You don't know what you're talking about. I love her," I tell him, feeling it in every inch of my body, every atom that makes up my being and soul.

Rodrigo's expression shifts into one of fury, his hands fisting at his sides. But it isn't the murderous look on his face that makes my stomach drop. It's the sharp gasp I hear behind me.

"Michael," Diana whispers.

I curse under my breath and squeeze my eyes shut before turning to face her.

"Michael," she says again. "You love me?"

This is definitely not how I wanted things to go down.

"I do." My heart races in my chest, beating so loudly I can hear it in my ears, but I don't hesitate to make it clear. What's the point? I love her and there's no going back. I wouldn't even want to.

A goofy grin spreads across Diana's face, eyes widening as she takes a step toward me. Suddenly, the distance between us grows intolerable, so I pull her to me and wind my arms around her waist. "I love you, Diana. I've loved you for a really long time, I think. It kinda started off real slow? But it's built into something I can barely parse into words."

I think I hear Rodrigo mock-gagging in the background, but it's hard to pay attention to anything else when I'm holding her like this, and she's looking up at me like she feels the same way.

Except she doesn't say it back. Why isn't she saying it back?

My smile falls when hers does, Diana's expression morphing from one of happiness and joy, to one of... dismay?

"I... Thank you *so* much, Michael," she says, with a forced smile.

The pain is insurmountable—I've never known anything like it. All of a sudden, I struggle to breathe. To string a set of words together well enough to form a sentence.

Rodrigo bursts out laughing. "What a priceless moment. God, I'm so happy I was here for this."

I ignore him. I'd like to say it's by choice, but most of my energy right now is going into *not* showing Diana just how hurt I am by what she said—or didn't say.

"Michael, I—"

"Shh, it's okay," I whisper, before pressing a soft kiss to her forehead. Because it is. There's still a chance she feels the same way and doesn't want to discuss this in front of this idiot. "We can talk later. When we're alone." I cup her cheek and smile down at her.

Diana swallows once—hard. "Thank you," she whispers.

"Who did you leave the girls with?" I ask.

"Lexi. She stopped by, saw I was a little distressed, and told me I should stop you guys from getting into a dumb fight," she whispers.

I smile. She's so adorable. "Baby, it was never going to get to that point. I would never have let it," I whisper.

"Now that we've cleared up she doesn't care about you that way, can we wrap things up?" Rodrigo cuts in. "What the hell are you doing out here, Diana? Michael and I came outside to settle this like men. Or I guess that's what I thought, before he backed out of a fight," Rodrigo says, crossing his arms in front of his chest.

"It was never going to be a fucking fight. I just wanted to talk," I remind him, reluctantly letting go of Diana to face him.

He rolls his eyes.

"Well, I came out to make sure it *wouldn't* evolve into a stupid fight. And also to let you know that your daughters are inside asking why their father, whom they haven't seen or spoken to in months, is suddenly looking *very* angry with Michael."

"As if they give a shit about Michael."

"They do, actually. Very much," Diana says, straightening her spine. Pride and love fills my chest. Knowing the feeling is mutual—at least with the girls—really is incredible.

"Please. He's nothing to them. Just your fucking boyfriend."

"He's been there for them, too, this entire summer—not just for me."

"I don't feel comfortable with the fact that you've let a man be this close to my daughters without asking me. Without me having met him first. That's fucked, Diana. And I expected better from you."

I take a step toward him, suddenly rethinking not kicking his ass, but Diana pulls me back.

"I need to talk to him alone," she tells me. "Would you mind going back inside? Plus, I'm sure Lexi can't afford to babysit our kids while we argue like children in the restaurant parking lot."

I glare at Rodrigo, then stare back at her before nodding. I take a deep breath and tell her, "Okay. But let me know if you need anything whatsoever. From a snide comeback, to an ass-kicking, I'm your guy."

A hint of a smile begins to form on her lips. "Noted."

I go in to place a peck on her lips, but decide to really go for it last minute. Diana and I are not ones for PDA, but this feels different. The caveman side of my brain needs to claim her—especially in front of this asshole—and this seems like the easiest way to make sure everyone knows she's mine. At least in this moment.

"Good luck," I whisper against her lips before walking away, leaving her breathless.

Chapter Thirty-Three

DIANA

Since it's clear Rodrigo is only hear to sow chaos, I manage to convince him to go back to Colorado after some back-and-forth—without saying goodbye to Cami and Emi. They've had enough drama from their father for one day, to the point where I felt an Irish exit might be easier on them than a dragged out goodbye.

Rodrigo being Rodrigo, he doesn't leave without imparting some kind of emotional destruction, of course. It was while we were waiting for his Uber that would take him back to the pool house to pick up his things that he managed to get in my head:

"You're letting Cami and Emi get attached to Michael when the relationship isn't going to amount to anything is cruel for everyone involved," he said.

"You don't know that. This thing between Michael and me—it isn't casual."

"Come on, Diana. Jokes and dickish comments aside, you don't *actually* believe this is going to work, do you?"

"Why wouldn't it?" I ground my teeth and crossed my arms in front of my chest, ready to respond to every single challenge he threw back at me.

"Well, let's start with the most glaringly obvious reason: you live in Colorado and he lives out here. And before you think about moving as an option, let me nip that in the bud: I'm not going to let you just take Cami and Emi out of state if things ever get serious between you two. They're my daughters, too, and they belong close to their father. So you can pretend all you want that you can make things last between the two of you, but it's not going to happen. He has his roots set here and you have them there.

"Second, I *know* you. I know there's no fucking way you're going to be able to be relaxed enough to have a long-distance relationship. I give it three months *max* before it all blows up. Before you drive each other crazy."

"What the hell is *that* supposed to mean?"

He shrugged, unbothered. "Just that I know how you can get. How abrasive and... *overwhelming*. Obnoxious up there on your high fucking horse. It won't be too long before he's asking you for space. Which will cause the opposite effect, of course. Because your type-A personality would just kick in and you'd try to *fix* everything, and end up making it worse. Imagine our marriage heightened by the stress of distance."

It was like getting kicked me in the chest. I wasn't really *that* horrible was I? I felt the stinging build in my eyes as I thought about the years I'd wasted on a man whois simultaneously calculatingly cruel and indifferent.

"I didn't *stray*—as your lawyer so kindly put it—because you were the world's best wife." Rodrigo looked at me expectantly. "This can't be news to you. I mean, yes, I fucked up. I cheated. But, you—you weren't exactly *perfect*, Diana. You were... demanding. Naggy. And, frankly, exhausting."

I knew what he was doing. I knew that he was trying to mess with my mind and my heart. And yet...

Every single word that came out of his mouth cut me like one of Michael's super sharp, super fancy knives. *"You have to be careful with them,"* he'd explained on one of the many nights he cooked us dinner. "*Because they're less dangerous than owning a dull knife, of course. But if you do accidentally cut yourself... Well, it'll be deep. And they're so damn sharp, at first, you don't even realize you've hurt yourself until the entire damn cutting board is covered in blood.*"

So when Rodrigo's words hit my ears, my first instinct was to laugh at his sad attempt to throw me off. But somehow he managed to weasel himself into my head. Into my heart. Somehow, his words wrapped around my brain and convinced me that he's right. That even though I *know* he's telling me all this to hurt me, he isn't exactly wrong.

"You're going to fuck things up. And it's going to fuck things up for my daughters, too. They're already too attached to the loser. My advice? End it. End it before they get even more attached. You're going to hurt Emi and Cami. And haven't they been through enough?"

I looked away, hating how much Rodrigo's words made sense in my head. Because he's right. The girls *have* grown attached—to Rachel and Michael. *I've* grown attached. And I'm not the easiest person to be in a relationship with. Especially not now. Not after everything.

As soon as I walk back into the restaurant, my eyes fall on our table. On the easy way Michael and Rachel and Emi and Cami interact. On the way he tells Cami, "This is the veggie dish I made you a couple of weeks ago."

"Oh, yeah," she says softly, smiling up at him. "I really liked that one."

He beams down at her. "It's why I put it on the menu. You guys are my toughest critics, so I thought if it was a winner with *you*, then..."

Emi giggles. "I'm not sure I would call you a *winner* just yet..."

Michael brings his hands to his chest, mock-dying from a gunshot wound, I suppose. "You're killing me."

"*Da-ad,*" Rachel whines, rolling her eyes.

And it's such a beautiful scene. Such a lovely, glorious scene.

I want to cry.

I do cry.

I cry because I want it. I want it every day of my life starting from this very second. I want him and Rachel and us together.

Family, I think. *This is family*.

And while I had exactly that growing up, it never translated into the one I tried to have with Rodrigo. He was lazy and neglectful —Weaponized Incompetency was his middle name. So I grew resentful and bitter. Tired of having everything fall on my shoulders *constantly*. Tired of always being the one taking care of everyone.

I've never truly had the familial experience I had this summer—only as a child. And even then, I was held responsible for my little sisters' actions. Asked to teach them how to act, make sure they were okay. That they were acclimating to the US as best as possible. I was parent 2.5, it feels like.

And now that I have a taste for it—the perfect partner, with the exceptional kids—I'm on the precipice of losing it all. Be it in one, two, six months—even a year—or now.

Now would be better.

Now would be the best thing for all of us.

Now would mean less of a mess—as clean a break as we can get.

It would save us time. Pain. Arguments and discussions. A lot of heartache.

It would upset the girls at first, I think. But over time, they'd see it would be for the best. They can remain long-distance friends without the pressures of having their parents be in a relationship. Without having the subconscious instinct to pick sides.

Rodrigo is right—letting Cami and Emi grow attached only to have another man they love disappear would be a nightmare. Too much for them to bear. And while I won't shoulder the entirety of the blame for the divorce—not even the majority of it—this would absolutely be on me.

Chapter Thirty-Four

MICHAEL

"Hey," I greet Diana with a smile. But something's wrong. I can tell as soon as my eyes meet hers.

"Hey. How's everything?"

"Good." I smile again, but this time it's forced. "We were just talking about the food. And Emi was asking me questions about the cooking process."

She looks at her daughter. "Oh, yeah? You into cooking now?"

Emi blushes and looks down at the table. "I mean, it's kinda cool. After Michael forced us to watch those episodes of that kid cooking show—"

I scoff. "*Forced*? You wish." My chest fills with pride, but I try to hide it. No need to tell a bunch of preteens I'm emotional over them liking *Masterchef Junior*.

Emi smiles a little. "*Anyway*, I thought it looked a little cool. So Michael was just explaining how he made it."

"That's amazing. What was your favorite part?" Diana's all smiles and enthusiasm for the food as Emi talks.

After, she congratulates the girls once again for their performance in the talent show, but the light in her eyes isn't there. The one that shone brightly in the dead of night in her bedroom as I made love to her the night before. Sure, it faded with Rodrigo's arrival, but it was still present. Now, though...

She fake-smiles through the rest of dinner, and apologizes to her daughters on behalf of their father for having to leave so soon without saying goodbye, leaving me with so much intrigue, it's almost painful. Cami and Emi take it better than I would've ever expected. And while I'm happy they aren't distraught and wailing, a sheen of tears the only sign of their sadness, something about the mildness in their reaction is louder than any tantrum could've been. It means they're used to being disappointed by him. In my opinion, that's even more heartbreaking since they deserve the goddamn world. They deserve to feel loved.

Diana's gaze flits to mine, and I finally see it. The anxiety. The concern. The clear signal that something isn't right. Before, she was hiding it. Now, it's obvious she's close to losing her grip.

Fuck.

What did he say to her? What did he do?

A fire lights within, blazing through my veins. I don't even know for sure what happened, but I know he's left, and she's upset, and that's enough of a reason for me to want to hunt him down and really teach him a lesson.

I won't though. Not that way, at least.

I've grown since my teens and twenties, and I know better than to fuck around and find out by starting a physical fight with anyone. No matter how much they deserve to have their nose punched in.

"Michael, can we go check out the kitchen? Lexi told us she'd show us around once we were done with dessert." Emi looks up at me with hope and excitement in her eyes.

I have a strict "No kids allowed in the back while the restaurant is open" rule, but if I don't get a few seconds alone to find out what that asshole said or did to Diana any time soon,

I'm going to lose it. So I put my trust in Lexi, tell the girls to stay clear of the chefs, warn them not to get burnt, and let all three go behind the kitchen doors in search of their next adventure.

"What's going on?" I ask Diana in a low voice, unsuccessfully keeping the panic out of my voice.

She shakes her head. "Nothing. Just... had to send him home."

I frown, going stone cold. There's obviously more to the story. But why isn't she sharing? "What happened? What did he say? What did he *do*?" I can hear the frustration in my voice. *Just tell me.*

"He didn't do anything. It was just... hard. It's always hard with him, you know?"

My stomach rolls, blood running cold. "Do you—" I stop. Swallow hard, twice. "Do you still have feelings for him?"

Mercifully, Diana snorts. "*God*, no."

"Then..."

She sighs deeply, as if trying to expel every single thing that weighs heavily on her chest. "Just... We talked about some things that were difficult. Things I need to process."

I groan. "Come on, Diana. You're being cryptic, and I have no idea why. You're shutting me out."

She bites her lower lip and looks away, but I don't miss the way her eyes sparkle with the sheen of incoming tears.

"What the—" I get up from my chair and take the seat beside her, scooting closer until my face is just inches away. "Diana," I whisper, taking her hands in mine. "What's going on? What did that fucker say? I'll fucking kill him."

She sniffs and looks back at me—*finally*—with a half-hearted smile. "Don't be silly."

"I would," I say, my voice gravelly. "I'd do anything for you."

Her face twists as if in pain at my words, and when a few

tears fall down her cheeks, she quickly wipes them away. "Don't. Don't say that, please."

I lean back in my chair, and stare back at her a little in shock. Suddenly, I realize what's happening here. It isn't a Diana-and-Rodrigo thing. It's an *us* thing. Diana-and-*Michael* thing.

"I'll say it if I mean it. And I do." I tighten my grip on her hands, pull myself closer to her, trying to communicate as best I can that I mean what I say. That I'm not like her loser ex-husband who is going to abandon her and her kids. That I'm going to be there for her and them in more ways than one. I'm here for good, and she needs to get used to it. "I'd do anything for you and the girls."

But something about mentioning Cami and Emi makes the whole thing worse, because her tears come freely now; she doesn't even try to hide them anymore.

"Baby," I whisper, bringing her hands to my lips. "What's wrong? Why does that upset you?"

She inhales sharply, a little ragged. Diana struggles to look me in the eye and speak at the same time, so I pull her in my arms. Holding her as she cries, I run my fingers through her loose curls, the scent of her hair filling my lungs.

God, how I wish I could bottle it up and smell it all day.

I look around nervously, making sure my restaurant patrons can't hear us. But when I catch a couple of people glancing our way, I pull Diana up to her feet and lead her into the office I share with Lexi.

"So we can speak privately," I tell her when I lock the door behind us. The last thing her girls need is to find their mother in tears minutes after Rodrigo's departure.

I maneuver Diana into a chair and crouch in front of her as she cries—more quietly, now. I place my hands on her smooth thighs to balance myself, but mostly it's just to connect. The need to feel her, to make sure she's real, is visceral.

I wait for the tears to stop almost completely, before speaking. "Will you please tell me what's going on? I know he left, and that's why you're crying, but—"

"That's not why I'm crying," she finally speaks, her voice breaking once.

I shake my head. "Then I don't understand. What happened? Is it something he said? Because if he hurt you..." My hands fist on her thighs, but I stretch them out once again, not wanting to lose control.

"I was the one who asked him to leave."

"Oh." That's... interesting. "Can I ask why? I mean, I know he's a pain in the ass, and believe me when I say I'm not sad to see him go. But I'm confused. I thought you wanted him around so the girls could spend time with him—especially since the fucker completely ghosted them this summer."

She winces. "I know. I know I should've let him stay because they missed him and he's their father but... But they don't need to see us fighting again. And they don't need to see more conflict."

"What were you fighting about?"

She shakes her head. "Dumb stuff." But she can't look me in the eye when she answers.

And since I'm not an idiot, I ask, "Was it about me? Were you arguing about me?" Because of course the guy is jealous. Three months of radio silence and suddenly he shows up as soon as his daughter mentions my existence in one of her letters? Come on.

She bites her lower lip. Another tear streaks down her cheek. "Yes," she admits in a whisper. "He's... he's not happy about us."

Bile rising in my throat, I scoot closer to her, my grip unconsciously tightening around her legs, preparing myself to keep her here before the universe tries to take her away from me.

"Why would he be? He's a narcissist who can't get over the fact that his gorgeous, brilliant, incredible ex-wife is moving on. To add insult to injury, this man she's moving on with—*me*—also cares deeply about said narcissist's daughters."

"Yeah."

I cup her face in my hands, dig my fingers in her hair, and bring her closer to me to press a kiss on her lips. Diana's hands come up to grip my shoulders, nails digging into me through the fabric. I groan, because I don't hate it one bit. Part of me wants her to mark me. Part of me wants a reminder that she was there everywhere I go.

Before the kiss deepens too much, I pull away but keep my forehead pressed to hers. We're quiet as we try to catch our breath, and it takes a minute. After all, one kiss is enough to light a fire inside us both.

"What exactly did he say about us that upset you so much?" I ask.

She scrunches her eyes shut for a few seconds before pulling away. "Nothing I didn't already know."

"Come on, Dee. Just tell me before I fucking go crazy here."

She shrugs once. "That we're not going to make it, Michael."

I think she calls my name, asks me if I'm okay, but my heartbeat is loud in my ears, and I can barely process what she just said. Because she told me she already knew the things Rodrigo upset her with. Which means she thinks we're not going to work out. And that's just... unacceptable.

I shake her off and pace in front of my desk. She gets up and catches me by the elbow, forcing me to look at her.

"*Michael.*"

"So you agree with him? You don't think we're going to make it?" I can hear the tremble in my voice, something I think

I've only experienced once in my life. The night I found out Jessie had died and Rachel was coming home with me.

"*I can't take her. I'm not meant to be a dad. This is a horrible idea. Find someone else,*" I begged Rachel's grandparents over the phone. It was a plea from a desperate man. The sound of pure denial and fear of a life you never imagined for yourself—one you believed with your whole being you never wanted. Yes, having Rachel come into my life as my daughter turned out to be the most incredible thing that ever happened to me. But I have a feeling that losing Diana will be the worst. I have a feeling I won't recover.

"I... I care about you. *Deeply.*" Her voice is shaky, her lips trembling. "B—"

"Do not say *but.* If you value my sanity, Diana, do not tell me there is a *but.*" I can barely get the words out, my lungs feel so constricted. "If you care about me deeply, do not tell me there isn't a way to work things out. Because we can do anything together."

"Michael." She takes a deep breath, and I know she's steeling herself to shatter my heart. "Michael, this isn't going to work out. I think we should break up."

No.

Chapter Thirty-Five

DIANA

The pain in Michael's face is clear and heartbreaking. Earth shattering. It burns every inch of my body, pummels every ounce of my soul, and pierces through my heart so sharply I can barely finish telling him how I feel. I'm sure it mirrors the look on my face, too.

But what I need to tell him and what comes next are necessary, because I know that if I let myself fall deeper than I already am—and I know I could—there's no way I would ever recover. The way I feel about Michael is stronger than anything I ever felt for any other man, and while right now I cannot fathom ever feeling this way for anyone else, I have to end it.

"You want to break up?" he asks. "Baby, we've barely even started! What the hell is going on? Tell me, because I'm going out of my mind. Did we not decide last night that we were going to try? Did we not agree that this was worth the trouble we knew long-distance was going to be? That we care enough about each other to try and make this work?" He runs both his hands through his hair, a wild look of desperation in his eyes. "I don't understand how you could be so callous about this."

"Callous?" I scoff. "I'm being the complete opposite. I feel like we're being callous in thinking this could work. In not considering how much this could hurt everyone involved. I'm not just talking about you and me, you know. Cami and Emi and Rachel... They love each other, too. And when this doesn't work out—"

"*When*? What do you mean *when*?" he hisses. "I have no intention of us not working out."

"You say that now," I say, taking his hands in mine. I want to comfort him just as much as I need his comfort. "But what about when we're a few months in and we're arguing all the time, or we're frustrated over not being able to see each other as often as we'd like? Or when the stress of the restaurant or of me navigating a completely different life starts to bleed into every single interaction we have? And where do you expect this to go, exactly? Because while I'd love to think this long-distance relationship will be enough, we both know we're not living in a damn fairytale, Michael. I mean, I can't leave Colorado—Rodrigo made it perfectly clear he'd never even entertain the idea of letting me take the girls out of state—and you *just* opened a restaurant in Long Island. How is this ever supposed to work? What is our end game?"

"Is that what he told you?" Michael practically growls. "He's holding the girls over your head legally to keep us away from each other?"

I grimace. "He didn't say that. He just doesn't want me to take his girls to the other side of the country—understandably so. He'd never get to see Cami and Emi."

"What difference would it make? He never sees them now. And it's of his own making. But suddenly, the mere suggestion that you might *eventually* want to move on with your life to be with someone else is a ridiculous notion and completely unacceptable? And yeah, maybe you'll never be able to move out of Colorado, but that doesn't mean that me and Rachel can't move out there. Why wouldn't we if we eventually decide to try and make it work as a real family?"

My breath hitches, the mention of us having a life together, really trying to turn this into a tangible, real thing—a *family*—is... the biggest fantasy I could've ever dreamed up. The idea of Michael and Rachel moving out there sounds like a dream but one that could easily turn into a nightmare.

"What if you do move? What if you uproot your lives and realize when you get to Colorado that it's not working out? That you moved halfway across the country for nothing. You take a chance on a relationship that was never going to work out, then, we will have hurt not just each other, but definitely done a lot of damage to our kids. *Especially* Rachel, since you'd be submitting her to a life-changing move. What if you make this huge life decision, and it all goes to hell?"

"And what if it fucking doesn't?" he roars, eyes wild and desperate, throwing his arms open wide. "What if it's the best decision we'll ever make? What if it's everything we've ever wanted and never dreamed to ask? What if we take this chance and finally accept that we're meant to be together? To be a family. To love and fight and laugh and fuck and live the rest of our lives as a team. What if you and me, and Rachel and your girls, are endgame, and you're throwing it all away over some irrational fear your ex-husband has somehow managed to get you to believe in? I love you, goddamn it, and we belong together. And there's nothing you can do or say that will convince me otherwise." His red eyes shine with the threat of tears. It tears me apart.

I feel the warmth of my own tears stream down my cheeks as I watch him breathe heavily. So strong and wild but utterly breakable before me.

"I love you, too," I finally admit, my voice barely a whisper.

Michael exhales in relief, as if hearing me say the words has released him from a built up tension that had him in a choke hold.

"But this can't go on." My voice breaks as the tears come faster, my breathing becomes a bit harder. "I—I can't risk all the hurt. My daughters have had enough of it."

"Your daughters or you? Either way, I'd never do *anything* to hurt you guys." He sniffs once, runs his hands through his hair, a wild man searching for a grip on reality.

"I know you'd never purposely do so, Michael. C'mon."

"Then what makes you believe I would ever let you go? What makes you believe I'd let this happen? Because us breaking up? Yeah, that's going to cause a world of hurt. To you. To me. And to our daughters."

"The girls will remain good friends. We'll make sure of it. And because I know you'll never let go... Well, it means I'm going to have to be the one to set us both free."

Michael inhales sharply before pulling me close. His hands dig into my hair at the nape of my neck, our faces mere centimeters apart. "Why are you doing this to us? Stop." His voice breaks, a desperate plea that destroys any chance at peace. "You're hurting us. Why? Just, please, Diana. Please stop," he whispers against my lips.

I do my best to turn away, to avoid his kiss. But I'm only human, and resisting him is impossible. He presses his lips to mine and winds one hand tightly around my waist, while the other digs into my hair, his grip firm and commanding.

The kiss is devastating yet hopeful. It rips me to shreds—breaks me into a thousand pieces and puts me back together—a constant series of contradictions, just like our entire relationship has been.

When his tongue presses to my lips and the kiss intensifies, I run my hands up his arms, feeling the corded muscles of his biceps beneath my fingertips. I'll miss the way those muscles, born out of hours of manual labor and hard work, felt like the safest and softest place I'd ever had the absolute pleasure to be in. I'll miss his plain white t-shirts, and the way he made them look almost luxurious. I'll miss his heartbreaking smile and the way he laughs at my quirks. Most of all, I'll miss the loyalty and devotion I see in his eyes—to his daughter, to my girls, and to me.

"You can't take this away from me, Diana. You can't take it away from *us*. It isn't fair," he breathes against my neck before placing a kiss at the base of my throat. He follows it with a harder-than normal bite.

I sob once before pulling his face back to mine, wanting to pour every bit of myself into him. Wanting to give him every part of my heart and soul for safekeeping. He can have it all. He can take every piece of me and keep it. After all, who else am I going to give it to? I know, even after only a few weeks of seriously dating, that I will never love another man the way I love Michael. It's how I know he'll never love anyone else as much as he loves me.

I want to give him everything. Instead, I'm taking it all away.

When his hands travel down the back of my thighs to pick me up and drop me onto his desk, I put a hand on his chest to stop him.

"Not right now. Not *here*." Is he crazy?

"Why not now?" he asks, making quick work of the button and zipper of my shorts, tugging them down in one swift movement. "I need you. I want to show you how much I love you. And you're so fucking beautiful and—*Fuck*, Diana."

"I—" I start, but am distracted by the speed at which he removes his pants, the way he makes room for himself in between my legs. The way his cock is hard and wet at the tip, eager to make its mark—to claim me. "We're in your office. In a restaurant. I'm sure this violates more than a few health codes."

"Fuck the health codes," he growls, kissing up my neck as he drags the tip of his cock over my drenched underwear.

"What about your patrons? Your employees? What about our daughters?" It's a wonder I'm able to even form words, considering the lack of oxygen in the room.

"No one will interrupt us. Door's locked."

I don't know why I want to argue when all I want is to give in to this. Luckily, as soon as he kisses up my neck, any sort of fight left in me disintegrates into thin air.

"Michael," I moan when he nibbles the delicate skin beneath my ear.

I'm a panting mess when he pulls me closer to the edge of his desk—closer to him—and I feel the hard ridge through his own underwear.

"Need you now," he growls against my mouth. And with that, he lowers his underwear with one hand just enough to free his cock. With trembling fingers, he moves onto my panties next, dragging his knuckles up and down the damp fabric before shoving it delicately to the side. Inside, I feel myself flutter with need, my breathing growing shallower by the minute.

We both watch as he drags the tip of his penis over me. I shiver in his arms when he taps my clit, so he looks up to meet my gaze and check in on me.

"Good?" he asks in a whisper.

I swallow once and nod, but it's a lie. Because: no, not good. Nothing is good. Not when I know this is the end. But I guess I need this just as much as he does. I guess we both need to feel loved and cared for. So, for good measure, I add, "Yes. I'm good."

With that, Michael pushes into me, groaning into my neck.

My lungs freeze in my chest when I feel him move in me, slow and rough. I hold on as tight as I can, as if it could change anything about this. But loving each other won't change the fact that we have responsibilities that are pulling us in different directions—literally.

He moans my name over and over into my ear, telling me a

million times how much he loves me, how much he loves *this*. "I'll never get over it," he tells me between ragged breaths. "How fucking wild you drive me. How amazing this feels. *God,* Diana. Nothing has ever felt as good as you and I together."

I come harder than I ever have, his words causing an avalanche of emotions that has my toes curling in my shoes, my neck snapping back, and my spine contorting in a way that almost accidentally breaks me free from Michael's hold. That doesn't deter him, though. Not at all.

"Fuck, I love watching you come," he says, his hips pistoning now, his movements growing rougher and faster like he's desperately racing to meet me at the finish line where I lie in post-orgasm bliss.

I let him use me and love me and hold me as tight as he can. Fingers digging in my skin, coin-sized bruises in my future.

After he comes, he stays inside me for a moment, face pressed into my neck as he presses soft kisses to my collarbone.

"Don't do it," he whispers after several minutes of silence. He's soft already, and I can feel him dripping from between my legs, but we don't move a single inch, neither one of us ready to say goodbye just yet. Maybe ever. "Don't leave me."

"I have to go back to Colorado, Michael."

He shakes his head but still can't meet my eye. "You know what I mean."

I take a deep breath and press my hands to his chest, push him gently away. When I manage to untangle my limbs from his, I hop off the desk and slip off my panties before pulling on my shorts. I'd rather go commando than wear dirty underwear.

"What are you doing?"

I keep my eyes downcast, the stinging in my eyes building. "I need to get back home. The girls must be wondering where we are, and they need to rest before we start packing everything up tomorrow."

"Diana. Please tell me you're not going to let this happen. You can't actually just end things like this." He pulls his pants up and readjusts himself as he speaks, his voice shaky.

"I have to go, Michael. I have to—"

But he cuts me off. Grabs me by the shoulders and forces me to look at him. "Stop. Please don't do this."

I take a deep breath as fresh tears begin the stream down my cheeks. "I've already made my decision. And it's the best one."

Chapter Thirty-Six

DIANA

Work keeps me busy for the most part. We're right in the thick of writing up the official contracts for the Bloom acquisition, and Edgar has been incredible in letting me participate and offer suggestions. The distraction is helpful, but overall not 100% efficient. My whole body aches, my entire system shut down. Most days, I'm nothing more than a robot going from task to task, pushing through life, waiting until the feelings I have for Michael go away. Unfortunately, it doesn't seem like something that's going to happen anytime soon.

The last time I see him is after the girls' final playdate, two days before we go back to Colorado. It's awkward and painful, and I can't help but be flooded by the thought that I'd rather be anywhere but here and simultaneously nowhere else.

He tries to talk about what happened, but I shut him down multiple times. Our ending was always inevitable, so why bother fix things? Why even try?

Just as he and Rachel ready to leave, while the girls say their emotional goodbyes, Michael looks me straight in the eye and whispers, "I hope happiness finds you, Diana. And I hope you're able to find someone who appreciates you and loves you the way you deserve. But most of all, I hope someday you'll be able to see in yourself what I see: a strong, smart, incredibly beautiful woman who deserves nothing less than the goddamn world."

I manage to hold back tears until later that night, when I cry in the shower, long after Cami and Emi have gone to bed.

Right back to where I started at the beginning of summer: miserable and alone.

Once I'm back in Denver, by the grace of a higher power, it doesn't take long to find a new place to live in a killer area. The rent is affordable and the space is reasonable—a combination that isn't always easy to find. It's like the universe felt sorry for me and my shattered heart, and decided to cut me some slack in this one area.

"That is the dumbest shit I've ever heard in my entire goddamn life," Rosie says over FaceTime when I tell her how things ended between me and Michael.

It's almost midnight, I'm two glasses of wine in, Cami and Emi are asleep in their shared bedroom in our new apartment, there are moving boxes all over the place, and the word *tired* has lost all meaning to me. The level of emotional and physical exhaustion I feel right now is immeasurable.

I'm supposed to be unpacking the rest of our things before the girls start school tomorrow. Instead, I'm being berated by my sister over the phone for making the right choice. Because it was the right choice.

"It had to end that way, and you know it," I tell her, almost in tears. The pain in my chest hasn't subsided for a single moment since leaving Michael's office after having sex. If anything, it's gotten worse with every day. Being buried in work, in the move, and in the kids' beginning of year school activities has done nothing to numb the ache and emptiness.

"Do I? Because it doesn't seem like it was the right choice." She *tsks* and takes a sip of her wine.

In the background, I can hear her fiancé, Asher, cleaning up their dinner. Recently engaged, my sister looks like she's glowing, and I can't help but feel a little jealous. I want that happiness for myself, but I know it's not for me.

"Sorry, weren't you the one who told me to have a fling this summer?" I ask, a hint of venom in my voice.

"Yes, but—"

"Exactly. Well, I had a fling. And flings, by definition, are temporary."

"The thing is, you didn't have a fling. Flings are casual, and you had a deep emotional connection with this guy."

I shrug and look away from the screen. It's useless to try to deny it.

"So that's it. You walked out, your panties in your pocket, and never spoke to him again?"

"*God*, that sounds so... crude." I grimace.

"Did you?"

"Of course not. We talked a bit after. I mean, we had the girls to face, you know? We had another playdate for the kids at my place before leaving, but... It was rough, to see them together one last time."

"And what about you guys? You just didn't talk about it again?"

"He... tried." I chew on my lip as I remember our last conversation. The look in his eyes, the broken sound of his voice as he begged me to discuss it once again. "But I held firm, kept my eyes on our daughters as they played in the pool and shut him down with a *No* so final it surprised even myself. It was awful."

There's a beat before either one of us speaks again.

"Dee, I've never seen you look so... *miserable*."

"Wow, thanks," I deadpan.

"I'm serious. You were so happy when you guys were hooking up, and I don't think it was just because you were having sex regularly. Even before the first time you slept together. Even when you still hated him, you had this spark in your eyes. Now..." She exhales and shakes her head. "Now you look really fucking miserable."

"You just said that."

"It's worth repeating."

I roll my eyes. "I'm fine. Like I said, it wasn't going to work out. How could it?"

She nods slowly a few times, considering my answer. "I understand the odds would've been stacked against you, but don't you think it would've been worth trying?"

"I didn't want us to destroy each other, Rosie. I mean, sure, things could've started off okay. But then what about once we'd get really busy? Or we had our first fight? What if I became so annoying he left me? Or what if we went too long without seeing each other that he cheated on me?"

"From what Barbara has told me about Michael—"

"*You've talked to Barbara about my love life?*" I ask, a little too loudly.

"She was the only one who could give me an actual character reference of the guy! I couldn't just go off of what you were saying. And anyway, I'm glad I did, because she only had amazing things to say about him."

"Of course she would—she's his friend." Though I know that isn't fair. I wouldn't have fallen for Michael if he'd been anything less than wonderful. Not after everything with Rodrigo happened.

"It's not just that, and you know it." She sighs. "She said he's never actually dated anyone before. Not really. But that he's a dedicated guy who doesn't do things halfway. Which she seemed to think meant that he wasn't just fucking around with you. If Michael just wanted something casual, he would've told you. But he asked to stay together."

"I know he meant it when he said he loved me," I tell her. There's no denying the look in his eyes, the determination. And after almost three months of spending time with him, of seeing him almost every day, I'd gotten to know him well enough to know he wouldn't just say that to anyone. Not even just to sleep with them.

"Then why are you doubting that he'd stick with this relationship?"

"It's too much." My voice breaks. *I'm too much.* "There's no end in sight to this distance. On the off chance that this does work out, and we figure out we want to be together in the long run—" The possibility of that sounds as likely as aliens in my head: mathematically probable, but unlikely at this point in time. "Michael has a restaurant in Long Island that he *just* opened—it's not like he can just leave it. And me and the girls wouldn't be able to move because Rodrigo specifically said he wouldn't even consider it. That he would try and stop me."

"Which is bullshit, if you ask me," Rosie says through gritted teeth. "Didn't you tell me he hasn't so much as called again since leaving Sag Harbor? Or paid child support since the divorce? What the hell does he care, anyway?"

I wince.

"Shit, sorry. I know it probably isn't nice to be reminded of the fact that your ex is a total dick."

I shrug once and look down at my hands. "You're not wrong, so there's no use in getting upset." I heave a huge sigh and look out the window of my new apartment, the city lights shining bright. "I can handle when Rodrigo's a jerk to me—I expect it. But I still haven't gotten used to him acting like the world's worst father to his children. Sure, he never would've qualified for the Dad of the Year award in his history of being a parent, but still. He can't check on his girls? Or return his daughters' calls once every so often?"

My sister's concerned face fills my phone's screen, pity in her eyes.

"Don't. Don't look at me like that. I'm fine."

"You're not. And neither are your girls."

"I'm doing my best here, Rose." And suddenly, I'm crying. Because being a single parent feels impossible most days. Because having two kids to take care of—one of whom has a very serious chronic condition—is overwhelming. Because I live in constant fear that I'm ruining their lives beyond repair. And because I hate myself for feeling like I have the right to even be a tiny bit depressed because the man I think might be the love of my life is no longer in it.

"And you're doing amazing, Dee. I promise. You're a freaking super mom."

I snort, rubbing my nose with the back of my hand.

"I'm serious. You've done everything you need to do to make their lives as close to perfect as possible. You moved into a great new place in their same school district, so they don't have to start fresh somewhere new. You took them on the summer trip of a lifetime. You fight for them with their dad every day. You restarted a career and work crazy long hours in order to be able to afford anything that they need. You are an outstanding caregiver to them, even if sometimes they might not thank you for it. I don't know many mothers who give so much of themselves to their kids."

I sniff once, wipe another tear away. "Thanks, but it's the bare minimum, in my opinion. If you're not giving everything to your kids, are you even a good parent?"

Rosie inhales. "Dee," she says, heartbreak in her voice. "You're allowed to be your own person. To have an identity and life outside of being just a mother. Especially one like you."

"Yeah," I mutter, not really believing that.

We hang up shortly after, Rosie sensing I need my space to

unpack more than just my things. I pour myself another drink and take a look around my apartment, praying it will quickly start feeling like home because I feel so lost now. It's like my heart doesn't feel like it belongs here anymore. It's like it decided a few weeks ago exactly where it's meant to be.

I miss Michael. I miss him down to my bones—a million tiny fractures constantly radiating an insurmountable amount of pain up and down my body. I miss feeling seen and having a teammate in life. I miss his company and partnership and love.

God, do I miss him.

I throw back the last of my third glass of wine and reach for my phone. With shaking fingers, I search through my contacts and call him.

It rings once, but the few seconds in between pressing *send* and that first ringtone may as well have been eons.

When he picks up, his voice is laced with confusion and hesitation. "Diana? Is this... Is this really happening?"

"Hi," I breathe, feeling my whole body loosening just from the sound of his voice. "God, it's so good to hear you."

There's silence on the other end of the call, which is... unexpected. "Are you okay? It's kind of late."

I gasp when I check the clock on the microwave. It's more than *kind of* late—it's one A.M. already. Three A.M. for him. "I am *so* sorry. I didn't realize what time it was. I'll let you go—"

"No, wait! Are you okay? Is something wrong?"

"No, I... I just missed you. Wanted to hear your voice."

Again, he doesn't say anything, leaving me pressing my phone to my ear, aching to hear him speak again.

"Michael?"

"Are you drunk? Have you had anything to drink?"

"I— I'm not *drunk*," I scoff.

"But you have had something to drink?"

Sudden embarrassment disguised as fury courses through

my veins. "I'm not *drunk*, though. Was just having a FaceTime session with my sister—girl talk, you know—and we had a few glasses of wine together. Virtually."

"Are you safe? I mean, are you home? Everything okay? Drinking isn't really like you."

I smile into my phone because he still cares—at least whether I live or die. "Yes. I'm safe. In my new place."

"Good." And I can hear the smile in his voice now. "So, what was so urgent that you had to call me at this hour, if it wasn't the alcohol doing the dialing?"

A little hurt, I reply, "I just wanted to say hi."

"Hi?"

"I guess?"

He chuckles a little, and the sound of his soft laughter loosens some of the tension in the air. "How are you?"

"I... I'm okay. How have you—" A hiccup cuts me off and I want to die of embarrassment. *Way to convince him you're not drunk.* "How's Rachel? And the restaurant?"

"Both amazing. Rachel's actually excited to start school this year, which is nice to see. I think the talent show sparked this showbiz bug in her, because she told me she'd like to join the drama club."

"That's so good! I heard theatre is great for shy kids. You just have to prepare yourself, because you might end up with a hardcore theatre kid, begging you to take her to Broadway once a month."

Michael snorts. "Yeah, I'm not doing that, no matter how much I love my kid."

I laugh. "Please. We both know you'd take her once and fall in love with it. It could turn into your thing."

He chuckles. "How's work going? And your new place?"

"New place is great. And work's amazing, actually."

"You still thinking about law school?"

I take a beat because I forgot I'd told him about it. "No, not at all," I lie. The truth is, I think about it almost as much as I think about him. Two things I want; two things I'll never have. "I was never giving it serious consideration. I don't think I'm the right fit, you know? I'm happy being a paralegal."

"...can't *believe* you're throwing it away for..." he mutters, but I can't understand him fully. "You and I both know that isn't true. That you aren't the right fit, I mean. You would be amazing at it. You're kind and loyal, so I know you wouldn't be one of those snake-like attorneys. And you're so smart, it's insane. A fucking turn on like I've never experienced. Just... the way your brain works is..." He sighs. "And no one would be more dedicated to her clients than you would be."

I melt, sinking lower on the couch as I let his words coat my heart like honey—warm, comforting, and so sweet.

I don't deserve them.

"I don't have the time or the money to go to law school. That automatically puts me under the 'not right fit' column. Immediately disqualified."

"You can make it happen. You're smart, and can get anything done when you put your mind to it. If anyone can manage everything that's on your plate, it's you."

"I think you may be overestimating my abilities," I say with an awkward laugh.

He scoffs. "You know, I'm real tired of you putting yourself down. More importantly, I'm tired of you putting yourself second, third, or even fourth."

His words—the *tone* of them—are like whiplash from his previous praise. "Michael—"

"Seriously, it's the same thing that happened with us. You think you're less than, so you decide not to fight for yourself, choosing instead to hurt both of us. You're doing the same here: not believing in yourself, settling for a paralegal position when everyone else knows you would be the best attorney at your firm."

I snort, but he doesn't find my attempt to relieve the tension a bit funny. "Me not going to law school is not about not believing in myself. It's about prioritizing my family and doing what's best for it. How many times do I have to tell you that?"

"How many times am I going to have to remind you that prioritizing yourself sometimes *is* what's best for your family. That, in this case, it's not an act of selfishness. That it's the possibility of providing a better future for your daughters."

I press my lips together. "Maybe it isn't an act of selfishness for other people. Or maybe it wouldn't be one if I didn't have so much going on. But there is no way in hell I could go to school while having to focus so much on keeping my daughters healthy and happy."

"Your daughters want to see you happy. *I* want to see you happy."

"Well, I don't see that happening any time soon." I don't mean for the words to slip out, but they do. A massive mistake, since we both immediately fall silent. And I know. I know he's two seconds from losing the surprising and admirable control he's maintained so far in this conversation.

"I'm sorry. I don't think I should've called. I guess I just... missed you. And wanted to see how you were doing."

A silence so dead leaves me checking to see whether the call dropped or not.

"Hello? You still there?"

Michael clears his throat once. "You're right. You shouldn't have called," he says, his voice a little rough, whatever hint of humor and lightness it held before now gone. "I don't think we should be having this conversation when you've been drinking. Or at all, to be honest. I don't think I have it in me."

"Michael, I—" The pit in my stomach I've been trying to distract myself from opens wide, a yawning abyss.

"You wanted this, Diana. You were the one who said you didn't want to be together long-distance. I wanted to fight for us, and you said no."

"I just wanted to see how you were doing," I say, my voice breaking. "I just—"

"Missed me, I know. I miss you, too. More than I could ever explain in words. But I can't just hop on a call with you and pretend everything is alright. And I certainly don't want to get these calls when you're drunk."

"I'm not—"

"Whatever. After a few glasses of wine. When you're feeling lonely. How do you think that makes me feel? Because I could tell you, if you'd like." He exhales, sounding just as broken as I feel. "I just... I can't do this. I can't be your friend or someone you call when you're just alone and... I thought I meant more to you than that. That you respected me more."

"I *do*. I care about you. Please know that I would never intentionally hurt you."

"Well, you're fucking hurting me." Now it's *his* voice breaking. "I... I've never loved anyone the way I love you. I've never wanted anything more in my goddamn life the way I want you. And while I respect your decision to kick me to the curb—"

"I did *not* kick you to the curb. I—"

"While I respect your decision to break things off, then, I need a clean break. I can't do this. I can't just keep waiting for you because *it is going to end me*, Diana. I can barely breathe as is, and excuse me, but I need to keep my shit together for my daughter. So... So I need to end this call, and you need to never call me again."

I bite my fist to keep from crying too loudly, squeezing my eyes shut. I don't want to wake the girls, or let him hear me cry.

He sighs. "I didn't mean that last part. Of course, if you ever truly need me—like *actually* need me—then I'll be there, no questions asked. But I don't think it's fair of you to call me a few glasses of wine in 'just to talk' because you miss me after the way we ended things."

"I'm so sorry, Michael," I say, voice wet and blubbery.

He sighs. "Goodbye, Diana."

Chapter Thirty-Seven

MICHAEL

"I've told you a million times *NOT* to use this olive oil as a finishing oil. *This* bottle is for cooking, and *this one* is the fancy shit for finishing," I seethe, reprimanding my cooks for what feels like the millionth time. "Again. Do it *again*. And you can be the one to explain to our customer why their order is late."

I turn on my heel and stomp off into the restaurant office before throwing myself into the chair behind my desk. Head in my hands, eyes squeezed shut, I wait for the inevitable moment Lexi walks through the office door.

"What the hell was that?" Her voice is as venomous as mine was. "What gives you the right to speak to our kitchen staff that way? I believe when you first wanted to open this place you vowed never to be like your former Chefs de Cuisine and treat people like garbage. And yet, here you are, being an absolute dick."

"I know," I mumble through my hands, more ashamed than words can describe. "There's no excuse for what I did. I'm sorry."

"Don't tell *me* that. Go tell George and the rest of the kitchen staff. The serving staff, too. You've been a nightmare to work with lately."

I free my face from my hands and nod. "I know."

"So, what are you going to do about it?"

I heave a sigh and sit up straight in my seat, trying to project confidence—though I'm sure everyone can tell it's an act. Losing the love of your life will destroy your sense of worth like that.

"I'm going to do better. I promise. It's just, the stress of the new business and gearing up for a new school year. You know, getting used to a new routine. It's been tough. Rachel and I have been—"

Lexi holds a hand up. "Okay, I'm gonna stop you right there. Because you and I both know your shitty attitude has nothing to do with the stress of the new business or the new routine you and Rachel are trying to settle into. Don't try to lie to me. *Or* yourself." She rolls her eyes. "You and I both know what it's about."

I chew the inside of my cheek, unwilling to admit to her why I've felt like dying most days. Why I've felt like running and never coming back. That the only thing that's held me together is my daughter and the blessing it is to have her in my life. That I've held onto her harder than before because my heart cannot stand another loss.

"I'm fine," I mutter.

"I don't think you are."

"I'm *fine*," I tell her again, this time with more insistence.

Lexi purses her lips and crosses her arms in front of her chest. "I'm going to need you to get up, apologize to your staff, and go home. Take a week off to decompress. Because you are *not* fine, cus."

It's safe to say I do not take Lexi's "request" easily—my first instinct is to argue with her, tell her it isn't true. But I can't deny I've turned into someone even *I* can't stand to be around. Miserable. Broken. Short-tempered. Argumentative. And what isn't good for me, isn't good for my daughter.

I sigh. "I'm not sure how getting away is supposed to help, if I'm honest." My loneliness follows me everywhere, after all. "And also, I don't exactly have the time. We *just* opened a restaurant, in case you forgot."

Lexi rolls her eyes at me. "They key word there is *we*. Meaning, I can cover for you while you go away. That's the whole point of having a partner—to share the load. So I say you need to get out and take a break."

"I don't think now's the right time."

"Now's the perfect time. Rachel doesn't officially start school until after Labor Day, right?"

"Yeah."

"So. You have this weekend. Why don't you guys take a trip? Bond before things get crazier. Go camping or something. At least for a night."

"I don't know..."

"Think about it. In the meantime, get your ass back in the kitchen and apologize."

I blow a puff of air and get to my feet, following Lexi into the kitchen.

CAMPING HAS NEVER EXACTLY BEEN MY THING—LEAST OF all during a holiday weekend when every single beach and campground is packed—but, in the end, a father-daughter bonding day with Rachel sounds pretty good, even if I know it won't fix my broken heart.

"So, what exactly do people *do* when they go camping?" Rachel asks, watching me as I pitch our tent.

I shrug. "I don't know. Hike. Fish. Hunt."

"*Right*. But there's no hiking here—everything is flat, so it would be more like *walking*. Fishing is kinda gross. And I would *never* hunt." She shivers, which makes me smile. No, she would never hunt—my daughter loves animals way too much.

"Well, we can also just hang out. Go to the beach."

She smiles. "Okay."

Later that night, after spending all day at the crowded beach, I wrap Rachel up in a blanket after grilling a couple of burgers in our portable grill, and teach her how to roast the perfect marshmallow (slowly, for a perfectly gooey inside and toasty outside texture).

"Did you have fun today?" I ask, opening up the conversation after a lull.

She shrugs once, not looking up from her marshmallow as it hovers carefully over the roaring fire. "Sure, it was fine."

I know she's partially lying, though. Because while we did enjoy the time we spent together, I know her feelings were hurt when she approached some older girls playing on the beach and they rejected her. It shattered my heart watching it all from afar, and while I wanted to march over there to give them a serious talking to, tell them that they're missing out on the best kid ever, I know it would've made matters worse for Rachel.

Still, I don't think the topic can go unaddressed.

"So, do you want to talk about what happened at the beach with that group of girls?"

She's quiet for a moment before answering. "No. Not really."

"C'mon, kid. Please?" Silence. "I just want to know you're okay."

She shrugs again, and I begin to wonder whether I'm finally entering those dreaded pre-teen and teen years everyone has warned me about. Is this how it's going to be from now on? Am I going to have to pull teeth to get her to talk to me about the difficult things?

I think back to *my* teenage years and answer my own question, because if my parents had cared to ask me for a single second what was going on (which they certainly didn't), I still wouldn't have told them anything.

"I'm fine. Just... a little sad."

I nod. "They weren't nice. Your feelings are valid."

"It isn't just that, really. Sure, they weren't nice. But mostly it just reminded me that—" Her eyes flash wide and she cuts herself off.

"What? Reminded you of what?"

"I... don't want to say."

I raise a brow expectantly.

With an overly dramatic sigh and an even more dramatic eye roll, she finally speaks: "It reminded me how much I miss Cami and Emi. And how much fun I had this summer. And those girls not letting me hang out with them... Well, it made me scared that I won't be able to make friends this year once school starts up next week. Last year was tough." A sheen of tears covers her eyes, so I get up from my seat and take one next to her. Wrapping my arm around her shoulders, I pull her close into me and press a kiss to the top of her head.

"I'm so sorry things have been so hard on you. Just know you are an *amazing* kid, and I know you're going to find your group of friends at this new school. Especially once you join the drama club."

Rachel smiles—barely. "I know. I have a good feeling. But it still doesn't take away the fact that I miss my friends. I don't even know when I'll see Cami and Emi again." She looks up at me with tears and heartbreak in her eyes, and it absolutely shatters me. "I didn't want them to leave. The girls *or* Diana."

"I know. This whole thing has been hard on me, too," I admit, though I probably shouldn't out loud.

"Why did you guys break up?"

"I—" I swallow once. "We didn't really break up. We were never really together."

Rachel shoots me a look that is way beyond her years—a *cut the bullshit* look that makes her look so much like her mother, it rattles me. As if Jessie had crossed over onto the plane of the living to give me a stern talking to for being an asshole, for letting Diana walk away from me—from us—so easily.

"C'mon, Dad."

I sigh. "It's complicated. They live in a completely different state, across the country, kid. It would've been... It would've been way too much." I try to give her the less complicated, kid-friendly version of Diana's motives for ending it, but it's easier said than done. Especially since I haven't completely come to terms with it myself.

"Does it also have anything to do with the girls' dad? Does Diana still love him?"

I smile, my daughter ever so perceptive. "It does have a little to do with their dad, but no, she doesn't love him. Sometimes, when parents get divorced, things get a little messy. And Diana is currently in a very messy situation."

She nods pensively. "I feel bad for them. Cami was really sad about everything. She used to tell me how much she missed her dad. How lucky I was to have you. I told her that when Mom died, you took me in and... I think for a minute there she got a little jealous that you *chose* to be with me after... everything. She mentioned that once her parents separated, she barely ever saw her dad."

"Yeah." I'm devastated to hear how upset Cami was. I've always known she was more aware of what was going on around her than she let on, but it's still difficult to hear. "He has his own set of issues."

"Not everyone can be as cool as you," she says with a shy smile.

I hug her close to me again. "That's the second time you've said I'm cool."

"Ugh. Don't get used to it."

I chuckle.

"You've been sad, too. I can tell."

I gulp, cursing myself for not having prepared to have this conversation. We've been skating around the girls leaving, but I knew it would come eventually.

"Yes. I... I *have been* upset about Diana and the girls leaving. We had a good summer together. I miss them."

"It's more than that, though, isn't it? Do you love her?"

I sigh and put my head in my hands. "I don't think we should be having this conversation. Aren't you a little young for this?"

"For discussions about love?" She shrugs. "I don't know. Probably? But I just want to understand. Because even before we *sort of* found out that you and Diana liked each other like that, the three of us could kind of tell you liked each other. You smiled a lot around her."

I chuckle. "Oh, yeah?"

"Yeah."

I sigh wistfully. "I don't know. I guess, yes. I love her. But you'll realize when you grow up that life isn't always black and white. That things aren't always so simple. Just because two people care about each other, doesn't mean that they can be together."

Rachel looks away as she seems to process my words, and it takes her a moment to respond. "I think that's dumb."

I sigh again. "I don't disagree."

Chapter Thirty-Eight

DIANA

THREE MONTHS LATER

"If I'm being honest, Diana, this might be a blessing in disguise," Edgar tells me, sliding a piece of paper to me over his desk. At the top, the document reads "Voluntary Relinquishment of Parental Rights."

"A blessing in disguise?" I scoff. "How? The father of my children has filed a legal document saying he's washing his hands of his two girls. Permanently. How is any of this okay?"

"Well," he purses his lips. "He did pay what he owed in back child support—though no alimony payments. Still, it's one less thing you need to worry about now. One less thing to chase. We can stop contacting his lawyer demanding he pay—which also means fewer legal bills for you, even if we do give you a discount here as an employee."

"I guess."

He sighs before he continues, a bit of pity in his eyes. I hate it. "Rodrigo has made it clear he wants nothing to do with the girls—" I wince—"and while that's horrible, it *is* better this way, if you ask me. They can finally start getting used to not having him around instead of hoping he'll show up for them for once."

I take a deep steadying breath. "Will there be a court hearing?"

"No, the judge didn't ask for one, and I don't believe you'd like to request one either, would you?"

I shake my head. Maybe Edgar is right. Maybe it's best if this is just... done.

"Didn't think so. I... also have to mention, he expedited this."

"What does that mean?"

"Just that he wanted to get this done as quickly as possible. My guess is to keep the amount of child support he had to pay you to a minimum."

"That asshole," I whisper.

Edgar's eyes widen in shock, never having heard me curse before.

"Sorry." I blush.

"Don't worry about it. It's well-deserved." He sighs and leans back in his chair. "How do you feel?"

"Upset, obviously." My voice breaks, the tears streaming down my cheeks. Normally, I wouldn't dream of ever crying in front of a boss, but Edgar was my lawyer through my entire divorce. He's seen me at my worst. "Saying he wasn't the best father is the understatement of the century, but still... I don't even know how I'm going to explain this to the girls. I'm... all alone now. *We're* alone."

"You know that isn't *really* true. You still have your extended family. That's something to be very happy about. And, more importantly, you're free now, Diana."

I look up into his eyes, a bit shocked. "Am I?"

"You can do whatever you want now. You'll never have to ask him for anything ever again. That's the bright side here. Do you know how many family law cases I've seen where former spouses use their children as weapons post-divorce? It's horrible, the way these children are manipulated or used as tools to purposefully make the other spouse's life difficult. You won't have that anymore. You and your girls can go, and live a stress- and Rodrigo-free life."

"I'm scared," I confess. "I understand what you mean that it's an odd sort of silver lining, but at the same time, I could've used that money. Or at least some kind of parental support, you know? Help once a week."

"Respectfully, you weren't getting any kind of support before this filing. So it's not like this made any difference, did it?"

I nod, attempting to swallow the ball in my throat.

"And, anyway... You've officially completed your six month probationary period here at the firm. Which means..."

He slides another sheet of paper, folded this time. When I open it, the top of the document reads "Porter, Jameson, & Webb Updated Compensation Package."

I inhale sharply. "A raise?"

He nods. "And an increase in responsibility, too. You're still a paralegal, of course. But some clients have taken a special liking to you, so we've decided to permanently assign you to some of those cases, which means you qualify for bonuses."

"Whoa," I breathe, reviewing the updated package.

"I hope this comes as a good early Christmas present," he says with a smile.

I sniff. "Yes, thank you. A fantastic one, actually. Definitely softened the blow of it all. I'm excited to have dedicated clients."

"Which leads me to my next point... You remember Jonathan Bloom, right?"

Manhattan looks like an entirely different city than the one I first visited in the summer. The streets are even more crowded than before, but the hot garbage smells have been replaced by the scent of literal roasted chestnuts, bright office building lights are now accompanied by endless string lights adorning every corner, and the sound of traffic comes with a side of holiday music blasting from stores, restaurants, and coffee shops. Before, I thought movies that showed New York over the holidays were representing a gross exaggeration of its reality—now I know that I've been wrong this whole time.

The city is beautiful and something out of a storybook.

Even Jonathan Bloom's building lobby has undergone a transformation. Previously cold, decorated only in a scheme of black and white marble, it feels almost welcoming with its updated holiday decorations. Every inch of the place seems to be covered in a combination of pine, bows, twinkle lights, and gold and red accents. I swear they even put the scent of pine in the air vents.

I was scared of coming back to New York, of accidentally running into Michael somewhere in the city, as unlikely as that sounds. I was scared of what it would do to me, because after months of no contact, after months of separation, there isn't a single part of me that feels any different. I'm still in love with him.

At the end of the day, though, I'm glad I'm here. This trip would not have been possible if Emi wasn't in a place where I could leave her with my parents. So the fact that I felt okay enough to let her and Cami stay with them while I'm away speaks volumes to how things have been going with her diabetes. I still obsessively check her CGM app to see how her glucose levels are—more so now that I'm in New York—but we've had fewer scares over the past few months. A huge relief for our entire family.

"You ready for this?" Edgar asks beside me.

I smile up at him. "I mean, you only gave me a couple of days to prepare for this business trip, but you know I'm ready."

He pats me once on the back. "Never doubted you for a second."

Seeing Jonathan again after so long is... odd. He greets me as kind and friendly as ever, with open arms, bringing me in for an unexpected hug. So sweet, in fact, it makes me wonder whether he doesn't know Michael and I aren't together anymore.

"Diana," he says with a smile. "It's *so* good to see you again."

A little dumbstruck, I let him lead us into his conference room. The warm greeting doesn't go unnoticed by my boss *or* Jonathan's legal team, but they all know better than to bring it up right now.

Jonathan asks us how our flight was, kicking off the usual slew of small talk that precedes every single meeting. Eventually though, we set pleasantries aside and thankfully get down to business.

"The contracts and negotiations have been finalized," Edgar notifies our client, passing the final documents to the client team.

"Finally," Jonathan heaves a sigh. "Not gonna lie, I was getting real tired of this back and forth. Who knew buying a small company in Denver was going to be so time-consuming?"

The team chuckles before reviewing every line of the contract together. When Jonathan and his team are fully satisfied, he smiles and thanks us for a job well done.

Knowing that I was a part of something big fills me with a sense of accomplishment I haven't felt in a long time, and it never would've happened if Rodrigo hadn't left me. So maybe Edgar was right in that his exit from my life has brought me incredible blessings. This job. A newfound strength I never knew I had in me. And Michael—even though I lost him.

This time, I do go out for drinks with the team in celebration of the conclusion of our business. Jonathan sits next to me at dinner, and it's nice. It feels like having an old friend, despite us not having known each other for very long. It doesn't take an expert to know that the ease I feel is one by association, because he's friends with Michael. And I want to ask him so much about the man I love, but I manage to keep quiet. To stick to business or trivial conversation. That is, until he broaches the topic...

"You know you can ask, right?" he says in a low voice, so only I can hear.

I play dumb. "Ask what?"

"Ask how he's doing. How *she's* doing. Both of them."

I attempt to swallow the sudden knot in my throat but struggle. "How are they?"

Jonathan smiles, those gorgeous blue eyes showing me kindness I feel I don't deserve. "Rachel's okay. I spoke to him a couple of weeks ago, and he mentioned she was doing some sort of winter play."

I nod, my heart twisting in my chest. "And Michael?"

His smile drops, brows pulled together in sadness. "He's... He's hanging in there. The restaurant is doing well. Getting rave reviews."

"Yeah, I've been keeping up." I set up a Google alert for it, actually.

"Of course you have," he says with a smile. "But it's been rough on him, you being gone. He doesn't say much because he knows you and I have been working together, but I've known him for a while. He still misses you."

"I miss him," I whisper. "A lot."

"So why aren't you together, again? I know long-distance can be tough, but—"

"It wasn't just that." I shake my head. "I mean, it was. But it was more so that there would've been no end to it unless he dropped everything and came to me. And he *just* opened H&H."

"What about you? I know the girls are in school and everything, but... the way you two looked at each other was something else. You wouldn't move for him?"

"It's complicated. My ex—he threatened me. Told me he wouldn't give me permission to move the girls out of state. Which is so stupid, because he just—" I cut myself off with a gasp. *"Holy shit."* I push from my chair in shock, pulling the attention of everyone from our table to me.

"Diana? Are you okay?" Edgar asks.

I flush, a bit embarrassed by my outburst, but the gravity of my realization keeps me from caring about it for too long. "He gave up his parental rights, Edgar. He gave them up." I stare wide-eyed at my boss and realize exactly what he was trying to tell me when he said I was free. "I can do *whatever* I want."

Edgar smiles across the table at me. "I told you."

"What's going on?" Jonathan asks.

"I—oh my god, I'm so sorry for the dramatics, but I have to go." I start to leave, before rushing back to the table, addressing my boss. "Do you mind if I take a couple of days off?"

He laughs. "Go do what you need to do."

I could hug him right now. So I do. "Thank you so much."

And without another thought, I grab my coat and take a cab all the way to Penn Station. I have a train to catch.

Chapter Thirty-Nine

MICHAEL

I've never been a fan of winter—but it isn't for the obvious reasons. It isn't because of the weather or the freezing cold temperatures, the dead vegetation or the end of year. It's mostly to do with the fact that, growing up in Sag Harbor, there would be a massive exodus once the temperature dropped to freezing levels. People with summer homes would stop visiting until the following spring, and tourism would drop substantially, leaving the previously-crowded beaches and towns empty. Almost ghost-like.

Many locals actually prefer it that way, to get their towns back from seasonal tourists. But as a teenager growing up with absent parents, I loved making new friends every summer. I liked getting to know people from different backgrounds. And the absence of the crowds, the end of the temporary relationships I'd form as a kid with transient people, multiplied my loneliness tenfold.

Nowadays, winter in Sag Harbor isn't as bad as it used to be. Over the last couple of years, many people have moved out here permanently, choosing to set down roots—whether it's to retire or start their families. Either way, it's been nice not to feel like you're living in the middle of a dead town. It's *especially* nice when you have a business that depends on people. And while it's normal for business to go down over the holidays in this, we haven't found it to be the case with H&H.

Nope. H&H is *thriving*. Dubbed by one of the most respectable food critics in the country as "the gem of Long Island," our restaurant has exceeded expectations. Patrons have loved my new elevated take on simple, easy-to-understand ingredients that they see in their own supermarkets every day. They appreciate the lack of sticker shock when they peruse the menu, and are wowed that they're getting Michelin-level tasting—and looking—meals without the price. So much so that it has become a destination restaurant for people all over the tristate area.

It's certainly been an incredible thing to witness my vision not just come to life, but to more than exceed expectations.

From the outside, life is going well. Rachel is doing okay in school, enjoying her drama club, and work is fantastic. But on the inside, I'm a fucking mess. I can't stop thinking about the last time Diana and I spoke, even though it was months ago. Can't stop thinking about how my words came across. I know they were necessary, but often times, when I revisit the conversation, I wonder whether I was too stern. Too aggressive. Whether I should've softened the blow when I asked her never to call me again.

But then I think back to the mindset I was in at the time, and realize it could've gone so much worse. Because I could barely get out of bed back then. The only reason I did was because I had a front to keep up for my daughter, and thank god for her, since I haven't been able to escape this heartbreak.

I see Diana in everything and everyone, every inch of this town a memorial to the shortest and most meaningful relationship I've ever had, and it's killing me slowly.

"Table six's roasted chicken is ready." Lexi breaks through my musings, passing over the chicken for final plating.

I come back to reality and get to work, carefully slicing the herb-roasted bird on a bias before fanning the pieces on the plate. I accompany the protein with a colorful trio of roasted beets, parsnips, and carrots, sitting atop a thin layer of buttery mashed potatoes. The ultimate comfort food meal for the winter, plated like a work of art. I prepare a second chicken dish, and ring the bell for pick-up. "Order's up for table 6!"

When a waiter comes around, I sag against the counter, and put my head in my hands until I'm called to plate again.

The kitchen doors swing open, our head waiter, Matteo, coming in with a confused look in his eyes. "Uh, we got an interesting order for table two. They ordered every item on the menu."

I look at him with a raised brow. "Table two is a two-person table. They want to taste everything? That's way too much food for a couple of people."

"Yeah, it's actually just one person." When I stare blankly at him, he shrugs. "I don't know man. This lady said she wanted to make sure she tasted everything since I told her you change your menu weekly—or sometimes even daily—based on what's fresh. Said something about living in the moment before you kick her out forever? I don't fucking know."

"Before I kick her out forever? What does that mean?" What the hell?

His shrug is noncommittal, like he's already checked out of this conversation.

"Huh." Curious, I step through the double doors of the kitchen, thinking it might be a good idea to meet this person with the limitless appetite. But I stop dead in my tracks when I see the woman that's been haunting my dreams every night sitting by the window. At table two.

I've often dreamt of what would happen if we were to run into each other again—especially after how we left things. It feels like my mind runs through at least five different scenarios a day just to keep me prepared for this exact situation. Except here I am, faced with the woman who took my heart with her when she left, and I have no fucking idea what to say or do.

What I *do* know is that I need to somehow begin with breathing, which I seem to have forgotten how to do.

As if sensing my presence, she looks up to meet my eyes. I watch as she inhales sharply, her back tensing and her eyes widening into two wide round circles, red-rimmed and bloodshot.

"Michael," she breathes. I can hear her soft voice even over the sound of the crowded restaurant, I'm so attuned to her.

Behind me, I feel two soft hands gently push me. "Go to her," Lexi whispers in my ear (and where the hell did she come from anyway?).

In a trancelike state, I do.

Diana motions for me to take a seat. "Would you like to sit? We can talk. Or... or I can go if you don't want me here."

And because I'm a fucking moron, all I can think to reply is, "Your order isn't even ready."

"I—uh, that's okay."

Duh, you idiot. She's not here for the food.

With a deep, shaky breath, I take a seat. Keeping my eyes on the table, I wait for her to speak first. It's a cowardly move, but I'm not the one who showed up out of nowhere.

"I'm so happy the place is doing well. Honestly, I didn't make a reservation or anything, and by the time I got here I was worried there wouldn't be availability. But as luck would have it, your hostess said there was a last-minute cancellation."

Dammit. I forgot how cute her nervous babbling is.

I finally look up, wincing at her expression.

"Obviously, I'm not here for the food. Despite knowing first-hand anything you cook is so good, I always come back for seconds."

"Is that what you're here for? Seconds?"

She swallows once. "No. I... I miss you."

I nod. Nod again. Keep nodding so much I could easily be confused with a bobble head until I make myself dizzy. "Right. Is that it, then?"

The hurt in her face is clear, but I couldn't help my response. I've asked her to stay away for my own mental health unless she really needed me. And now she's here in my restaurant? Telling me she misses me like I haven't been dying slowly from the same feeling for the past three months of my life?

"Are you in trouble? Is that why you're here? Did Rodrigo come after you or the—"

"No. *No.* It's, uh... it's the opposite."

I raise a brow. "He sent you here?"

She snorts and wipes her nose with the back of her hand. In my own heartbreak, I hadn't realized the tears that had started to build in her eyes. "No, it isn't that. Rodrigo is gone. He waived his parental rights."

I exhale, a wave of devastation for Diana's daughters falls over me. Who the fuck would ever think of leaving them? I already thought less of Rodrigo for being dumb enough to throw Diana away, but to leave all three of them? There was a time when I would've killed to have them in my life forever. Still would. And this guy just willingly cast them aside?

Madness. Absolute madness.

"How are the girls handling it?" I ask, because I need to know how hard I'm going to destroy the motherfucker the next time I see him.

"Surprisingly well. Or at least much better than I expected. I think they gave up on their dad a couple of months ago, if I'm being honest. When school started, and he stopped coming around again, definitely."

"How about you? Are you okay? Do you need help? Is that

why you're here?" Because I know what giving up parental rights means: it also means giving up *responsibilities*, as in financial ones. Maybe Diana needs money? But I can't ever see her asking anyone for money unless her daughters were literally inches away from living on the street. And I certainly wouldn't be the first person she'd go to. Not now. Even though I would probably still give her anything she asked for if she did.

"I'm here for *you*."

I never used to be one to struggle with breathing before meeting Diana, yet it feels like almost every time I'm around her I suffer from an anoxic event. Like now, for example.

After growing a bit too lightheaded for comfort, I finally manage to suck in a breath.

Her lower lip trembles, and I can see just how difficult this is for her from the way her hands shake on the table, the pale skin on her face. Still, doesn't she know it's impossible for *me*?

"You're here for me?"

She hesitates. "Well, I was actually in New York for a work trip and—"

Ah. There it is.

"Just thought you'd stop by for a visit, then?" The disappointment is vicious and runs *deep*. Despite still having feelings for her, the pain is still unexpected. Until this very moment, I thought I had accepted my fate. And yet, for a minute there, I actually believed she was here to ask me to get back together. That she was here to tell me she loved me. And I wanted it.

But I was wrong.

"I... Not really. Or I guess, yes. But..." She sighs heavily, as if the entire weight of the world were on her shoulders. My first instinct is still to help alleviate some of it. My second, to walk away and protect myself from the world of pain that's sure to come my way.

"Listen," I start, my voice a little too shaky for comfort. "I don't know exactly what's going on here, but if you felt like you had to come visit the restaurant or me just because you were a couple of hours away, please know that you didn't have to. You don't owe me anything. You never did. All I wanted was to make your life easier, and by the look of your face, this conversation is not one you want to have. So please, enjoy your dinner—it's on me. I would recommend the duck, but you already ordered everything on the menu—and I hope you have a fantastic trip back to Colorado." I get to my feet and quickly turn on my heel, leaving the woman I love behind as I go hide in my office like a coward, leaning on my desk as I try to process everything.

A knock at the door interrupts the thoughts running through my head.

"Yeah?" But I already know who it is.

"It's me." The soft tone of her voice does something to the inside of my chest, an aching pain that seems to start right below my ribs and end in my stomach.

This love for her, it just might kill me.

Diana doesn't wait for me to tell her to come in. She doesn't ask permission either. Instead, she pushes the door open, slipping quickly inside the office, and shuts it behind her.

Suddenly, it's too much. This space is too small to hold everything I want to say, all the things I feel.

"You shouldn't be back here. This isn't for patrons and..." I shake my head.

Out there, her scent was almost disguised by the smell of food and other people. But locked inside this office, I'm overwhelmed by peaches and honey—by the smell of something so familiar, tied to so many visceral memories that have kept me in a chokehold since the moment I laid eyes on her, I involuntarily relax and tense at the same time. The concentrated scent of a collection of moments—some perfect and others not so perfect—that have kept me up at night for over three months.

The day we met.

Our first kiss.

The first time I cooked for her.

The last time she was in this very office.

I wince and squeeze my eyes shut, praying this is just a very, very painful nightmare that I'll soon wake up from.

"I know, I'm sorry," she says. "I just... I *need* to say something, and then I promise you can send me away forever."

My eyes stay closed for another moment before I'm able to take a deep breath and finally look at her. *Really* look at her.

For the first time, I see the true exhaustion in her deep-set eyes. I notice the permanent frown on her face, like she's forgotten how to smile. I take in the pale color of her skin, which goes way beyond the fade of a tan or being cooped up at home in the dead of winter.

For the first time, I begin to wonder whether she's just as devastated by our separation as I am.

"Okay," I say with a sigh. "What is it that you need to say?"

"I'm sorry."

My whole body tenses into a rock—no air comes in or out of my lungs.

"I'm *so* sorry, Michael. I never meant to hurt you. But please know that I only pulled away because I thought I was doing the right thing, and that I truly believed it was the best way to minimize pain on every front. Because it wasn't just about us anymore. We had to think about our daughters, and how close they had gotten, and how close *we* were.

"But while I am *very* sorry I hurt everyone involved in breaking up before we let things get too serious, I don't regret it. I did what I thought was best for my daughters at the time. Yes, I hurt myself in doing so, too, but I thought it was necessary. There was no way out. No way for us to be together. We would've had to wait years before I'd be able to move—a decade until my girls turned eighteen—or you would've had to pack up your restaurant, and come to us."

"I would've done it," I manage to rasp. "I would've packed it all up for you. My entire life. Rachel and me. For you and the girls."

"Eventually, maybe. But I don't want that for you. You're doing so well already and..." She sighs, smiles softly. "I would've never forgiven myself for taking this from you."

"Have you forgiven yourself for taking what could've been half my family away from me, then? You and the girls? Because that's what it felt like you did by going. And I realize now, with time, that Rodrigo really fucked us over, but I would've loved you through the distance. Through however many years it would've taken for us to finally be together in the same space physically. I would've spent every dollar I have to fly out and see you as often as possible. I would've—" I shake my head, and stop myself before I let the anger and hurt boil over. "I don't want to talk anymore. Gonna end up saying something I don't mean. Or do mean, but don't want to say." My voice breaks, and I look away.

She nods, tears streaming down her cheeks. "I understand. Still, I want you to know something."

"What's that?"

She takes a deep breath before speaking, her voice shaky. "I love you."

The sharp pain in my chest almost knocks me off the desk.

"I love you, and I don't think I'm ever going to stop. I don't ever want to. And while I understand that you probably hate me now, I really wish you wouldn't. Because I can do this now. Because Rodrigo giving up his parental rights means we can move out of state without his permission. Because it means my daughters and I are free to love and be loved by the right man. And I know listening to what I have to say, you might be thinking I'm only here because Rodrigo is officially out of my life. And that's partly true, of course. But I doubt I would've been able to make it another month without you. Without knowing that, in some distant future, we could be together. Because I was done trying to get through a single day without us. Through a single *hour*. I've been done with pretending that I'll be fine without you for quite some time now.

"I love you, and I want you back. I want us to work together to figure something out because while I *can* live without you, I don't want to." She stops to take a breath. Squeezes her eyes shut as if readying herself to say the most important part of her speech. "For the first time in my life, I've decided to choose myself and what I want. And I want *us*."

I stare at her, dumbstruck.

Is this real life?

She clears her throat, her cheeks suddenly crimson red. "That is, if you'll have me, of course. If you still want me."

If I'll still have her? If I still want her?

I take a deep breath, too upset to be embarrassed by the stinging in my eyes or the knot in my throat. I haven't cried since Jessie died, and it had probably been decades since then. But with Diana, it's like every emotion is magnified, and I can't help myself.

"I don't know what to say. Except that you destroyed me, Diana."

I watch the way my words hit her square in the chest, and now it's *her* who can't breathe.

But she needs to listen to this, and I need to say it. We both need this in order to move on.

"You leaving like that, taking yourself from me so suddenly. It killed me." I take a deep breath, try to settle my thoughts before I go off. "I had to keep going for Rachel, but it was the hardest moment of my entire life. It was short, the time we had, but it rocked me to the core, and changed me for good. It showed me what I want in life. And that's you and Rachel and your girls. It's a family. The kind I never had and never thought I'd even want. And it felt impossible to go on every day without you. It still does. So while you can live without me, I need to confess that I'm pretty sure *I* can't live without *you*."

She inhales sharply, finally taking a breath. "What are you saying?"

"I'm saying that I don't care anymore. That I don't want to be proud. That I'll take any bit you give me at this point because I'm done trying to survive a life without you. I need you, Diana." I exhale. "I love you, and yes, I accept. I still want you. I'll still have you."

I reach out and take her wrist, pull her in one smooth and quick movement into my arms. Suddenly, I'm overwhelmed by the feeling of her body pressed against mine, the scent coming from her hair, and the absolute beauty that is *her*. I wrap one arm around her waist while my other hand digs into her hair, holding her close to me.

"I never thought I'd have this again. Never thought I'd have *you*," she whispers against my lips, her hands fisting my chef's coat, white knuckled.

"You have me forever, now."

I press my lips to hers—*finally*—and melt. Because even though we're in the middle of winter, it tastes like summer.

Epilogue

MICHAEL

FIVE YEARS LATER

"Did you get everything done?" I ask, my phone pressed between my shoulder and my ear as I chop up some cucumbers for tonight's dinner.

Diana sighs over the phone—but it isn't a frustrated sigh. It isn't a stressed out one, either. It's the sound of her relief. That after five years of hard work—during which she spent one year of LSAT prep, four years of law school which she attended part time, all while having a full-time job, managing a cross-country move, and being the best mom to her kids—we're finally going to be able to reunite our family and be in one place. Diana, Emi, and Cami are finally coming home to Rachel and me.

"Yes, I'm done. The movers left about half an hour ago, I'm handing over the apartment keys tomorrow morning, and immediately taking the train out East after."

I can't help the wide smile that spreads across my face. "I can't wait."

"How are the girls?"

I look over at Rachel and Diana's two daughters, watching TV on the couch and talking excitedly as they click through YouTube videos with Rachel. Diana sent Cami and Emi ahead of time so they could start at their new school while she wrapped things up in New York City.

Once Diana got into law school and Rodrigo's voluntary relinquishing of parental rights was finalized, Diana and the girls moved to Queens. For the past four years, she'd been attending law school part-time at Cardozo School of Law in the city. Since then, she's been working in Jonathan's company's in-house legal counsel department after she asked for a job. Edgar, knowing her situation, happily let her go so long as she promised to always look out for herself and her kids first.

It's been a dream come true, having her so close. To get to see her and the kids every weekend for the past four years. To spend every holiday together as a family, either here or in Colorado, has been an incredible gift I have never nor will ever take for granted.

"We're doing great here. Settling into the new house." A ranch-style home I bought for our new blended family. Diana was hesitant about it at first, but I wanted to show her just *how* committed I am to us and to Cami and Emi by having the house under *both* our names. And if the house isn't enough to show her how much I want this to work, I'm sure the emerald cut sapphire I got her will give her an idea. But she doesn't know about that yet.

She's it.

"They're not causing any trouble, are they?"

I set the knife down and laugh. "So what if they are? They should feel comfortable enough to."

I can practically hear her roll her eyes. "You spoil them."

A wistful sigh. "I'm weak, what can I say?"

Diana laughs, though, because she knows just how happy I am. "Has Cami told you her new thing yet?"

I chuckle. "Oh, yeah. Sourdough."

"She's been watching bread baking videos non-stop for the

past couple of months. Said she can't wait for you to teach her how to do it right. So far, all she's done is make gloopy messes in my kitchen." She chuckles.

My heart swells in my chest. I love that I've been able to connect with Cami when it comes to cooking and baking. We've come a long way. "Yeah. We're gonna make a starter from scratch tomorrow. She's already challenged me to a bake-off."

"WHEN ARE YOU PROPOSING?" CAMI ASKS IN A WHISPER.

"Shh, kid. You're gonna kill the surprise." I should've never told the girls. But then again, there was no way I was ever going to ask Diana to marry me without the approval of all three.

Cami rolls her eyes at me, her face covered in flour from our latest round of experimental bread loaf baking. It took us about ten days to get a sourdough starter going, and Cami and I haven't been able to stop baking since. "She's in the shower! It's not like she'll be able to hear us," she whisper-yells.

I chuckle. "Sorry, I'm nervous."

"Are you proposing tonight during your date night?"

"Maybe." I wiggle my eyebrows.

Cami gasps. "Emi! Rach! C'mere!"

"*Shhhh*!! Dang, be cool, Cami," I beg, my heart sprinting.

"*She's in the shower*," she repeats with *another* eye roll.

Ah, the joys of having a fourteen-year old girl.

Emi and Rachel run into the kitchen, eyes wide.

"What's wrong? What happened?" Emi asks.

"He's doing it *tonight*," Cami whispers.

Both girls gasp.

"Yes!" Emi punches the air.

"Oh my god, *Dad*. This is amazing." Rachel jumps in place, smile broad.

And yeah, it is.

Without thinking, I wipe my greased up hands on my nicest button-down.

"*Fuuuuuckkk*," I mutter under my breath. "Fucking fuck, fuckity fuck fuck!"

"Everything okay down there?" Diana asks, getting out of the cab of the truck to meet me where I'm bent over the engine.

"No. Fuck. *Yes*. Just stay inside of the cab. We're in the middle of the highway—this is super dangerous." I use the flashlight on my phone to try to see what's going on with my engine, but it's impossible through all the smoke.

"Do you know what you're doing?"

No. "Yes, I think." Obviously, it's a lie. I'm stalling while I figure out what to do.

"Let's call triple-A or something." Diana bites her lip, looking like she's afraid my truck's a few seconds away from exploding.

Honestly, at this point, it might be.

"A tow truck will take too long," I grumble. "We'll miss dinner."

"So, we'll miss our dinner reservation. It's fine. We can go out tomorrow."

"This is the only time we could get a babysitter for weeks." Another lie, of course. I'm not worried about a babysitter nor am I worried about missing a reservation. What I *am* worried about is missing the sunset at the beach where we met, because that's where we're *really* headed tonight. She just doesn't know that yet.

My phone buzzes in my pocket, so I pull it out.

Lexi: where the hell are you guys? I'm hiding in the dunes with the photographer.

I groan. "This is a nightmare."

"What is? Sure, the car not working sucks, but it's not the end of the world. We just need someone to come pick us up. You call a tow truck, and I'll call Lexi and—"

"*No*! Don't call Lexi," I say in a panic. "I— Sorry. Just, this isn't something you should be bothering her with."

Diana narrows her eyes at me, hands on her hips. "What the heck is going on here, Michael? You've been acting weird ever since we moved in together. Jumpy." Her expression suddenly shifts, face falls and pales. "Do you regret this? Us moving in?"

My stomach drops, horrified. "Baby, *no*." I go to her, and, even in my greased up shirt, pull her into a hug. "No, it's not that."

"But it *is* something," she says against my chest, her voice breaking. "Because you've been acting so weird. Like you're hiding something. And— I know it was a big change, but we've been talking about this for a while, so it's not fair to suddenly change your mind. But if you have, there's nothing I can do about it, so—"

"It's the opposite. God, it's the opposite. I'm trying to fucking take you out to the beach where we first got into an argument on the night we met and propose to you, goddamn it. But this car is fucking dead, and the sun's about to go down, and Lexi keeps texting me, asking where the hell we are because she's hiding with her photographer friend in the dunes hoping to get a photo of me on one knee, and hopefully you smiling when I ask you whether—"

"You want to marry me?" Her eyes well with tears; she brings her hands to her mouth.

I laugh in disbelief at her doubt. "*Of course* I do."

"I don't know your life," she says with a blubbery laugh.

"You *do* know my life, because you and those three girls *are* my life. So yes, I do want to marry you. And the plan was to do it tonight, but it all went to shit. So now you're going to have to wait for me to plan a new thing *all* over again and—"

"What? No. You can't do that to me. You can't just dangle the carrot and take it away. You can't just be all 'uh, yeah Diana, I was gonna propose, but things happened so now it's gonna be another time.'" I'd find her imitation of my voice hilarious, if it weren't so cute.

"That supposed to be me, huh?" I chuckle.

"Oh, yeah. Hundred percent," Diana deadpans.

"So what do you suggest I do, then? Propose to you here in the middle of the highway while my car smokes beside roadside trash in my greased-up shirt?"

She smiles, cheeks flushing. "Honestly, I can't think of anything better. It means I get to be with you forever."

I take a beat as I feel the widest smile spread across my face. With my heart beating a drum in my chest, I take her hands in my dirty ones, and drop to one knee.

THE END

Acknowledgments

This book took a lot of time, research, and help to write properly. I want to thank Kerri Buckley, Cindy Guinn, and Dr. Lorena Rasquin León for their help and research. While I did use a lot from my own experience of being diagnosed with a life-threatening chronic condition from a young age, Type 1 Diabetes is a completely different beast. I could not have properly written this book without the help of these three people.

This is the last baby in this series and man, it was so much harder to let go than I thought it would be. While I've been aching to move on from this series, it's also brought so many incredible things to my life. So I'd love to thank all of you for sticking with me through every single one. To every single person who helped bring this series to life. To the readers who fell in love with my characters just as much as I did. To Dreamscape Audio. To my agent, Jenissa Graham. To Tracey. To my family. And to my husband.

Thank you, K. None of this would be possible without you.

And with that, I'm ready to close this chapter (pun intended) and move on from *Seasons of Love*.

About
CAROLINE FRANK

Caroline Frank is a Venezuelan indie author and self-proclaimed shoe addict. She currently resides in Philadelphia with her husband, two crazy cats, Señor Kitty and Salem, and her German Shepherd, Tilly.

She spends her days reading, crocheting, crafting, writing, and biking. Her favorite things include the first sip of an iced-cold Coke and using self-deprecating humor to get through the day.

Though she always planned to eventually take over the world, she thinks writing fun stories every day is pretty freaking awesome and plans to continue to do so for the foreseeable future.

ALSO BY CAROLINE FRANK

<u>Seasons of Love Series:</u>

Fall Into You (Book 1)

Shall We Dance? (Book 2)

Happily Ever Disaster (Book 2.5)

Second Chance Snowmance (Book 3)

Tastes Like Summer (Book 4)

Stand-Alone:

Reply All

Chosen, Eternally (novella)

One Last Thing Before You Go

www.ingramcontent.com/pod-product-compliance
Lightning Source LLC
Chambersburg PA
CBHW030025260826
50375CB00077B/560
* 9 7 8 1 9 6 0 1 0 6 1 0 0 *